Murder On Friday Street

Russell Cooper

Red Balloon Press

Books by Russell Cooper

Florence Fairweather Spy Mystery Series:

Milton Park

Aubrey Hall

Red Cottage

Friday Street Murder Mystery Series:

Murder On Friday Street

Easier Dead Than Done

A Murder Worth Dying For

Murder ME Tomorrow

For Rachel

Very few of us are what we seem.

— Agatha Christie

Chapter One

Berlin, November 1989

On a secluded wooden bench high up on a hill overlooking Berlin, a woman and four young men watched in silence the historical activities unfold in the city below.

Silver sparks from pickaxes and long-handled hammers zipped into the dark, moonless sky as the frenzy continued into the small hours. The five witnesses on the bench watched as the graffiti-covered Berlin Wall crumbled piece by concrete piece, and they saw Russia's grip on the world loosen with each stolen lump of the infamous wall.

And what became of the five?

Two of them died and came back to life.

Two of them were murdered.

Three of them solved the crime.

But that makes seven, and what of the murderer?

The murderer nearly got away with it. *Nearly*.

Present Day, Friday Street, England

Plum Pudding Lane bursts with colour during late spring when the rhododendrons parade their purple blooms. A local gardener says his father planted the seedlings a hundred years ago and tells anyone in earshot that King George VI took a cutting wrapped in wet newspaper for Buckingham Palace's top lawn. True or not, it's a charming tale.

Halfway down Plum Pudding Lane, a narrow section that resembles a pinched Victorian waistline makes it impossible for two vehicles to pass, but with a stretch, you can touch a purple flower head on either side. Young children attempt the feat, while older children, with more important things to do, ignore mother nature's grandest colour show.

Friday Street is an impossibly pretty village surrounded by rolling carpets of lush fields divided by thickets and hedgerows full of wildlife. Nobody leaves Friday Street unless they've secured a move to the coveted and prize-winning Shere Village a few miles away, but that's rare. Rarer still is for someone to move away from the Surrey Hills all together; somebody did, but that was a long time ago.

All of it is simply lovely—the greenest corner of England tucked neatly into a pocket of land a stone's throw from the bustling commerce of London. Spring gracefully stood aside for summer three weeks ago, when the chilly fresh mornings switched to warmer sunny starts, and now the whir of a distant lawnmower fills the air with the unmistakable sound of Sunday.

From a distance, the house at the top end of Plum Pudding Lane looks like an oil painting with its smudged lines and irregular form. The wrap-around Virginia creeper, or Parthenocissus Quinquefolia, as the owners will tell you, turns crimson red in autumn and looks for all the world like the house is on fire. It's not entirely certain if the house is holding the Virginia creeper up or the other way around; either way, it's a spectacular sight worthy of an annual photograph.

A dry-stone wall and a dense hedge hinder you from getting a straight-on view of Tanglefoot Farm, so instead, you must lean this way and that and crane your neck through ninety degrees, but it's worth it, as Tanglefoot is Friday Street's finest home.

The three-hundred-year-old Georgian house nestles in mature gardens full of fluttering butterflies and busy bees and has been in the same family for a hundred years. The owners remain off the radar and live in secrecy, as do quite a few residents within the eighteen dwellings in Friday Street, the smallest village in the Hills.

There's no point looking for Plum Pudding Lane as thick brambles on one side and the tendrils from a willow tree on the other obscure the entrance, although a villager in the know will tell you the brothers at Tanglefoot Farm, Cedric and Ambrose, are retired MI6 spies of some sort. You can't keep a lid on things in Friday Street: everyone knows everything that goes on there.

Tanglefoot Farm, with its pantry full of homemade honey, is a picture postcard place to live. Rarely do you see a house and know in that instant you could leave everything behind and move in with nothing but a suitcase, yet with Tanglefoot Farm, you could do such a thing and not look back.

<><><>

Chapter Two

Friday Street, ten years ago

The local newspaper ran the headline "Murder on Friday Street", which made the killing sound more like an Agatha Christie novel than a serious crime. Friday Street is a narrow lane, and somewhat confusingly, also the name of the village, or hamlet, to be precise. And with only a handful of cottages, the death of the local man created quite a dent in the population.

It was a Wednesday, an hour before daylight began to fade, when they found the body. Ten years ago, a week or so to the day, a small group of ramblers saw the partially submerged body in the lake. The newspaper referred to the pond as a lake, but it's a pond the size of six grass tennis courts or half a football pitch. Some call it a lake, but it is a pond—Friday Street's pond. Finding a bloated body in the water must be a traumatic experience, especially after an early pub dinner.

Statements from the ramblers offered nothing of usefulness to the investigating detective, Colin Beard, who took charge of the case. Not that anyone expected a clue to be floating next to the body. And much later, as details were eked out with the slowness of a glacier, it was understood the dead man in the pond was Randolph Vine, a local who had lived in Friday Street for twenty years.

Everyone in Friday Street knew Mr Vine, and they all had a cheery story to tell, but after he died, they realised they knew nothing about the man, and that's not as unusual as it sounds. Everyone knows someone like that, a fellow dogwalker, a commuter, or a villager. Yet, we don't know anything about them other than those shared, repetitive moments talking about dogs, late trains, or the upcoming planting of the flower borders in front of the church. Those in Friday Street agreed he was an amiable, good-natured man who always stopped to talk and pass the time of day.

Randolph Vine was an agent in MI6, and during his younger years, around the time the Berlin Wall fell, he played a significant role in the Cold War when Russia was the enemy and blamed for everything—you've got to blame someone. Britain pointed the accusational finger at Moscow for everything from our high-interest rates, the impending nuclear war, and of course, the weather. The headlines ran with all sorts of nonsense, and among the silliness, some of it was probably true—you just never knew which bits.

The murder of Randolph Vine soon became a cold case and a crime the world forgot, but not the people of Friday Street—they didn't forget, and rumours circled and still do, that Randolph was bumped off by a hitman from Russia. However, the police didn't buy into the extravagant story.

'You've been watching too much American television,' said one officer. Adding, 'It was a mugging gone horribly wrong. Nothing more than that.'

And that's where things were left: a mugging that had turned nasty where a man died, and his body was dumped in the pond. A mugging ticked all the boxes of the investigation, so any appetite to proceed further was lost, especially not to explore Russian involvement.

The flapping yellow and black tape wrapped around the trees near the pond and the white tent erected to protect the crime scene disappeared after twelve days, and the police never returned. Case closed, unsolved unless you believed the convenient mugging verdict.

And this is where Cedric and Ambrose from Tanglefoot Farm took a central role in looking after Randolph's daughter, Charlotte. Although if you called her Charlotte, she would correct you to say Charlie, and if you called her Charlotte following the correction, the second warning would come with bristly rudeness; she took after her mother that way. Charlie Vine was a few months from turning eighteen when her father, Randolph, was murdered. Her mother died in a car crash when Charlie was eight, so it was just the two of them.

And it worked.

They were as close as any father and daughter could be, and a genuine bond sealed them together like wallpaper to a wall.

Cedric and Ambrose became Charlie's guardian angels, and you'd struggle to find two men more ill-equipped to offer parental advice during a crisis. Fortunately, Randolph's affairs were in good order, and he left a clear charter for Charlie's schooling and the role Cedric and Ambrose should adopt.

'I hate boarding school,' Charlie would tell them on the weekends she visited Tanglefoot Farm.

'I hated it, too,' Ambrose would say.

'You're not helping, Ambrose, dear boy,' came Cedric's reply with an acerbic undertone. 'Our role is to guide the girl, not agree with her.'

A local school for Charlie morphed into Cambridge University, and that meant boyfriends. Cedric and Ambrose were of little help there, too.

'Charlie, my girl, that boy is not suitable,' Cedric would tell her at first sight of someone she brought to Tanglefoot Farm at the weekend. 'The boy has too many tattoos on his head and rides a motorbike that looks unsafe. Has anyone checked the tyre pressure?'

'I like him,' Ambrose would add.

'You're not helping, Ambrose, dear boy,' Cedric would say again.

Due to Randolph's imposing imprint left upon the Intelligence Service, Charlie began work at the Foreign Office, with brief spells at GCHQ in Cheltenham and finally at MI6 at Vauxhall Cross in central London. And during those transitions, the motorbike boys were left behind, but her love of all things fast remained. Charlie quickly took to her various roles in the Service; she got that from her father.

Charlie inherited her father's cottage near the pond in Friday Street and spent a few weekends and the occasional night in the cosy place. However, the view across the pond proved too challenging, and one morning she marched up Plum Pudding Lane to Tanglefoot Farm with two suitcases and announced to Cedric and Ambrose that she was moving in with them.

'How long are you staying?' Cedric asked, looking over

his soft-boiled egg without concern for the brusqueness of his question.

'Forever,' replied Charlie without concern for the presumptuousness of her answer. She put her cases down, and that was the day she moved into Tanglefoot Farm.

'I think I'll make a pot of tea then,' offered Ambrose.

'With a dash of honey?' asked Charlie.

Ambrose and Cedric looked at her as if she had just asked the most ridiculous question.

'Obviously,' they chimed.

That was ten years ago, and the topic of her leaving was never discussed again.

Cedric and Ambrose loved having Charlie live with them, and they fussed over everything like a couple of mother hens and, in their minds, became quite the parental team. Charlie, bit by bit, moved into the east wing of Tanglefoot Farm with separate access to the double garage and wooden toolshed where she hung her black leather motorbike jacket and open-face helmet, which did little to hide her extravagant crow-black long hair inherited from her Italian mother, and her dimpled jaw and high cheekbones from her father. No wonder she attracted a long line of boys, but not one could get past her two watchful gatekeepers.

From Charlie's bedroom window, if she stood on tiptoe, she could see the beehives, and just beyond, she could see the butterflies cheerfully occupying the expansive wildflower garden. And in a way, Cedric was a stinging bee, and Ambrose was a loving butterfly—such were their differences. Charlie snorted at her comparison of the two men.

Charlie's first year at Tanglefoot Farm dovetailed neatly with her last year at school and her transition to Cambridge. How she wrapped the hapless pair around her finger and tugged at their untrained parental heartstrings like a harpist was a work of art. She quickly discovered the slightest cough was rewarded with at least one day off school accompanied by a trip to the coast to recuperate in the warm sea breeze. She managed a trip to Paris on the Eurostar when she told them she might have caught bird flu. Cedric and Ambrose probably knew she was bluffing; they went along with it all the same.

Charlie missed her dad, and that first year brought a deep, unwavering pain every day.

<><><>

Chapter Three

Present Day

Charlie Vine is edging towards twenty-eight yet still catches herself, occasionally gazing into space, thinking about her lovely dad. And it's always the same: her initial thoughts are laced with sadness, and within a few minutes, she remembers how he'd make her laugh uncontrollably, and she'd begin to smile, and magically, her sorrow rolls into a beautiful memory.

Charlie isn't lonely or alone because Cedric and Ambrose see to it that her life is fulfilling. However, the odd night at home painting her nails would be a fine thing, but Cedric and Ambrose always turn up with something of vital importance that requires her help.

And this evening, with her nailbrush loaded with mocha-coloured varnish and an inch from her big toenail, Cedric shouts upstairs.

'Charlie, come quickly. We need your help.'

She puts the tiny brush back in the bottle, screwing the lid on tightly, knowing that she'd not return to finish the job —four toenails varnished and six still needing their coat of mocha is a record.

'Coming,' she yells downstairs.

Tanglefoot Farm traps voices in hallways and archways, making it insufferable to hold a conversation between rooms or between floors. Yet, every creak and groan that echoes from the Georgian pile can be heard with pinpoint clarity. She dashes downstairs to see Cedric and Ambrose standing in the library.

'We need your opinion on something,' says Cedric. 'Let me take that back. It's not so much your opinion we require; it's—'

Charlie waves her hand, indicating he should move quickly to the point.

With a dismissive sniff, Cedric says, 'We can't decide on the correct choice of blazer. Ambrose prefers his one, which is clearly the wrong choice, and I am dead set on this one.' He runs his fingers under the lapel of his stripey jacket, looking for her approval.

Charlie stares at their jackets and walks in a slow circle around them. 'Is this one of your silly tests?'

'Test? Why would it be a test?' Ambrose says.

'Because the blazers are identical,' says Charlie.

'I told you it was pointless asking the girl,' says Cedric. 'After years of the finest schooling and the benefit of our gifted minds, she can't tell the difference between your lilac and green jacket and my green and lilac one.'

'You can hear yourself, can't you?' says Charlie, looking them up and down. She howls with laughter, telling them, 'You look like a couple of deckchairs on Eastbourne beach.'

'Heavens above, it's as obvious as an out-of-tune bell in a bell tower,' says Cedric. 'Mine is green and lilac, and Ambrose's is lilac and green. It's about the dominance of the first colour.'

'We can't blame her. She lives her life in a leather jacket,' says Ambrose.

'We should have known better,' says Cedric.

Charlie looks at her toes with a smile, guessing the mocha varnish will chip off long before she gets the chance to finish the job. Still, four out of ten toes was the most she'd managed in years.

Cedric and Ambrose read the daily newspapers—the ink-on-paper kind—the real kind, as they will tell you.

The newspaper boy from the next village, Abinger Hammer, rides like fury each morning up the lane with *The Times* and *The Telegraph*. On Sunday, he delivers the heavy weeklies and supplements, including the Russian newspaper, *The Nezavisimaya* and the Greek paper, *The Kathimerini*. And for the paperboy's efforts, waiting for him every Sunday is a jar of Tanglefoot Farm honey and a crisp ten-pound note as a tip.

It's always Cedric and Ambrose, and not the other way around. No different from fish and chips, salt and vinegar, or knife and fork. Cedric is the eldest by nine essential minutes.

'I'd be the King if we were both princes. King Cedric,' and he says it often enough to be more than an off-the-cuff remark.

Ambrose rolls his eyes, 'It sounds more like a remedy for Lupus.' He looks out the window to check the weather,

'Let's take Winnie for a walk to the end of the lane and back.'

Winnie, the all-too-clever toy poodle, can sleep all day and all night; her capacity for sleep is unrivalled. As usual, she's curled up on the sofa in Charlie's half of Tanglefoot Farm, where she spends most of her time; they have an understanding, a bond.

Ambrose jangles the lead, trying to tempt Winnie for a stroll. If dogs could talk, Winnie would ask if it was raining, and if so, say to put the lead away. She can communicate all of this with the slightest flicker of an eye.

Ambrose calls into Charlie's half, 'Come on, Winnie, it's not raining.'

The harness and lead are for show because Winnie isn't going to chase a rabbit or dig a hole to bury a bone or attack another dog.

Tanglefoot Farm is equally divided: two girls, Charlie and Winnie, in the east wing and two boys in the west. The boys never stood a chance!

Ambrose calls upstairs to Charlie, 'We're going for a walk. You coming?'

'I will if Winnie goes?' she calls back.

'She will if you will,' says Ambrose.

Charlie appears and takes the lead, and with Winnie close at heel, they set off as if a starter's pistol was fired. Ambrose joins Cedric, who is waiting by the front gate, staring into the sky.

'I think it might rain,' says Cedric.

He always thinks it's going to rain; it's his default setting.

Ambrose always thinks the sun will shine; it's his default setting.

Charlie runs ahead with her arms outstretched like a

child pretending to be an aeroplane weaving from side to side down Plum Pudding Lane, with Winnie running behind her, barking at nothing. Charlie touches the purple rhododendron heads on either bank of the narrowest part of the lane, sending petals spinning in the summer air. Cedric and Ambrose saunter down the lane a fair distance behind Charlie and Winnie.

Ambrose says, 'Next week, it will be ten years since the ramblers found Randolph in the pond. How can ten years fly by so fast?'

Cedric doesn't say anything for a while. Instead, he stops and scratches his head. 'I still can't believe how the police messed it up. They said they had no clues and nothing to go on. Poppycock!'

Cedric and Ambrose didn't accept the *mugging gone wrong* theory and couldn't entirely buy the idea it was a Russian hit squad. Moscow would have boasted because they wanted you to know how far their murderous reach extended, so you had nightmares thinking Russians were lurking in the dark.

Cedric looks to the heavens, not for inspiration, but to check for rain. He carries his umbrella everywhere—even on a trip to Luxor, Egypt, one of the driest places on earth.

He says to Ambrose, 'There's a letter from Linus Pope on the kitchen table. I'd recognise his pompous handwriting anywhere.'

'I saw it,' says Ambrose. 'You going to open it?'

'No, you?' asks Cedric.

'We'll get Charlie to do it,' says Ambrose, and they nod in agreement.

From halfway down Plum Pudding Lane, Charlie shouts, 'Charlie can do what?'

'I'm sure that girl has the hearing of a bat,' says Ambrose.

'What was that?' shouts Charlie.

'I said we might sit in the garden for a cup of tea and a chat,' says Ambrose.

Charlie shouts, 'In that case, I'll bring Linus Pope's letter from the kitchen table and read it to you, considering you aren't brave enough to open it.'

Cedric and Ambrose wait for Charlie to run back up the lane to join them and decide, without consultation, that whatever Linus Pope wants, their answer will be an emphatic no.

Linus Pope, together with Cedric and Ambrose, made up three of the five members of the Friday Street Spy Ring. They used to meet on Friday evenings for a beer at the Stephan Langton Pub near the pond.

During those meetings, they chatted over beer and chips about inter-departmental problems and offered each other ideas to streamline the Intelligence Service. It usually took until the second round of drinks before they began criticising each other and casting blame for one problem or the other. By the fourth drink, they were best friends again and had forgotten why they were at the Stephan Langton in the first place. Each Friday was the same, light chat, blame, and then best friends again. The beer was always good, and the chips were the best in the Surrey Hills.

The Friday Street Spy Ring's last meeting was ten years ago. The death of Randolph Vine ended their weekly tradition that started in the late eighties when Linus Pope moved to Friday Street. They lost their appetite for their Friday get-togethers, and a distance grew between them.

Cedric would say on more than twenty occasions a year

that Linus Pope was not his cup of tea and could bore the pants off someone who professionally seeks boredom.

'What can that man possibly want with us? He does remember we're retired from the Service, doesn't he?' says Cedric.

Winnie jumps up at them, landing her dusty paws on their mustard-coloured corduroy trousers. Cedric and Ambrose momentarily freeze as they stare at the dirt.

'Oh, for goodness sake,' says Charlie. 'It's a bit of mud. When it's dry, I'll brush it off for you. Come on. Let's get you back to the safety of Tanglefoot Farm, and I'll make you a lovely cup of tea with a slice of cake.'

The word cake catches Winnie's ears, who runs like an Olympian around to the gravel courtyard and waits by the kitchen door. Moments later, the water boils, and Charlie makes a pot of tea and cuts three slices of cake.

'What are you doing?' asks Cedric.

'I thought we might—' Charlie was cut short.

'Look at the time,' says Cedric. 'It's two-thirty! We have Assam tea at two-thirty. Everybody knows it.'

Charlie puts her hands on her hips and looks at the two men, who are fraught with paralysis that their two-thirty cup of Assam tea may be in danger.

'A change might do you good,' she says.

Cedric puts his hand up like a stop sign, turning his head away, saying, 'We've had Assam tea at two-thirty every day since the first Wednesday in June 1978.'

Charlie picks up the letter from Linus Pope and holds it to the light, trying to see what it says. 'It might be important.'

'Nothing from that man can be important,' says Cedric. 'I can see the man's house from our study, so if it's important, he can knock on our front door and tell us the news himself.'

'Whenever he knocks, you never answer the door,' she says.

'Precisely,' says Cedric. He pours from the pot, then scrunches his face at the colour of the tea. 'A tad weak.'

Charlie opens the envelope and takes out the letter. She remains silent for a while, not that Cedric or Ambrose notice as they devour their slice of cake and sip their two-thirty Assam.

'The letter,' she says. 'It's about my dad.'

<><><>

Chapter Four

When Cedric and Ambrose still worked in the Service at Vauxhall Cross, the morning ritual was the same each day.

Linus Pope would drive halfway up Plum Pudding Lane to Tanglefoot Farm. Of course, if Cedric and Ambrose had ever decided to purchase and, indeed, ever answer a phone, Linus could have told them he was waiting in the lane at the pinch, the narrowest part.

Instead, he would toot his car horn, and as ever, no rapid movement or inquisitive faces ever appeared at the window. Linus Pope would toot several more times before the front door finally opened, and Cedric and Ambrose ambled out.

Pope watched them check the hanging baskets before they wandered down the lane in their matching grey pinstriped suits and royal-blue silk ties at a pace more suited to a retired couple admiring the purple blooms with neatly rolled umbrellas in hand. However, with all the will in the world, they were not for changing, and Linus Pope knew since his Cambridge days the world moved at one pace, and Cedric and Ambrose moved at another. They would clamber into the back seat, bickering about the perfect time to boil an egg or the correct height for the lawnmower blades.

Pope reversed his car down Plum Pudding Lane. He was a relatively calm man, yet the narrowness of the lane annoyed him every morning.

'Ever thought about cutting the hedgerow back a bit?' he would say, straining to look over his shoulder.

'What for?' Cedric would say.

'So a car can get further than halfway!'

'We don't own a car,' Cedric would say.

'Or a damn phone!' added Pope.

Each morning they would drive to Vauxhall Cross, which involved conversations about international concerns and debates on how to solve them.

'*We should do this, and we should do that,*' came the suggestions from the backseat. Ambrose's knowledge of history merged into Cedric's memory of political literature, which led to a one-sided debate with anyone else—especially Linus Pope.

And on every drive to work, Pope would raise his voice a note and turn his head over his shoulder like a taxi driver, 'Just because you both agree on something doesn't make it right.'

'I think you'll find it does,' said Cedric.

The countryside's blur of colourful tapestry outside the car windows slowly merged with the colourless swell of city life. Pope lowered his voice before he steered his Jaguar through the security gates of MI6.

He said, 'Randolph Vine told me he might be in danger.'

'Danger?' asked Ambrose.

'He will tell us tonight at the Friday Street meeting.'

And that was the day Randolph Vine didn't show up at the meeting, and the next day, the group of ramblers discovered his body in the pond.

Charlie collects Linus Pope's letter. She slips through the kitchen door, crunches across the gravel courtyard, and opens the garage doors, where her father's gleaming black Jaguar's chrome bumpers sparkle in the daylight.

The driver's seat is Charlie's safe haven—her refuge when the weight of the world bares down on her. She slumps onto the worn cream leather, and Winnie jumps up on her lap, taking the opportunity to close her eyes. The classic Jaguar triggers Charlie's childhood memories as she grips the steering wheel, picturing her father dropping her at school. Her memories are only ever of the two of them.

The Jaguar and Charlie are both twenty-eight years old, and from the comfort of the driver's seat, she connects with her father and takes out the letter to read it again.

Dear Charlie,

I suspect you've opened the letter on account of Cedric and Ambrose's lack of contact. I've taken possession of some items from your father's case. I invite you, Cedric and Ambrose to join me at the Stephan Langton pub on the pond, where you can open the box.

Shall we say Friday, 7:30 pm?

Linus.

Charlie runs her fingers across the words *your father* while stroking Winnie from head to tail. Slow footsteps crunch across the gravel, and Charlie sees Cedric and Ambrose strolling across the courtyard towards the garage. They open the Jaguar's rear doors and sit together in the backseat.

Cedric sighs, already annoyed with the answer. 'What did *the* Pope want?'

Charlie hands them the note and waits for them to absorb the information.

'Items?' asks Ambrose. 'What items, and why now?'

Cedric turns the note over and holds it to the light. 'The Stephan Langton pub. It whiffs a bit of our old Friday Street Spy Ring.'

Charlie snatches the note back.

She says, 'We're going, and that's that—no ifs, buts, or maybes. So I suggest you take the rest of the afternoon to figure out what you're wearing tonight. I'm leaving here at seven-twenty-five on the dot.' She steps out of the Jaguar and crunches back across the courtyard.

The silence in the car is palpable. Cedric and Ambrose watch until Charlie and Winnie slip through the kitchen door before they speak.

'I'm thinking blue blazer, white trousers, and a long sleeve soft salmon shirt,' says Cedric.

'Perfect,' nods Ambrose. 'Blue suede shoes and yellow socks?'

'Naturally,' says Cedric. 'We don't want to overdo it.'

By virtue of a ploughed field and a thick hedgerow, the line of sight from Linus Pope's bedroom window looks directly into Cedric and Ambrose's study. He has a telescope on a tripod permanently trained on their bookcase—it's the only part of Tanglefoot Farm he can see.

Linus focuses his telescope lens on the third shelf, where a photograph of Cedric and Ambrose are making a rude two-finger gesture. Linus convinces himself they are sticking their fingers up at him as it's their sort of schoolboy humour. He reads the handwritten note that leans against the rude photograph: *See you at 7:30.*

Good for you, Charlie. Good job.

After a safe, ponderous career, Linus Pope heads up the Administration Department at the Service, and his office at Vauxhall Cross, although north facing, has no view of the Thames.

<><><>

Chapter Five

'Come on!' shouts Charlie, standing at the foot of the stairs. She yells once more. 'Come on, you two.'

Cedric's head appears over the upstairs bannister. 'What's all the fuss?'

'It's already after seven-fifteen,' she says.

'And?' says Ambrose, whose head appears on the other side of the bannister.

'The invitation says seven-thirty,' says Charlie.

Ambrose stares at her. 'You should hurry up yourself and get changed.'

'I am changed,' she says.

'You're going as a biker?'

'Oh, come on, you are a couple of fluffs,' says Charlie. 'Don't give Linus Pope another reason to think you hate him any more than you do. And anyway, I want to see what's in the box. I'll see you in the car.'

In their blue blazer and white flannel combination, Cedric and Ambrose take a final look in their full-length mirrors.

'I rarely say it,' says Ambrose. 'But we look fetching.'

'You say it all the time. Come on, let's not keep Miss Angry waiting.'

They skip down the stairs and across the gravel courtyard to the revving black Jaguar.

'We're early,' says Cedric, checking his watch as he climbs in the back seat.

'Hardly,' whispers Charlie.

She presses the accelerator and races the Jaguar around Tanglefoot Farm and down Plum Pudding Lane. Flurries of purple rhododendron petals flutter in the evening breeze as Charlie races through the narrow pinch without slowing. Cedric and Ambrose close their eyes.

'Grandma Lizzie was a fast driver during the war. No doubt she would have approved of your sporty efforts,' says Ambrose.

At the end of the lane, Charlie shoots across the narrow track surrounding the pond and heads towards the Stephan Langton pub.

'When was the last time you saw Linus Pope?' she asks.

'At our retirement dinner a couple of years ago,' says Cedric.

'But you can see his house from your study,' Charlie says.

'Not if you look the other way,' adds Ambrose.

'What is it with you and him?'

'We'll need a week to tell you everything,' says Cedric.

Charlie parks the Jaguar opposite the pub and steps out.

The Stephan Langton pub boasts a Tudor look with a timber and brick frontage and a porch with a pitched roof where mature clumps of moss peep between the tiles. The green front door is invitingly half open, and the aromatic joys wafting from the kitchen to greet Charlie take her back to when her father brought her here for Sunday lunch.

'Fancy roast beef, Charlie Girl?' he'd ask with a wide smile.

Sundays in Friday Street were Charlie's best days. And it was always the same; a lazy morning followed by a walk where her father would tell her about the American stash of munitions buried in the wooded hills above Friday Street. The deep bunkers, now full of brambles and thick undergrowth, were attempts by the German Luftwaffe to destroy the underground ammunition. The allied bombs and bullets are long gone, but the craters remain, and today the only reminder of yesteryear is the "No Swimming" sign in the pond. The locals say too many unexploded bombs hit the water and nestled somewhere in the mud and reeds. Her father said that Friday Street was a place spies came to hide.

Those were the days.

Charlie marches inside with Winnie while Cedric and Ambrose study the overhanging roses, taking their time to amble into the pub. It's a delaying tactic, and wild horses couldn't have pulled them along any quicker; such was their reluctance to meet Linus Pope.

Charlie loops her arms through theirs and guides them with some force to a round table in a darkened alcove. Linus Pope stands and tries to hide his disbelief that Cedric and Ambrose are there, in the flesh. Charlie pushes them into the alcove and waits a beat with Winnie for the three unwilling men to greet one another.

'Pope,' says Cedric without any emotion or eye contact.

'Cedric,' says Pope.

'Pope,' says Ambrose, equally dismissive.

'Ambrose,' says Linus Pope.

Charlie squeezes into the alcove and invites everyone to sit at the table.

She says, 'I'm so happy you three didn't make that any more awkward than it needed to be,' her tut cemented her sarcasm. Winnie jumps onto her lap.

The carton in the middle of the table is the size of a shoebox. Charlie stares at the worn edges and scuffed corners, wondering how many hands her father's items have passed through before she finally gets to see inside. She reads her father's name and his date of birth and death on the faded label on the lid.

Charlie expected a grander box, something more fitting, like mahogany or oak with red silk inlay. Instead, her father's unfinished life was reduced to fit into a shoebox—and a tatty shoebox at that.

A lady appears to enquire what they would like to drink and hands them dinner menus while reciting the day's specials. She retreats to the bar with their order and returns a moment later, carrying a tray of glasses and a bottle of white wine poking out from an ice bucket.

Four pairs of eyes stare at the box.

'Shall we?' says Linus Pope. 'Charlie, will you do the honours?'

She looks at Cedric and Ambrose, more for confidence than permission. They both give the slightest nod, watching as Charlie uses the steak knife from the table to cut the parcel string and cut through the official government seal.

With a slight tremble in her hands, she lifts the lid.

There was nothing to say—not yet.

They lean forward and peer inside the ten-year-old time capsule to see a brown padded envelope with the name Randolph Vine scrawled across the front.

'Are you ready to order?' asks the lady as she fills their wine glasses.

'A few more minutes, if that's alright,' says Ambrose, not wanting to break the spell, and the lady pads away to attend to the needs of another table.

An underwhelming feeling bristles among them as Charlie tears open the envelope and empties the contents onto the table. She then looks inside for anything else. But that was it—a set of keys and a crossword book.

'That's it?' says Ambrose, picking up the box and checking inside the brown envelope.

'Hardly a bounty of missing treasure, is it?' sniffs Cedric.

Charlie picks up the crossword book and flicks through the three hundred or so pages from back to front. Her blank expression matches the blank pages.

'Your father wasn't one for crossword puzzles. He believed they were for imbeciles,' says Linus Pope.

'We love crosswords,' says Ambrose.

'Case closed,' says Linus, impressed with the ill-timing of his joke.

Charlie examines the four keys to her father's Friday Street cottage and holds them in her hand. A long moment passes before she picks up the book, fanning through it once more.

'I'm sorry there isn't more, Charlie,' says Ambrose, and reaches out to touch her hand.

With a pen at the ready, the lady reappears, raising her eyebrows and chin and asks what they would like to order.

Cedric orders the chicken and leek pie with chunky chips, and Ambrose nods, saying he'll have the same.

'Me, too,' says Linus.

'Make that four,' says Charlie.

The conversation jumps from subject to subject, and Cedric and Ambrose work in a pincer movement, catching Linus Pope out at every turn. Charlie frowns at them, and they lighten their attack slightly once the topic turns to their homemade honey production.

Two members of staff bring four plates of food into the alcove, and a basket of warm bread rolls is placed on the table next to the shoebox. For a few minutes, there's no conversation, only the light clatter of cutlery.

'Why did the four of you cram yourselves into this little spot every Friday for your meetings?' Charlie asks.

'Four?' says Linus. 'There were five of us in the Friday Street Spy Ring.'

'Five?' asks Charlie. 'Who made up the fifth spot?'

Cedric and Ambrose cast Linus a disapproving look, but Linus ploughs on and resorts to a half-whisper as if divulging a state secret, and in many ways, he is.

'Naturally, there was your father and these two over-dressed fuss bags,' he says, waving a finger at Cedric and Ambrose. 'Me, of course, and Joshua King.'

'Joshua King?' she says. 'Who is Joshua King?'

Cedric coughs over Pope's words, drowning him out to prevent him from continuing, then lowers his voice to the faintest sound, 'You do understand we were a spy ring—secrets and all that, and not some sort of social group with a list of names posted on the pub wall.'

'It couldn't have been a social group with him in it,' says Ambrose, pointing at Linus Pope.

Charlie puts her cutlery down. 'Come on, out with it! Who the hell is Joshua King?'

Nobody lifts their eyes to answer. Instead, it was heads down to focus on the chicken pie and chips.

'This is delicious,' says Cedric. 'The chicken is so tender.'

'And the pastry is so light,' adds Ambrose.

Charlie uses her knife to point at the three men doing their absolute best to ignore her question. She demands they offer a morsel of information. 'One of you had better come up with something.'

'Cedric, you should tell her,' says Ambrose.

Cedric steeples his hands as if in prayer, letting out a sigh. 'It's most likely, I mean it's highly probable, that Joshua King killed your father.'

<><><>

Chapter Six

'He did what?' screeches Charlie, waving her knife and fork.

'When I said Joshua King killed your father, I didn't mean he killed Randolph in the way you'd normally mean it,' says Cedric.

Ambrose puts his hand up as if requesting to speak.

'What my lack-of-tact brother is stabbing at so crudely in the dark is that Joshua King accidentally went public with the Friday Street Spy Ring members. Then, two days later, your father was found in the pond.' Ambrose laid his hand on Charlie's hand—the one holding the knife. 'We've thought for the last ten years that the spy ring leak and your father's death were linked.'

'Where's Joshua now?' asks Charlie. 'Was he interrogated by the police?'

Linus hovers his hands, palms down, over the table, imploring for quiet and waits for everyone's attention. 'That is not what happened,' he says in a slow monotone voice. 'The police made it clear it was a mugging that went wrong, and we've no reason to believe foul play played any significant part in your father's murder. Not Joshua King, and not the Russians.'

'And that right there is why we haven't spoken to *the* Pope for years!' snaps Cedric. 'He couldn't find the end of his nose with a map and a funnel, and he can't accept that someone from the spy world killed your father.'

Charlie's eyes well up, and tears overflow down her cheeks.

She stands in a hurry, bashing her leg against the table and knocks a couple of glasses over before running outside with Winnie.

'Nice job! Are you happy now, Pope?' Cedric says, his lips spread thinly to reveal his teeth in a show of exasperation.

Ambrose adds, 'Pope, you get to go home and think no more about churning up what happened ten years ago while we'll spend ages consoling her, just like we did when she first lost her dad.'

Cedric and Ambrose leave the pub and step across the track to wait by the Jaguar, watching Charlie walking with Winnie along the edge of the pond.

'Poor girl,' says Ambrose, kicking his shoes at a stone sticking out from the track. 'I must admit, I was hoping for a little more than a book of unsolved crossword puzzles and Randolph's house keys in that shabby old shoebox. What was the Service thinking?'

Cedric exhales in agreement, and snaps, 'Even that fool detective in charge of Randolph's murder might have caught the killer if there was a note in the box explaining the killer has a long ginger beard and lives at 18 Buttercup Drive, answering to the name Bob—damned incompetence and uselessness. If I ever meet that detective, I'll—' his words trail off.

'Exactly,' says Ambrose.

They stand by the car, muttering angrily about the police while waiting for Charlie to meander a slow lap around the pond. Sometimes, and only by chance, they know when she needs space.

When Randolph died, they smothered Charlie in close-quarter kindness; it was sensory overload for her. What they lacked in quality time, they more than made up for with quantity time. Even so, Charlie pushed back.

They were out of their depth as they'd never dealt with a bereavement like that before, and on top of everything, they were grieving, too. Their best friend was murdered, and his daughter, who howled in pain like a wild animal, moved into Tanglefoot Farm. They didn't know anything about young girls—they didn't know anything about girls of any age. So, looking after Charlie was a steep learning curve, and any mistake that could be made was made repeatedly.

Ambrose asks, 'What do you think happened to Joshua King?'

'Maybe he did the decent thing and fell on his sword somewhere near the South Pole, so his frozen body could never be found.' Cedric says, tapping his foot against the tyre.

'A tad harsh, Cedric,' says Ambrose. 'Maybe we should try and find him.'

'What for?'

'I don't know. I thought—' He stops speaking when he sees Pope walking out of the pub.

Linus walks towards the Jaguar and looks lovingly at the gleaming paintwork. 'I've always loved this car,' he says. 'So ministerial and so elegant. It suited Randolph perfectly; he was the best of us.'

Cedric and Ambrose give a sideways nod, showing a reluctance to engage further.

'I miss him too, you know,' pleads Linus, glaring at Cedric and Ambrose. 'He was my best friend at Cambridge and the firm.'

'Yes, and you know he was murdered,' barks Cedric. 'And yet you carry on the charade about the police's buffoonery of a mugging—'

Ambrose cuts across Cedric's words, saying, 'What my less-than-sensitive brother is trying to say is: you're a first-class arse!' A moment of silence follows before he adds, 'I'm sorry, Linus. That didn't come out as I intended.'

'I thought we're meant to be on the same side,' says Linus. 'I'm fully aware Randolph was the victim of a murder, not a mugging. I was trying to protect the girl from further hurt.'

Cedric sighs through each word. 'Protecting someone from the truth does not protect them from pain. If anything, it adds to it.'

'Whatever you think,' says Linus. 'It won't bring her father back. He's long dead, and the case is long cold.'

'Cold? You say. The case is colder than the iceberg that sunk the Titanic,' says Cedric, stepping in front of Linus Pope's face to make his point. 'It was a cold case the moment they found Randolph floating on the pond. The police showed no interest once the pieces of their investigation led them to believe it was a mugging. They quit and gave up. Worse than useless, the lot of them.'

Charlie heads towards the parking bay to see the three men in a huddle. They seem to be talking civilly for once. Winnie runs on ahead as if to warn them Charlie is approaching.

'Have you made friends?' she says aloud from twenty paces.

'Something like that,' says Linus. He steps over to his car and opens the door. 'It was nice seeing you, Charlie.'

Cedric waves at Pope. 'It was nice seeing you too, dear.'

Linus Pope gazes up at the skies and performs a standing count of five to calm himself.

'We must do this again,' says Charlie.

Cedric adds, 'And remember, Pope, please be a stranger.'

Charlie unlocks the Jaguar, and her protective guardians clamber into the back seat. Winnie jumps onto the passenger seat, waiting for Charlie to settle behind the wheel before leaping onto her lap.

She says, 'I don't believe Linus is convinced my father was the victim of a mugging gone wrong.' She turns the wheel full lock and eases the Jaguar out of the bay before driving alongside the pond and across the track towards Plum Pudding Lane. Her whisper is barely audible, 'Maybe this Joshua King fellow did kill my dad.'

'He couldn't have done it,' says Ambrose.

'Why not?'

'Because he was on an aeroplane to Australia the evening your father died, and we haven't seen him since,' says Ambrose.

Charlie stares at the crossword puzzle book and the set of keys on the passenger seat. She hoped for so much more from her father's possessions.

'Where's Dad's wallet?' she asks.

'The police say the mugger took it,' says Cedric.

'Oh yes, the mugging,' she says. 'Or the murderer threw it in the pond. It could still be in there. We could dredge—'

'It was ten years ago, Charlie, so any trail has gone cold,' says Ambrose. 'Anyway, do you want to rake over all that pain again?'

'It's painful whether I rake or not,' Charlie says, driving at a frightening speed through the pinch on Plum Pudding Lane, treating the road as though it was the width of a runway. She looks over her shoulder at the two men who have their eyes closed, and in a chirpy voice, she says, 'Let's not forget that we have two clues.'

'We do?' asks Cedric. He opens his eyes and glances at Ambrose, who still has his eyes shut from the speedy driving experience.

Charlie moves her hand across to the passenger seat and lifts the crossword book, and then rattles her father's bunch of four keys. She lets Cedric and Ambrose out of the car and then parks her father's Jaguar in the garage. Winnie jumps from the driver's seat and stretches as though they'd just returned from a long European drive.

Charlie stays a moment longer in the garage before taking off her leather jacket and slinging it over her shoulder. She wanders across the courtyard and into the house to find Cedric and Ambrose at the kitchen table, looking at a beehive brochure.

'Tea?' says Charlie.

Cedric and Ambrose look at the clock on the wall; it reads nine-thirty-five. Their rules for drinking tea and coffee are clear: No coffee before seven-thirty in the morning and not after four in the afternoon—tea with milk only in the morning and honey or lemon in the afternoon. Evenings are tricky, but no hot beverages after nine-thirty, hence the hesitation. However, they do have a caveat to their rules: if they receive a royal visit, then there will be a complete suspension of all beverage timings, and they agreed to follow suit with King Charles.

'It's five minutes late for the last tea of the day, but I think it's worth the risk,' says Ambrose.

'Me, too,' adds Cedric.

'You brave soldiers,' says Charlie.

There's a knock at the front door, and Winnie barks.

'Who can that be?' says Ambrose.

'I can't begin to think,' says Cedric.

Charlie sighs, 'I'll open the door and find out, shall I?'

She leaves Cedric and Ambrose, weighing up the possibilities of who could be knocking at this hour and opens the front door to see Linus Pope.

'Linus, how nice to see you again so soon.'

'May I come in? I've something vital to tell you and the other two.'

Charlie stands aside and waves him through to the kitchen.

'Look who I found outside,' she says.

Cedric and Ambrose look at Linus.

'Oh, for the love of Christmas, did we not split the food bill accurately?' says Cedric.

'No, it's not that.'

'Oh, I know,' says Ambrose. 'You've come to apologise for upsetting Charlie.'

'He didn't upset me,' she says.

Linus puts his hands on his hips, saying, 'I've come to tell you some news.'

'Your emigration papers have come through, and you're heading to Peru in the morning?' says Cedric.

Charlie puts a pot of tea on the table and fills four cups, waving her hand at Cedric and Ambrose to suggest Linus ignores them.

Linus shovels two teaspoonfuls of sugar and pours a three-second shot of milk into his cup before stirring vigorously and tapping his spoon on the side of his cup.

'I'm grateful King Charles isn't here to witness this,' says Ambrose.

'What's that?' says Linus.

Ambrose coughs. 'What news? You come bearing news.'

Linus bites into a ginger biscuit, looking around the kitchen like a man about to divulge a secret, then lowers his voice to a whisper, 'Joshua King is dead.'

'Dead?' shouts Ambrose.

'Joshua King, dead?' shouts Cedric.

'Dead?' repeats Ambrose.

Charlie puts her hands up to stop another cycle. 'Why didn't you say so in the pub earlier?'

Linus sits up straight and squares his chin. 'Because the Service deemed his death necessary to be kept a secret and under wraps for ten years.'

'And ten years is up now?' asks Charlie.

'Just about,' says Linus.

'How did he die?' asks Cedric. 'Painful, was it?'

'In a car crash on a lonely stretch of road a hundred miles out of Sydney.'

'And there endeth the lesson in karma,' says Ambrose.

<><><>

Chapter Seven

Joshua King waits in line with his passport in hand. He's not been home to England in a decade—how could he have? He's been dead for ten years.

The security officer at Sydney Airport waves him forward, and Joshua has flown enough to know the drill, so his belt, wallet, keys and coins lay in the grey tray beside his phone. He watches it trundle away through the X-ray machine on the conveyor. Once through the scanner, he rethreads his belt while pocketing his belongings before heading to his departure gate. The bookshops overflow, as do other retail outlets, rinsing the remaining pennies from the tourists.

Joshua quickly converted to life in Australia and took a job in a computer software company. He buried all traces of his past, and nobody suspected he was a spy who died in a car crash on arrival to Australia and became Alan McQueen, the man who rose from the ashes.

As Alan McQueen, he endured a decade in middle management, keeping well back from the leaders at a safe distance—a man hidden in plain sight. Few of the staff knew him, yet knew nothing about him. They won't miss or remember him. Joshua King, living as Alan McQueen, was a somebody and a nobody, and for a tall man, that was quite an accomplishment. As of today, he doesn't need to be someone else.

He arrives at the departure gate and sits on a metal seat with the thinnest leather cushion. He has two hours to wait for his flight, but there's no chance to get comfortable, what with this metal seat and his mind flip-flopping from thought to thought and from concern to concern.

Thirty minutes into his wait, the announcer explains the flight will be delayed by an hour. There's a brief apology, but no explanation for the extra wait, and a gaggle of passengers surround the defenceless young man at the desk. Joshua decides to find a coffee shop—he sees no point having it out with the poor chap—he'll know nothing, and the aircraft will still be delayed. Joshua steps on a travelator and spots a coffee shop at the far end. He saunters up to the counter and stares at the board.

'What would you like?' says the lady behind the counter.

Joshua looks at his watch, shrugging his shoulders with a nasal tut, thinking about old habits dying hard. Cedric and Ambrose always, and probably still do, look at their watch before explaining it is either too early for this or too late for that and how on earth can you drink your tea with milk at this hour?

'A black coffee and a blueberry muffin, please,' he says, knowing it's not the right time for either coffee or cake and how Cedric and Ambrose would persecute him for the next hour.

It's not unusual for Joshua to reflect on the days when Cedric and Ambrose dominated his life and work. A rare smile spreads across his face as he takes his tray to a table in the corner of the busy coffee shop. He misses the old days, he misses Friday nights with the boys in the spy ring at the Stephan Langton pub, he misses his old job, and he even, at a stretch, misses that old stickler, Linus Pope.

A jab of pain runs through him, momentarily rendering him defenceless as he remembers Randolph Vine. He was a brilliant agent—better than everyone. Randolph had a sense of fair play, a kindness that so few had at that time. Most did their job competently, but Randolph did it with compassion, and what tortures King the most is knowing that his actions killed Vine.

He tries cutting his muffin with an inadequate wooden coffee stirrer, and crumbs tumble into his lap. A nervousness washes over him as sinister thoughts pepper him about his trip. Ten years was a long time to be dead, and he's slowly grown used to being Alan McQueen. Being dead has its benefits.

The Service kept Joshua King's death a secret. Only a handful of people knew, although that is about to change, as the ten-year blanket of silence is about to be lifted. Joshua King's death is a week away from becoming public record.

The blueberry muffin doesn't survive King's prodding, and crumbs scatter around the small plate. Furthermore, he let his coffee go cold, and it's quickly becoming an altogether miserable experience. Joshua glances at the board above his gate for an update; there's nothing new. His thoughts once more turn to his days working with Cedric and Ambrose, Randolph Vine, and a woman, the deep sleeper, who was their leader. An invisible team who pulled the strings behind the scenes, preventing a nuclear war, a third world war, or any war.

The five on the Berlin bench—what a night!

Joshua and Randolph were the doers, the tip-of-the-arrow agents in the field who engaged head-on with danger. They understood the twisted deceptions of Russian spies and forged associations within the underbelly of the communist regime.

The Cold War was a game for grown-ups, and their deep-sleeper leader in Moscow knew all the tricks. She was a force of nature, a wild fearless woman who called the shots.

All Secret Service organisations rely on intelligence gathering. Cedric and Ambrose were the best in the business, and without fear of appearing conceited, they would tell you they were the Intelligence part of MI6—they weren't "M" for Military; they were "I" for Intelligence.

Without Cedric and Ambrose, The Cold War would have been colder and bleaker. They deciphered and decoded and dug deep into the triple-play Russian games. They knew the smoke and mirror tricks because Cedric and Ambrose were a two-man encyclopaedic force of deception, politics and history. They released thousands of slight truths to bury a story, preventing the press from printing a headline.

Every team needs a manager in the background to ensure timesheets and expenses are correct, and Linus Pope filled that role. He revelled in the numbness of complex administration and could muster an agreement on foreign policy in a heartbeat with a legally bound paper padlock that no government could unpick. Although annoying, Linus Pope was vital to the success of the Friday Street Spy Ring. Another brief announcement explains further delays to Joshua's flight and he orders another black coffee.

<><><>

Chapter Eight

'Smell this!' says Ambrose.

Charlie turns, and Ambrose dramatically wafts his jar of honey under her nose. She bats his arm away, but Ambrose, in his white beekeeping overalls, edges the jar of honey towards her nose again.

He says. 'Please smell my honey. It's the best I've made.'

'You told me bees make the honey.'

'Nobody likes a smarty pants,' he says.

Charlie sighs and rolls her eyes as she gives in and inhales. The warm, complex aroma captures Tanglefoot Farm's wildflower garden, reminiscent of her favourite spot under the weeping willow. There's a hint of summer, a dash of spring, a spoonful of autumn, and a pinch of winter, all finding their way through the golden syrup. Charlie closes her eyes, lost in the complexities of Ambrose's honey.

'Well? What do you think?'

'I suppose it's okay,' she says without lifting her head.

'You suppose it's okay! Sadly, you've inherited your nose from your father. Randolph couldn't tell the difference between a West Bengal hand-picked tea leaf and a cup of milky tea in a dirty enamel mug.'

'I'm teasing you,' she says. 'Your honey is like sunshine dripping slowly over a mountain top.'

'You're a chump, Charlotte Vine. A first-class chump.'

Charlie smiles and gazes through the kitchen window at nothing in particular.

Ambrose puts the jar back on the shelf. 'I detect something is not quite right, Charlie.' He steps back as if recoiling from his thoughts, saying, 'It's not a boyfriend problem, is it? I can't help you if it is, nor can Cedric. We aren't qualified to help with anything like that.'

'No, it's not that,' she says.

'Are you constipated?'

'No!'

'So why the long face, Red Rum?' He asks.

She gives him a quizzical look.

'Racehorse,' he says, leaving her to figure out the rest.

Charlie opens her bag and takes out the crossword book. The undertones of disappointment are present as she says, 'Why did dad have this in his pocket? The cottage keys, I understand, but crosswords? I keep flicking through the pages hoping to see the faintest message, but there's nothing there.'

Cedric walks into the kitchen, wearing an artist's blue smock, holding a pallet covered with daubs of light peach paint.

'Have you been painting?' asks Charlie.

Cedric points his brush to emphasise his words, 'Your ability to state the obvious knows no bounds.' He turns to Ambrose, 'I've finished the doorframe leading into the library. It needed a light touch-up.'

Charlie says, 'Why did you dress up like Monet to paint a doorframe?'

'It's my painting outfit,' says Cedric.

Ambrose explains that Charlie is wondering why her father had a book of crosswords on him when he was murdered.

Cedric scratches his head. 'It's certainly a mystery because Randolph was useless at crosswords.'

'My dad, useless at crossword puzzles?'

'Quite useless, I'm afraid,' says Cedric. 'I'd say he was as useless as a tetera without a kapáki.'

Cedric and Ambrose roar with laughter—as they always do when they mix their Latin and Greek to comedy effect, especially when they confuse their prey.

'You idiots,' says Charlie.

'Stultus,' says Cedric.

'Vlákas,' adds Ambrose, and they laugh again, walking away from the kitchen to the library to admire Cedric's painting.

Charlie has always made a point of ignoring them when they pivot into their foreign language humour. She flicks through the pages once more, yearning for inspiration to strike her, but there's nothing other than a book full of unsolved clues—across and down.

She reaches into her bag and takes out her father's small bunch of keys. Four keys on a ring is hardly a clue.

Charlie sidles by Cedric and Ambrose, who are preoccupied contemplating wallpaper patterns for the library wall and more than likely won't notice if she pops out for an hour. She checks her watch; there's an hour and fifteen minutes before it's time for morning coffee and lemon drizzle sponge. She walks out the front door with Winnie and sets off down Plum Pudding Lane.

The identifiable sounds of a Saturday morning are as distinct as church bells are to a Sunday morning. There's a pleasurableness to Friday Street like apple crumble with steaming custard and a vicar riding a bicycle.

Halfway down the lane, just after the narrow pinch, Charlie climbs over a wooden stile hiding in a gap among the rhododendrons and clambers up the grassy bank.

Charlie brushes stalks of dried grass and dust from her jeans with her hands, attempting to tidy herself a little, and then walks across the field to the rear gate leading to Linus Pope's house.

Earlier, from the landing window at Tanglefoot Farm, she saw the top of Pope's head pottering about his garden, so she knows he's home.

She knocks.

The door opens with a slowness, and Linus beams an awkward smile before waving Charlie indoors.

'Cedric and Ambrose with you?' He asks with deep lines furrowing across his forehead.

'They're studying wallpaper patterns for the library.'

'As long as it's something of national importance,' says Linus. 'I've made some lemonade. Would you like a glass?'

She nods and follows Linus into a corner of the garden, where the sunlight dapples through the leaves of a gnarly old apple tree. The wrought iron garden chairs, complete with soft yellow cushions, are far more comfortable than they look, and Winnie quickly settles on Charlie's lap.

Linus hands her a lemonade, and she takes a long drink before placing the glass on the table. Without preamble, she asks, 'Was my father any good at crosswords?'

Linus takes an even longer sip of his lemonade, clearly delaying saying anything until it becomes apparent he's avoiding the question.

'Was he?' she pushes.

'Randolph had many fine qualities, but—'

'I know all that,' she says. 'But was he any good at these?' she holds up the crossword book.

Linus's eyes follow the book as Charlie waves it around. He clears his throat and puts his hands on his knees.

He says, 'For all of your father's wonderful talents, none sadly lay in the art of solving crossword puzzles. He was a dazzler, a smooth negotiator, and a fierce field operative. Randolph and Joshua King were a double-act of danger who flew from here to there at frightening speeds.' Linus uses his hands to demonstrate an aircraft. 'Cedric and Ambrose were, *are*, the masters of cryptic puzzles, and I'm sure they've told you how good they are at Greek and Latin conundrums.'

'Too often,' she says, lifting her chin and looking Linus dead in the eye. 'Why have I never heard about Joshua King? And when I do, I find out he died ten years ago.'

Linus is quick to answer.

'You only met Cedric, Ambrose and me. Many would say we are the soft face of the Service. You must remember your father and Joshua King were ruthless agents who performed... let's just say, unpleasant assignments for our crown and country. Your father always wanted that part of his life kept far away from you.' Pope lets his words settle with her a while before adding with a more genial voice, 'Annoyingly, Cedric and Ambrose are geniuses, making life unbearable for everyone else. But you should have seen them back in the day. They could unravel the most complex code and uncover the tiniest clue to avert danger. The Service would then send your father and Joshua King to pull the trigger.' Linus sits back in his garden chair and begins to recount a moment when Britain was in peril. 'This one time—'

Charlie sits forward, making it clear she's not in the mood to hear another story. Linus cocks his head to one side in preparation to listen, showing no sign of taking offence.

'I know you don't believe a mugger killed my father, so let's stop playing those games,' she says. 'Tell me what you know about Joshua King. There must be more to what you told us last night.'

Linus leans forward, steepling his fingers. 'Joshua King died ten years ago. I saw the photographs of the car crash, and I can tell you nobody could have survived that wreck.' He leans back in his garden chair as if his duty is complete and sips his lemonade.

'Who identified King's body?'

'The local police force,' says Linus.

'And?'

'And what?' he says.

'And what else?' says Charlie. She stares at Pope. 'It's a bit convenient that King's email identified my father as a British spy who was killed two days later, and then, Joshua dies in a car crash on the other side of the world the next day. A near-perfect alibi, wouldn't you say?'

'When you piece it together like that, I suppose it sounds a bit—how did you put it? Convenient!'

'How did the Australian police know Joshua King was an MI6 agent?'

'They didn't.'

'So how did they know not to publicise his death?'

'They did publicise his death, but not the correct details. The Sydney police didn't know anyone named Joshua King,' says Linus.

'I don't follow,' says Charlie.

'Field agents never travel using their real identities, so when Joshua King died, the only detail the local police knew was that a British tourist called Edward Jenkins died in a car crash outside Sydney.'

Charlie sits back in her chair. 'And Edward Jenkins was Joshua King's alias?'

'You've got it. The authorities down under notified the British consulate, and their computer system would have triggered them to connect with the British Government, which trickled through to the Intelligence Service. As a result, a hush order was sanctioned for Joshua King's death for ten years.'

'Why ten years?' asks Charlie crossing her legs. Winnie rolls with the movement like a surfer riding a wave.

Linus moves closer and lowers his voice to a whisper, 'It allows us to continue working on any cases King was working on by pretending the agent is still alive.'

'Was Joshua working on a case?'

'I can't tell you.'

Charlie looks at her watch: it's nearly coffee and lemon drizzle time. She wants to pump Pope for more information, but delaying the coffee and cake is more trouble than it's worth. And anyway, she can scramble across the field to ask him more questions at any time. Pope was surprisingly forthcoming, she thinks.

'Come anytime,' says Linus. 'You're always welcome.'

She thanks him and takes off towards the field behind his house.

Linus calls out, 'There is one more thing.'

Charlie turns to face him by the garden gate.

'King's wife is the only civilian who knew King died ten years ago.'

'Joshua was married?'

'Why is that so strange?'

'Only that nobody mentioned that he had a wife. What's her name?'

'Polly. Polly King.'

'Where in the world is she now?'

'She lives in Shere,' he says, pointing to the village over the hill from Friday Street.

Charlie thanks Linus, then runs across the field and clambers down the grassy bank to the wooden stile and speed-walks up Plum Pudding Lane. She skirts around the courtyard at the rear and slips in through the kitchen door to find Cedric and Ambrose still staring at wallpaper books.

'Coffee and lemon drizzle?' she asks, leaning through the library door.

They both look at their watches. 'Perfect timing,' they say.

'We've decided on dark green and gold stripes,' says Ambrose.

'And a pair of brown corduroy reading chairs,' adds Cedric.

'Then it's a good job your morning hasn't been a total waste,' says Charlie, walking into the kitchen.

<><><>

Chapter Nine

'Would either of you like another slice of lemon drizzle?'

'We aren't children, Charlotte Vine,' says Cedric. His tone is borderline acerbic.

Charlie raises her eyebrows to the highest level and tilts her head forward. 'Well?'

'Yes, please,' says Cedric; his tone now contains no hint of bitterness, adding, 'This time, I should get the bigger slice.'

Charlie cuts two slices of cake and pours more coffee from the cafetiere. Cedric and Ambrose study each other's cake and nod their approval.

'What do either of you know about Polly King?' she asks.

'How do you know about Mrs King?' asks Cedric.

'Linus—'

Cedric raises the flat of his hand to prevent her from giving further information and says, 'That man is useless at keeping the Crown's secrets.' Cedric continues muttering under his breath as he eats his cake like a mathematician, cutting his slice into precise triangles, ensuring each mouthful has the correct sponge-to-lemon drizzle ratio—fussy yet neat.

Now impatient, Charlie switches her attention to Ambrose, asking, 'How long was she married to Joshua King before he died?'

Ambrose waves his dessert fork, humming to hint that he knows the answer. He gobbles his slice in three large mouthfuls: no fuss, no bother, and not surprisingly, their eating styles do not betray their frames: Ambrose is shaped like an apple, while Cedric is like a stick of celery. One round and always happy, the other thin and easily irritated.

'One year,' says Ambrose. 'It was a whirlwind romance. They met and married all in one go. Polly King was an attractive man catcher.'

'Was?' asks Charlie.

'I'm sure she still is, but we've not seen her for ten years,' says Ambrose.

Charlie clears their plates away, talking while she loads the dishwasher, 'Linus told me she lives in Shere, so she's no more than fifteen minutes away from Friday Street.'

Cedric sits with a straight back and employs his acerbic undertone again, saying, 'Or a lot longer than fifteen minutes if you have no intention of ever going there to see her.'

Charlie says, 'Polly King practically lives around the corner, and you haven't seen her for ten years. Any reason for that?'

'You're quite authoritative today, Charlotte Vine?' says Cedric.

She ignores that he ignores her question and mumbles, 'I think I'll drive over and introduce myself. She might know something about my dad.'

'She'll definitely know something about your dad because she—' Ambrose is cut short mid-sentence.

'There's no need to go into all that today,' says Cedric, attempting to laugh it off.

Charlie stands in the doorway, preventing them from slipping away unchallenged. She purses her lips and waits to hear more, then opens her eyes wide as if peeping over an invisible pair of spectacles.

'We're cornered,' says Ambrose.

'Don't say anything,' whispers Cedric. 'Not a word!'

'She's staring at me,' says Ambrose. 'I'm not sure I can hold out.'

'Whatever you do, don't tell Charlotte anything,' says Cedric, continuing to whisper.

Charlie steps toward them. 'Stop calling me Charlotte.'

Ambrose gestures for Charlie to sit at the kitchen table, saying 'Very well.' He breathes out in resignation. 'I suppose it's time you should know.'

Charlie sits and waits for them to join her, but her impatience gets the better of her, snapping at them to hurry up.

Ambrose clears his throat several times.

He stammers, 'Well... well, the best way to say it is like this. I mean, the only way to explain, and I'm not altogether sure how to say it. The... the thing is, Charlie—'

Cedric cuts in. 'Your father and Polly-fancy-pants had the briefest affair before she flashed her eyes at Joshua and switched horses.'

'And when you say switched horses, you mean she switched from dad to Joshua?'

'Like I said, she switched horses,' says Cedric.

Charlie's bombardment of thoughts provides no usable questions, so Cedric and Ambrose, noticing her blank expression, take the opportunity to escape from the kitchen to the sanctuary of the library. Cedric scribbles a note that reads: *Charlie somehow knows about Randolph's dalliance with Polly.* He places it against the photograph of him and Ambrose making a rude gesture. They're confident Linus Pope will see the message sometime today. He doesn't miss a trick.

'What do you think Charlie will do?' asks Ambrose.

'Other than stirring up trouble, probably nothing,' says Cedric. 'There's so much she doesn't know, and all of it should be kept under wraps.'

In the kitchen, Charlie is unable to remove her swirling thoughts about Polly King from her head. Finally, she looks down at Winnie, saying, 'I have an idea; let's drive to the delicatessen in Shere and buy some pistachio flavoured ice cream.'

Winnie turns in excitable circles about going for a drive. Charlie pops her head into the library to say goodbye, but Cedric and Ambrose are not there. She runs upstairs, and there's no sign of them there either.

Outside, across the courtyard, Charlie sees colourful ribbons from two straw boaters bobbing about in the back seat of her Jaguar.

Those two will be the death of me!

She runs across the courtyard and opens the driver's door, steps inside, and Winnie jumps up on her lap, ready for the off.

'We thought we'd come, too,' says Ambrose. 'We can't have you running about the Surrey Hills, meeting up with your father's mistress. You never know what you might learn.'

'I'm not a child. I can handle the truth,' she says, revving the engine before easing the Jaguar around Tanglefoot Farm onto Plum Pudding Lane. 'Did either of you know Joshua King died ten years ago?'

Cedric leans forward and says, 'We found out he died when you did.'

Ambrose also leans forward, adding, 'And, Charlie, let's go slowly. This lane is too narrow to race at full pelt, and there's enough mishap in Friday Street without you adding to it.'

Charlie turns to face them and says, 'I'll go slowly if you tell me something I don't know about my father. You are both full of secrets, and it's about time you coughed up something useful.' She revs the powerful engine in readiness to charge at the pinch in the lane. 'Ambrose, you can begin.'

Ambrose roams his eyes back and forth and clicks his finger. 'I've got one. Randolph had a small lock-up in the basement of an old MI6 disused warehouse in London. We saw it once, didn't we, Cedric?'

'Oh yes, it was full of pistols and poisons, false beards and fake passports. Your father was quite the collector.'

'Where is it?' asks Charlie.

Cedric says, 'If we tell you, you'll promise to drive slowly?'

'Yes. Yes,' says Charlie, eager to hear the information.

He sighs, 'Waterloo bridge, under an arch, there's a building that looks like an empty shop. It's nondescript, no signage, not even a number, just a door. However, I'm certain it would have been cleared out years ago.'

Charlie turns to face down the lane, presses the accelerator pedal, and hurtles towards the narrow pinch.

'You said you wouldn't drive fast if we told you a secret,' yells Ambrose.

'This isn't fast!' says Charlie. 'Now, this is fast!' she

drives her father's Jaguar at top speed while her backseat passengers close their eyes. The wing mirrors brush the rhododendrons on both sides of the pinch.

'I suppose we didn't die,' says Cedric.

'Your Grandma Lizzie was a fast driver, wasn't she?' says Charlie.

Ambrose, slowly opening his eyes, smiles and says, 'During the summer holidays, we'd stay with her at Tanglefoot Farm, and she would drive us around the Surrey Hills as if she was in a Grand Prix. Everyone on the road had to be overtaken.'

Cedric adds, 'She told us she killed a top German Spy attempting to escape from a beach during the second world war, and her actions caught the attention of an all-female spy team.'

Ambrose pops his head between the two front seats. 'She was amazing, flying Spitfires, speaking French and German, and Winston Churchill gave her a cigar and a bottle of Pol Roger champagne on her birthday, but you know how these stories get embellished over the years.'

Cedric says, 'In many ways, young Charlie Vine, you are the reincarnation of Grandma Lizzie.'

Once inside the deli, they stare into the glass cabinet at the assembly of colourful tubs, and following an eternity of decision-making, mostly by Cedric, who changes his mind five times, the three of them walk across the quiet street to a wooden bench under a willow tree next to the babbling stream.

'This is a gorgeous little village. I should come here more often,' says Charlie nodding at an old lady sitting on the next bench.

Cedric, who chose honey ice cream, but only after questioning the poor girl behind the counter about the certification of the bees, lets the sunshine settle on his face.

'Where does Polly live?' asks Charlie.

'We don't know,' says Cedric.

'Remember, it's a hot day and a long walk home over the hill,' says Charlie.

'In a cottage opposite the church,' says Ambrose.

Charlie stands in front of them, finishes her ice cream and says, 'Do you know what I would do if I had your combined brainpower?'

'Dress better?' suggests Cedric.

Charlie ignores him. 'I would become a sleuth.'

'Like Miss Marple and Sherlock Holmes?' asks Ambrose.

'Precisely,' she says. 'I would solve unsolvable crimes, and you both could help. You could be Marple and Holmes.'

'They both wear hats,' says Ambrose.

'Good, that's settled,' she says. 'Come on, let's put your mighty brains to work and knock on Polly King's front door.'

'Hold on! Wait a minute,' says Cedric. 'We can't go barging around talking to people. How are we supposed to know about Joshua King's death? It's meant to be a secret.'

'Let's not get bogged down with facts,' says Charlie.

<><><>

Chapter Ten

A mix of terracotta flowerpots and hanging baskets add a colourful garnish to the front of Polly King's pink cottage. Shere is full of prettiness, and every cosy home could equally pose for the village postcard.

Charlie leads the way to the front door and knocks while Cedric and Ambrose hang back, admiring the blooms, although a sign of trepidation may have more to do with their lack of boldness.

Polly King answers the door, and Charlie explains who she is while pointing to Cedric and Ambrose, who do their best to remain preoccupied with a large pot of flatleaf parsley.

Once the flurry of reintroductions is complete, they follow her into the neat, low-ceiling cottage, where Polly invites them to sit.

Cedric and Ambrose sit on a small two-seater, and Charlie takes her usual seat where she can see the whole room and both doors—the passive power position, her father used to call it.

Polly King is in her late forties—a slim, attractive woman who exudes confidence with her looks and posture. She tilts her head slightly upwards, asking if they would like tea.

Cedric and Ambrose nod, checking their watches.

'Do you have Assam?' asks Cedric.

Polly shakes her head. 'Sorry, no. Do you take milk?' she asks in her soft creamy voice.

'No. Lemon, please,' they say.

Polly heads to the kitchen to search for a lemon, and Charlie whispers, 'Milk wouldn't kill you this once.'

Cedric cranes his neck to check Polly isn't standing in the doorway and says, 'Those are my principles, and if you don't like them... well, I have others.'

Ambrose sniggers at Cedric's impersonation of Groucho Marx, and Charlie, as always, takes it in her stride and ignores them.

Polly returns with a broad smile and a small plate with six slices of lemon neatly set in a semi-circle, saying how lovely it is to see them for what must be the first time in ten years.

Cedric raises a finger and, before speaking, catches Charlie's eye. He lightens his tone, 'Nine years, eleven months and twenty-five days, but ten years is close enough.'

They settle into a light chit-chat about the old days in Friday Street, and Charlie waits patiently for an opening. She slides in with the finesse of a cat when a pause finally presents itself.

She says with as much curiosity as she can muster, 'I understand you knew my father quite well.'

'Yes, we were good friends,' says Polly. 'I met him just before I met Joshua, my husband.' Her face turns from joy to one of genuine sorrow as she says, 'I was sorry to hear about Randolph's death; it was a terrible shock and must have been hard for you being so young.' Polly speaks and pours from a teapot with a picture of the Queen emblazoned on the side while offering the lemon slices to Cedric and Ambrose. Polly looks like someone who is invariably well-dressed with immaculate hair and nails.

'I was sorry to hear about Joshua,' says Charlie. 'From what Linus Pope told me, your husband sounded quite the adventurer.'

Cedric and Ambrose glare at her in disbelief. Even with their best unyielding stare, they are unable to prevent Charlie from babbling on about high-level, confidential information—there she is, blurting it out all over Shere Village to the only person who is supposed to know Joshua King is dead.

Polly sips her tea and nods towards a silver photo frame on the shelf above the fireplace.

'That's us in Barcelona a month before his—' She stops herself in her tracks and, in a quieter voice, adds, 'You know, before his car crash in Australia while on a work assignment.'

Charlie reaches out to touch Polly's arm. 'I'm sorry. I didn't mean to churn up sad memories. We only heard yesterday from Linus Pope about the death of your husband.'

'It was a long time ago, a lifetime ago,' says Polly. 'I've run out of tears.'

Cedric walks over to the fireplace to look at the photograph and says, 'Barcelona is a wonderful city. Did you get a chance to swim in the river Besòs?'

The lines on Polly's forehead deepen. 'I don't remember,' she says. 'We travelled a lot back then, and it was probably a flying visit. In and out. More tea?' she holds up the pot.

Cedric and Ambrose both decline.

'This was Joshua's cottage, if I remember,' says Ambrose. 'Lovely frontage. You've done wonders with the place.'

Polly nods. 'Yes, Joshua loved it here and drew up plans to extend the back with a conservatory and add a bathroom upstairs.'

Cedric says, 'It was his mother's place before she went into an old people's home. I remember coming here for Bakewell tart. Joshua was so proud of his mother's cooking.'

'Best Bakewell tart and homemade custard in Surrey,' says Ambrose in agreement.

'She was a wonderful cook,' says Polly. 'I only met her a few times before she entered the nursing home, and Joshua always boasted about her legendary cakes.'

Cedric and Ambrose both slap their thighs. It was their way of bringing any meeting or visit to an end.

'Thank you for the tea,' they say, giving a quick, synchronised nod, bidding Polly their polite farewells.

Charlie carries Winnie outside into the sunshine, and Polly waves from the front door until they are out of sight.

They walk, single file, along the narrow, well-trodden pathway into the church graveyard.

'That was nice,' says Charlie. 'I'm glad I met her.'

'Polly King is a delightful liar,' says Cedric, and wanders off with Ambrose among the ancient gravestones while Winnie darts around the summer tufts of grass, enjoying her moment of freedom.

'Delightful liar?' asks Charlie, catching up with them.

Ambrose crouches to read a weathered gravestone. 'This poor fellow died in the war in 1914. He was only eighteen. Half the young men in Shere and the other villages in the Surrey Hills died in that war, and the ones who survived lost their sons in the next war.'

'Bloody waste!' barks Cedric.

Charlie follows them both towards the church porch. 'You said Polly was a delightful liar. What does that mean?'

Cedric and Ambrose sit on the wooden bench inside the porch, using their boaters as fans to cool their faces. Charlie stands in front of them while Winnie sprawls out on the cold tiles.

'Firstly,' says Ambrose. 'Joshua's mother was a dreadful cook. Everyone knew it. She was actually famous for making the worst Bakewell tart in Shere. The woman couldn't make a cake to save her life, and she would be only too happy to tell you how bad a cook she was.'

Cedric whispers, 'Also, the photograph wasn't taken in Barcelona. Polly has confused the river Besòs with the river Spree.'

'Meaning?' asks Charlie.

'Meaning the photograph was taken in Berlin, not Barcelona.'

'I don't know anything about those rivers, so what does all this mean?' she asks.

'I don't know,' says Cedric. 'But I feel like Sherlock Holmes.'

'And I have a touch of the Miss Marples about me,' says Ambrose.

They put their boaters on and stroll through Shere towards the black Jaguar. On the way, Charlie stops at the corner grocery store and selects a punnet of sun-ripened tomatoes, some white button mushrooms, a large garlic, and a box of thin spaghetti.

Cedric and Ambrose study the contents of Charlie's

shopping and choose two bottles of Chianti and a loaf of crusty bread.

'Sleuthing is a hungry business,' says Charlie. 'And you two earned yourself dinner on the terrace.' She hands them the bag of groceries while she threads her arms through theirs, steering them back to the car.

'Polly is glamorous,' she says.

'She always dressed elegantly,' says Ambrose. 'We never saw her with a hair out of place.'

'Would you like me to cook?' asks Charlie, packing the shopping bag into the front seat.

Cedric and Ambrose burst out laughing and slide into the backseat.

'What's so funny?' Charlie says with a snap.

Charlie never cooked—there was no need. The kitchen at Tanglefoot Farm was a smooth production line of fabulous food. Over the years, Cedric and Ambrose have entertained fascinating people from stage and film, authors and politicians, to artists and academics.

Charlie cooked a disastrous stir fry mince when she first moved into Tanglefoot Farm as a way to thank them for their generosity.

She looks in the mirror, saying, 'My stir fry mince mishap was ten years ago!'

She starts the car and eases the Jaguar out of the village.

'Friday Street is better,' says Ambrose, looking at the perfect cottages lining the lanes of Shere.

'Quite so,' says Cedric. 'You can't beat Friday Street.'

In the courtyard at Tanglefoot Farm, Charlie grabs the shopping bag and walks through the back door.

'So how was your first day sleuthing?' she asks.

'I loved it, and we have another candidate for our suspect list,' says Ambrose.

'Polly?' asks Charlie. 'You think Polly could have murdered my dad?'

Cedric hangs his boater on a hook in the kitchen. 'There's more to being a sleuth than jumping to conclusions,' he says.

'What's Polly's motive?' she asks.

Cedric shrugs his shoulders and thinks for a moment. 'I don't know.'

'What's her alibi?' she asks.

'I don't know that either,' says Cedric. 'But we've learned that sleuthing gives you a big appetite.'

Ambrose opens a bottle of Chianti and pours three glasses, handing one to Charlie, then points to the garden table. 'Go and get comfortable, and we'll make a start on dinner.'

Charlie walks out to the terrace, and Winnie curls up on her lap.

'I know how you feel,' says Charlie. 'Let's go to London tomorrow and look around my dad's lock up.'

Winnie's eyes were already closed.

The wildflower garden runs from the terrace to the top hedge, and the wafts of summer scents blend effortlessly with the spaghetti and tomato sauce topped with shavings of parmesan cheese. Cedric refills their glasses, and Charlie breaks the garlic bread into thick chunks.

She raises her glass and says, 'To finding my father's killer.'

'Cheers,' says Cedric. 'And here's to our first two suspects.'

'Polly, and—?' asks Charlie.

'Joshua King,' says Cedric.

'But he's dead,' she says.

'Being dead doesn't mean he didn't do it,' adds Ambrose.

'Well, that's true,' says Charlie. She loads her fork with spaghetti and begins to eat. 'What shall we call the case?'

'How about, Murder on Friday Street,' says Ambrose. He looks at Charlie with a grimace, adding, 'Too much?'

'Murder on Friday Street,' she says. 'It works.'

<><><>

Chapter Eleven

Joshua King waits in his seat, fighting to contain his impatience with a passenger, a short angry man struggling with his bag, who somehow managed to wedge his case into the overhead locker.

When you couple twenty-four hours of travel with delay upon agonising delay, it's no surprise everyone's level of tolerance is running low. All the seats ahead of Joshua King's row are now empty, and the man continues his failing attempts to free his bag while trapping fifty passengers who are unable to pass him.

If looks could kill!

'Let me,' says Joshua, unfolding himself to his full six-foot-seven height and plucking the bag from the locker without effort. He smiles at the red-faced man.

'You're so lucky being tall,' says the man.

Not really, thinks Joshua.

And he was right. A tall spy has its disadvantages: you stick out, and the one thing you don't want to do as an agent is to stick out. You are memorable. How can you be forgettable when everyone you meet remembers how tall you are?

So, Joshua, through practice, mastered the art of sitting, leaning and avoiding standing next to short people. He crouches in photographs and never stands at the back, where he towers over everybody.

In a way, his height made him a better agent as he constantly thought about standing out, and by doing so, he blended in, apart from when he helped someone with their luggage. If this were a Cold War mission in Russia back in the day, he would have been caught and killed by now.

Joshua King exits the aircraft, appreciating the burn in his leg muscles brought on by his long strides up the ramp leading to the arrivals hall at London's Heathrow Airport.

It's good to be home.

He travels light. One bag—his life on his back.

Joshua King's secret history will remain sealed in a box for a further handful of days, leaving him free to complete his assignment in Friday Street. Some people know he's dead, while others don't know what happened to him. Either way, for the first time in ten years, Joshua King, now reborn, gulps lungfuls of England's sweet summer air.

King is a planner. A careful forecaster. Someone who takes adventurous steps only after calculating the risks ahead. Randolph Vine taught him never to open a door unless you knew what was on the other side—it was a metaphor for their profession.

In stark contradiction to Randolph's own philosophy, he constantly urged Joshua to stop dithering and kick the bloody door down.

King stands in the taxi rank outside the terminal, waiting his turn. He needs to go to Friday Street, but London is easier to lose yourself. He's far too tall to hide in a tiny village with nothing but a handful of cottages, a pond, and a pub.

A London taxi pulls up, and the driver pops his head out the window.

'Where to Guvnor?'

Joshua makes his decision. He slings his pack over his shoulder, saying, 'Do you know a village called Friday Street? It's in the Surrey Hills?'

The driver gives him a London smile. 'As it 'appens, mate, I do. Hop in. It'll take an hour or so.'

Sunday mornings at Tanglefoot Farm are usually quiet, but not this one. Before Cedric and Ambrose stir, Charlie is out with Winnie for a long walk around Friday Street, and as she treads through the lowlands, the fresh air suggests a warm day ahead.

Winnie trots to heal like a show pony, and Charlie chats with her. 'If you had to put some of our money on it, who do you think killed my dad?' Winnie looks up, expecting to receive a treat for listening.

Charlie mulls over her suspects. Firstly there's Joshua King, and according to the sleeping beauties, Sherlock and Miss Marple, Polly King now finds herself on the list. But there must be others, so who would have benefited from killing my father?

The clues aren't much to go on, scraps, really. Hopefully, her trip to the lock-up will prove fruitful. Her ambling takes her to Linus Pope's front door. She knocks without thinking through why she's there.

A moment later, Pope's uncombed, morning head appears. He puts his glasses on and requires a moment to focus.

'Charlotte, I mean Charlie, good morning,' he stands straight and runs his hand through his messy hair. 'Did I miss a note on the library photograph from Cedric and Ambrose?'

Charlie smiles, 'We're going to my father's lock-up in London this morning, and I think you should come with us.'

Linus scratches his head and croaks, 'But it's empty.'

'I know. I want to see it all the same.'

'Can I ask why?'

Charlie picks Winnie up, 'Because Cedric and Ambrose have agreed to help me find my father's killer.'

'After ten years?' asks Linus.

'I have a couple of weeks leave over the summer, and today is day two of the case.'

'Day two?' he asks.

'We went to see Polly King yesterday.'

'How charming,' says Linus.

'She's on the list,' says Charlie.

'List?'

'Our list of suspects,' she says.

'Oh good God,' mutters Pope. 'Am I on it?'

'Probably, yes, along with Joshua King.'

'Not much of a list, is it,' he says.

Charlie leans to one side as a form of agreement and tells him to be at Tanglefoot Farm in an hour. She scampers across the field and slides down the grassy bank, then climbs through the hedge onto the lane.

Pope was right—it wasn't much of a list, especially as nobody looks guilty, apart from Joshua King, and he's dead.

Charlie stomps across the courtyard and opens the kitchen door, where the aroma of freshly ground coffee wafts out to greet her, and the buttery bouquet of warm croissants pulls her to the kitchen. She hears movement upstairs; no doubt there are complications about what to wear.

She leans against the butler sink, devouring the croissant in two bites and sips her coffee, then charges upstairs, shouting to Cedric and Ambrose, asking if they are ready.

Cedric walks in front of her across the landing to Ambrose's room, and she hears them discussing if the mustard-colour corduroy blazers set the right tone for an underground warehouse facility. After thirty minutes, they appear wearing salmon-tailored shorts, yellow shirts and white Panama hats.

'How do we look?' they ask.

'Perfect,' she says. 'Oh, and prepare yourselves; Linus Pope is joining us this morning.'

They nosily huff a long exhale, and their shoulders slouch, much like a teenager after being asked to clean their bedroom.

'Doesn't he have a job to go to?' says Ambrose.

'Linus Pope is such an Oizys,' says Cedric.

Ambrose bursts out laughing in full loud belly laughs. 'Oh, that takes me back to the office,' says Ambrose. 'We called Pope, Oizys. He never once cottoned on.'

Charlie narrows her eyes, and her forehead frowns. 'Come on, then. Fill me in on the joke of the year.'

Between bouts of uncontrollable laughs, Cedric tells her that Oizys is the Greek Goddess of misery.

Ambrose added, 'And Pope never got the joke because he's terrible at Greek mythology—it's his Achilles' elbow.' He laughs again.

A gentle tap on the front door signals Linus Pope's arrival, and Charlie waves at him through the glass to go around the back.

Winnie barks with excitement and runs in circles before charging out of the kitchen door and across the courtyard. Cedric and Ambrose take their time watering the herb garden before making themselves comfortable in the Jaguar's backseat. Charlie walks with Linus across the courtyard and points to the passenger door.

'Mind your Achilles' elbow,' says Cedric.

Giggles from the backseat halt when Charlie races around Tanglefoot Farm at top speed, accelerating down Plum Pudding Lane. She notices Pope's face drain, turning a ghostly pale.

'Open the window if you're feeling uncomfortable,' she says.

'Or you could drive a hundred miles an hour slower,' Pope says.

At the end of the lane, she turns right, following the twists and turns, and then joins the main road. Charlie darts in and out, passing the Sunday morning drivers as if she's dealing with slow backmarkers on a race track.

Her head is full of busy ideas without securing the first step of a plan. She guides the smooth Jaguar effortlessly towards London, noting that Sundays are good days for getting things done.

Linus turns around and asks, 'Am I really on your list of suspects?'

Cedric and Ambrose look at each other and sigh.

'Sadly, no,' says Cedric. 'But if you're annoying, you'll go straight back on.'

Ambrose adds, 'I feel good about today's visit to the lock-up.' He holds up his magnifying glass with its ornate wooden handle and some plastic bags to collect evidence.

Linus Pope tuts, 'In that case, you'll crack the case by lunchtime.'

<><><>

Chapter Twelve

King steps out of the cab and stretches his long limbs.

He's been travelling since the day before yesterday, although it feels like an agonising month filled with miniature seats and processed food.

'Do you want me to hang around for you, Guvnor?' says the chatty driver, who managed to talk without listening for the whole trip. 'There 'ain't much 'ere, mate, apart from a pub and a pond.' The airport driver sticks his nose through his open window and coughs as he breathes the oxygen-rich air, his London lungs unable to cope with the freshness of it all.

Although there's a smidgeon of temptation to make a speedy getaway to the capital, Joshua pays the man and watches the London cab disappear up the twisty steep lane away from Friday Street.

King walks towards the pond, saunters along the pathway, and steps into the Stephan Langton pub.

It feels like yesterday, like a Friday Street Spy Ring day.

There's something unusual, almost spiritual, about

revisiting somewhere familiar after ten years. He sits at the bar and orders his first English beer in a decade. He takes a sip, releasing a long *ahh*.

He thinks about what he has to do and takes another sip.

He doesn't have a plan—a *goal*, yes, but not a plan.

Joshua looks out of the pub's bay window across the pond, noting that nothing, and at the same time everything, has changed. Why should Friday Street change? How could it? It's a perfectly formed oasis of beauty.

From the window, leaning as far to the left as possible, he can see Randolph's cottage. And, of course, the pond where it all happened.

The few tourists who venture off the beaten track take in the view and then leave with a reluctance to tell others to prevent the tiny hamlet from becoming overrun with gawpers. Turning Friday Street into a goldfish bowl would be a crime. So when Randolph Vine's body was discovered in the pond, the Intelligence Service placed a media muzzle over the release of details, and the public knew nothing of the grisly crime. And because of that, Friday Street remains in the shadows.

Joshua casts his eyes over the menu and orders a roast beef Sunday lunch with roast potatoes, Yorkshire pudding, and all the trimmings. For ten years, he's dreamt of a pub Sunday roast, so he orders an extra Yorkshire pudding to compensate.

Joshua closes his eyes, half expecting Linus, Randolph, Cedric and Ambrose to be waiting for him to join them for a Friday Street Spy Ring meeting. His food arrives, and he takes his roast and pint to the alcove and immerses himself in Friday evening memories. It was the same every week:

field operatives versus the office—spies versus Intelligence, with Linus Pope playing the referee.

King smiles—they were great evenings, the best of times.

One Friday evening, Joshua explained how Randolph always did the same thing when stepping into a crowded elevator, wherever they were in the world: he would say to the strangers, 'You're probably wondering why I called this meeting?'

Cedric and Ambrose loved listening to Joshua and Randolph's life on the road, their life on the edge. They didn't crave it, and there was no jealousy. Their world was Intelligence, not action.

Joshua eats his roast lunch and orders another pint of ale, wondering if Cedric and Ambrose ever suspected him of killing Randolph Vine. How could they? They believed he was on a plane heading for Australia.

Charlie pulls the Jaguar to a smooth halt outside the archway underneath Waterloo Bridge. From the outside, the Government lock-up looks like a shop that closed for business several years ago; such was its state of abandonment with dozens of ripped posters glued at irregular angles, one on top of the other, faded by age and weather.

The bricked-up archway to the right looks equally abandoned, and the archway on the left is a Polish nightclub and bar.

'Is that it?' asks Charlie.

On workdays, hordes of commuters walk by without registering the rundown archway shop, focusing only on getting to work. At weekends, the tourists pass by, scurrying to a place of interest.

Linus looks through the passenger window, admiring the invisible lock-up. 'It's perfect,' he says. 'The Service has storage units and safehouses like this one all over the city.'

'All derelict?' says Charlie.

Linus Pope nods as he clambers out of the car and approaches the front door. Winnie wakes up and sits bolt upright on Charlie's lap.

Ambrose says, 'How do we get in?'

Charlie points at Pope, 'Why else do you think I brought the man with the code and the key.'

'You're just like your father,' says Cedric. 'Randolph was never short of cunning, even if it meant putting up with the Pope for an hour in the car.'

They amble towards the shop, and Linus holds the door open. They walk inside, where dust particles tumble in rays of light from the torn posters on the window.

'I like what you've done with the place, Pope,' says Cedric.

Linus selects a key from his bunch and opens a door at the back of the shop. He flicks a grubby light switch, which dimly illuminates a staircase that disappears down into a black hole.

Charlie nudges Ambrose, 'You'll need your magnifying glass to see your way down there.'

'I'm more concerned about getting my pink shorts dirty,' he says, peering into the abyss. 'I'll stay up here and keep watch.'

Charlie tilts her head, 'Are you scared, Ambrose?'

'Of course I am. I should have stayed at home.'

She ignores him, saying, 'That's good. Lead the way.'

Ambrose holds the sticky bannister and takes his first step into the dimming light. Cedric follows, and then Charlie with Winnie in her arms.

Linus Pope locks the front door and joins them, clomping their way down into the darkness.

He shouts to Ambrose, 'There's a light switch at the bottom of the stairs.'

'Could you have found an eerier place for MI6 to keep their secrets?' says Charlie.

Linus Pope says defensively, 'The Service bought this place in the nineteen fifties because it has an underground storage area. Nobody will ever think this is a secure Government site.'

Ambrose flicks the light switch at the bottom of the staircase, and an endless row of overhead fluorescent lights begin to hum, slowly flickering to produce an unflattering cast of yellow light.

Hundreds of floor-to-ceiling wire cages with heavy-duty electronic locks line the walls—the dank concrete floor smells of mould from an age of unpleasantness.

'Well, this is decidedly the worst place I've ever seen,' says Cedric. He tuts, adding, 'Next time, I suggest the Service doesn't buy a storage unit under the River Thames. I can smell the sludge.'

Ambrose stands with his hands in his pockets, looking at the grim basement. 'I'm not touching anything.'

Each cage displays a code on a metal square in the top right-hand corner with department initials and dates to form a nine-digit alphanumeric encryption.

'This could take forever,' sighs Charlie. 'I thought this was a storage unit where you put your sofa and a box of books when you move house. It stinks of dead things down here.' She holds onto Winnie.

Linus Pope uses a small torch to illuminate the codes, walking quickly from cage to cage. The others tag along.

'He seems to know what he's looking for,' says Ambrose. 'He's in one of his "take charge" moments.'

Pope's pace slows until he stops in front of a cage with the code: FOR-2012-RV. He points, saying, 'Field Office Russia. 2012. Randolph Vine.'

Nobody moves for a minute.

Charlie slowly edges towards the dark cage and runs her finger over the thick wire frame. 'Are all these cages for dead agents?'

'No, not all of them,' says Pope. 'Most contain boxes of old case notes, and some will store confiscated evidence, while others have remnants from the lives of turned foreign agents. It's a real treasure trove down here.'

'But it's unguarded,' says Charlie.

'It's monitored,' says Pope.

Charlie looks confused.

Pope points to the strip lights on the ceiling.

'They might look like old neon lights from a school classroom, but they are cameras. The whole facility locks down if you punch in the wrong code on the cage.'

'A little dramatic,' says Charlie.

'Everything about MI6 is cloak-and-dagger dramatic,' says Ambrose. 'They can't boil an egg without a fanfare.'

'Concentrate then, Pope,' says Cedric. 'We could be stuck down here until tomorrow morning waiting for some spotty underpaid junior of yours to look at the film footage.'

Pope takes out his notebook and taps a seven-digit code onto the keypad. A green light flashes twice, and he turns the key. The cage door pings open.

'*Voilà*,' says Pope, holding the door open for Charlie, who takes a few tentative steps into the dark cage. A sensor buzzes, followed by a shower of white light from an overhead bulb. Four plastic boxes are stacked in one corner, and a cardboard box sits in the other.

Charlie steps to the corner and removes the lid from the top plastic box. It's empty. The one beneath is also empty, as are the bottom two.

She says, 'Why would Dad store empty boxes?'

Nobody answers.

'This makes no sense!' Charlie says, scooting across to the cardboard box in the opposite corner. She rips off the packing tape and peers inside the empty box. 'Please tell me this is the wrong cage.'

Linus Pope looks apologetic. 'I did say it was empty.'

Cedric takes Pope's torch, saying, 'That's true, but you are often wrong.' He shines the torch around, muttering, 'This wasn't Randolph's style.'

Charlie looks up at him. 'What do you mean?'

Cedric crouches next to her, whispering, 'Randolph loved clues. He lived for the dramatic and would have loved this place. Your father's empty cage is telling us something.'

Charlie puts Winnie on the concrete floor, and after a minute or two, she begins sniffing and scratching the cardboard box.

'What is it, Winnie?' says Charlie.

Pope says with an ounce of impatience, 'There's nothing here. Our boys searched every inch of this cage from top to bottom after your father died.'

'Wait, what's that?' says Charlie lifting the box closer to Cedric's torch beam.

Ambrose moves his magnifying glass back and forth to look at a faint line of text inside the box. He whispers, 'Pope, write this down: OSGR 12756 45789.'

'What does that mean?' says Charlie.

'I don't know, but it could be a clue,' says Ambrose.

Pope's impatience bubbles over, and he snorts, 'It could be anything, but probably, nothing.'

'OSGR,' says Cedric. He mutters it several times under his breath before clicking his fingers and speaking slowly, 'How about Ordinance Survey Grid Reference?'

'That's it,' says Ambrose. 'It's a map reference.'

'For what?' asks Charlie, stretching her back.

'I don't know,' says Cedric. 'There are millions of grid references.'

'How do we find out what it is?' she asks.

'We need to go to our map box in the library at Tanglefoot Farm,' says Ambrose. 'We've got thousands of maps.'

'Or I could look it up on my phone,' says Charlie. 'Come on, let's leave this creepy place.'

Pope shuts the cage door, enters the code, and the flashing green light locks the unit.

On the climb back up the narrow staircase, Charlie's phone finds a signal, and she taps in the coordinates. She stops dead in her tracks, and the others come to a standstill behind her. Charlie enlarges the image on her phone and turns to show Cedric and Ambrose.

They look at each other.

'Well, I wasn't expecting that,' says Cedric.

'Nor me,' says Ambrose.

'Let's go now!' says Charlie, bounding back up the staircase to the uninhabited shop.

Linus Pope arrives at the top of the staircase and turns off the lights.

He asks, 'So what is it?'

'A mystery garage,' says Charlie.

<><><>

Chapter Thirteen

Charlie is upbeat about the grid reference.

She had no idea her father owned a garage in Friday Street. You can never know everything about someone, especially when it's your dad.

Charlie fires up the Jaguar and is happy to pull away from the dank, abandoned, stinking lock-up under Waterloo Bridge, although the smell from the basement clings to her clothes.

She buzzes the window down, and the rushing summer air freshens her hair.

Linus Pope chats on his phone, attempting to sort an administration mishap at the office, while Cedric and Ambrose mutter while checking their shirts and shorts for basement dirt. They vigorously rub at marks and dirt patches with their white handkerchiefs, tutting as they go until they're satisfied they are presentable.

Charlie mulls over the new clue her father scribbled on the cardboard box, and her heart sinks as she considers it might be from someone randomly dumping it in her dad's underground unit. However, it would be hugely coincidental if somebody else had a garage in Friday Street and a cage in MI6's underground lock-up. Although, Friday Street is a village of spies.

Linus Pope was nearly right. The lock-up was empty. But a clue is a clue, and her mind turns somersaults, speculating what's in the garage.

Charlie contemplates the possibilities while zooming around the roundabout at Elephant and Castle faster than other road users and notices Pope is chatting on the phone with his eyes closed.

Cedric says, 'It's nearly time for a cup of tea.'

Charlie says, 'I know a lovely place on Chelsea Bridge.'

'Is it one of your biker places?' asks Cedric.

She says, 'You'll love it.'

'I doubt it,' says Cedric. 'We'll probably catch Lupus.'

Pope finishes his call and says, 'It might toughen you up a bit.'

Charlie swerves hard right, and Pope bangs his head on the car door. He lets out a high pitch squeal.

'No singing in the car, Pope,' says Ambrose.

Charlie parks the Jaguar on the kerb next to a tea hut on the south side of Chelsea Bridge and turns off the engine. She faces the backseat and forbids Cedric and Ambrose to ask if the man has Assam tea and lemon slices.

Cedric's face scrunches, and he nudges Ambrose, pointing to the large enamel mugs on the tea hut's counter.

They all step out of the car and join the end of the queue where three burly construction workers, a delivery driver, a biker, and a mother and daughter from Chicago wait in line.

Charlie points to a spot at the end of the line and says to Cedric and Ambrose, 'Don't say anything, and don't do anything to attract attention.'

'This isn't our first time ordering a mug of tea from a place liable to transmit a sexual disease,' says Cedric.

'Right there. That's what I mean,' says Charlie shaking her head. 'Put your thinking to better use. What do you think is in the garage?'

'Your father did everything for a reason,' says Ambrose. 'No doubt it's full of his spy stuff.'

Charlie orders four mugs of tea and four slices of apricot sponge from the man in the hut, who tells her with brimming enthusiasm that his wife made it, which makes him happy.

Cedric takes a bite and makes a humming sound. 'It's delicious,' he says, looking baffled. 'It's genuinely good.'

They finish their tea and cake, and Pope returns the mugs and plates to the hut.

'Time to go, buttercups,' says Charlie.

She has her father's garage on her mind and heads towards the Jaguar, where the conversation in the car on the way home switches from topic to topic when Ambrose asks Pope a good question.

'Apart from the mugging theory, did the police follow any other line of enquiry?'

Linus Pope says they interviewed a man called Kevin Hall. Nothing came of it, as he had a strong alibi for the time of the killing.

'Who is Kevin Hall, and what was his alibi?' asks Charlie.

'I don't know any more,' says Pope.

'We should track him down and ask him ourselves. Where does he live?' asks Charlie, adding an extra spurt of power to an already uncomfortable speed.

'I don't know anything more than what I just told you,' says Pope.

'You're the only one who knows anything at all,' she says.

'Maybe you can look up Kevin Hall on your clever telephone,' says Cedric.

Charlie doesn't respond. Her eyes narrow as the mental and emotional machinery begin to grind, contemplating the case. After ten minutes of silence, she turns to Pope.

'I'll drop you home on the way through.' The words spill out as a firm statement, not a question which means he isn't going to the garage—Linus Pope is going home. She stops outside his house and jumps out, hugging him goodbye.

Cedric and Ambrose watch Charlie from the backseat.

'Why is she hugging him?' asks Ambrose.

'Because she's clever,' says Cedric. 'She'll need more information from the old bore, so she's keeping him sweet.'

'Clever girl,' says Ambrose.

'She's too clever for Pope, just like her dad,' says Cedric.

Charlie clambers back into the Jaguar and waves enthusiastically at Pope as he walks up his garden path. She calls out from the lowered car window and tells Linus he's a lifesaver.

'Lifesaver is a little over the top,' says Cedric.

Charlie launches the car like a rocket down the lane, and Winnie balances on her lap, leaning like a seasoned pillion with each corner.

'Who the hell is Kevin Hall?' she says.

Cedric leans forward. 'I don't know. It's the first I've heard of him.'

Charlie steers along the lane in Friday Street, past the Stephan Langton pub, and parks outside the green door at the far end of a neat row of garages.

'This is it,' she says.

They exit the Jaguar, and Winnie runs around on a small patch of grass. Charlie tugs at the garage door handle, but it's locked and doesn't move an inch. She pushes the top of the door, kicks the bottom, and then leans against the sides, but it doesn't budge.

'Do either of you have a crowbar?' she asks, laughing and snorting at her question.

Ambrose puts his hands on his hips and stares at the door. 'Randolph wouldn't send us here unless he knew we could get in, so there must be a simple solution staring us in the face.'

Charlie clicks her fingers and opens the Jaguar driver's door, grabbing her father's bunch of four keys that came with the crossword book in the shoe box.

'*Voilà!*' she says, jiggling the keys. She unlocks the door and lifts it up and over in one smooth movement.

Ten years of undisturbed dust swirls in a shadowy cloud until the gloom finally clears. Cedric and Ambrose sharply draw in air over their teeth, then whistle as they exhale.

'I was not expecting that,' Ambrose says.

'I hoped I'd never see the old girl ever again,' snaps Cedric.

Charlie takes a few tentative steps into the garage. 'What is it?'

Cedric and Ambrose point to what is taking up half the garage.

Ambrose says, 'Charlie, meet Elsie.'

'Who the hell is Elsie?'

<><><>

Chapter Fourteen

Charlie

So, here I am, standing in my dad's mystery garage in Friday Street.

'Go on then. Who's Elsie?'

I didn't mean for my tone to be quite so impatient.

Cedric and Ambrose loop their arms through mine and walk me slowly towards what I can only describe as the most beautiful machine I've ever seen. I reach out and touch Elsie's curves, and the evocative smell of engine oil wafts up my nose and tingles like a glass of champagne.

'Elsie belonged to Grandma Lizzie,' says Ambrose. 'She thought it was too dangerous for us to have.'

Cedric unconvincingly says, 'I think, given time, I could master a machine like this.'

I stare at him, and he does his best to appear slightly alpha. My giggle puts him straight.

Elsie is a classic Norton motorbike with a rocket-like, silver sidecar that has a whiff of the Second World War about it. A coating of dust has settled on the paint and chrome trim from its years in captivity. However, it's a work of art with its retro styling and, dare I say; it looks ready to ride.

I swing my leg over the bike and sit on the saddle; what a beast she is—everything about Elsie screams speed and power: my two favourite words. The sidecar has two red leather seats with comfortable cushions.

'Did you two sit in there?'

Ambrose nods, cautiously opening the glass lid. He climbs in the front seat, and Cedric clambers into the seat behind.

'Oh look,' says Ambrose with a note of jubilant surprise. 'Our green corduroy motoring caps are still here.'

They put them on, and I do all I can not to burst out with laughter. Naturally, the caps suit them, and after a minute of fussing over the angle of the material, they look at me for appraisal.

I tell them, and mean it, that Grandma Lizzie would be proud.

I open the fuel cap and see the silvery glow of petrol shimmering at the bottom of the tank. Surely this old beauty won't start.

There's no key in the ignition—it could be anywhere, lost forever.

A thought flits through my mind, so I climb off the motorbike and step over to the garage door and take the keys from the lock. The smallest of the four keys fits perfectly into the ignition on the handlebars. I turn it, and coloured lights illuminate inside the old glass dials.

I thrust my weight downwards on the kickstarter, and the engine coughs and splutters before guffing a dark plume of fumes from the exhaust.

My two passengers attempt to climb out of the sidecar, but not before I bear down on the kickstarter once more. And this time with success. The engine roars like a growling racing car. I flick the bike into first gear with my foot, release the brake, and ease Elsie out of the garage.

The throb of the engine vibrates through every bone in my body.

Just a little test run, I tell them above the ear-shattering roar.

I put on the pair of goggles that hang from the handlebars and open the throttle. The Norton responds. Grandma Lizzie certainly loved power and no doubt enjoyed frightening her two grandsons just as much.

'Not too fast,' shouts Cedric, knocking on the glass sidecar cover. He looks fearful as I trundle past the Stephan Langton pub. I pick up speed, and the wind flicks at my hair. I turn the collar up on my leather jacket and lean slightly forward.

Ambrose screams, 'Oh no, she's leaning forward.'

'Hold on,' I bark and race around the pond.

The tyres squeal, and the engine roars as I chase up the hill. This is a flying machine. I bet the sidecar boys were scared half to death when Grandma Lizzie whizzed around the countryside. Whoever tuned the engine knew what they were doing.

'Do you have to ride quite so fast?' shouts Cedric as the sidecar wheel lifts off the ground. The baritone roar from the exhaust pipes drowns out his voice, and if I'm honest, I can hear him well enough but choose to ignore him.

Oh yes, I could get used to this.

The gear changes are fluid, and the cornering is effortless, even with those two sacks of potatoes crying out for me to stop. I take one more lap down the hill and around the pond before parking Elsie in the garage.

The Norton engine ticks as it cools, and my nerve endings jangle as I gradually calm down from the adrenaline rush. Cedric and Ambrose climb out of the sidecar, and apparently, according to them, I'm as reckless as Grandma Lizzie—I take that as a compliment.

The back wall of the garage is lined with shelves crammed with overflowing boxes, stacks of books and messy piles of documents.

Unusual for Dad to be so untidy. He wasn't fussy, but he was never this messy.

Cedric and Ambrose rub their backs from the trip in the sidecar and look as surprised as I am about Dad's shambles on the shelves.

Although Cedric and Ambrose find the shelves interesting, I can't take my eyes off the flying machine and say, 'How did Elsie end up here?'

Ambrose says, 'Grandma Lizzie rode her until she was over eighty-five, and we were both delighted when she finally hung up her goggles. To be honest, we had no idea Elsie was here.'

'We had no idea this garage was here,' says Cedric.

'And why do you call her Elsie?' I ask.

'It's a Norton L.C,' says Cedric. 'As kids, we always thought Grandma Lizzie was calling it Elsie, not L.C, and it stuck.'

To me, it's a thing of beauty. It's rustic, charming, fast, and more than likely dangerous, probably illegal, and better still, it scares the living daylights out of Cedric and

Ambrose. I'll walk back later this evening with Winnie and ride Elsie back to Tanglefoot Farm and park her next to the Jaguar.

I look at the bodywork, and from a cursory glance, the motorbike and sidecar are in good condition. A good clean, and thorough service should ensure the moving parts—keep moving.

I notice a tall man walking away from the pond. I can't be certain if he was looking at me. Tourists come to walk around the Surrey Hills, and often, by chance, they stumble across Friday Street. You can drop a pin on a map and find somewhere breathtaking to visit around here. A thousand shades of green fill the forests, and tiny pathways meander around the countryside, so it's not unusual for people to stand and stare.

Dad spoke to everyone, and a chatty exchange was effortless for him. I wish I was more like that. A whole week can pass before I realise I've not spoken to another soul. I don't count Cedric and Ambrose.

They fuss over their green corduroy caps. Heaven forbid some dust landed on the material! They take turns looking in the motorbike side mirror, then carefully place the caps in the tiny glove box in the sidecar.

Their encyclopaedic minds are full of codes, intricate details, languages and historical facts, yet it amazes me how they spend an unusual amount of time deciding what to wear.

My thoughts shift to the police. Can I speak to the police? What do they know? Nothing new, probably. They've stuck with the mugging theory for ten years, so I've no reason to think they'll suddenly get a change of heart. Shame I was a kid back then. Obviously, I didn't see myself as a kid. Who does at eighteen? If Dad died now, rather than back then, I would not stop banging on the door of the officer in charge.

Kevin Hall comes to mind, and I mention to Cedric and Ambrose that I'll look him up once we're back at Tanglefoot Farm.

'This Kevin Hall fellow could potentially be your father's killer,' says Cedric. 'Should we be poking the bear with a stick?'

'The police believed his alibi,' Ambrose reminds him.

'Alibis can be fabricated,' says Cedric.

'The name Kevin doesn't sound like a killer's name,' says Ambrose.

I tell them that I knew a Kevin at Cambridge who was arrested for drugs. I know that's not the same, but it puts the name Kevin in question.

I lock the garage and look at the keys in my hand. I assumed they were Dad's keys to the cottage—that's how easy it is to miss a clue. Maybe I should take another look at the empty crossword book.

Winnie waits for me to sit in the driver's seat, then launches onto my lap. I kiss the top of her head and reach for my phone. I scroll through the contacts and click on Linus Pope's name.

He answers on the first ring.

'Hello, Linus.'

'Hello, Charlie. Any luck at your father's mystery garage?'

I tell him about Elsie and that I'll need time to rifle through everything. I suggest I take a week off before my summer break and ask if he can arrange it for me in my softest voice, adding that I don't know what I'd do without him.

Cedric coughs, saying, 'Manipulator.'

Ambrose laughs, and I wave a hand to shush them.

Linus Pope agrees to fix it for me. He's good like that. I drive around the pond at Friday Street and head for Tanglefoot Farm.

Kevin Hall is back on my mind. He might have murdered my dad. I race up Plum Pudding Lane and park in the garage. It's late afternoon, and Cedric and Ambrose are beginning to flag, so I offer them a slice of cake.

Finding Elsie was not a mighty step forward in the case, but somehow I felt Dad was guiding us. After I've had a cup of tea, I'll walk the long way across the fields to collect Elsie. A good march will get my brain ticking over.

I tap Kevin Hall's name into my computer while I wait for the water to boil. At work, I have access to a database that could find him and locate his position in a heartbeat, but I can't use it. Not even Linus Pope can use it unless it's an official operation. And this is absolutely unofficial.

Social media sites work just as well as MI6's databases, and I find two possible Kevin Hall's by the time the water has boiled.

'There's a Kevin Hall in Holmbury St Mary,' I say.

'That's no more than a casual jog over the hill,' says Ambrose.

Cedric snorts, 'You, Jog? You haven't jogged since we were in Berlin being chased by the Stasi.'

I suggest a drive-by tomorrow.

'I don't think we should shoot him quite yet,' says Ambrose.

Confronting Kevin Hall is exciting, but what do we say to him? I casually float my thoughts.

'We don't confront him,' says Cedric. 'We are Intelligence Officers. We gather intelligence. That's our task. We aren't field agents.'

Ambrose eats his slice of cake in two mouthfuls, and crumbs tumble down his yellow shirt. He says, 'First, we locate this Kevin Hall chap, and then we dive deep into his life.'

I circle the island in the kitchen, thinking we need a central base for our case. I click my fingers, saying, 'Let's make the garage our operations room.'

'We'll die of asthma,' says Cedric.

'No, not in my father's mystery garage. Let's set up our ops room in the garage around the back where I park the Jaguar and where I'll keep Elsie.' Things are coming together. I can feel it.

'Can we have a wall for our suspects?' asks Ambrose.

I'll leave them to arrange photos of our suspects. They'll spend hours measuring and sticking and making sure the colours match. Heaven forbid I use the wrong colour pen.

I announce I'm taking Winnie to collect Elsie and kiss them goodbye before setting off down Plum Pudding Lane. Winnie keeps up as I quick-step left, right, left, right to the bottom, then cut through the gate and across the field. My marching feet keep a good pace while my mind floods with thoughts, doubt mostly, followed by a hit of confidence, then an override of certainty that I'm doing the right thing to find my father's killer.

Am I?

I clamber over a few more fences and follow hedgerows taking the long way around the fields until I arrive at the pond in Friday Street.

I take Dad's keys out of my pocket and open the garage. Elsie makes me smile. I put Grandma Lizzie's goggles on and lift Winnie into the sidecar to sit on the cushion. My first stamp of the kickstarter fires up the raucous engine, and I steer Elsie out of the garage. I jump off and lock the door.

The tall man I saw earlier walks into the Stephan Langton pub.

On my return to Tanglefoot Farm, I think about tomorrow and the drive-by and vow *not* to punch Kevin Hall in the face.

<><><>

Chapter Fifteen

Incomplete grieving has a tendency to leave wounds in the heart, and grief left completely unattended over time festers and turns on the host. Joshua King's heart has festered for ten years, and the overwhelming guilt has finally crushed his spirit.

He calls a taxi from the Stephan Langton pub and steps outside to wait. The late hour in Friday Street offers nothing more than a few lights shining through gaps in curtains and a distant voice trailing off to leave a stillness he's not experienced for a long time. He looks at his watch and checks for his taxi, reflecting on his first day in ten years in Friday Street which delivered a host of surprises.

After lunch, he left his backpack behind the bar and spent the afternoon strolling around the pond, eventually settling on a bench overlooking the water where Randolph Vine's body was found. King stared into the water, wishing things had turned out differently.

His afternoon contemplation was interrupted by a car speeding down the hill—the vehicle was Randolph's unmistakable classic black Jaguar which took him by surprise.

Joshua watched the dark blur speed along the lane, past the pub, and shudder to a cloudy halt outside the last in a row of garages.

He watched a young woman in a motorbike jacket, a white T-shirt, and jeans step from the driver's door with a tiny poodle.

That couldn't be Charlotte, not Randolph's girl. Her age was about right; she'd be twenty-eight. King slumped out of sight on his bench and watched Charlie Vine and two men who stepped out from the backseat. A tall thin man and a short round man who wore salmon pink shorts, yellow shirts, and Panama hats—Cedric and Ambrose!

They're alive! Good.

Joshua watched as the three stepped into the garage's dark abyss, slipping from his view. King moved from his bench and walked around the pond to find a better position. The sound of an engine backfiring came from the garage, and a moment later, through a plume of dirty exhaust, a motorbike and sidecar trundled out.

He watched as Charlie rode the motorbike, and Cedric and Ambrose perched in the sidecar along with their white faces and green caps, giving her commands, no doubt about speed and safety. And that was Joshua's chance to see inside this mystery garage.

He clambered over the pub wall and ran into the garage. The shelves on the back wall of the garage were crammed with books and maps, jars and oddments. The decade of grey dust would have shown his fingerprints if he moved anything, so Joshua slipped from the garage and hid in the pub garden before the motorbike and sidecar sped back up the lane. He waited for them to leave in the Jaguar and sauntered around the pond again. Nothing and everything in Friday Street had changed.

The rest of his afternoon flittered away, and he ordered a sandwich and a beer while waiting for a veil of darkness to descend over the village. From out of the gloom, he saw Charlie and her small dog walk briskly up the lane. King stepped back into the shadows of the pub and watched her open the garage and, a moment later, ride the motorbike and sidecar off into the night.

The dark of Friday Street is now total, and the headlights of his taxi are visible from over the top of the hill. He clambers into the back seat and gives the driver the address of his hotel. Jet lag finally kicks in like a punch to the head, and his last thought before his eyes close is the image of Randolph's dead body floating in the pond.

<><><>

Chapter Sixteen

Cedric wakes with a start.

Last night's frightening ride inside Elsie's wretched sidecar churned up memories he'd squashed deep down into his gut from when he and Ambrose first moved into Tanglefoot Farm with Grandma Lizzie as young boys.

His torment begins to calm, and his thoughts gently shift to the new ops room. He tells himself it'll need managing at a leadership level, but not until after a good breakfast.

Identifying a killer is an intellectual process of careful precision steps, taken one piece of irrefutable evidence at a time. The problem is people lie, and Cedric knows from his time in the Service that people lie all the time. He always told the truth and quickly discovered that people recoiled from the truth when he told them their clothes were wrongly coordinated, or their hair was too grey, or their house was in the wrong street. People just don't like the truth—they prefer the convenience of lying to others and themselves.

Cedric's mind is foggy after the bottle of crispy Sancerre they drank last night to recover from the spin in Elsie. Of course, the fogginess might have been the bottle of Chablis they drank before—or the glass of dry sherry before that. What was he thinking? They had nothing to celebrate, yet Charlie kept pouring as though they'd landed on the moon, and Ambrose has an innocent way of making the wine flow—of course, he's to blame; he's nine minutes younger.

Egg on toast and freshly squeezed orange juice should see him back to his enthusiastic best to track down Randolph's killer.

Ambrose taps on Cedric's bedroom door, waits for the agreed seven seconds, and enters with a cup of tea.

The twins concluded that seven seconds allowed for any compromising situation to become uncompromised before opening a door. They discussed every possible length of time between knock and entry, and it took all of September 1979 to arrive at seven seconds.

'Thank you, dear boy,' says Cedric, taking the cup of tea. 'Is Charlie up yet?'

'She's gone for a run.'

'Where?'

'To Shere and back,' says Ambrose.

'Why?'

'She set off in running shoes and a black hat, so I'm guessing some sort of exercise,' says Ambrose, sipping his tea. 'I could have been a runner. I have runners' feet.'

'No, you have athlete's foot,' says Cedric. 'It's quite different, like the time you had tennis elbow during Wimbledon.'

Winnie is still sleeping in Charlie's bed. Technically, she's Cedric and Ambrose's dog, but when Charlie came to live at Tanglefoot Farm after her father died, she sobbed herself to sleep every night. Winnie went to comfort her, and they've been inseparable ever since—the little turncoat.

'Poached or scrambled?' Ambrose asks.

'Scrambled,' says Cedric, meaning he'll have to cook. For all his outstanding qualities in the kitchen, Ambrose can't scramble an egg. Cedric has tried to show him how it's done properly, but for the love of Moses, the man refuses to learn.

Monday's clothing colours are preset to blue and cream, so with blue blazers and cream trousers, Cedric and Ambrose head to the kitchen to begin breakfast.

'This Kevin Hall chappy,' Cedric says. 'Shall we play good cops, bad cop?'

'Charlie being the bad cop, right?' confirms Ambrose.

Neither of them have *bad cop* bones and jointly conclude that if Kevin Hall needs ruffing up, Charlie is the designated fighter who can put the frighteners on Hall by grabbing his lapels and pushing him around.

Charlie walks into the kitchen with sweat dripping from her chin, picks up a glass of freshly squeezed orange juice, and gulps it down. She explains in quite a robust way that nobody will be grabbed by the lapels, pushed around, or roughed up. And there will be no good cop, bad cop drama, adding, as she heads upstairs for a shower, that they are only gathering intelligence.

Cedric calls after her, 'If you're thirsty, you should drink water.'

She returns in record time with wet hair and stands at the kitchen island, eating a plateful of scrambled eggs on thick sourdough toast, two hash browns, and mushrooms.

'Chairs are an excellent invention, you know,' says Cedric. 'You eat like a horse!'

Charlie ignores him and loads her fork with the last hash brown while making a naying sound like a horse. She feeds Winnie a small piece of toast with bits of egg.

She says, 'I saw a tall man in Friday Street last night when I collected Elsie. I saw him earlier, too. It was as if he didn't want to be seen.'

'That's a lovely story,' says Cedric, lifting his chin to appear taller.

Cedric is six feet tall, and he'll tell you he's the standard height for a man. However, his doctor in Harley Street measured him when he was twenty-five, and apparently, he stands just under five foot eleven inches, but he never told Ambrose. He never told anyone.

Cedric changed doctors the following day.

'I'll print photos of our suspects,' says Ambrose. 'Colour I think. Black and white will make them look too spooky.'

'We have a corkboard somewhere,' adds Cedric, searching for office supplies.

In the Service, Cedric and Ambrose loved the days when Randolph and Joshua popped into HQ after a mission. They would sit on the corner of a desk and regale them with their recent adventure. Cedric and Ambrose's activities were less aggressive, involving embedding complex codes in a user manual for a toaster in the Greek language section for one of their agents in Eastern Europe.

Neither Cedric nor Ambrose have been involved in a fight. Conversely, Charlie was brought up on a diet of Kung Fu, boxing and fast cars, encouraged entirely by her father.

Randolph's parents were gentle, softly-spoken teachers, and he turned out to be a spy. Cedric and Ambrose's father was a violent heavy drinker, who punched them in the face one Christmas to toughen them up, and they turned out... well, they turned out.

Their father died in an industrial meat grinder accident at work, and Cedric and Ambrose moved into Tanglefoot Farm at the age of eight and a half to live with Grandma Lizzie, and that was that.

'What do you think of these mugshots?' asks Ambrose waving his freshly printed portraits for the suspect gallery.

'Lovely,' says Charlie. '

'Ambrose kissed a communist,' says Cedric. His words blurt without any connection to the morning's conversation.

'Cedric!' yells Ambrose.

'And where exactly did Ambrose kiss this communist?' asks Charlie.

'Moscow,' says Cedric.

'I mean, where on the body?'

'On the lips. It was all very seedy. Ambrose was being used as a honey trap—'

'Cedric!' yells Ambrose. 'We agreed to take some secrets to the grave.' He stands before him to block any further words from tumbling out of Cedric's mouth. Of course, it doesn't.

Cedric, now unstoppable, adds, 'We needed some vital information, and we knew this Russian spy was strangely attracted to short-fat Englishmen. So, we sent in Ambrose, the human love missile. I saw him kiss her, and honestly, it's been the source of nightmares my whole life.'

Charlie wraps her arms around Ambrose. 'You sneaky devil, kissing the girls—'

Ambrose yells, 'It was one kiss, and I did it for England.'

Cedric laughs and carries a foldable card table across the courtyard to the garage ops room and assembles it in front of an old three-seater leather sofa. He places the crossword book on the table.

'Not much of a *clues* table, is it?' he says.

The three-car garage is big enough to house the Jaguar, Elsie and the ops room. Grandma Lizzie stored her memorabilia from the Second World War in boxes and suitcases, and most of it is still there in the corner.

During the summer holidays, Cedric and Ambrose would spend days rummaging through documents, uniforms, ammunition, and all sorts of oddments; In many ways, it's why they ended up in the Service.

Ambrose hangs the corkboard on the wall opposite the sofa and directs two ceiling spot lamps to shine on the suspects: Kevin Hall, Polly King, and the deceased Joshua King.

Cedric and Ambrose sink into the soft leather sofa while Charlie glares at the corkboard.

After a few minutes, she says, 'How did you catch killers when you were in the Service?'

'We didn't,' says Ambrose. 'We gathered intelligence, solved problems, and exchanged coded messages with our agents.' He reminds her for the umpteenth time, they were the *Intelligence* part of MI6, not the *Military* part—the "I" bit, not the "M" bit.

Charlie uses her pen to point at the photographs, and with the slowness of an elephant trudging upstairs, she says, 'One of these three could be my father's killer.'

'Excellent,' says Cedric. 'The girl is halfway to cracking the case.'

'Technically, she's a third of the way,' says Ambrose. 'She's got a one-in-three shot of being right.'

They both burst out laughing, slapping their legs. Charlie waits for them to simmer down. She knows they sometimes see her as an eighteen-year-old girl whose father has just died. Charlie works in Linus Pope's department with a sensitive job on the logistics desk—she's clever, Cambridge clever.

Looking directly at them, she says, 'Cedric, I need you to dig up everything on Polly King. And, Ambrose, I need you to find out Joshua King's final movements.'

Cedric writes Polly King in his small black notebook and bites the end of his pen.

Charlie hands him her mobile telephone. 'Use this,' she says.

Without looking up, he says, 'I taught your phone everything it knows. It will be quicker to do it my way.'

Ambrose writes Joshua King in his notebook and underlines it several times. He, too, waves the phone option away.

Charlie stands behind the sofa, looking at the ops room with three photographs on the suspect wall and a crossword book clue on the table.

'Perfect,' she says. 'Let's go and rattle Kevin Hall's cage.'

'I thought we were gathering intelligence,' says Ambrose.

'Yes, we are,' she says. 'But first, we rattle!'

<><><>

Chapter Seventeen

Charlie sits astride Elsie, kickstarts the engine and a beautiful baritone note roars from the exhaust pipes, reverberating around the garage. She puts on her goggles and slides the open-face crash helmet over her long hair.

Cedric and Ambrose, somewhat tentatively, step into Elsie's sidecar, one behind the other. Winnie jumps in and sits on Ambrose's lap in the front seat.

Charlie secures the glass cover and smiles as her reluctant passengers don their green corduroy caps. She revs the engine and spins the rear tyre, racing out of the garage and around Tanglefoot Farm onto the lane. Cedric and Ambrose close their eyes as Charlie shoots through the pinch at full speed.

Kevin Hall lives in Holmbury St Mary, a charming village close to Friday Street. The quiet lanes twist this way and that in a blur of high hedgerows and countryside browns, yellows and greens. Earlier, Charlie narrowed the man's address to a road running out of the south side of the village. On Kevin Hall's profile, he proudly displays a range of snaps of his bright yellow car with darkened windows. The buildings in the photograph provided enough general information for Charlie to pinpoint his location to within a dozen houses.

Charlie brought Elsie to a slow standstill in a parking spot under a tree next to the turning for Kevin Hall's road.

'We'll go on foot from here,' she says.

'Maybe we should stay here and keep a look out,' says Cedric. Ambrose nods in agreement, saying he's already spotted a few shady-looking people roaming around. They remove their green corduroy caps and fold them neatly while remaining in the safety of the sidecar.

'We're all going,' Charlie says, leaving no room for discussion. She lifts the sidecar lid, and Cedric and Ambrose step out, peering up and down the quiet street. Charlie sets off at a brisk pace, with Winnie trotting along-side her.

'Let's not forget this chap could be the murderer,' says Ambrose, trying to keep up.

'A stone-cold, ruthless killer,' adds Cedric, already beginning to puff and pant.

'Stick close to me then,' says Charlie. 'He's not expecting us, and he murdered my dad ten years ago. If he is the killer, he thinks he's got away with it, scott-free.'

'For all we know, he could have been murdering someone every month for a decade,' says Ambrose. 'Your assessment doesn't stack up.'

Charlie glares at them to stop any more nonsense and leads them into Kevin Hall's road. A bright yellow Ford with dark windows is parked in front of a rusty garage door halfway down the street.

'There!' shouts Ambrose pointing to the yellow car. 'It's that one!'

'It's hard to believe you both had distinguished careers in the Intelligence Service,' says Charlie. 'Obviously, it needs saying; we're in stealth mode.'

They walk on the opposite side of the road to the parked yellow car, attempting to look like a family taking their dog for a walk.

'What's the plan?' asks Cedric.

'At this point, don't make sudden movements,' says Charlie. 'Easy, does it.' She crosses the road, peers inside the yellow car, and then waves for them to join her.

'It's not much of a plan,' says Ambrose.

The outside of the car is clean. Conversely, the inside is full of empty deep-fried chicken and pizza takeaway boxes.

'It must smell in there,' says Cedric. 'Look at the seats, they're greasy.' He steps back from the window as if being too close would cause him to catch a tropical disease.

Charlie looks over the garden hedge to check the coast is clear. She opens the gate and walks up the scruffy pathway to the house. Holmbury St Mary has a reputation for neatness, so this messy front garden must be an eyesore for Kevin Hall's neighbours. Nobody wants to live next door to a house like this. Charlie half expects to see a worn-out sofa in the garden or a washing machine, such was the state of the dump.

She edges up to the front door and crouches down to look through the letterbox. It's too dark inside to see anything, and it's quiet, suggesting nobody is home. An empty house has a still, recognisable silence perfect for thieves to steal televisions and raid jewellery boxes, knowing they won't be disturbed.

Charlie barges her shoulder against the door.

It's locked.

In a loud whisper, she turns and says, 'Keep a look out.'

They look baffled at the request. 'For what?' they say with hunched shoulders and upturned palms.

'For Elvis!'

'Elvis?' says Ambrose, looking more confused.

'Kevin Hall, of course,' she barks.

Cedric takes one step up the garden path towards her. 'And what shall we do if we see him?'

'Warn me!'

Ambrose steps beside Cedric, 'As a warning, shall I do my owl hoot?' He cups his hands, puts them in his mouth, and makes soft hooting sounds.

'Or, you can brush feathers against the window,' she says.

'Sarcasm is the lowest form of wit,' says Cedric.

'So am I doing the owl hoot or not?' asks Ambrose.

'Yes, but shout a warning as well. Let's be on the safe side,' says Charlie.

'A warning?' asks Cedric. 'We should agree on the word.'

'Maybe something confusing, like pineapple or banana,' says Ambrose.

'I think shouting out a fruit is an excellent idea,' says Cedric. 'Tomato is a fruit,' he adds. 'Not everyone knows that, and the idea of tomatoes with custard rather ruins the notion of it being a fruit.'

Charlie puts her hands on her hips, and they stop talking.

She sighs, 'Shout a fruit or a salad or a vegetable, anything that warns me that Kevin Hall is here.' She slips around the back of the house.

'I'm doing my owl hoot,' whispers Ambrose.

'Just a thought, dear boy, owls are nocturnal,' says

Cedric. 'I'm not certain they hoot during the day. Can we risk Kevin Hall knowing this?'

'I hadn't thought of that,' says Ambrose. They walk down the garden path and out through the gate to stand behind the bright yellow car, constantly looking up and down the quiet street.

'I should have brought the photograph of Kevin Hall,' suggests Cedric.

'We don't know if he's short or tall,' says Ambrose. 'People lie about their height all the time.'

'People lie,' says Cedric, swivelling his head up and down the road.

Charlie uses the method her father showed her to pick a lock and the back door of Kevin Hall's house pings open. She steps inside and creeps along the hallway. Her ears sting from the pressure to hear any sound—all is quiet.

Hall's house is messy, messier than the front garden, and messier than his car. The countertops in the tiny kitchen are covered with dirty plates and mugs. She smiles, knowing Cedric and Ambrose would recoil, claiming they've contracted legionnaire's disease.

Charlie scopes the fridge door for photos and rifles through a pile of unopened mail next to the food-splattered microwave. One letter is from the local council, and she raises it to the window light to see the letter inside. She can't make out the wording, but there's lots of red ink, which usually implies an overdue payment.

She tucks the letter in her jacket pocket and walks to the front room, where the curtains are closed, and there's a rancid smell of stale food. A glint of sunlight pierces through a tear in the curtains onto a leather chair positioned in front of a giant television screen. Alongside the wall, a two-seater sofa is covered with creased clothing. Charlie half expects to see a dead body as she uses her pen to move the garments aside.

Kevin Hall, you need to clean your house!

There's nothing under the pile of vile-smelling clothes, so she steps out into the hallway and creeps upstairs. On the way up, Charlie peers through the railings on the landing—apart from the stairs creaking and groaning under her feet, all is quiet. There are three doors: two bedrooms and a bathroom. The smaller of the two bedrooms is full of cardboard boxes from what looks like a recent house move, and the larger bedroom is a mirror image of the lounge downstairs with clothes strewn everywhere. The bed is unmade, and the stained duvet is on the floor.

The bathroom is full of clutter, and a bucket overflows with empty beer cans. Charlie shuts the door, thinking the case will remain unsolved if the clue to her father's killer is in this stinking house.

Outside, Cedric and Ambrose continue to scan the road. They decide *pineapple* is the correct warning word.

'Charlie is fearless,' says Ambrose.

'Like her father,' agrees Cedric.

Ambrose shuffles his feet and begins to breathe heavily, and his voice is barely audible, 'A bald-headed man with a large dog is approaching.'

Cedric turns to look at the oncoming man whose neck starts from his ears, and his oil-stained t-shirt pulls tightly across his muscular chest. 'Holy mother of—'

The man swaggers towards them and shouts, 'Oi, Tweedledee and Tweedledum! Get away from my car!'

Cedric whispers, 'Sound the alarm, Ambrose. It's Kevin Hall.'

Ambrose cups his hands and blows, producing a near-silent owl hoot.

'Charlie won't hear that,' whispers Cedric.

Ambrose shouts a near-silent and husky, 'Pineapple!'

The bull-man barks again, 'What are you two doing looking at my car? And why is that idiot saying pineapple?'

'My brother has a condition called pinappleous whisperous,' says Cedric.

'Are you two clowns pulling my chain?' says Hall.

'We are taking our dog for a walk and admiring the houses on the road,' says Cedric pointing at Winnie and then at the houses.

'Bugger off, you couple of creepy weirdoes.' Kevin Hall's menacing tone hangs in the air like an unwelcome morning fog. Seemingly, he's used to pushing his weight around.

'Is there a post box near here?' asks Ambrose. 'We have a letter that needs posting to our aunt. You see, she's not been well, and we thought a letter might cheer her up. She lives in Devon, near the coast, in a beautiful—'

'Oh, shut up, podgy!' Kevin Hall's anger swells, and his fidgety eyes flick from Cedric to Ambrose.

'Well, it's been delightful. We must be off,' says Ambrose, and nudges Cedric to start walking. Cedric holds his ground for a moment.

He lifts his chin and says, 'We are causing you no harm, young man. We are looking at houses.'

Kevin Hall lunges at them, roaring like an animal. Winnie barks, lifting her back feet off the ground with each little snarl. Hall looks down and says, 'And you can shut it, too!' Kevin Hall's dog starts barking, and the howling booms up and down the road.

Ambrose pushes Cedric away from the scene, and they begin walking in the wrong direction—at this point, Charlie emerges from a house three houses up from Kevin Hall's.

'Pineapple,' whispers Ambrose. 'Charlie, code pineapple!'

Cedric says, 'Ambrose, dear boy, she can't hear. I can barely hear your warning cry.'

Charlie approaches them and says, 'That's Kevin Hall.'

'Yes, we know,' says Cedric. 'He's like an angry horsefly in need of blood.'

'Why didn't you warn me?' she says.

'I gave owl hoots and several pineapples,' says Ambrose.

Cedric adds, 'Don't look now, but Mr Angry of Holmbury St Mary is walking over to us.'

Charlie turns to face the big man and says with a chirp, 'What's up, buttercup?'

'Are these two fools with you?'

'Yes, what of it?'

'Get them out of my face,' barks Hall.

Charlie steps closer to the man and says, 'Why don't you go and cool down?'

Hall's intricate snake tattoos wrap around his forearms and poke out from his t-shirt, circling his neck. His dog continues to snarl.

Kevin Hall clenches his fists and says, 'I'll give you ten seconds to get out of here before I start swinging.'

Charlie laughs. 'Are you a girl hitter?'

'No, but I'll punch them,' he says, pointing at Cedric and Ambrose.

'I'm afraid that's the same thing,' says Charlie without breaking eye contact. 'My work is done here.'

She steers Cedric and Ambrose up the road and around the corner to where Elsie is parked under the tree. She opens the glass lid and helps them clamber inside. She sits astride the Norton and fires up the engine.

She says, 'No offence, but it would have been easier if I was with my dad and Joshua today rather than you two.'

'Offence has been taken,' says Ambrose, straightening his corduroy cap.

'We played our part,' confirms Cedric. 'We kept lookout and raised the alarm.

Charlie tuts and peels away from Holmbury St Mary, drowning out the voices from the sidecar. She got what she came for today and possibly confronted her father's killer.

<><><>

Chapter Eighteen

The ride back in Elsie from Kevin Hall in Holmbury St Mary is uneventful, apart from Charlie's attempt to break the land speed record.

Ambrose shivers as the adrenalin leaves his body from their near-death experience. 'Hall is definitely a killer,' he says to Cedric turning to face him. 'We faced death squarely in the eye today.'

Cedric looks pale and peaky, which is unlike him. He's the robust and often the rude one on account of being nine minutes older and taller—it's not a scientific fact—it's just something he decided. Cedric can upset a complete stranger in a shop with a casual comment by informing them their outfit clashes with the carpet.

The two men are thrown around in the sidecar as Charlie zig-zags at speed away from Holmbury St Mary. Ambrose looks out for Kevin Hall's yellow car and considers the possibility that he has a different vehicle for murdering people from his bright yellow one. Surely a witness would have noticed a brightly coloured car at the scene of the murder.

Yes, officer, the killer was in his early forties, bald-headed, plastered in tattoos, drove a yellow car, and then sped off towards Holmbury St Mary, where he lives in a stinking mess.

Murderers surely have a plan. They can't be cavalier about murder without thinking through the consequences of driving a yellow car. Ambrose concludes Kevin Hall must have two vehicles: a two-car murderer. Is that a thing? There's no other explanation. He turns around to see if Kevin Hall is following them in a different vehicle, but the coast is clear. Anyway, how can anyone follow them? They're travelling at the speed of light.

'Is Kevin Hall our killer?' Ambrose shouts so Cedric can hear him above the din inside the rattling sidecar. He continues, 'Hall fits the bill, but what would be his motive? Killers have motives. A random killing in Friday Street doesn't make sense. And why kill Randolph Vine? Maybe we should start at the motive and work backwards.'

Ambrose taps on the glass canopy and signals Charlie to pull into a side road. She stops, unclips the lid, and fresh summer air wafts into the sidecar.

Ambrose assembles his thoughts. 'What are the possible motives for killing your father? Randolph must have had an enemy with a serious enough motive to kill him.'

'Are you suggesting we focus on the motive rather than look for suspects?' says Cedric.

'Good thinking, everyone,' says Charlie.

Ambrose suggested it, but the idea landed in the melting pot of chatter before he could claim it, and nobody will remember that he pointed out the obviousness of a motive. Charlie steps off the motorbike and removes her helmet and goggles, then runs her fingers through her hair.

She says, 'Ambrose, that's an inspired idea.'

'It's not such a breakthrough idea,' says Cedric with an edge of cantankerousness. 'I think we were all thinking the same thing.'

Ambrose says, 'Who benefited ten years ago from killing your dad?'

'If they knew that, the police officer in charge would have wrapped up the case ten years ago,' Charlie says.

Cedric scoffs, 'Even if the killer was caught in the act, with six witnesses, and later admitted to the murder in a written statement, I think the bumbling officer in charge would still have found a way to mess it up.' Cedric tuts, adding, 'What a buffoon that chap must be!'

Charlie looks gloomy and puts her crash helmet back on. And with a look of tiredness and sadness, she says, 'Come on, let's head home.'

'Oh look, it's tea and cake time,' says Cedric, looking at his watch while missing all the flashing signals of Charlie's demeanour.

Although Charlie slows, she still overtakes every other road user and rides as though they are on fire. The calm and safety of Plum Pudding Lane is a welcome sight from their escapade with the deadly Kevin Hall. Charlie whizzes around into the courtyard and comes to a standstill in the garage in a cloud of dust.

Charlie jumps off Elsie and slumps heavily onto the sofa. 'Kevin Hall has probably murdered somebody, but why would he kill my dad?'

'I'll make tea,' says Cedric, scurrying across the courtyard.

Ambrose tries to keep up with him, saying, 'How would a thug from Holmbury St Mary know Charlie's dad?'

Without slowing, Cedric says, 'I don't know, but I'll

definitely think better after a pot of Assam and a slice of lemon drizzle.'

When deprived of tea and cake, an academic's brain reduces its ability to function at the correct oscillating speed in order to produce intelligent thought. Cedric read about it in a report from Harvard, or he made it up. He can't remember. Either way, he believed it to be true.

Cedric pours the boiling water onto the Assam tea leaves in the teapot while Ambrose cuts the cake. The scent of zesty lemon fills the kitchen.

Ambrose is a master bread maker and cake baker, cooking everything tasty and fattening. Cedric specialises in sauces, meats and fish. They rule Tanglefoot Farm's kitchen and grow pensive when Charlie starts banging pots and pans in an attempt to cook something. However, more annoying than her noisy cooking sessions is when she empties the dishwasher and puts everything the wrong way around in the cupboards.

Cup handles to the right!

They look out the kitchen window at Charlie, who continues to slump on the sofa with one leg dangling over the arm.

Ambrose touches Cedric's arm and says, 'We must remember Randolph was her father. She lost her dad. So, a few steps of tenderness wouldn't go a miss. Look at that poor girl's gloomy face.'

Cedric breathes a long, thoughtful sigh, 'Naturally, dear boy, you are right. However, her expression could be from constipation. Remember our Aunt in Devon? She suffers from constipation and has the same look on her face as Charlie.' He carries the tray across the courtyard to the ops room, places it on the card table, and begins to pour.

'Cedric wants to know if you're constipated,' Ambrose asks, sipping his tea.

'What's wrong with you?' she says.

'Here,' says Cedric, passing her a cup. 'Tea always helps.'

'I'm not constipated!' she says. 'I'm drained, that's all.'

They drink tea and plough their way through the cake, sitting silently while staring at the photographs on the corkboard.

'What was Kevin Hall's house like?' asks Cedric. 'From the look of his garden and car, I imagine it was contaminated. Did you gel your hands before you ate your lemon drizzle? You can catch all sorts from people's houses. I knew a man who caught Dengue fever from a washing machine.'

Charlie sips her tea and says, 'The bathroom was—'

Ambrose stops her in her tracks. 'Let me eat my cake before you splatter me with details.' He gulps his slice in two mouthfuls.

Charlie waves her hand, indicating there's no need to explain the griminess of it all. She takes a white envelope from her jacket pocket and puts it next to the crossword book on the clues table.

'Did you steal it?' Ambrose asks. 'From Kevin Hall's house?'

'Borrowed it,' says Charlie. 'That's different from stealing.'

Cedric sits up straight. 'Do you intend to take it back?'

'No,' she says. 'It's unopened, so Kevin Hall won't know it's missing.'

'She's got a good point,' says Ambrose. 'We should steam it open. That way, nobody will ever know we opened it.'

Charlie nods, picks up the envelope and rips it open.

'I thought steaming it open was the idea,' says Ambrose.

Charlie scans the letter and explains it's a reminder for Hall's overdue Council tax payment. She says, 'Kevin Trevor Hall. That's his full name. Why would *he* want to kill my dad?' It's a good question. 'Tell me about my father's cases at work. Did he have enemies?'

Cedric and Ambrose know the list of his enemies is endless. They won't tell Charlie this, obviously. In most countries where Britain was seen as the enemy, Randolph was a wanted man.

'Nothing springs to mind,' Ambrose says. 'Although in his line of work, I'm sure he's upset one or two along the way.'

Cedric adds, 'We should correlate cases and people and time scales to find a common thread. The murderer will be in there somewhere.'

'How are we going to do that?' says Charlie.

Cedric looks at Ambrose, and they share a long knowing look.

Ambrose says, 'Should we?'

'Lord knows we have no choice,' Cedric says.

'Would one of you tell me what you're wittering on about,' says Charlie.

They look at Charlie and utter the two words they were certain they would never say again.

'Verity Fanthorpe,' they say with as much forbearance as they can muster.

'What's a Bertie Fannyrope?' asks Charlie.

'It's not a what but a who,' says Cedric. 'Verity Fanthorpe was a legend in the Intelligence Service.'

And it's true.

Verity Fanthorpe, who is either retired or dead by now, was Britain's best-ever sleeper spy. And to be the best, you have to be tested when you're at your lowest level of physical and emotional exhaustion and yet you still have the ability to dig deep into your reserves to help the person next to you. Verity Fanthorpe proved herself over and over again. And after thirty distinguished years on enemy soil, Verity returned to England to run the foreign operations desk.

'Where is she?' asks Charlie.

'We don't know, but we know a man who might,' says Cedric. 'If you want to know about a line of unbreakable code with a reversible double turn divisible twist, you would come to us. But if you need to know about paperclips or someone's address, then sadly, we'll need to ask Linus Pope.

Charlie sits upright on the sofa with no signs of sluggishness and asks, 'Do you think this Verity Fanthorpe can help us?'

'When Verity retired from active service in Moscow, she became our boss and gave us quite a torrid time of it,' says Ambrose.

'Then I like her already,' says Charlie.

'Are you sure you're not constipated?' asks Cedric.

<><><>

Chapter Nineteen

'Pope is popping over,' Cedric announces, quickstepping it across the courtyard to the ops room.

'Does he know what happened to Verity Fanthorpe?' asks Charlie.

'We didn't say anything over the telephone,' he says.

Cedric and Ambrose rarely use a telephone, and when they do, they assume someone is listening, picking up snippets of chatter, most of which make no sense in isolation but, when pieced together, could form a valuable chunk of a bigger secret. So, their motto is: *say nothing at all*, which has served them well. Plus, Cedric and Ambrose are dab hands at talking utter gibberish. For three decades of Cold War listening, the Moscow agents would have gleaned nothing from listening into their telephone calls. Nonsense was the name of the game.

Charlie walks with Winnie around the garden of scented wildflowers. Her thoughts fight a tug-of-war between excitement and disappointment. Kevin Hall was a thug; that was obvious, but how could there be a connection with her father? They lived in different worlds. Charlie couldn't fathom a scenario where her dad and Hall would be face to face, resulting in her father floating dead in the pond in Friday Street. Hall didn't show the talent to outsmart her dad, but she couldn't rule him out. He was still a suspect and would remain on the corkboard.

Her excitement comes from the possible introduction of Verity Fanthorpe. Is she any good? Does she have any oomph left in her life to help?

Linus Pope follows Cedric's instructions and walks around Tanglefoot Farm, crossing the gravel courtyard to the garage, where Cedric and Ambrose sit waiting on the sofa in the ops room.

'What do you want with Verity Fanthorpe?' asks Pope. His words blurt out like a defensive statement rather than a question.

'And a good afternoon to you, too,' says Cedric.

Pope walks over to Elsie and runs his fingers over the glass canopy. 'Did you find this old wrecker in Randolph's mystery garage?'

Cedric nods, 'And it's just as fast and just as dangerous in the hands of Charlie as it was under the spell of Grandma Lizzie.'

'Both of you scare too easily,' says Pope. He wanders around the garage, adding, 'Well, something must be brewing if you want Verity Fanthorpe. That woman ran your lives ragged. Are you sure you want her back on the front line?'

Cedric nods as if weighing up a complex conundrum. 'We're bringing Verity in for Charlie.'

Ambrose offers Pope a cup of tea and holds up a plate of lemon drizzle.

Linus Pope takes the cake and chomps it without

savouring the delicate flavours. 'Cake and tea? Anyone would think these are bribes.'

'Any idea where the old girl is hiding?' asks Cedric. 'I doubt she's still with the firm, is she?'

Pope looks at the photographs on the corkboard. 'Is this all you've got?'

Charlie returns from the wildflower garden and walks into the ops room, and says, 'No, Linus, we have a pile of clues and photographs to put up, but we've been too busy chasing down leads.'

'And who is this unsavoury-looking hooligan?' asks Pope, pointing at Kevin Hall's photograph.

'You don't know?' asks Charlie.

Pope shakes his head, brushes cake crumbs from his shirt, and claims never to have seen him before.

'That's Kevin Hall,' she says.

'It's not,' says Pope. 'Kevin Hall is at least sixty years old.'

'This chump is definitely Kevin Hall,' says Ambrose. 'We confronted the monster.'

'Well, you're the experts,' says Linus Pope, his tone lilting on the side of mocking. 'When are you planning to confront the *real* Kevin Hall, the one who was questioned by the police in relation to Randolph's murder?'

'We're talking to him later,' says Charlie. Her retaliation is solid and defensive, even believable. She tells Pope they wanted to ensure the police didn't make a mistake ten years ago by questioning the wrong Kevin. 'We're off to see the *real* Kevin Hall tonight. Isn't that right?' She glares at Cedric and Ambrose.

They play along with an overly dramatic wave of nods, knee slaps, and a stream of agreements.

Charlie sits on the sofa and puts her arm around Pope's shoulder, 'Now, about Verity. We need your help.'

'The last thing I heard,' he says, looking over his shoulder as if in the field, 'Old Fanthorpe lives in a rusty camper van on Newlands Corner. But you won't get much out of her.'

'Why not?' asks Cedric.

Pope slurps his tea. 'Years of living a double life and taking too many experimental military drugs during the Cold War have taken their toll on her sanity. Her brain is scrambled—you'll get nothing out of her other than rambling stories about how she brought the Berlin Wall down.'

'Is she at Newlands Corner, now?' asks Cedric.

'She comes and goes,' says Pope.

Charlie taps on her mobile phone and shows Pope a photograph of a man in his early sixties, asking if he recognises him.

'No, why should I?'

'Because it's Kevin Hall, the real one,' she says.

Pope picks up the crossword book and flicks through the pages.

He says, 'I suppose if your father wrote the killer's name in here, the killer wouldn't have left it in his pocket when they murdered him.' Pope slings the book back on the table and finishes his cup of tea.

'Goodness me, where are my manners?' says Ambrose. 'Let me see you out.' He escorts Pope across the gravel courtyard and around Tanglefoot Farm before waving a hearty farewell and returning to the ops room.

'Let's agree never to mention our wrong Kevin moment ever again,' says Charlie. 'Understood?'

Cedric and Ambrose nod in agreement.

'Anyone fancy a trip to Newlands Corner?' asks Charlie. 'We'll visit Kevin Hall on the way back. He lives in a cottage in Silent Pool.'

'Let's pray he doesn't own a snarling dog?' says Cedric.

Charlie swings her leg over the motorbike, and with a hefty jump on Elsie's kick starter, the engine roars into life. She lifts the glass canopy on the sidecar and beckons Cedric and Ambrose to climb aboard. Winnie, too.

Charlie races around Tanglefoot Farm as Cedric and Ambrose rock to-and-fro as they put on their corduroy caps before shutting their eyes as Elsie shoots through the pinch in the lane.

Newlands Corner, just a handful of miles from Friday Street, is famous for Agatha Christie's disappearance in December 1926 and boasts spectacular views across the Surrey Hills. Essentially, it's a place where people come to sit and do nothing other than look out across the majesty of England's untouched land. It's one of those breathtaking spots where, momentarily, the world stops for no reason other than for you to view its natural beauty.

Charlie parks Elsie in the near-empty parking area surrounding a small tea shop. There's no sign of a camper van or anyone resembling Verity Fanthorpe. Three bikers mooch around in black leathers looking at each other's motorbikes. A young couple with their child and two men standing at the back of a car drinking from a flask are the only signs of activity at Newlands Corner.

Charlie walks over to the tea shop and asks the young girl behind the counter if she knows anybody who fits Verity Fanthorpe's description.

The trouble with today's youth, Cedric told Charlie a minute earlier, is that they don't pay attention to anything other than their phones. They stare at a small screen and miss the world around them.

'I know who you mean,' says the young girl.

'When was the last time you saw her?' asks Charlie.

'Two, no, more like three hours ago,' the girl says. 'She's lovely. I see her most mornings, and she's so friendly.'

Charlie gives the girl her phone number and asks her to pass it on to Verity.

'I don't think she has a phone, but I can message you if you like.'

Charlie thanks the girl and returns to Elsie, where Cedric and Ambrose test each other on the Latin names for the various trees.

'So what can you tell me about Verity Fanthorpe?' says Charlie.

Cedric kicks at a tuft of grass, and Ambrose becomes busy with a strap inside the sidecar, but Charlie persists and asks again.

Ambrose gives in, saying, 'When Verity was taken out of the field on account of her age, she became our boss. She wasn't suited to corporate life as her management skills lacked subtlety. Once, she threatened to cut a young trainee's fingers off with a machete because he mistakenly sent the wrong file to Moscow. The poor boy needed a week off to recover.'

'I like the sound of her more and more,' says Charlie.

'Yes, we knew you would,' adds Cedric. 'Verity chased that young boy around the office, screaming with the machete above her head, swishing it left and right, chopping plants in half and sending piles of paper flying.'

They stand silently, looking at the hazy patchwork countryside beneath them, until Charlie states the obvious.

'We aren't doing very well, are we?' she says. 'We broke

into the wrong Kevin's house, and the real Kevin Hall looks like he wouldn't say boo to a goose, let alone kill my dad. No wonder the case is still cold after ten years.'

Ambrose loops his arm through Charlie's and nestles close to her while Cedric stands to attention, admiring the late afternoon view.

'We'll catch a break,' says Ambrose. 'In our darkest days in the Service, we always caught a break.'

Charlie didn't say anything in case she ruined Ambrose's promise. It was a half-promise at best, but it was all she had. Her phone pings with a message from the tea shop girl saying Verity's campervan is chugging up the hill towards Newlands Terrace.

Maybe Verity is her break.

With more rust than paint, the campervan bumps and rattles into the parking area. It pumps a foul stream of choking fumes from the exhaust pipe and parks next to the tea shop. The engine continues burbling long after the ignition has been turned off.

Charlie watches a lady spring from the driver's door and walk with a bounce in her step, up to the tea shop, and following a brief exchange, the girl points over to where Charlie is sitting.

Ambrose draws breath over his teeth, tuts twice and says, 'I thought this day would never come. And to think all this time, Verity Fanthorpe has been living a few miles from Friday Street, and when I say living,' he points at the campervan with its engine still burping, 'In that thing!'

Verity strides with purpose towards them.

Winnie wags her tail with excitement.

'Hello, boys,' says Verity. 'I bet you thought you'd seen the back of me.' Ambrose offers his hand, but she slaps it away and pulls him in for a warm bear hug. 'That's what you need, my boy, a proper hug.' She turns to face Cedric, who takes a step backwards behind Charlie. 'Come along, Cedric, give me a hug.'

There is no escape as she pulls Cedric into a warm embrace, squeezing him until his bones crack. Verity looks Charlie up and down and says, 'And you must be Randolph's girl. You weren't much to look at when you were a kid, but you've turned out to look like your mother. She was a beauty.' Verity shakes Charlie's hand with vigour.

'It's lovely to meet you,' says Charlie.

'I imagine these two brainboxes didn't mention me until they needed help with something,' says Verity. She takes a treat from her pocket and bends down. 'There you go, my lovely. It's great to meet you, too.'

Verity Fanthorpe looks at Charlie and shakes her head, 'I can see your father in your eyes. I shouldn't have favourites, but your dad was my favourite.'

Verity, whose glasses peep out from a tangle of wild grey hair on top of her head, is wearing flared burgundy trousers and a bright orange shirt with sturdy, heavy-duty boots.

'How long have you been up here on Newlands Corner,' asks Charlie.

'On and off for years. Linus Pope occasionally checks that I'm still alive.' Verity puts her hands on her hips and looks at Cedric and Ambrose. 'Well, boys, what do you need?'

Cedric clears his throat, 'Verity, I'm sure you're too busy, but a minute of your time is all we need, and then you can return to whatever it is you do.'

Verity says, 'Who do you need bumping off? Knife, poison or natural causes?'

Cedric clears his throat again, 'I'm sorry, but there's no killing involved.'

'What do you want me for then?' she kicks a stone with an edge of disappointment on her face.

Charlie says, 'We need you to correlate cases and people and time scales to find a common thread. To help us find my father's killer.'

Verity stands with her hands on her hips. 'You certainly need help. You've been flapping about like a bunch of amateurs.'

'Have you been following us?' asks Cedric.

Verity nods, saying, 'Of course, I've been following you. I laughed watching you two drink tea from enamel mugs on Chelsea Bridge, and who do you think that little old lady was on the bench next to you in Shere eating ice cream? By the looks of things, you need all the help you can get. When you went to the wrong Kevin Hall's house, I was ready to scream!'

Ambrose says, 'You should come and visit our ops room at Tanglefoot F—'

Verity raises her hand, saying, 'Way ahead of you, dear boy. I must say, the sofa is very comfortable.'

'Is there anything else we should know?' asks Charlie.

Verity looks at the three of them and says, 'Well, I saw Joshua King yesterday.'

'Impossible. King died ten years ago,' says Ambrose. 'In a car crash in Australia.'

Verity smiles. 'I'm sure someone died in a car crash who was identified by the police as Joshua King, but I saw him here yesterday drinking a cup of coffee at the hut, standing no more than three feet from me.'

Charlie clicks her fingers. 'Did he see you?'

'No,' says Verity. 'And I watched him standing in the

doorway of the Stephan Langton pub when you flashed by on the lovely Elsie.'

'How could you know that?' says Charlie.

Verity says, 'I've followed you since the moment you decided to track down your father's killer. Now, come on, look lively. Let's go and talk to the real Kevin Hall.'

<><><>

Chapter Twenty

Charlie

Wow! I mean, wow. Verity Fanthorpe.

I feel I've been injected with a jolt of power from meeting an amazing person. My arms are shaking, and I'm fizzing all over.

I stand on Elsie's kickstarter to roar its engine to life and watch Verity give a hearty wave to the young girl in the tea hut before jumping into her camper. She gives me an enthusiastic thumbs-up sign from behind the steering wheel.

I would give anything to go back in time to race around the world with Verity and Grandma Lizzie, but I was born too late and seemingly missed out on all the fun.

Cedric and Ambrose chat in the sidecar. Their green corduroy cap-covered heads bob about, no doubt with lots to say about Verity. I'll get to the bottom of why they kept her at arm's length from me all these years. She's here now and very much involved.

Oddly, I find it funny that she's sat on our sofa in the ops room. Usually, I'd say something, but not this time—I feel normal rules aren't going to apply to Verity Fanthorpe. She's made an immediate impact on me, what with her flared burgundy trousers and baggy orange shirt, but it works. I'm not even sure how, but it does.

Verity is a force of nature, and her grinning face fills my side mirrors as she follows me out of Newlands Corner in her rusty campervan. Whatever happened in the past, Verity is back in the game helping us to hunt a killer, and I'm glad she's on our side. I tap on the sidecar's canopy, and Cedric, Ambrose and Winnie look up at me. I give them a Verity-style thumbs-up, and they roll their eyes. They can see I'm quite taken with her.

And so to business.

The real Kevin Hall lives down the hill from Newlands Corner in a tiny place called Silent Pool. If he is my father's killer, I'll put him in an armlock and make a citizen's arrest—is that a thing? It's too late to look it up as I take a sharp left at the sign for Silent Pool. Some say it's a haunted pool: that's if you believe such things. I don't!

I follow the narrow road until it peters out into a dirt track leading to a dead end. No other tyre tracks lead in or out. I unclip the canopy, and my sidecar passengers look at the muddy track.

'We'll stay here as lookouts?' says Ambrose. 'It's standard procedure for a stakeout.'

I tell them it's an excellent idea, but if they see the crazy axeman of Silent Pool, they should run for their lives, or shout pineapple, or hoot like an owl. They step out of the sidecar and tuck their trousers into their socks, preparing for a muddy walk in the woods.

'You're not funny, Charlotte Vine,' says Cedric.

Verity's campervan chugs along the track and pulls up next to Elsie, and after two minutes, its tired engine finally stops puffing and rattling. Verity jumps out and adopts a crouching tiger position as if under fire, all the while scanning the area in a three-hundred-and-sixty-degree sweep.

'The war is over,' says Cedric.

'It's never over,' she says and leaps up to a standing stance. 'Shall we take guns? I've got a bag of ammo and a hand grenade.'

'This is a scouting assignment, not a shooting mission,' I say.

I imagine all sorts of scenarios that could happen in the next ten minutes because I've never waded so far out of my depth before. I follow Verity at a soldier's marching pace into the marshy woodland. I keep lengthening my stride, trying to keep up, but she can move. I turn to see Cedric and Ambrose stepping carefully over fallen branches. If they could hover above mud, they would.

The muddy pathway winds its way to the back of two cottages, where I stand beside Verity behind a tree. I'm so close to her that I can feel her breathing. I'm buzzing with excitement and try my hardest to play things down.

One cottage has children's toys strewn across the garden, and the other has an abundance of flowerpots: far too many for a small yard. Kevin Hall is too old to have young children. I shouldn't judge—not because judging is wrong, but the last time I judged, I broke into the wrong Kevin Hall's house. He could be a grandfather, and would a killer have this many flowerpots?

Winnie reaches me and taps my knee to be picked up.

She's muddy, and I'm wearing a white T-shirt. Verity bends down and picks her up.

'You're a beauty,' she says.

Winnie kisses Verity on her chin.

'Have you two met before?' I ask, sensing the answer is yes.

'Only when you've been out of the house, and I've happened to be pottering about in your garden.' She says it as if we've been old friends for years. And oddly, I don't mind.

Cedric arrives and says, 'Ah, the two-cottage conundrum.'

Ambrose puffs and pants his way to the tree, where the four of us stare at the rear of two cottages.

'Flowerpot man is overcompensating for something,' says Verity.

I ask Verity where she was when my father was murdered in Friday Street.

'You sound like a clumsy policeman, dear,' says Verity.

'I didn't mean it like that. I mean, where were you at the time?'

'That's the same question,' she says. 'I was a sleeper agent in Moscow.' She flashes her eyes at Cedric and Ambrose, who nod in agreement.

Verity Fanthorpe couldn't look more like an eccentric Englishwoman if she tried. Wild hair, glasses, uncoordinated clothing, and a cheerful bossiness. How did she blend into the local community in Moscow? She's the opposite of a spy.

'Those were the days,' Verity says. 'I'll tell you all about it over a bottle or two of claret. When your father was murdered, the details were sketchy at best. To be honest, it felt like a cover-up of sorts.'

'You mean he might have been killed by our own side?' I ask. I hadn't contemplated that.

'We can't rule anything out, Charlie,' Verity says. 'It was certainly not a mugging.'

'So which cottage, toys or flowerpots?' asks Ambrose.

'Flowerpots,' I say.

Verity agrees.

I suggest that I'll go in and take a look around. I get that from my father. He always wanted to be the first through the door. I heard one time he was in East Berlin and didn't have any money in his pockets. So, my dad walked into a German bar late at night and told the young boy behind the counter that he was the new owner and needed to cash up. He acted so confidently that the boy emptied the cash register into a bag and handed it over. Dad walked out the door and ran off through the streets.

There wasn't much money in the bag, but enough to get him over the border and make a home run. A few weeks later, through diplomatic channels, he sent the bar owner an envelope with the night's takings and a note to say thank you. Dad always made it sound like you had to think on your feet back then, a bit like right now.

'Plan?' asks Verity.

'I don't have one,' I say.

'I like your style. No restrictions,' says Verity. 'I'll be right behind you.'

'Maybe you should stay here and look after Cedric and Ambrose.'

'Don't be soft,' she says. 'I'm coming with you or going instead of you. Lead on.'

I creep out from behind the tree, carefully placing my feet to avoid making a sound. Meanwhile, Verity walks up to the wooden gate and kicks it clean off its hinges. It shatters, and splinters of wood fly in all directions.

This was not the stealthy entrance I had in mind.

Verity looks at me with a wide grin, saying, 'No time to fanny about, dear. If this Kevin Hall chappy is your father's killer, then let's shake him up a bit.'

I glance at Cedric and Ambrose, who smile and give me a look that says, we told you so!

Verity marches through the minefield of flowerpots and knocks on the tiny cottage's back door with the side of her fist: Gestapo style. My adrenaline fizzes my nerve endings to a state of red alert.

Nobody answers. Who would? The door pounding would scare anyone half to death.

On Verity's third Gestapo knock, the door opens—so someone isn't scared half to death. A man in his early sixties stands in the doorway. Is this my father's murderer? He fixes his gaze on the pieces of the gate.

My senses are shaken and rattled—Verity's are not.

'Kevin Hall?' she barks in a commanding voice.

'Yes,' says the man. His eyes dart to me. I think he sees me as the good cop. He murmurs, 'What happened to my gate?'

Verity smiles and reaches out her hand to introduce herself, saying, 'I'm such a clumsy old sausage. I never know whether to push or pull.'

'I saw you from my bedroom window. You kicked it off its hinges.'

'Let's not get bogged down in details.' Verity's voice switches to a soft, rich tone. I love how she doesn't break eye contact with Hall as she smiles and tilts her head a little.

Oh, she's good, dangerously good. I could get used to this. I am used to it.

I do my best to sound like somebody from the council and want to ask him about my dad. I try to slow my heart-beat and engage in a more natural rhythm.

I say, 'I understand the police spoke to you about Randolph Vine ten years ago. Do you remember?'

'I remember,' he says, then politely adds, 'I told them everything back then, and I've got nothing new to say.'

Kevin Hall makes his first mistake by attempting to close the door, but Verity is too fast and wedges her foot on the doorstep. Her steel-toe-cap boot acts like an immovable anvil: the door won't close no matter how much Kevin Hall tries. I want a pair of those all-purpose, practical boots.

Verity's smile widens as she invites herself into Hall's cottage. I follow her inside. It's surprisingly clean. I suppose in my mind, I wrongly associated this Kevin Hall with the wrong Kevin and his disgraceful foul-smelling mess of a home. The neat cottage is tastefully decorated, and from a cursory glance into the kitchen, there's no visible pile of dirty plates. You can tell a lot about someone when you peep into their kitchen. The front room looks out onto a well-kept front lawn with a brown Volvo in the driveway—no sign of a bright yellow anything.

Kevin Hall rubs his hands on the side of his legs and looks down at his polished shoes.

'May we sit?' I ask politely. We are inside now, so there's no need for pushiness. I hope Verity sees it the same way.

'Please, yes,' he says, waving his hand toward a two-seater sofa.

We sit, and Verity's tone, thankfully, changes, asking, 'How long have you lived here, Kevin? It's delightful.'

'Seven years,' he says. 'My wife, Doreen and I always promised ourselves we'd live in a little cottage. Sadly she died before we moved in, but it's exactly what she would have wanted.' He looks at a photo above the fireplace. It must be Doreen. She looks like the female version of Kevin Hall. 'We were teenage sweethearts,' he adds.

'Why did the police question you about the murder in Friday Street?' asks Verity. She could be asking directions to the town hall, such was her gentle line of questioning. She's a pro in how she changes from kicking down a wooden gate to gently asking about the murder.

Hall says, 'I had nothing to do with it.'

'Quite so,' says Verity. 'But why did they question you?'

Kevin Hall pauses for a long while, almost to the point where I'm about to jump in and ask the question again, but Verity places her hand softly on my knee to stop my blurting out. Verity stares with the softest eyes at Hall, how a grandma looks adoringly at her grandchildren. She doesn't hurry or harass. Instead, she sits with her hands clasped, resting in her lap, waiting for Hall to open up.

And he does.

Kevin Hall looks up at us with doe eyes, and with tears falling, he says, 'It was our wedding anniversary. Doreen and I decided to book a table at the Stephan Langton pub. We had a lovely meal, and on the way back to our car, I noticed a man staggering about. He bumped into me.'

'Who was it?' I ask, unable to contain myself. I check with Verity, but she's still eye-locked with Hall.

'I didn't know him, but later I discovered it was Randolph Vine.'

'You saw him the night he was murdered?'

Kevin Hall nods.

Verity shifts slightly on the sofa and asks, 'What happened next?'

'Nothing,' he says.

I'm expecting more than nothing, so I push a bit. 'Did you speak to him?'

'Sort of,' says Hall. 'I asked if he was alright.'

'And?'

'He was mumbling,' says Hall.

'Drunk?' asks Verity.

'Not drunk. It was as if he was sedated. He grabbed at my jacket, trying to speak, but he was all over the place.'

'Did he say anything?' I ask. I suppose I'd get some comfort if I find out my dad's last words.

'It was mumbo-jumbo,' says Hall.

Verity clicks her fingers as if snapping the man out of a trance. 'The police pulled you in because they found strands of your clothing under his fingernails. How did they know it was your jacket?'

'They said an eyewitness saw the man grab me,' says Hall.

Verity stands, and I stand next to her. I'm unsure if she's going to attack Hall or comfort him. 'What did the police ask you?' she says

'They seemed convinced I was tangled up in some London gang who wanted Randolph Vine dead. I didn't know him. I work on the railways, which I've done all my life. I'm an engineer, not a killer.'

'What gang?' Verity asks.

Hall waits a beat before saying, 'Some gang in London, Fulham, I think. A Russian name. Vlad something. Vlad Niki.'

Verity nudges me towards the door. She reaches into her pocket and takes out some money, and hands it to the bemused Hall, explaining it's for the gate. He doesn't take it, and Verity returns the money to her pocket.

I've never heard of Vlad Niki, but whoever he is, the

name spooks Verity. I've only known her for two hours and assumed she was unspookable.

Verity darts through the broken gate and runs to the tree where Cedric and Ambrose are discussing deciduous leaf configurations and whether Aristotle outshone his tutor, Plato.

Verity beckons us to head back to the vehicles. So, I pick Winnie up and head back toward Elsie. We walk quickly in silence along the pathway to the clearing where we parked.

At Verity's campervan, I ask, 'Come on then, out with it. Who is this Vlad Niki?'

'Vladimir Nikitin,' says Verity. 'Not Vlad Niki.'

Cedric and Ambrose freeze like a fleeting pause in their life as if someone's turned off their power supply. I watch their faces pale at the mention of Vladimir Nikitin. I've never seen them react this way before.

'And who is Vladimir Nikitin?' I ask.

'My husband,' says Verity.

<><><>

Chapter Twenty-One

Verity jumps into her campervan and scurries down the lane at high speed in reverse. All the while, she clips branches and spits dirt in the air until she's out of sight.

Charlie puts her hand on the glass canopy, preventing Cedric and Ambrose from climbing in, and says, 'I need an explanation.'

Cedric says, 'It's complicated.'

Charlie looks at Ambrose and probes him for more.

He draws air through his teeth and whistles, then says, 'It's very complicated.'

Charlie swings her leg over Elsie and kickstarts the engine while Cedric and Ambrose clamber into the sidecar. At the end of the lane, Charlie spends a moment deciding where to go before turning right and speeding up the hill toward Newlands Corner. Verity's campervan is parked next to the tea hut, and she's standing at the counter talking with the young girl and a couple of motorbikers.

Charlie stops and climbs off Elsie removing her helmet and goggles as she walks up to the tea shed. The two bikers look Charlie up and down, but she's too focused to notice their glare. She looks over to Cedric and Ambrose and makes the letter tea shape with her hands while raising her eyebrows.

Verity leans in and says, 'Those two beauties won't want a cup of tea from here. They don't stock Assam, and too many people have used the mugs.' And right on cue, Cedric and Ambrose shake their heads and walk Winnie towards the grass.

Charlie orders two mugs of tea and steers Verity away from the hut.

She says, 'Two things. One, were you really married to Vladimir Nikitin, a Russian gangster?'

'He was a midlevel mobster, and it was my cover in Moscow, and the other thing?'

'Where do I get a pair of boots like yours?'

'I'll sort you out with the boots, but Vladimir Nikitin is a long story,' says Verity.

'Good. I love long stories, so come to Tanglefoot tonight for dinner. Those two will cook, and we can chat over a bottle of claret in the garden?'

Without any delay, Verity says, 'I'll see you at seven.'

Charlie smiles and sips her tea, walking with Verity side-by-side. They do a few laps of the parking area on top of Newlands Corner and catch up with Cedric and Ambrose.

'Verity is coming for dinner tonight,' says Charlie, putting her goggles and helmet on, then lifting her leg over the motorbike before jumping on the kickstarter.

Ambrose pops his head out of the sidecar and says, 'Verity comes across as calm and loveable, but there's a screw loose in there somewhere.'

Charlie revs Elsie and says, 'Well, I like her, so put

those culinary brains to good work and figure out what to cook.' She steers Elsie out of Newlands Corner and down the hill past Silent Pool, thinking how Kevin Hall turned out to be a funny fish and not the type she had imagined who would kill her father, but no doubt Verity will have some thoughts on him.

<><><>

Chapter Twenty-Two

Joshua King does his best to nestle on the bed. For a tall man, a single bed is of little use.

His knees brush his chin as he fails once more to get comfortable. But it's no use, in the same way, it's no use a giraffe trying to get comfortable on a bicycle.

King pulls a wooden chair in front of the bed and rests on it a tripod with high-powered binoculars attached to the mount. He focuses the eye-piece and trains the viewfinder on Polly King's cottage on the other side of the lane in Shere Village.

Joshua scans the cottage through the military-grade binoculars. If someone is home, there would be signs of life by now, but there's no movement, not a flicker.

Stakeouts are a battle of the mind. They start with controlled enthusiasm, and within an hour, your concentration wanes, your hunger cravings create hallucinations, your inner voice convinces you this is a waste of time, and your flask of strong black coffee ceases to perk you up. But this is not Joshua's first stakeout. He's completed thousands of them worldwide, although this is his first in ten years, and ten years of inactivity in Australia has dulled his senses.

He scopes the cottages on either side of Polly's. The one to the left, with the blue flowers around the doorway, has a light on in the bedroom. What are those blue flowers? Cedric and Ambrose would know the Latin name of the flowers and give him a ten-minute lecture about planting, pruning and seasonal blooms. Joshua snorts a laugh as he's reminded of those two old fusspots.

On their return from warzone missions, Joshua and Randolph embellished their stories, and Cedric and Ambrose listened like excited kids.

A woman at the upstairs window of the cottage on the right rifles through her wardrobe and places a few dresses on the bed. Now King feels like a peeping Tom—he keeps looking all the same. He takes a sip of his cold black coffee, and a few minutes later, the lady from the window appears in a long green summer dress at the front door. Good choice.

A weekday afternoon in Shere would never be hectic. Cars come and go, and the bell on the grocery store door pings now and again. A few schoolchildren walk beside the stream, and a group of ladies, on a rambling trip, sit outside the pub with glasses of white wine and baskets of chips.

Nothing is going to happen, so Joshua stands and stretches. Then, he notices a man walking towards Polly's cottage. It could be nothing. He knocks on Polly's door and then stands back before looking up as if expecting Polly to pop her head out of an upstairs window.

The lady in the green dress chats with the mystery man and points down the quiet road. What is she pointing at? Joshua trains his binoculars on the man's head, waiting for him to turn. What are they talking about? This is a long conversation, and she's pointing again. Joshua follows the line of her finger, but it's not a definitive point, just a general finger-point as if to say Polly's not here, although she might be over there somewhere.

The man turns around, and Joshua snaps a photograph. He tracks the man through his binoculars to the end of the lane, where he disappears from sight. Everything is a potential clue: the lady in a green dress talking to the man, the blue flowers, and even the ramblers eating chips.

Joshua King half lays on the bed with his feet on the floor. He lights a cigarette and blows smoke rings at the ceiling even though the landlady told him twice yesterday it was a non-smoking room. His landlady has a sense of smell as keen as a police sniffer dog, so Joshua sprays a solution of three parts cider vinegar and one part warm water into the cloud of smoke.

The warm evening sunshine is lost on Verity as she speeds up Plum Pudding Lane with her elbow sticking out the campervan's window. She doesn't slow for the narrow pinch and clips the flower heads on either side, sending petals into a restless spin. She tugs on the steering wheel of her rusty mobile home and races around the back of Tanglefoot Farm before coming to an abrupt standstill.

She steps out of the still-chugging camper and bends down to kiss an excited Winnie, saying, 'Hello darling.'

Charlie beckons Verity over to the ops room and hands her an extra-large gin and tonic.

Verity says, taking a long sip. 'Essentially, this is a British health drink. Juniper berries are a superfood, and the quinine in the tonic water treats malaria.'

'There's not much malaria in Friday Street, is there?' asks Charlie.

'I'm not taking any chances, dear,' says Verity, downing her drink in one go.

Charlie pours Verity another without asking. Anyone who shoots their drink this fast will not say no to another. She beckons Verity to sit in the command centre.

Verity sits on the sofa and makes herself comfortable. 'Very nice,' she says. 'You can build an empire from here.' She rummages in her wild grey hair, locates her glasses, and studies the photographs on the wall.

'We don't have much,' says Charlie. 'The case is so cold that clues have been lost to time.'

'Nonsense,' says Verity. 'Clues last forever. Yes, they might be harder to find, and memories fade, but it's all there for us to find.' She looks around, 'Where are the two irritating walking encyclopaedias?'

'In the kitchen, discussing the ratio of honey to balsamic for the poached salmon dressing and haggling over the difference between two regional Dijon mustards.'

Verity rolls her eyes and says, 'It never changes with those two. They hated me when I was their boss at MI6.' Then, she laughs aloud, 'I used to give them an impossible code to crack that nobody else could solve and tell them that a junior team from MI5 cracked it in under two hours. Of course, I never told them that the CIA, FBI, and ten other sets of acronyms had been trying to crack it for six months.'

They clink their glasses together.

Charlie asks, 'And did they crack the code?'

'Every time! They can be righteous and exhausting, and annoying, but the number of times they saved the day because of their bionic intelligence is countless. But don't tell them I said that. I quite like having them fear me.' Verity springs to her feet to take a closer look at the photographs. 'You're keeping Kevin Hall on the board, right? There's something about the man that I can't put my finger on yet. But we will.'

Charlie reaches over and picks up the crossword book, slowly flicking through the pages. 'Not much of a clue, is it?' she says.

Without turning around, Verity says, 'No dear, an empty book gives little away, and remember, not everything points to the murderer.' She takes a few steps over to the black Jaguar. 'This is a beauty. Your dad loved this car.'

Randolph's gleaming black classic Jaguar was the only one in Friday Street, and the neighbours knew his comings and goings from the sightings of his car. On days home from university, Charlie found herself sitting in his car behind the steering wheel—a lazy few hours here and there in the Jag, sitting, reading, thinking or doing nothing at all. Cedric and Ambrose became overdramatic and checked in on her in case she was suicidal after reading up on teenage behaviour mood swings. And it was their compounded over-reactions that led Charlie to feel protected and loved.

Verity picks up the crossword book and sniffs the pages. She asks, 'One day in the water?'

'I think so,' says Charlie.

'Joshua is in Friday Street for something,' says Verity. 'He snooped around for an hour at Newlands Corner, then left.'

'Did he see you?'

'Goodness, no. The tall man spends too much of his life trying to be inconspicuous and misses half the things going on around him. He was a good but limited agent, a quick thinker, but poor at stealth on account of being ten feet tall. It's like a woman having dazzling long blonde hair and large bosoms. They stand out too much, and spies who stand out tend to get shot.'

Charlie joins Verity at her father's Jaguar. 'So why has Joshua risen from the dead? Cedric and Ambrose think he had something to do with Dad's murder.'

Verity doesn't respond right away. Instead, she thinks in a meditative state and says, 'Don't force it—it will come to you.'

'You kicked Kevin Hall's gate off its hinges,' says Charlie.

'Sometimes you've got to force it,' says Verity.

Cedric calls from the kitchen for them to get ready for dinner. The smells floating across the garden promise a table of tasty food.

'I've been spoiled for ten years,' says Charlie with a hint of guilt.

Verity loops her arm through Charlie's, saying, 'Everyone laughed when your father left instructions for them to look after you, and nobody was surprised that they took to motherhood like a duck to bricklaying. And then, slowly, very slowly, they got the hang of it.'

At the table, with the dexterity of talented Italian waiters, Ambrose and Cedric serve four platefuls of poached salmon, asparagus and artichoke salad, broccoli with Dijon mustard and a basket of garlic bread with grilled mozzarella. Cedric opens a bottle of chilled Frascati and pours four glasses as they take their seats.

Verity raises her glass and says, 'Boys, it's good to be back.'

'Good to be back,' they all say together.

'Do you mean that?' Verity asks.

'Of course not,' says Ambrose. 'You scare the living daylights out of us.'

'Jolly good!' says Verity. 'Just like old times, then.'

They eat as the butterflies soak up the last of the day's sunshine, among the wildflowers of Tanglefoot Farm's garden—a peaceful setting more suited to discussing watercolours rather than Randolph Vine's murder on Friday Street.

Cedric cuts his salmon into quarters while Ambrose loads his fork and eats without fuss. Charlie tops up the wine glasses and takes a slice of garlic bread. Verity is a hearty eater, although, from her sparrow-thin frame, you'd be forgiven for thinking she rarely ate.

Between mouthfuls, Verity says, 'We had a vegan at MI6 called John Hunter, so we nicknamed him Gatherer.'

Charlie roars with laughter.

Verity asks, 'What did the investigator tell you about your father's case?'

Cedric cuts in, saying, 'According to Pope, the worse-than-useless lead officer retired right after the case was closed.'

'Is he still alive?' asks Verity. 'If so, let's take him to the crime scene and pepper him with questions.' She loads another spoonful of food onto her plate and adds, 'If he needs a firework shoving up his backside, then I'll happily light the touchpaper so we can get on with the case.' Verity shows no sign of slowing down or veering away from danger for a seventy-five-year-old.

'We'll talk to Pope first thing tomorrow afternoon,' says Cedric.

'Why not first thing in the morning?' says Charlie. 'We've gathered a bit of momentum.'

'Tomorrow is the first Tuesday of the month,' says Ambrose.

'And?' says Verity. 'What does that mean?'

'We visit our tailor and cheese purveyor in central London.'

Verity pushes her chair back, stands up, and says, 'I need a few things in London, so we'll go together. Do you want to come in my campervan? I'm assuming you still can't drive.'

Cedric and Ambrose look at the rusty ramshackle in the courtyard and then at Charlie.

'I'll drive,' says Charlie. 'Verity, why don't you come with us in the morning, and when the boys are in Saville Row visiting their tailor, we can grab a coffee and a cake, and you can tell me all about your husband, Vladimir Nikitin.'

Verity refills her glass and says, 'And then we can stick a firework up the officer's backside.'

<><><>

Chapter Twenty-Three

Verity

At seventy-five, you can be rude, and people give you a pass as if you don't know any better. I do know better, but I don't have the patience to tell them. Honestly, I could get away with murder!

For the record, I was not a member of the ridiculously named Friday Street Spy Ring. I say ridiculous only because I was not a member. If I were—well, if I were a member, then it would be the best private spy club in the world. However, I was a member of the famous five who sat on the bench above Berlin the night the wall came tumbling down. And anyway, I didn't need to be a Friday Street Spy Ring member because I bugged the table where they sat every Friday in the Stephan Langton pub.

I listened to their secret evenings while they chomped through grilled steaks, baskets of chips and guzzled bottles of wine and talked total tosh. Cedric and Ambrose are creatures of habit and always sat at the same table in the alcove at the same time every Friday evening. It's a terrible trait for a spy, so that's why they were based at HQ and spent very little time in the field.

Funnily enough, the bug is still there, and I pop in to change the battery from time to time. If I'm bored, I listen to people's conversations. It's a terrible thing to do, but I'm a spy. It's what I do.

I spent most of my working life in the Soviet Union during Russia's uglier years of communism. And when I say uglier, I mean ruthless, although we were also ruthless. The Cold War was a lot more than spies in trench coats leaving chalk messages for each other on park benches. And at that time in Moscow, it was vodka, kissing, and more vodka. Russian men are wonderful kissers. Russian women are excellent vodka drinkers. I think it was their way to get through the unpleasantness of hardline Socialism.

My overriding memory of the Soviet Union was the cold, and because of the cold, I drank vodka, which led to a lot of kissing and more vodka, which led to... well, you get the general idea. And through the haze of kissing and drinking, I met Vlad—my gorgeous Vladimir Nikitin.

In those days, I dressed in leopard prints and leather miniskirts. I deliberately looked slutty. You have a slight edge if your opponent thinks you are incompetent or stupid because your clothing is non-conforming. People underestimate you for various reasons, and my advantage has always been my appearance. My jackets have a deliberate drop of egg on the lapel, and my outfits are designed to clash. It's liberating.

I loved yesterday.

Everything about it made me feel like a reborn agent,

from kicking down Kevin Hall's garden gate to having dinner with Cedric and Ambrose and staring at the photographs with Charlie in the ops room. Hence, at seventy-five, it's good to be back on the job.

I truly loved Charlie's dad, Randolph Vine, and I always knew he was murdered. And the fact that Vladimir Nikitin's name came up at Kevin Hall's house yesterday afternoon took me by surprise. I haven't seen my husband for twenty-five years.

I can't move too fast as my head hurts a bit this morning.

I stayed in my campervan at Tanglefoot Farm after too many gin and tonics last night. And now, sitting on the step of the camper, I'm drinking a strong cup of black coffee with the rising sun warming my face. I've always tried not to follow a fixed schedule, and after years of living off my nerves, it's good to let life flow in any direction that feels good.

After yesterday's exertions, my legs hurt, my arms hurt, and my head hurts. I put it down to ninety-eight per cent gin and tonic and two per cent age.

The birds, the bees, and the colourful butterflies busy themselves in Tanglefoot's garden, and I watch them going about their morning with a business-like intensity. My mind wanders from thought to thought when Charlie crunches across the gravel courtyard with a couple of plates in one hand and two mugs in the other. More coffee I hope.

I like Charlie. I can happily avoid most people, but Charlie has something about her that I've taken to already. She reminds me of me: that's why I like her. She's basically me!

She hands me a mug of black coffee.

'How did you sleep?' she asks.

'Like the dead,' I say. 'You?'

'Not well,' she says. 'My mind is too busy to rest.'

She's definitely me!

And she's right, of course; her head must be full of ifs, buts and maybes about her father's murder. Unfortunately, I was in the old Soviet Union and missed the murder on Friday Street, but Linus, although annoying, did keep me informed. He has his uses.

Charlie hands me a toasted egg and sausage sandwich with a dollop of brown sauce and sits on an upturned bucket in front of me. It's vital you know when to use ketchup and when to use brown sauce.

Charlie got it right because Cedric and Ambrose would have trained her from day one about the correct usage of a teacup, all food accompaniments, suitable clothing to match seasonal changes, and when to use brown sauce. Good girl!

I point to Tanglefoot Farm with a mouthful of sandwich, saying, 'Those two muffins have spoiled you. But if anyone had to take me in, I would choose Cedric and Ambrose. Charlie Vine, you're the luckiest girl in the world.'

We chink coffee mugs.

'I know,' Charlie says. 'They've done everything for me. Sometimes, they are overprotective, but I can't fault them. And then there are times I could kill them with a blunt instrument.'

I tell Charlie I've dreamed of killing them a hundred times, and we laugh. Winnie trots across the courtyard and nestles in Charlie's lap.

We munch our way through our scrummy breakfast, and she starts peppering me with questions. Good ones, and I knew at that second that Charlie would make a great field agent.

'Joshua King: Good or bad?' she asks.

'Do you mean, did he kill your father?' It's best to be clear about what you think someone has asked you. I interrogated the wrong person in Johannesburg because of a misunderstanding—John of Jamestown, not James of Johnstown. It was an easy mistake, and he was terribly nice about the punch to his face I gave him.

Charlie nods and looks at me. She wants more.

'Joshua King had the skills and could have taken the flight the day after the one we thought he was on and still have time to die in his fake car crash. But what motive?' I ask.

'I don't know,' says Charlie.

'The man is a good agent, and he could have easily killed Randolph and then slipped away down under. He's a suspect for sure.'

Charlie sips her coffee and gazes off into space. I tap her foot with my boot. 'A penny for your thoughts.'

'I don't think I'm doing a very good job of this,' she says.

I stop myself from agreeing with her and say, 'Let's focus on gathering information and keeping a clear head. We had a productive visit to Kevin Hall yesterday, and he threw the name Vladimir Nikitin into our pathway.'

'Will it be awkward seeing your husband?'

'Very.'

'Why?'

'He thinks I'm dead,' I say.

'What?'

'At the end of the Cold War, the best way out of Russia and out of my marriage was for me to die. So, I poured a couple of pints of pig's blood over me and had a few horrifically staged photographs taken from inside an upside-down car, and Vladimir bought the lie that I was dead. MI6's dirty tricks department sold the lie perfectly, and within a week, my husband held a funeral service in Moscow. It was a beautiful service with candles and a choir.'

'How do you know?'

'Because I sat at the back of the church. I sang, and it was very moving. However, I'm sure I can smooth things over when I see him.'

'If I were Vladimir, I'd be furious.'

'That's why we'll take a bag of money and a gun.'

Unfazed by the mention of a gun, Charlie points at my steel-toe-capped boots. 'I want a pair of those.'

I nod. I've got a spare pair somewhere.

'We should get going,' says Charlie.

From painful experience, I know Cedric and Ambrose won't be derailed from their monthly visit to their tailor in Saville Row or their cheese purveyor in Jermyn Street.

Lord save me.

<><><>

Chapter Twenty-Four

Verity wraps her arms around Charlie's waist while Cedric and Ambrose make themselves comfortable in Elsie's sidecar with Winnie. They wanted to travel in the Jaguar and put their argument forward with intellectual force but somehow found themselves outvoted two-to-two.

A week ago, Cedric and Ambrose feared the Jaguar. And now, with the arrival of Elsie and Verity, they long to be in the backseat of the car rather than the teeth-chattering, vintage sidecar.

Charlie kickstarts the motorbike and swerves around Tanglefoot Farm, racing down the lane at high speed. Verity, half-standing, stretches her arms as wide as possible as they whizz through the pinch and slaps the blooms on either side, sending petals spinning in the air.

Tuesday morning's traffic in London is moderate, and Charlie cuts in and out of the cars to reach Saville Row in record time. Verity pats her on the shoulders for a job well done, but Cedric and Ambrose look shaken with their speed ride as they step into the store to see their favourite tailor, Alfred.

Charlie says, 'Alfred has made suits for—'

Verity stops her mid-sentence and says, 'Princes, Kings, and Emperors. They've told me a million times.'

'The good news is that they'll be gone for a couple of hours,' says Charlie. 'They're being measured for their new autumn blazers and have already spent nine days looking at suede elbow patches.'

Verity suggests they grab some tea and cake. Charlie clips on Winnie's lead, and they walk to a small coffee shop, where they order a pot of tea and two slices of Victoria sponge.

Charlie pours the tea.

Verity takes a bite of her sponge and says, 'Let's get Linus Pope to ask the retired police officer to meet us at the pond in Friday Street this evening.'

'I imagine police officers hate that.'

'I imagine you're right,' says Verity. 'But that's not a reason for us not to meet him there.'

Charlie nods, 'You're right, of course. What do you expect to get out of it? Cedric is convinced the officer must be an absolute buffoon.'

Verity wipes sponge crumbs from her bright red trousers, saying, 'Back in the Soviet Union, you couldn't walk about dressed like this. They would have pulled you in for being a hippie and straightened you out.'

'I thought your unconventional dress code was your secret to success,' says Charlie.

Verity flips open a battered old wallet and shows Charlie a photograph of a striking woman with long, curly blonde hair, a leather micro short leather miniskirt and knee-length high-heeled boots.

'Who is that fire-cracker?' says Charlie.

'That's me in Red Square the day I married Vladimir Nikitin.'

'That's you?' says Charlie. She puts her cup down and looks closer at the photograph. 'That's you? I thought you always dressed like... well, like you.'

'I always aim to shock,' says Verity. 'I was a sleeper spy in Russia for most of my working life and began to think like a Russian, drink like a Russian, fight like a Russian, and ended up marrying a Russian.' Verity returns the photograph to her pocket where it belongs: out of sight.

Charlie begins asking three questions all at once, but nothing other than a jumble of words pops out. 'What I'm trying to say is that you were stunning.'

'I had my moments,' says Verity. 'It's easy when you're young, but on my way to seventy-five, things have sagged in all the wrong places.'

'I think you're lovely,' says Charlie.

'And, of course, you're absolutely right.'

They both laugh, and Charlie takes out her phone and clicks on Pope's name. It's answered on the third ring. Charlie turns on the loudspeaker.

Pope's voice squeaks from the phone. He says, 'I'm guessing you want something.'

Verity leans closer to the phone, 'Morning, Pope.'

'Verity Fanthorpe, is that you?'

'Yes, dear. Now listen, I need you to drop that box of paper clips you're counting and contact the investigating officer on the Randolph Vine case. Tell him to meet us at the pond at six-thirty this evening. Thank you. Bye!' Verity presses the red button and ends the call. 'That will make him as angry as hell. When he calls, tell him I'm in a meeting.'

Linus Pope calls back within five seconds.

Charlie answers, saying, 'Verity is in a meeting. I'll say you called. Bye!'

Verity smiles. 'Good. In five seconds, he'll send a message. He's as predictable as a teenage boy chasing a girl.'

Linus Pope's message pops up on Charlie's phone: *Investigating officer retired.*

Verity takes Charlie's phone and taps a message: *Fully understood. Excellent work. Verity thanks you for your sacrifice.*

Three minutes pass before Pope's next message: *Investigating officer Colin Beard will meet you @ 6:30 - Friday Street Pond.*

Charlie says, 'Is Linus scared of you?'

'I told him once how many people I killed as an agent, including one poor soul I killed with a carrot and a tub of butter. Pope's been wary of me ever since.'

Charlie pours the last of the tea, and they sit, watching the world pass by the window for a few minutes. Winnie enjoys a few stray crumbs and sits on Charlie's lap, sighing with contentment. Charlie strokes Winnie's soft apricot hair, thinking about what to ask the police officer.

'We must find Joshua King,' says Verity. 'He's back in Friday Street for a reason.'

'And what's that?'

'More than likely, to kill again.'

'Are you serious?' says Charlie.

Verity lowers her voice to a whisper, 'If Joshua didn't kill your father, why would he risk breaking cover to return to Friday Street? He was safe in Australia, living as someone else, and nobody here was any the wiser. So it makes sense he's returned to kill again.'

'Kill who?'

'Only Joshua has the answer to that,' says Verity. 'As it stands, he's our prime suspect, which is a shame.'

'Why?'

'Because I like him, and he saved my life once. We were in Spain chasing two members from a terrorist cell through the back streets of Malaga, and this young fellow got the jump on me. Joshua turned up at the right time and kicked the bandit in the kneecaps.'

'Would you like more tea?' asks Charlie. She walks to the counter, knowing Cedric and Ambrose will be sitting in the back of the tailor's store, reserved for Alfred's most important clients, taking their time poring over materials and buttons, patterns and stripes. *The nap of the cloth is everything*, they painstakingly explained one arduous morning.

'And more sponge,' shouts Verity. 'We can't catch a killer without more sponge.' Her voice booms across the coffee shop when there's a natural silence. A handful of shocked faces glare at Verity, who, in return, shows no concern for her murderous outburst.

Charlie returns with more tea and cake.

'We must be tactful with this Colin Beard tonight,' Charlie says. 'It will be easy to upset him. We are, after all, unpicking his case.'

'Colin is a dependable name,' says Verity. 'You don't get many idiots called Colin. However, I sat next to a boy at school called Colin, and he burnt the science block down.'

Charlie leans back in her chair, and Winnie reclaims her spot on Charlie's lap. She turns to Verity, who is already halfway through her second piece of cake. 'You knew my dad's methods in the field, so what strikes you as odd about his murder?'

Verity thinks for a moment. 'Your father had a highly

tuned sixth sense and knew when danger was ahead. So whoever murdered him either knew him or posed no threat because a stranger would never have got that close.'

Charlie ran through the names of those who knew him. Joshua King, of course, Polly King, but why would she have killed him? Kevin Hall didn't know him but ran into him outside the Stephan Langton pub, and that doesn't seem reason enough to murder him.

Verity reaches out to touch Charlie's knee, whispering, 'My dear, your dad did many murky things as an agent for the Crown, and when you upturn the apple cart in people's lives, you should expect some pushback.'

'Are you saying his death could've been payback? A revenge killing of sorts? Who would want to do that?'

'The Russians love a bit of dramatic revenge; you only have to listen to their music and poetry to know that. But, mind you, so do we Brits! I can't lie. I did a bit of revenging myself once when I jabbed a Frenchman with my poison-tipped umbrella in Paris, not to kill him but to paralyse him for an hour or two. Scare him—you get the idea.'

'Spy revenge stuff?' asks Charlie.

'Good God, no. Nothing like that. He was a French boy I liked. We went on a romantic date in Paris, and he ran off with a pretty girl he met when I was in the loo. The toad left me to pay, so when I caught up with them on the metro, I pricked him with my brolly, and he cried like a baby. What is it with men?'

Charlie listens to Verity's words while holding her tea cup close to her open mouth. 'So my dad's murder could have been revenge-motivated?'

Verity finishes her second thick slice of jam sponge and swigs her tea. 'We know it wasn't a mugging, and we know he couldn't have been taken by surprise, therefore it was someone he knew, but unlikely a revenge killing. He would have seen that coming.'

Charlie slumps back into her chair and says, 'I feel like we keep ending up back at the beginning.'

Verity sits forward in her chair and looks around her to check no one is listening in to their conversation. 'Your father didn't leave loose ends, if you know what I mean.'

Charlie looks up at Verity and raises her left shoulder an inch. 'No, I don't know what you mean.'

Verity says, 'No loose ends means there's nobody left who can take revenge. In the Russian mafia, they have what they call NBL. Have you heard of that?'

Charlie shakes her head and suspects something unpleasant is coming her way.

Verity spins around once more to check for eavesdroppers. 'No Blood Left. They kill every relative, leaving nobody alive who could take revenge.'

Charlie puts her teacup down, realising that she could be next on someone's revenge list and says, 'Oh hell. . . No blood left means me.'

Verity sits back and says, 'We must consider everything.'

Charlie forces a smile when her phone buzzes with a message: *Come now. Immediate assistance required! C&A.* Charlie shows Verity the message and says, 'There's a crisis at the tailor.'

Verity stands and stretches. 'I didn't think they had a phone.'

'They don't. They use other people's phones to send me messages.'

Verity tuts, 'What sort of emergency? Incorrect buttonhole stitching or the lapel width too narrow.'

'Something like that,' says Charlie.

. . .

Joshua King hides in the shadow of an empty shop's doorway on the far side of Saville Row, and from the dark, he watches Charlie and Verity walk from the coffee shop to the outfitters. King knows how regular Cedric and Ambrose are with their tailor trips, and no doubt, next, they'll go to Jermyn Street and visit Paxton & Whitfield, the finest cheesemongers in the capital.

Taking a calculated risk, Joshua sets off at a brisk pace from Saville Row to Jermyn Street to get ahead of Charlie and the sidecar. He finds a hiding spot in a covered corner where he can see into the cheese shop across the narrow street. Once settled in his new position, he sets up the sights on his rifle.

<><><>

Chapter Twenty-Five

'Ah! The smell of paradise,' says Ambrose, sniffing the air in his favourite cheesemongers.

The emporium never fails to find something interesting for Cedric and Ambrose to taste on arrival, and today, it's Moliterno with truffles: a creamy sheep's milk cheese from Sardinia.

'Oh, that's good,' says Cedric. 'If there's a God, heaven will surely be made of cheese.'

The manager suggests champagne or a deep claret to compliment the Italian cheese perfectly.

Cedric and Ambrose have been Cheese Club gold members for many years. A varied cheese board kept them going through the darker nights of code-breaking.

Cedric samples some artisan biscuits while Ambrose fills a box with cheeses from France, Italy and England.

'Don't look!' says Verity.

'How can I not look?' Ambrose says.

Verity waves everyone over, and they stand in a circle with their heads pressed together.

Cedric looks at Ambrose's selection in his basket. 'Oh,

good choice, dear boy. I love a mature Wookey-Hole Cheddar.'

Verity pokes him in the chest, 'I'll give you a Wookey-Hole in a minute. Listen carefully, and whatever you do, don't react, but across the street, a man is hiding in a dark corner. He spied on Charlie and me in the coffee shop and is now staking us out from over there,' she flashes her eyes over her shoulder.

Ambrose can't help himself and lifts his head, peering towards the dark corner across the street. Verity tugs his tie and yanks his head back into the circle.

'What did I tell you? Don't look!' she says.

'I spent ages getting my Windsor knot just so this morning, and now you've ruined it,' says Ambrose.

Charlie lowers her voice, 'Who is spying on us?'

'Joshua King,' says Verity. 'He's been on us since we left Tanglefoot Farm this morning.'

'Why didn't you tell us before?' asks Ambrose.

Verity sighs, saying, 'Because I thought you'd immediately start staring at him.'

'You make a fair point,' says Ambrose, adjusting his tie, adding, 'I might have whiplash.'

'What does King want?' says Charlie.

'I don't know,' says Verity.

'What's our move?' says Charlie.

Verity whispers, 'I don't want anyone to accidentally look at him on the way out, so when we leave here, turn sharp right and right again, and we'll work our way back to Elsie via St James's Square.'

'Is he here to bump us off?' asks Cedric.

'I think King is just stalking us,' says Verity.

Cedric and Ambrose continue adding cheeses to their selection, but now that they are being watched from across the street, their attention swings from cheese to a clean getaway.

'Would you boys get a move on?' says Verity. 'There's a man over there with his finger on the trigger, and you're looking at a new cheese knife.'

'Unfortunately, some people don't realise the importance of cheese. And when I say some people, I mean Verity unkind Fanthorpe,' says Cedric.

When Verity was their boss, she was frustrated not to be in the field as a sleeper spy. She was MI6's ace in the Russian hole and didn't adjust well when recalled to live out her working life in Vauxhall, London. From Moscow's high life to corporate lowlife was quite a comedown for Verity. She was used to marking her own homework, and the constraints of office management came as quite a shock.

Cedric whispers to Ambrose, 'How did Verity become part of our hunt-for-the-Friday-Street-murderer gang so quickly?'

'That's her superpower, and Charlie likes her,' says Ambrose.

They follow Charlie and Verity onto Jermyn Street, carrying their two reassuringly heavy bags of cheese, and the front door pings shut behind them.

They clip along at a snappy pace and are soon out of sight of Joshua King's dark corner. The four of them breathe an all-round sigh of relief.

'King has time to move to a new location,' says Verity. 'We are sitting ducks.'

'Now you tell us!' says Ambrose.

'It's better if we run,' says Verity.

'I'm not a runner,' says Ambrose.

They reach Elsie after an exhaustive number of left and

rights, and Cedric and Ambrose gasp for air, but not Verity. She's hardly puffing.

Charlie opens the canopy, and the comforting sound of the engine sends them on their way out of range of Joshua King's rifle.

Cedric taps Ambrose on his shoulder and shouts above the sidecar's rattles, 'Excellent cheese run today.'

And from the safety of the sidecar, they watch London blur as Charlie swerves in and out of the traffic. Her busy eyes take in the cars up ahead with frequent glances in the mirrors, constantly checking for Joshua King. She embraces danger as much as Verity. They are like two peas in a pod. Verity smiles as she sways with the motion of Elsie on their way to Fulham to meet Vladimir Nikitin.

Cedric and Ambrose retired from the Service to make honey, tackle crosswords, and reread the classics. Their plan did not involve running around London to avoid murderers lurking in dark corners and knocking on the door of a Russian mid-range oligarch. Vladimir wasn't one of Moscow's leading mobsters, but Verity played him like a violin all the same.

Cedric taps Ambrose's shoulder and shouts above the sidecar's hullabaloo, 'We are supposed to be retired, dear boy, reading Dickins!'

<><><>

Chapter Twenty-Six

Verity urges Charlie to go faster.

Charlie obliges by pushing Elsie through impossibly small gaps in the traffic toward Fulham, London's exclusive southwest corner.

Charlie parks Elsie halfway down the street from Vladimir's white, double-fronted, three-storey house with high brick walls and a long sliding electric gate. Some would say the house is stunning, while others would say it's tasteless—Cedric and Ambrose would say that, adding it's overly showy and gaudy.

'Did you ever live here?' Charlie says.

'No. I only lived in Moscow with Vladimir. London living for rich Russians is a relatively new phenomenon, but they've always had sleepers living among us. Now, they live out in the open, surrounded by opulent wealth. No, this isn't for me; give me my campervan on Newlands Corner any day of the week.'

They crouch behind a wall, and Winnie takes the opportunity to do her business. Ambrose brought his bags of cheese, and the strong whiff, together with Winnie's recent doings, makes for an unpleasant experience.

'How are we going to do this?' says Charlie, pointing at Verity, adding, 'Vladimir thinks you're dead, so you can't knock on his front door.'

Verity nods and says, 'And Cedric and Ambrose can't knock on the door either.'

'Why can't we?' says Ambrose.

Verity sighs, 'Listen, boys, you're not field material. Vladimir will have you in a headlock in two minutes.'

All eyes turn to Charlie.

'It's me, isn't it,' she says. 'I have to go in and poke the Russian bear.'

They hobble together a basic plan where Charlie takes Winnie to the Russian's front door, pretending to look for her other dog.

'I'm not sure it's the best plan,' says Charlie. 'What if Vladimir thinks I am a spy?'

Verity looks Charlie up and down, 'Dear child, you look like James Dean with your leather jacket, jeans and white t-shirt. Spies don't dress like that.'

'But isn't that the idea of a spy?' Charlie says. 'To blend in and not look like a spy.'

'You're wasting time,' says Verity. 'Knock on the door and take three steps back. It will make you look innocent.'

'I am innocent.'

'There you are then,' says Verity. 'You've nothing to worry about.'

Charlie steps out from behind the wall and walks along the tree-lined street towards Vladimir's house. She prepares a few opening lines in her head and forces her shoulders to relax. On arrival, she presses the button on the panel to the right of the gate and looks into the camera.

'Can I help you?' comes a man's voice through the speaker.

'Hello,' says Charlie, summoning her inner young girl, and lifts Winnie's face to the camera lens. 'I've lost one of my mother's dogs. She looks just like this one.' Charlie sniffs a few watery sniffs and rubs her eyes. It's quite a show.

'There's no dog here, sorry,' says the man.

'I think she might have crept through the railings of your gate,' says Charlie, adding a few more sniffs.

There are a few pips and a bit of static from the video phone, and then he says, 'Wait there. I'm coming out to take a look.'

The gate clicks, sliding gracefully to the left, revealing a sweeping driveway with a fountain in the middle and room for six cars.

Charlie takes a tiny step onto Russian soil. She knows it's not Russian soil, but property owned by an ex-Soviet somebody is reason enough to be cautious. Winnie stays rooted to Charlie's feet. The front door opens, and a lady dressed in a housekeeper's white uniform holds the door for a man to walk through.

He's too young to be Vladimir and too good-looking to be the bodyguard, although Kevin Costner—

'Good afternoon,' says the good-looking man.

'Good afternoon,' says Charlie, walking toward him.

The man, in his mid-thirties with dark hair and darker eyes, bends down and reaches out his hand for Winnie to examine.

'She doesn't normally like strangers,' says Charlie.

'Nor do I,' says the man, running his hand over Winnie's head. Winnie enjoys the attention and moves closer to her new friend.

'What's her name?'

'Winnie.'

'That's a nice name.'

'Winnie the poodle,' says Charlie.

The man laughs as he stands, towering over her. 'There's nothing sadder than a lost dog. What's its name?'

Charlie hadn't thought about that. In rapid-fire, her mind churned through unsuitable names: Tango, Ian, Norman, Cedric, Ambrose, Linus. Oh, God! Come on, brain. Finally, she says, 'Verity! Yes, Verity is my dog's name.'

'Verity, that's a new one on me,' he says.

'She's loud and mad and forceful,' says Charlie.

The man walks to the front gate and shouts, 'Verity! Verity! Come here, girl. Verity!'

Charlie joins in, calling, 'Verity. Verity, come here, girl. Verity.' On reflection, Tango would have been a better choice. Charlie looks across the road to where the team are hiding, hoping Verity doesn't pop her head above the parapet.

The young man begins to whistle.

Charlie suggests, 'Maybe Verity managed to sneak into your back garden.'

The man nods with widening eyes and motions for Charlie to follow him through a side gate and along the pathway. The house goes back further than it is wide. It's like a hotel. There must be a dozen bedrooms and a dozen bathrooms. The back garden has a swimming pool, a grass tennis court and a sunken firepit with soft cushions neatly arranged on the circular sofa.

'I love your house,' says Charlie. She waves her hand, adding, 'I love your garden, too. Verity certainly chose a beautiful place to disappear.'

The man looks under the firepit furniture and around

the back of the pool house, taking his time to search the grounds. Charlie takes this opportunity to chat with him.

'Have you lived here long?'

'Yes,' he says.

Charlie looks under the bushes at the rear of the garden, calling out for Verity, and when she stands, she notices him looking at her: the kind of look a man gives when he's interested in what he sees.

'It's hot this afternoon,' she says, taking off her jacket.

'May I offer you a glass of something cold?' And only in the word cold could Charlie detect the slightest Russian twang. It might have been slight, but it was there.

'That would be lovely, thank you.' Charlie's phone rang. She didn't recognise the number, which meant it was either Cedric or Ambrose.

'Hello,' she says.

'This is Verity. I'm calling from a telephone box, don't act surprised,' whispers Verity.

'Yes, thank you, Mother.'

'Good girl. Have you met any Russians yet?'

'Yes, that's right, Mother.'

'Now, it's two-thirty, so I'm taking Cedric and Ambrose to get a cup of tea and a slice of something. See you back at Elsie in an hour. I love your choice of name for your lost dog. Tell the Russian that Verity has turned up at home. If you understand, say... that sounds perfect.'

'That sounds perfect, Mother. I'll see you at Elsie's in an hour,' says Charlie and hangs up the phone.

'My name is Yuri,' says the man, handing her a tall glass of something fizzing with fruit slices and a mini umbrella. He raises his eyebrows towards her phone and asks, 'Is everything alright?'

Charlie takes a sip while thinking a thousand miles an

hour, 'Ooh, this is delicious,' she says, playing for more time. 'I'm Charlotte, but everyone calls me Charlie. That was my mother on the phone telling me Verity made it safely home.'

'I'll call off the search party,' says Yuri. His smile is as perfect as his hair shining in the afternoon sunlight, and his neatly tailored shorts show enough muscular thigh to reveal his fitness level.

Charlie sits on the sofa surrounding the firepit and takes in the exquisite garden. 'Do you garden?'

Yuri shakes his head. 'That was my father's department. I don't have any aptitude for it, although I love sitting out here.'

'Your father is talented; it must keep him busy.'

Yuri took a slow sip of his drink before putting his glass on the table. 'My father spends most of his time taking in the sea air in Eastbourne.'

'Eastbourne is lovely this time of year,' says Charlie, adding a smile. 'Do you ever go and visit him?'

'I'm going this week,' says Yuri. 'I try and go at least once a week.'

Charlie takes a long, slow look around the garden and returns the glass to the table. 'This drink has saved me, but may I use your loo?'

Yuri gives directions, and Charlie sets off toward the house, leaving Winnie on the sofa. The open bi-fold doors reveal an expansive marble kitchen. Too much marble, Cedric and Ambrose would say.

Charlie stops in the hallway to look at the photographs on the wall, and there it is, a black and white snap of a gorgeous couple, Vladimir and a blonde woman in a short mini skirt. Verity. Charlie quickly uses her phone to take a photograph and then pops into the lavish downstairs restroom with gold taps and plug.

. . .

In a red London telephone box on the corner of Vladimir's street, Cedric and Ambrose crowd Verity in the tiny space. They press their heads against the earpiece, and the strong-smelling blue cheese in the cramped space wafts into their faces.

'What did she say?' asks Cedric.

'Is she safe?' says Ambrose.

They stare at Verity for a full debrief of the call.

She pushes the door open for some much-needed fresh air and says, 'I can barely think above your cheese. Charlie is a resourceful girl.'

She shoos Cedric and Ambrose out of the cramped telephone box and begins filling in the scant details as they walk to Parsons Green to find a coffee shop.

Verity knows this is where the rubber hits the road for Charlie. Every plan can blow up in your face the minute you engage with the enemy. And if Russia is somehow involved in Randolph's murder, Vladimir is the enemy. She wonders how he's aged; he'd be seventy-seven but undoubtedly still handsome.

In the coffee shop, she orders tea and cake while Cedric and Ambrose find a table outside in the sunshine.

'There's only so long you can talk about a missing dog,' says Ambrose.

Charlie takes after Randolph, and he mastered the art of staying engaged in a conversation way beyond the original starting point. Charlie's lost dog scenario creates sympathy, and that's her starting point. After that, it's about compliments and easy questions to keep your opponent engaged because people love compliments and love to talk about themselves.

'This tea is outstanding,' says Cedric, topping up his cup.

Ambrose launches into the cake, making short work of the walnut and coffee cream slice. The dappled sun dances on the silver teapot from the leafy trees surrounding the green—an idyllic spot to consider their next move.

'About Randolph's murder,' asks Verity. 'Poisoned would be my guess.'

'The details have been kept under wraps for ten years, so it's unlikely we'll learn much,' says Ambrose.

'This police officer, Colin Beard, could be the key to it all,' says Verity.

Cedric sighs, 'Remember, he's the one who believed it was a mugging gone wrong, so I doubt he'll have a fresh idea a decade on. Trust me, the man will be an utter waste of time.'

Verity says, 'Come on, drink up and let's return to Elsie in case Charlie has run out of chatter. This is her third day in the field, and she might freeze.'

'Charlie, freeze?' says Cedric. 'That girl is made from iron and fire. She'll have those Russians eating out of her hand by now.'

Verity sets a fast pace back to Elsie, which leaves Cedric and Ambrose puffing and panting for air. She leans forward, much like a sprinter running through the line and touches the sidecar. She declares race victory.

'We weren't racing,' says Ambrose, loosening his tie and removing his jacket.

'Everything's a race,' snaps Verity, looking around for Charlie and Winnie, but they are nowhere to be seen.

Cedric checks his watch. It's gone three-thirty.

He says, 'She's never late. Maybe we should go and get her.'

Verity throws a couple of air punches as if fighting a boxer in a ring and then takes a dozen deep lunges on each leg.

She pulls her wild hair back, saying, 'No, I'll go in alone!'

'Oh, God,' says Ambrose. 'Verity's going to thump a Russian.'

<><><>

Chapter Twenty-Seven

Charlie

I'm trying my hardest to remain professional in front of Yuri.

However, here I am wearing a leather jacket and oily jeans and, for all the world, looking like a sweaty biker. My one pretty summer dress is hanging up in my wardrobe. It could be worse—I could be stuck in the sidecar on this sweltering hot day with Ambrose's bags of ripe cheese.

While Yuri heads inside to top up my summery drink, I take in the grandeur of the house. Seven theatrically curved steps lead up to the doors that open to the marble-laden kitchen, and on the upper floors, six ornate balconies overlook the manicured garden. Before he returns, I glance at the photo I snapped of Verity on my way to the loo. She looks glamorous and genuinely happy. What a wild and exciting life she led. No wonder she kicked off when the Service recalled her to the corporate world in London.

Yuri sits back on the sofa and puts my refilled glass in front of me. This is my chance to ask a searching question.

'Your dad must miss you. What's his name?' I could kick myself! That was clumsy and blunt, but the words spat from my mouth before I could stop them. I clench my teeth to prevent anything else from coming out unfiltered.

I urge myself to smile with as much self-control as I can muster. Instead, an awkward grin spreads across my face. No wonder Cedric and Ambrose thought I was constipated.

'I miss him,' says Yuri. 'My father's name is Vladimir.'

The arithmetic in my head begins performing somersaults as I try to figure out if Yuri is Verity's son. She would have said, wouldn't she? There was no mention of a son, just Vladimir. Yuri looks nothing like Verity. In the photo, Verity looks nothing like Verity.

Before I say something stupid, I stand, and Winnie pulls on the lead to make a move.

Yuri takes my glass, and I thank him for his kindness. I'm moving slowly to make the moment last without appearing too obvious. Why doesn't he ask me for my number? It's the James Dean look, isn't it?

'It would be lovely to see you again,' he says.

Halleluiah!

I lean my head to one side because years ago, I read a magazine article, How to Attract a Man in Five Easy Steps, that leaning your head to one side is attractive. I forget the other four steps, but leaning your head plugs into a man's brain.

Yuri is talking, but I'm still leaning to one side. I need to straighten my head and say something.

'And you can meet Verity.' As soon as I said it, I knew it was a foolish thing to say. I add, 'Shall we swap numbers?'

And we do.

'Maybe we could picnic on the seafront at Eastbourne,' says Yuri.

My brain ping-pongs images back and forth of eating egg sandwiches with Yuri while Verity interrogates Vladimir.

'That sounds perfect,' I say, finally straightening my head. My neck aches, but I restrain myself from rubbing it. I'll do it later.

Yuri shows me to the side gate, and I follow him along the path to the front driveway. He clicks the electric gate open, and I walk through with Winnie. I feel like I'm doing the walk of shame, but all I did was enjoy a glass of fizz and arrange to go to Eastbourne for a picnic with a man I met an hour ago. Thank goodness I wasn't wearing my pretty summer dress. I wave at him and awkwardly run from his house to where I parked Elsie.

Verity walks towards me, saying loud enough for the whole street to hear, 'Well, how did it go?'

'We're going for a picnic in Eastbourne,' I say.

'How lovely,' says Ambrose. 'I'll make a list of things to put in the hamper, and—'

Verity cuts across him and asks, 'You're going on a picnic with Vladimir?' She looks put out.

'No, your son, Yuri,' I say.

'My son, Yuri? Who's Yuri?' she says.

Cedric clicks his fingers as if asking the question of the century, 'Did you kiss him?'

I sit astride Elsie, explaining I didn't kiss anyone and kickstart the engine, sending a reassuring roar down the road. Cedric and Ambrose sit in the cheesy sidecar, discussing luncheon hampers, while Verity keeps the questions coming.

'Did you meet Vladimir? How did he look?'

I rev the engine and give Verity a fifteen-second recap of my hour with Yuri. I ask, 'So, is Yuri your son?'

'No,' she says, 'I don't have children.'

And for the first time since meeting Verity, I notice a lull in her high-octane character. She taps my shoulder and points in the direction of Tanglefoot Farm.

I'll ask questions later. Cedric and Ambrose know everything there is to know about everything. I'll book a table for six at the Stephan Langton pub tonight. The four of us, plus Colin Beard and no doubt Linus Pope, will turn up like a bad penny. He did organise for Beard to be there tonight, so it's only fair if he gets a seat at the table.

I steer Elsie through the late afternoon traffic and hammer down the power on the straight road leading to the Surrey Hills.

Yuri is on my mind. How could he not be? It's not every day you meet someone like him. From my peripheral vision, I see Verity making hand signals into the sidecar and feel her laughing. She's an amazing woman with a headful of memories and a renewed interest in Vladimir's world. I imagine she'll take most of her secrets with her.

Thoughts of Yuri fade, not entirely, though, and I begin to think about this evening with Colin Beard. He probably hasn't given my father's case a second thought and is only coming to keep Linus quiet. I hope Cedric isn't right about the man being a useless buffoon.

I give Elsie a juicy burst of power and whizz around Newlands Corner at top speed, heading for home. Verity cheers, putting her hands in the air as I turn into Plum Pudding Lane. She shouts at me to ride flat out. I look at my passengers, who grip the sidecar handles and close their eyes. I lean over the fuel tank and race the meaty engine. I wanted more adventure in my life, and this is it! Elsie speeds around the courtyard, and I park in the garage. There's someone in the ops room.

'Oh, crap!' I say.

'Oh, huge crap,' says Cedric.

'Language,' says Ambrose.

I point to our ops room, where Polly King is looking at the photograph of herself on our suspect corkboard.

'Oh, huge crap,' says Ambrose.

<><><>

Chapter Twenty-Eight

Polly King stands motionless, glaring at the photograph of herself on the wall, seemingly oblivious to the noisy motorbike's arrival.

'Is she dead?' asks Verity. 'I heard about people who die standing up, rigor mortis takes hold, and there they stand like a stuffed idiot.'

Polly turns around and says, 'I'm not dead, and I'm not deaf, but I am curious as to why my face is on your wall under the heading... suspects?'

Verity strides over to Polly King, thrusts her hand forward, and introduces herself, 'I'm Verity Fanthorpe.'

Polly shakes Verity's hand. 'Yes, I know. You worked with my husband, Joshua.'

Cedric and Ambrose stay in the safety of the cheesy sidecar for a moment while Charlie joins the conversation in the ops room by asking how they can help.

Polly loses her confidence and power pose before slumping onto the sofa and letting out a long sigh. Cedric and Ambrose take this as their cue to clamber out of the sidecar and offer their guest a cup of tea.

'Do you have something stronger?' asks Polly.

'How about a glass of elderflower wine,' says Ambrose. 'We made it last summer when we had that burst of hot weather and—'

Charlie puts her hand up, 'It's a lovely story, but I'm sensing a gin and tonic is required.'

Cedric and Ambrose turn and walk towards the kitchen door, reliving their summer of elderflower wine with each other.

Polly King fidgets on the sofa and fiddles with the straps on her high-heeled sandals. Verity secretly raises her finger to stop Charlie from saying anything. *Let your subject do the talking*. The fiddling finally stops, and Polly looks up and says, 'I think my dead husband, Joshua, is alive and is trying to kill me.'

Verity twirls with the grace of a ballerina and slides next to Polly on the sofa. She waits a full minute before saying, 'What makes you think he's alive?'

'I saw him,' sniffs Polly.

'Yes, dear, but he's dead.'

'I know,' says Polly.

'Where did you see him?' asks Charlie, checking with Verity if asking a question is alright. Verity doesn't move.

'Yesterday, in the cottage opposite mine. He was spying on me and again this morning. I couldn't turn a light on or answer the door and hid in my back bedroom like a prisoner the whole time.'

Verity places her hand softly on Polly's knee, 'And why do you think he's come back to life and trying to kill you?'

'Why else is he spying on me?'

'I really don't know,' says Verity. 'Many years ago, I was in love with someone who was spying on me. I was sad when he died.'

Polly looks at Verity, 'How did he die?'

'Oh, I shot—' Verity coughs. 'That's not important right now.'

Polly dabs her nose with a tissue while looking Charlie dead in the eye. 'Why is my photograph on your wall? You came to my house and had tea, and now I'm a suspect.'

Charlie steps over to the corkboard and looks at the three faces: Kevin Hall, Polly King, and Joshua King. She begins to waffle, ignoring Polly's question, when Cedric and Ambrose arrive with a tray of elderflower wine and a large gin and tonic, directing everyone to sit at the garden table under a large umbrella.

Polly sips her gin, taking in the beauty of it all. And through gentle sobs, she says, 'Your garden looks so natural.'

Charlie says, 'These two are keen apiarists and lepidopterists.'

Cedric and Ambrose look up open-mouthed, nodding their heads in appreciation, while Polly has the classic look of someone deciding whether to ask the obvious.

'Bees and butterflies, dear,' says Verity. 'Nothing more than bees and butterflies.' She takes a long sip of her elderflower wine and splutters until her eyes stream. 'Heavens above! This is like high-octane jet fuel!'

'It's stronger than that,' says Cedric. 'We've been working on our elderflower wine recipe for forty years.'

Ambrose takes a sip without a grimace and smacks his lips, looking at his wine. 'Good body. Nice finish. Long legs.'

'Is he talking about me?' asks Polly.

'I shouldn't think so, dear,' says Verity. 'Ambrose once kissed a girl in the eighties and hasn't fully recovered.'

Charlie hovers the bottle of elderflower wine over Polly's empty gin and tonic glass and raises her eyebrows.

Polly says, 'No thanks. I'd better keep a clear head.'

Verity asks, 'Did you walk here? I didn't see a car outside.'

'A friend dropped me off and is picking me up from the end of Plum Pudding Lane in a few minutes.'

Charlie stands, 'I'll walk you down.'

Polly stands and says, 'That's kind, but you look comfortable, and I need some quiet time to think. I'll saunter down the lane and enjoy the evening air.'

Nobody moves until Polly King is out of sight, and her footsteps can no longer be heard floating on the late afternoon breeze.

Verity speaks first, 'Polly asked a reasonable question about her face being on our wall.'

Cedric says, 'We picked up the trail of a ten-year-old cold case which had been woefully mishandled by the police and began by listing the people who were close to dear old Randolph.'

Ambrose says, 'They all qualify to be on the wall and must remain there until we can rule them out.'

Charlie looks at her watch. 'Let's walk to the pond; it will clear our heads and might even shake some good questions loose to ask Colin Beard. Oh, and one more thing, I've booked a table for six at the Stephan Langton pub for seven-thirty.'

'For six?' says Cedric.

'We should take Linus for dinner to thank him for organising the meeting with the police,' says Charlie.

Cedric tuts and frowns. 'Do we have to?'

As the gang walk down Plum Pudding Lane to the Friday Street pond, Verity and Charlie hang a few paces behind

Cedric and Ambrose, who changed into matching tweed suits and brogues for the evening's cross-questioning of Colin Beard.

'When did you first meet those two?' asks Charlie, pointing at the dapperly dressed twins.

'I met them when they were young boys. I worked in the Service under the guidance of Lizzie Denton, their grandma Lizzie, and was at Tanglefoot Farm the night they moved in following the death of their father. I kept tabs on them and recruited them straight out of Cambridge,' says Verity. 'Their intelligence caught my attention, but for a long time, they had no idea they were working for MI6. Sometimes, it's best not to tell people. They had an aptitude for languages and cryptic puzzles and scored off the chart in their IQ tests. But my goodness, what a pain in the neck they could be at times.'

'And still are,' laughs Charlie.

Winnie skips along, sniffing at the scented air, and Charlie loops her arm through Verity's as they pick up speed and catch up with Cedric and Ambrose. They clamber over the stile at the end of the lane and take a shortcut across the bone-dry field to Friday Street.

The pond is mirror-still, with nothing more than the faint mist of dusk clinging to its surface. Frantic midges bunch in shadowy swarms, forming dark mystical patches above the reeds around the water's edge.

'I love it here,' says Ambrose, standing with his hands on his hips, taking in the view. 'There's not a prettier sight in England.'

'Everyone says that about their little spot of heaven,' says Charlie. 'But you're right about loving it here. I do, too.'

Verity says, 'This evening, the only thing we need to do is avoid peppering this Colin Beard chap with questions about the case the minute we meet him. Let's steer him gently to the scene and let him dictate the pace. Let's not bombard the poor fellow.'

'Understood,' they say, knowing that Verity has questioned her fair share of people over the years, so if she says back off, then back off, they will.

They mooch around the pond and approach the only car parked facing the water. A large man, larger than most, wearing a Hawaiian, short-sleeved shirt, steps out of the car and starts walking to meet them.

Charlie whistles through her teeth and says. 'Cedric, please let me watch when you tell this giant wrestler that he is an utterly useless police officer.'

Cedric watches the slow-moving man amble closer to them. He says in a high-pitched voice, 'I don't remember saying anything like that. I'm an enormous fan of the police.'

On arrival, Colin Beard reaches out his shovel-sized hand and introduces himself. After a round of names and handshakes, Colin bends down and strokes Winnie's head.

'She doesn't normally like people,' says Charlie. 'The last policeman she met, she bit his finger.'

'I haven't been an officer for years,' says Beard. 'I guess the sinister smell of crime has finally washed off.'

Everyone waited silently until Colin Beard stood, towering over them like a bear, in readiness for the questions to begin.

'It's good of you to come and see us,' says Charlie. 'Linus told us you'd retired.'

Colin has one of those faces with a permanent, easy smile. He says, 'Pretty much after your father's case, I took early retirement. It was tough at first missing out on the action, and I admit, I still get under my wife's feet.'

Charlie takes a few slow steps, and the party begins walking to the far side of the pond.

'I thought Pope would have shown his face this evening,' says Verity.

'Talk of the devil,' says Ambrose, pointing to a man striding around the pond to meet them.

'Mr Beard, are you armed?' asks Cedric. 'You're welcome to fire a few warning shots over this clod's head.'

Linus Pope catches up with the group and immediately commandeers the attention of Colin, and like an amateur, asks him question after question about the Randolph Vine investigation.

'Someone wasn't at the briefing about peppering the poor chap,' says Ambrose under his breath. 'There's always one. And if you don't know who it is, then it's probably you!'

Verity carefully steers Beard away from Pope to the back of the group to chat with Charlie. Winnie trots along between them, and Charlie slows, letting the group drift ahead out of earshot.

'Thank you for seeing us this evening, Mr Beard,' she says.

'Call me Colin, please,' says Beard. 'I must admit, I was apprehensive about meeting you. Especially here at the... well, you know.'

Verity was right about letting Beard dictate the pace, and they chat with him for a lap of the pond and rejoin the others.

Verity puts Pope straight about questioning Beard, and he slinks away to hide his ashen face.

Colin Beard takes a firm hold of a tree branch, easing himself down the muddy bank to within a few inches of the water's edge.

Cedric and Ambrose look at the mud and then at their

brogues. They stay on the dry footpath while Charlie and Verity scramble down the bank to join the ex-policeman. The ever-persistent Linus Pope begins to make a move, but Cedric and Ambrose block his pathway, suggesting this is Charlie's time to be alone with the officer.

'Verity Fanthorpe is down there,' says Pope.

'Yes, we can see that,' says Ambrose. 'This is her world, not yours. You are more administration—Verity is more castration.'

At the water's edge, Charlie and Verity wait for Beard to start speaking.

'When I arrived on the scene, it was already getting dark,' he says, pointing to a spot on the water fifteen feet out into the pond. 'Your father was over there, face down. He—'

Charlie puts her hand on his arm, 'It's alright, Colin. I've waited ten years for this moment, so please take all the time you need and leave nothing out.'

Verity reaches out and touches his other arm. 'Colin, don't worry about Charlie. She's as tough as she looks.'

Beard continues telling them how two officers waded out and brought Randolph's body to the bank. They checked for signs of life, but there was no pulse. A scene of crimes officer took photographs and samples of water and mud, and Beard points to where a white tent was erected. The whole area was sealed off with police tape.

'How did he die?' asks Charlie.

'Your father didn't drown. The pathologist said he was dead before his body entered the water. The bruising around his arms and neck showed the hallmarks of restraint. It was a professional job, not a chance killing.'

'You said it was a mugging in your report,' says Charlie.

'I never agreed with that,' says Beard. 'My report was different from the official version. A trained killer murdered your father and made it look like a mugging. I've seen far too many muggings to know the difference. The home office soon took over once they discovered it was Randolph Vine.'

'Were you hushed up?' says Verity.

'I was strongly offered early retirement from the job I loved,' says Beard. 'I was never told as much, but it was clear to me that my retirement was because of your father's case. I don't think the ministry wanted the information made public about a British spy floating face down in a pond in Friday Street.'

Charlie looks at Verity for confirmation, 'Does that happen?'

Verity lets out a long sigh, 'I'm afraid it does. Colin is right. News about spies dying during the Cold War was kept quiet. Even when we took down a top Soviet target, it was hushed up. It's not only a secret service; it's a silent service.'

Colin Beard looks upwards as if wanting to offer more.

He says slowly, 'Your father had four keys on a ring and a blank crossword book in his pockets, which wasn't much. I expected more because when someone is murdered, they have lots of what we call pocket litter. You know, things like tickets, coins, and money, but your dad had none of that.'

Verity digs around in her pockets and finds a vegetable peeler, a flick knife, a short length of knotted rope, a syringe filled with yellow liquid, three orange tablets, an old twenty-pound note covered with phone numbers, and a walnut.

'You're prepared for most things,' says Beard.

'It's my basic survival kit,' says Verity as if carrying such a cache of weapons is the most normal thing.

Charlie pulls herself, tree branch by tree branch, to the track. Ambrose and Cedric reach out to help her with the last step. Verity sticks her shoulder behind Colin and pushes him back up the slippery bank. They set off the opposite way around the pond to the Stephan Langton pub.

Charlie walks with Colin Beard. 'Will you join us for dinner?' she asks, pointing to the pub on the pond.

'I'd love to,' he says. 'It's my wife's bridge night, and the Stephan Langton is one of my favourite pubs.'

They amble into the pub and squeeze into their favourite alcove, and order drinks while looking at the menu.

'This is the old Friday Street Spy Ring table,' says Linus.

Ambrose leans close to Linus Pope and says, 'And the first rule of spy club is what?'

'Don't talk about the Friday Street Spy Ring,' says Linus, looking sheepish.

Colin Beard sits next to Cedric and whispers, 'Linus Pope told me you think I'm an utter buffoon and that I made a complete mess of the investigation.'

'I-I-I wouldn't say that,' says Cedric.

Beard wraps his massive hand around his pint glass and takes a long, quenching drink of his beer. He wipes his mouth with the back of his hand and says, 'The thing is, Cedric, you're right. A mess was made of the case, and I was in charge, so I was responsible for the whole damn show.'

Cedric straightens up, clearly relieved about what could have been a far more awkward situation. His eyes dart from side to side as if contemplating something complex to say. 'The fish here is always good on Friday.'

'It's not Friday,' says Beard.

'Every day is Friday in Friday Street,' says Cedric.

<><><>

Chapter Twenty-Nine

Verity

I like Colin Beard. He's a solid copper, a good detective, but the Service's takeover crushed his investigation. I could feel his authenticity when we chatted in the Stephan Langton pub. He's a bear of a man who carries the weight of disappointment in not finding Randolph Vine's killer. I appreciate that.

It's late, nearly midnight, and the sky is a dark blanket of twinkling stars. Living free and wild in my campervan has been revolutionary for me. For decades, I lived on my wits in military-aroused countries, keeping my head down and ears open for morsels of intelligence. Although I loved it, my life of constant near-death experiences and shredded nerves eventually ended. So I moved on, or rather, I came home to a desk job where I bossed Cedric and Ambrose around. They pretended to hate it, but I knew deep down they had a soft spot for me.

Charlie, who I liked instantly, is sitting on the steps of my campervan and asks me what I'm thinking about. I top up her glass with some of Cedric and Ambrose's violent elderflower wine and then squeeze in next to her. I tell her that she looked satisfied with Beard's account of her father at the pond and afterwards around the dinner table.

'He took the right approach,' says Charlie. 'I think Colin must have been frustrated for a long time about not being allowed to sink his teeth into the case. When we crack this whole bloody thing open, we'll visit him and tell him our findings. So let's keep our fingers crossed that it wasn't a mugging gone wrong!'

I gaze at the stars and take in the peacefulness of Tanglefoot Farm's surroundings. Cedric and Ambrose renovated this place and are the only two men on earth who could have made it more old-fashioned.

What do we want the internet for? They said to Charlie.

My thoughts dart between our evening with Beard and the afternoon re-engaging with Vladimir's world. He's like a missing tooth when you can't stop yourself from running your tongue over the raggedy edges. Charlie delights in showing me the wedding photo from inside the house. I had no idea my Russian husband would still have my picture on the wall.

For me, it was a step-by-step, carefully orchestrated extraction from an undercover operation—for him, it was the tragic loss of his wife in a car accident. And now the silly old Soviet goose prefers Eastbourne to London. What's he doing there? I tell myself to stop thinking about him.

'More elderflower?' I ask.

Charlie lifts her glass, and the glug, glug momentarily drowns out the crickets' nighttime chorus as we sit and look into the endless sky. Cedric and Ambrose retired to their bedrooms after our return from the pub to colour-coordinate their new collection from their tailor. Life for them is beset with non-existent stressful bumps in a smooth road—lives of bliss.

After our fish pie and chips, Colin told us about his interview with Kevin Hall, which came about because of fabric caught under Randolph's fingernails.

'How did you know to interview Hall?' Charlie asked Colin. It was a good question, as Hall's jacket fibres wouldn't necessarily have been on the police database.

Kevin Hall came forward, Beard told us, so there was no need for a nationwide manhunt. And while charging through his apple crumble and custard, he added that Randolph's black Jaguar was seen driving around Friday Street in the afternoon. I was impressed with Colin Beard; he's someone we can revisit if the need arises.

I nudge Charlie on the step and ask when she and her Russian lover-boy are going to Eastbourne.

'I'll call him in the morning,' she says, ignoring my taunt.

I suggest she message Yuri now and tell him she's in bed but can't sleep, and it's all his fault.

'Verity!' shouts Charlie. 'I'm not doing that.'

I tell her she doesn't need to.

'Why?'

'Because I stole your phone and sent the message when I topped up your wine,' I say.

'What? You're crazy!' she shouts, recoiling from the steps.

I say, 'I know it's wrong, but sometimes throwing a spanner in the works moves things along.'

Charlie runs up the steps and dives into the campervan to retrieve her phone. A moment later, she yells, 'Oh, God! Verity!'

Charlie shows me the image on her phone of Yuri in his half-unbuttoned shirt, sitting in his bed.

'Now he's got the wrong idea about me,' sighs Charlie.

I urge her to calm down and smile at her. She smiles back. I like her; she's got style and guts. I'll find that other pair of steel-toe-cap boots in the morning. We hug each other goodnight, and I listen to the gravel crunch under her footsteps as she disappears into the darkness of Tanglefoot Farm.

I lean back and rest my head against my campervan door. Vladimir would not have survived today's Russia. I knew everything about him. He was a romantic, seductive man who had no idea I was a spy, and in a different world, one where he was born in England and went to Cambridge, we would have made a genuine couple very much in love. I crushed him when I died, and from the reports I read from other field agents, he was a mess of a man. Alternatively, I took being dead in my stride without looking back at the carnage I'd caused. I always saw that as my strength, but now I think it might be my weakness.

I've been mooching about in my campervan since leaving the Service, and I love being carefree, but being tethered to Tanglefoot Farm with hot and cold running water reminds me of the basic pleasures of life.

Was Vladimir involved in Randolph's death? Kevin Hall dropped Vladimir's name into our conversation the day I kicked his gate off its hinges. I don't usually get played —actually, never! Was I played? Of course not!

I stir a huge spoonful of Cedric and Ambrose's golden honey into a cup of herbal tea and stroll across to the ops room to look at Kevin Hall.

Randolph's crossword book is on the table, and I rest my cup next to it as I stare at Hall's photograph until my eyes defocus, and I drift off into thought. I pick up the crossword book and flick through the empty pages.

Wait! What was that?

The faintest pinhead of light appears on one of the pages. I flick through the book again and find the smallest pinhole on page fifty-seven, next to a clue.

Eighteen down: *The European measurement for speed* (3).

Kilometres Per Hour, I mutter, KPH.

I run into the house and chase up the stairs, shouting to see if Charlie is awake.

'Everyone is awake, you noisy clown,' says Cedric, standing at his bedroom door in his pyjamas.

I ask Cedric what Kevin Hall's middle name is.

'I've got no idea,' he says. 'Charlie will know. That door leads to her wing,' he says, pointing to a door at the end of a hallway.

I charge down the hallway and barge through the door.

Charlie and Winnie jump out of bed and stare at me as if I'm about to announce news of a meteor heading to earth.

'What's Kevin Hall's middle name?' I'm eager for her to say Peter or Philip or—I can't think of another P name for a man.

'And you need to know now?'

I explain the tiny pinhole next to the clue in the crossword book.

Charlie says, 'You think dad made the hole because Kevin Hall was going to kill him?'

'I don't know, but this is a breakthrough,' I say.

Then Charlie shouts loud enough so Cedric and Ambrose can hear, 'Ops room, two minutes!'

<><><>

Chapter Thirty

Joshua looks through his binoculars at Polly's cottage.

His life with her was a lifetime ago, and following that, he'd spent a decade as somebody else, only to return to England to feel his emotions churn inside his empty stomach. He should have eaten. And now his long days are taking their toll. His trip to London to watch Cedric and Ambrose visit their tailor and then onto their monthly cheese run is playing havoc with his knees. His fitness is not what it should be, and he rubs at a cramp in his leg.

As he relieves the aching cramp, he smiles at the thought of them quick-marching from store to store, taking lefts and rights, scurrying back to their motorbike and sidecar.

At the pond in Friday Street last evening, Joshua could only watch from a distance how they and Linus Pope chatted with a large man in a Hawaiian shirt. Verity and Charlie spent the most time with him, even clambering down to the water's edge. Who was he? Why were they at the pond? Was there new incriminating evidence?

It's after midnight, and King needs sleep, he needs food, and above all he needs answers. He drinks his glass of water, and his eyes slowly close as he slumps uncomfortably in his chair with tiredness.

But it isn't tiredness.

Joshua is slipping from this world into the next. He has no sense that he's dying, no indicator that he's drifting. Joshua King is dying as he sleeps and doesn't know it.

King, if asked, would tell you through bluff and pride that he expected to die in the field, fighting for the crown and country, defending his beliefs while taking down the enemy as he fell. But it's not going to be that way as death slowly takes him, rasping breath by rasping breath with no last words, no note, no witness. There's no time to say goodbye or say sorry, or to explain. There's nobody to record the tall man's final thoughts as he exhales his last breath, slumped in a chair that's too small, his binoculars still trained on the cottage across the street.

King's last breath is drawn alone, and a single heartbeat later, he is dead.

Verity places a soft red blanket over Cedric and Ambrose's knees once they settle on the sofa in the ops room.

'It's gone midnight,' says Cedric. 'Are you sure this can't wait until the morning?' He looks at his watch and then glares at Ambrose, who rolls his eyes in agreement.

Ambrose, who needs his sleep, begins to say, 'I need a square eight hours, and I have to say, medically—'

Verity stops him talking and says, 'If there's time after our briefing, then we can hear your medical explanation about your festival of sleep, but in advance of hearing it, I can tell you, it's nonsense.'

'Watch what Verity found,' says Charlie, using a flashlight to highlight the pinhole on page fifty-seven. She says, 'Eighteen down, three letters. The European measurement for speed?'

'Kilometres Per Hour,' Cedric and Ambrose say together, then they shorten it. 'K-P-H.'

'Kevin *something* Hall?' suggests Verity.

Cedric and Ambrose sit forward together.

'Are there any more pinholes?' asks Ambrose.

Charlie holds the flashlight while Verity slowly flips through the pages one at a time. The light shines through another pinhole.

Verity whispers, 'This is old school tactics, like chalk messages on a park bench or a rolled note stuffed behind a loose brick in a church wall.'

'They must be messages from Randolph,' says Cedric.

Charlie looks at him and says, 'Let's not get ahead of ourselves.'

Verity pushes her glasses up her nose and clears her throat. 'Nine across. A small team that defeats a bigger team—five and six.'

'Giant killer,' says Cedric.

Charlie picks up a piece of chalk and writes *KPH* and *giant killer* on the board, then sits on the sofa between Cedric and Ambrose while Verity paces up and down in front of them, tapping her temples.

Charlie takes her phone from her pocket, and her fingers dance across the screen before shouting, 'Peter! Kevin Hall's middle name is P for Peter.'

'K-P-H,' says Verity, drawing several circles around KPH on the board with the chalk. She snarls, 'Every fibre in my body is aching to climb on Elsie, ride over to Hall's house, drag the murderous toad out of bed, and interrogate him until he admits his guilt.'

Cedric nods slowly, raising his hands as if seeking to keep the peace, and says, 'Or is this an enormous red herring? A coincidence, maybe?'

Charlie leaps up from the sofa. 'It's not a red herring! It's not a coincidence! Let's go and get Kevin Hall!'

Charlie and Verity run toward Elsie, eager to catch their man in the middle of the night.

Ambrose stands and says, 'My sleep pattern is a shambles now, so I'm making some toasted cheese and pickle sandwiches. Do you two crime busters fancy one before you wrench Kevin Hall from his slumber?'

Cedric adds, 'Your murderer has no idea you're on to him. He's fast asleep without a care in the world.'

Verity and Charlie stop dead in their tracks.

'We can make time for one of those,' Verity whispers to Charlie.

They stomp across the gravel courtyard to the kitchen, where Charlie and Verity make themselves comfortable on the bar stools and watch Cedric slice a loaf of sourdough bread. Ambrose turns on the grill and opens the cheese box selection they bought in London. Cedric toasts and butters the bread while Ambrose grates the mature Wookey Hole Cheddar.

'My mouth is watering,' says Charlie.

Cedric pours four large glasses of port and arranges plates with napkins for his toasted masterpieces. Ambrose began making homemade pickle seventeen years ago, and two shelves in the pantry are dedicated to his hobby.

He runs his finger along the labels and says, 'I assume everyone fancies my tomato and wild mushroom pickle?'

He returns to the grill to watch the bubbling cheese begin to golden.

'Giant killer is a strange term,' says Cedric. 'Why would Randolph tell us about a giant killer?'

Ambrose serves the sandwiches, saying, 'Maybe it references David and Goliath. Randolph is Goliath, while his slayer, Kevin Hall, is the smaller, weaker David.'

'Or it's a code name for an operation,' says Verity. 'We can prise it out of Kevin Hall.'

Ambrose wipes his mouth with the napkin and pushes his plate away in an intentionally slow movement, saying, 'I'm assuming you mean torture when you say, prise.'

'Torture is such a strong term,' says Verity.

'Torture doesn't work,' says Ambrose. 'People will say anything to stop the pain. Instead, we should invite him here and give him a glass or two of something strong, then watch his body language when we mention giant killer.'

'Or we could thump him until he tells us,' says Verity.

'We must use our brains and not our fists,' says Cedric. 'K-P-H might not relate to Kevin Hall's initials; it might have to do with whatever giant killer means.'

Verity stands and walks around the kitchen, lifting lids on pots and looking inside. Then, she says, 'And let's not forget, our key suspect is Joshua King. We should also invite him to sit on our sofa in the ops room and ask him about giant killer and K-P-H.'

Cedric and Ambrose clear the plates and glasses while Charlie walks Verity back to her campervan.

'Maybe we were a tad hasty,' says Verity. 'Those couple of pickle makers in there are right about people saying anything when they're tortured. But I do miss charging around at midnight on fast motorbikes to catch the bad guys.'

'We can still go for a ride if you like, and you can bring your hand grenade,' says Charlie.

'The moment's gone, but thank you anyway. Your job is to get invited to Eastbourne with Yuri.'

Charlie wishes Verity goodnight and walks back towards Tanglefoot Farm before turning to ask one more question, 'What was your spy name in Russia?'

Verity turns from the campervan's steps and says, 'Katia.'

'Katia,' repeats Charlie. 'That's a nice name, but you look like a Verity.'

'Well, I do now,' says Verity. 'But you should have seen me back in the day.'

Charlie's phone pings with a message from Yuri, and she reads aloud, 'I'm heading to Eastbourne tomorrow to see my dad. Fancy a trip to the coast?'

'I told you it would work,' says Verity. 'I know my Russian men. Tell him, yes, thank you. Sweet dreams, dear.'

<><><>

Chapter Thirty-One

Cedric is lying in bed, floating on a heady mix of port, toasted cheese sandwiches and tiredness. Unable to sleep, he squashes his pillow over his face in a feeble attempt to drown out the two people talking loudly in the courtyard.

He knows it's impossible for two people to make as much noise as Charlie and Verity, who've quickly developed a need to shout at each other while discussing every topic.

Cedric's unique chiropractic pillow muffles the voices, and he recalls when Verity was a sleeper spy in Moscow, outsmarting everyone with her fieldcraft. Cedric and Ambrose set up a system to send her messages via *Pravda*, the Communist Party newspaper—a paper you had to read by law in the old Soviet Union. *Pravda*, or the truth, was a cumbersome operation where the left hand didn't even know what the left hand was doing, let alone the right hand, so it was easy for them to leave coded messages for Verity.

A message from them placed in 'Obituaries' meant a new kill order. A message in 'Marriages' meant someone was joining her in Moscow, and a notice in 'Births' indicated a new operation. They used a complex code of letter swaps and mathematical backspacing. Not surprisingly, they only showed the code to Verity once, and she understood it immediately.

On her return to London, Verity protected them from bullies in the Service who thought they were strange—they were strange, of course, and Verity used her swift uppercut to bring an end to anyone pushing their weight around.

Night moves casually aside for morning, and outside, nature's dawn chorus is in full chirp across the Surrey Hills. The surrounding villages connect through a network of well-trodden pathways through the patchwork of colourful fields, and Friday Street is at the centre of it all—a secret spot reserved for those in the know.

Cedric has a chaise longue next to his bedroom window, which overlooks the garden. It's where he does his best thinking, sitting there drinking coffee. He used to smoke and still craves cigarettes. He once asked his chain-smoking doctor if he gave up smoking, would he live any longer? The doctor said *no, it would just feel like it.* Cedric changed doctors again.

Charlie is preparing to meet Yuri, and Verity will ride Elsie to the coast with Cedric and Ambrose in the wretched sidecar. Of course, they'll moan about it, but secretly, they're getting used to it all and enjoy the fuss.

Ambrose knocks, waits seven seconds, and then walks into Cedric's room with a tray of coffee and admits they should have spotted the pinholes in the crossword book.

Cedric sips his coffee on his chaise longue and imagines smoking a cigarette. He says, 'We would have seen it if Randolph marked it with a red cross, not a micro-size pinhole.'

'How long did you stay awake thinking about the meaning of K-P-H and giant killer?' Ambrose asks.

'All night. You?'

'Same. And I've got nothing to show for it,' says Ambrose.

Cedric stands, looking out at the expanse of garden that stretches up to the top hedgerow, murmuring, 'Kevin Hall doesn't seem like a killer to me.'

'Quite so,' says Ambrose. 'He's a railwayman, not a murderer.'

Charlie barges into Cedric's room. 'Ops room, now!'

'What's the emergency? Has someone died?' asks Cedric.

'Yes,' she yells, running back down the stairs.

'We must tell her about the seven-second rule,' says Ambrose.

<><><>

Chapter Thirty-Two

Linus Pope's telephone rang at eight-thirty, and five minutes later, he called Tanglefoot Farm to break the news.

Charlie told him to come for breakfast, and that's where Linus Pope finds himself, walking across the gravel courtyard and into the kitchen.

Charlie pours him a cup of coffee, and he sits at the kitchen table while Charlie runs upstairs to tell Cedric and Ambrose about the death of Joshua King. The two men descend the staircase and bustle into the kitchen a moment later.

'What's going on?' says Ambrose.

'Joshua King is dead,' says Linus Pope, delivering the information like a newsreader announcing the death of the King.

'What, again?' says Cedric.

Linus fills in the scant details he received a few minutes earlier. 'King was found dead in a small cottage in Shere village. No gunshot or obvious signs of foul play,' he says. 'From what the police say, it sounds like a heart attack.'

'A heart attack? Joshua King? I doubt that,' says Ambrose.

'Where's Verity?' asks Cedric.

'She ran across the fields to Shere to look at the crime scene,' says Charlie.

'Crime scene?' says Pope. 'It's a bit premature to assume it's a crime, isn't it? The police didn't say anything about a crime scene.'

Cedric refills his coffee cup and says, 'A spy who died ten years ago in a car crash in Australia is found dead, again, in a small Surrey village is the very definition of a crime scene.'

'Anyway, the show must go on,' Ambrose sighs, taking a minute to gather himself. 'Charlie, you have an important day ahead,' he says, placing a Fortnum & Mason wicker hamper on the kitchen table, taking care to polish the leather handles with a soft cloth. A well-rehearsed thirty minutes see the two men fuss over a variety of neatly cut sandwiches, mini scotch eggs, swirls of smoked salmon, a tiny pot of Russian beluga caviar, a cheese board, and a chilled bottle of crispy Chablis.

'And I made these myself,' says Ambrose, holding up two scones with a pot of clotted cream and a jar of strawberry jam.

Pope half stands, licking his lips and asks, 'I've always wanted to know, does one say *scone* to rhyme with Ron—'

'Good Lord, man!' shouts Cedric, cutting him off. 'We're in Surrey, so it's *scone,* like bone and throne!'

Pope sits back down.

Charlie puts a plate in front of Linus with two halves of a scone topped with a spoonful of strawberry jam and a generous dollop of clotted cream. 'Breakfast of champions,' she says. 'Pay no attention to the hamper boys.'

Cedric momentarily stops placing items in the hamper. 'Pope, as you can see, it's cream on top of the jam. Wars have started for putting jam on top of the cream.'

'Ignore them,' says Charlie.

Verity bursts through the door and stands in the middle of the kitchen, stretching her hamstrings with a series of lunges. Her run across the fields to Shere from Friday Street is a demanding cross-country sprint, but the morning dash has barely brought Verity out in a sweat.

'What news of Joshua King?' asks Cedric.

'He's dead!' says Verity, stretching her arms.

'Yes, but how?' he asks.

'Well, a battalion of busy people in various uniforms are racing about looking official. I think we should ask Colin Beard what he's heard.' Verity's attention centres on the kitchen table. 'Ooh, breakfast, fabulous idea!'

No sooner does Verity finish her final deep lunge then Charlie puts a plate with a scone, jam and cream in front of her with a cup of coffee and a glass of freshly squeezed orange juice.

'Perfect! I love a scone,' says Verity, saying it to rhyme with Ron. She downs her orange juice and begins to spoon the clotted cream on the scone first, followed by a spoonful of jam.

Cedric glares at Verity and says, 'Thirty years of Russian vodka and countless punches to your head have clearly damaged the part of your brain in charge of correct etiquette.'

Verity doesn't look up as she says. 'Dear boy, when I was at Buckingham Palace to meet the Queen, she offered me a *scone* pronounced like Ron and then proceeded to put the cream on first, and this was thirty minutes after she pinned a medal for outstanding valour on my chest.

So, I'll take my lead from our Royal family and not from you.'

Linus Pope smiles as he finishes his last mouthful.

Cedric and Ambrose direct their energies toward Charlie's hamper and complete it with artisan crackers and a small jar of pickle. All the while, a discussion takes place as to what Charlie should wear to meet Yuri.

'Your James Dean look is a lovely ensemble,' says Cedric. 'Maybe it's time to wow him with a summer dress.'

Charlie's one summer dress comes out for garden parties and gentile company. *It's very girly*, Charlie says every time she puts it on, and then Cedric and Ambrose convince her how lovely she looks and how proud her father would be if he could see her swishing around in the pretty dress.

Charlie announces, 'I'll wear clean jeans.'

Cedric and Ambrose lift a long white box onto the kitchen table and nod at Charlie.

'What is it?' she asks. 'Is this for me?'

Ambrose says, 'It was delivered yesterday while we risked our lives outside the Russian mobster's house in Fulham.'

Charlie lifts the lid and moves the yellow tissue paper aside. She slowly feels the soft fabric. 'Is this really for me?' Charlie whispers, lifting the burgundy V-neck button-through dress with tiny white petals out of the box. She puts it against her body, swishing left and right.

'Try it on,' says Ambrose and Charlie runs upstairs.

Verity nods her approval, asking, 'How did you know what to order?'

'We watched a movie the other week,' says Cedric.

'About dresses?' says Pope.

'No. A movie about a young woman whose husband

was murdered, and she took violent revenge on the men who did it—she looked a lot like Charlie and wore the exact same dress,' says Cedric.

Pope had no further questions.

Charlie skips down the stairs and enters the kitchen to a round of applause. Cedric and Ambrose fuss with the buttons and adjust the ribbons on her wide-brimmed summer hat, declaring that she looks as pretty as her mother.

'I'm wearing my boots,' she says. 'So don't think I'll be prancing around in high heels.'

Verity clicks her fingers as if remembering a distant thought, then strides across the courtyard to her campervan and begins rummaging through an untidy cardboard box under the passenger seat. Knotted cables and wires overflow from the entanglement of oddments. Verity keeps all the things she considers useful, most of which were last functional during the Cold War. She pulls out a black metal box the size of a house brick and grabs two long curly wires, then walks across to Charlie's Jaguar.

'How do I look?' says Charlie, twirling on the gravel.

'Lovely,' says Verity without looking up. 'Pop the boot lid, dear. I want to put a tracker in your Jag.'

'What's that black box?' asks Charlie.

'It's a tracker, do keep up.'

'It's not what you'd call a microchip, is it,' says Charlie.

'This thing will last another five hundred years. Back in the day, Britain made equipment to last.'

Charlie leans against the Jaguar, watching Verity, who swears non-stop while fiddling with the wires.

Charlie asks, 'What if Yuri wants to take his car?'

'He can't!' Verity says with certainty. She stops fiddling and sits on the lip of the Jaguar's boot. During her active years in Moscow, she put trackers in hundreds of cars and kept tabs on everyone—somehow, it was easier back then.

'Let's say, for argument's sake, Yuri says we're going on the train,' says Charlie. 'Then what do I do with your enormous tracker?'

'What do you suggest?' says Verity.

'I've got a *phone tracker* app. I'll connect it to yours so you can track me wherever I am.'

'Connect it to my what?'

'To your ph—' says Charlie, stopping herself before adding, 'You don't have a phone, do you?'

'Of course, I don't!' says Verity. 'I don't want to be tracked.'

Charlie says, 'My friend's mum tracks her and can even see how fast she's driving. The other night, she had the fright of her life while tracking her daughter hurtling at a hundred and forty miles an hour through the countryside, only to find out her daughter was on a train.'

Linus Pope crunches on the gravel as he makes his way to the Jaguar and says, 'Charlie, I've got that app on my phone.'

'Good,' says Verity. 'Then you're coming with me instead of Cedric and Ambrose. We can disconnect the motorbike from the sidecar.'

Linus Pope shuffles into the ops room and slumps on the sofa to hide from Verity's request. He knows it wasn't a request but a statement of fact.

'The experience will do you good,' laughs Verity. 'Fresh air and all that.'

'And when you say experience, you mean riding at thunderous speeds in hot pursuit,' says Linus.

Verity removes the tracker from Charlie's Jaguar and puts it back into the box of oddments in her campervan.

'What's giant killer and K-P-H?' asks Pope, staring at the board on the wall.

Charlie explains the pinholes and clues in the crossword book and asks, 'Was giant killer an operation or a code for something?'

'It means nothing to me, I'm afraid.' Linus Pope picks up the crossword book and flicks through the pages to find the pinholes and once seen, they are glaringly obvious. 'How did all of us miss them?' He uses Ambrose's magnifying glass from the table and focuses on a small mark on page seventy-three.

Verity sits on the back of the sofa, trying to look through the magnifying glass. 'What are you looking at?' she asks.

'There's a mark next to the clue eleven across.'

'Read it out,' says Charlie.

'The omission of a sound or syllable when speaking?' He says.

Charlie shrugs her shoulders, then runs across the courtyard and shouts for Cedric and Ambrose to come to the ops room. They appear at the door wearing aprons, wiping their hands on a towel.

Verity waves them over and nudges Pope to reread the clue.

'The omission of a sound or syllable when speaking?' he says.

Cedric says, 'Elision.'

Ambrose adds, 'Elision is the absence of a sound in words like *I'm* or *let's*. An apostrophe connects two words with the removal of at least one syllable. The *elision* is the missing sound. For example, let us becomes let's.'

'Who knows nonsense like this?' says Charlie.

'Annoyingly, these two,' says Linus Pope.

Verity agrees while helping Charlie to unbolt the sidecar from the motorbike.

'Try not to get oil on your new dress,' says Ambrose. 'It's a devil to get out.'

Charlie and Verity prepare the vehicles for Operation Eastbourne, and Pope syncs his phone.

'How does this app-thing work?' asks Verity.

Ambrose says, 'The locations are set by satellite, and—'

'I'm sure it's a fascinating story,' says Verity. 'Tell me this evening when we get back.'

'Really?'

'No,' says Verity.

Ambrose clears the plates and coffee cups away, following their second breakfast of scrambled eggs on toast. He returns from the kitchen and asks, 'Are we going to talk about Joshua King, or are we just getting on with our lives?'

'Up until an hour ago, he was our chief suspect,' says Charlie.

'Just because King is dead doesn't mean he didn't kill your dad,' says Ambrose.

<><><>

Chapter Thirty-Three

Verity

Joshua King could have killed Charlie's dad. Of course, he could.

We can't bring him to justice, but we can prove he was guilty of murdering Randolph Vine. I would have preferred to grapple him to the ground and land a few punches on his chin before handing him over with a folder full of evidence.

Although I haven't spoken to Joshua King in ten years, I will miss him.

This app thing on Charlie's phone is clever, and when I say clever, we would have won the Cold War in half an hour with technology like this. We had chalk crosses on red post boxes, and I mustn't forget the coded messages in *Pravda's* births, deaths and marriages section. I felt connected to Cedric and Ambrose and their cleverness. They were the good old days, but I'm enjoying these days just as much. I'm in the middle of this mystery and loving every minute.

If Joshua King was not Randolph's killer, then did the same person kill Joshua King? We might have a double killer to catch, and as I mull over these thoughts, I kickstart Elsie, minus the sidecar, and rev the engine.

Charlie eases her Jaguar onto the gravel courtyard and steps over to me. She looks lovely in her new summer dress, especially with her hair tumbling over her shoulders, and the steel-toe-cap boots I gave her don't fashionably match her outfit, but I'm happy she's wearing them. I knew I had another pair somewhere in the campervan.

'You look gorgeous, Charlotte Vine,' I say.

She ignores me and asks, 'Who killed Joshua King?'

I tell her that we'll get to the bottom of it sooner or later.

Charlie turns around and then turns back to me, 'And why did Joshua King come back from the dead... only to die again.'

I say I don't know. I really don't. I wish I did. I really do.

Charlie clambers into the car and lets the engine settle into a harmonic hum. I lean in through her window and get a whiff of old leather and wood polish. I tell her I'll be close behind her, tap the side of my nose and then pat my trouser pocket.

'Have you got a gun?' she asks.

I take a cigar tube from my trouser pocket and remove a syringe with yellow liquid, saying, 'One jab will stop a rhino and revive a rhino, for that matter.'

'Who is it for?' asks Charlie.

'I'm seeing Vladimir, so I need to protect myself.'

Our plans changed, and Linus, rather than Cedric and Ambrose, will accompany me to Eastbourne. So, instead, they will walk over to Randolph's mystery garage and get to grips with the piles of mess on the rear shelf. It promises to be infinitely safer than tracking down a Russian gangster on the coast, and they also love sorting things out.

It's a win for everyone... except Linus, who looks a bit peaky.

Charlie sets off at a cracking pace, and I follow on Elsie. I feel Linus's arms hugging me tightly as we take off after the black Jag. Cedric and Ambrose wave white handkerchiefs until they fade from view.

It's a struggle for me to comprehend that I'm heading to Eastbourne to confront my husband. In the Cold War, Russia was the enemy, but Vladimir was not the enemy to me. He was a kind man who was feared by others.

Joshua King's death was a blow—a bigger blow for him, obviously, and a blow for Charlie, too. We pinned our hopes too much on King being Randolph's murderer, and now that he's been killed, he drops down our suspect list. My gut now tells me he didn't kill Randolph, but gut feelings are pointless if you can't back them up with evidence. Maybe that's why he was murdered: the killer noticed us sniffing around the case.

Linus taps me on the shoulder, and I flick the switch on the handlebars to engage the crash helmet intercom system.

He shouts, 'Turn left!'

'No need to shout,' I shout at him.

I lean this way and that, weaving in and out of the heavy morning traffic following Charlie's blue dot on Linus's phone screen. Kicking Kevin Hall's gate off its hinges led to this moment, and I can't help thinking about the possibility of a wild goose chase. Hall couldn't have known Vladimir socially, and I never met him in Moscow or anywhere in the Service, so the questioning from Colin

Beard would have been his only point of contact. I'll ask Beard when I see him next.

'Turn right,' whispers Linus.

Elsie grips the road like industrial adhesive, and her exhaust bellows sweet music as I speed along with the wind in my face. Nothing makes you feel more alive than racing on a death machine hunting for a killer. My nerve endings tingle just like they did when I lived in Moscow, living on the edge, married to Vladimir. He'd shout my name with his booming voice like my father did whenever I was in trouble.

Katia, come down here!

Katia, where are you?

Katia!

Each time Vladimir's voice thundered that way, I thought my cover had been blown and a room of secret police were waiting for me, only to find he'd bought me some flowers.

No wonder my nerves were ripped to shreds by the time I left active duty. Spies, as a rule, don't age well. I'm seventy-five and put my secret to semi-longevity to living off the grid in my campervan—and gin. Mostly gin.

'Tell me about Kevin Hall,' I say to Linus.

'You know more about him than I do,' says Pope. 'You kicked his gate down and frightened the man half to death.' And that was true; I did frighten him, but my internal spy radar was bleeping. It still is.

I say, 'When we return, I need you to do two things. Firstly, can you check at the Stephan Langton if Kevin Hall and his late wife, Doreen, were booked in to eat the night Randolph died?'

'It's a country pub. They won't have records dating back ten years.'

'Ask anyway,' I say.

'And the second thing?'

'Go to your paymaster in the Service and call in every favour you can to find out how Randolph Vine died. I don't want to hear about a mugging gone wrong. I think whoever murdered Vine poisoned him, so get your eyes on the official toxicology report.'

Pope has never operated behind enemy lines, so his spy receptors are untuned, but he has contacts on the inside who should be able to help.

He taps my shoulder, and his breathy voice pipes through the intercom, 'Take the next right and pull up at the end of the road. Charlie has stopped outside Yuri's house.'

Charlie has cleverly positioned her car in front of Yuri's sliding gate with the passenger door wide open, making it impossible for him to take his car. I watch her step through the gate and wait for her date.

'What's she doing?' says Pope.

'Being bloody clever,' I say. 'She's a natural field agent. You're wasting her in whatever department you've got her stashed, gawping at a computer screen all day. That kid should be operational. You can't teach this level of skill.'

'Haven't you heard, Verity, the war is over?'

'So I keep hearing.'

Wars rumble on often without resolution and bleed from one conflict to the next. Charlie is talking to Yuri while pointing to her black Jag. The hot-blooded Russian male will hate being driven by a woman. I can't help but laugh.

Cedric and Ambrose brought me into their Friday Street gang to glue the pieces of this mystery together. So far, I'm failing as I can't quite get my hands around the moving parts.

We watch Charlie's black Jaguar ease along to the end

of the road and turn right in the direction of Eastbourne and Vladimir.

It's becoming a reality.

I should start thinking about what to say to my ex-husband—*hello, Vlad. It's me, Katia. As you can see, I'm not dead. I was just passing and thought I'd pop in and ask if you had anything to do with the murder of Randolph Vine. Would you like a cup of tea?*

<><><>

Chapter Thirty-Four

Ambrose puts away the plates and cups from breakfast while Cedric runs around with the vacuum cleaner.

'Is Charlie safe with Yuri?' asks Ambrose.

'You mean, is Yuri safe with Charlie,' snorts Cedric. 'She ruined that pretty dress with those ruffian boots. I blame Verity.' He pushes the vacuum cleaner with vigour, adding. 'I hate to admit it, but life has become exciting with Verity at her old whirlwind pace.'

They've spent lots of time since discovering Randolph's mystery garage discussing how to tidy the laden shelf on the back wall. Nothing excites them more than to colour code and alphabetise an unwieldy stack of papers.

They set off with their stationery supplies at a good pace, and Winnie trots ahead down Plum Pudding Lane, stopping to sniff each tuft of grass.

'Are they there yet, do you think?' asks Ambrose.

Cedric looks at his watch and says, 'No, not yet, even though Charlie and Verity set off like the devil on fire. It's

Linus I'm concerned about. He's not used to the thrust of active fieldwork.'

Ambrose laughs uncontrollably and says, 'Poor chap. There's nobody quite like him who can find a pound of misery in an ounce of happiness.'

They laugh and chat while ambling to the end of the lane, then turn onto the track leading to the row of garages by Friday Street's pond.

'Giant killer, K-P-H and elision,' says Ambrose. 'What was Randolph trying to tell us?'

Cedric says, 'The clues are random and from different pages in the book. Two pinholes and a mark.'

'Morse code!' shouts Ambrose. 'My goodness, why didn't I see that before? Morse code! Dot, dot, dash.'

'Or, dash, dot, dot,' replies Cedric.

'Or dot, dash, dot,' suggests Ambrose. 'The letters U, D, and R,' he murmurs.

'U-D-R,' says Cedric. 'The University of the Dominican Republic?'

'Or R-D-U,' suggests Ambrose. 'The Royal Defence Unit. You don't feel we're overthinking this as usual, do you?'

'Us? Overthinking? Of course we are. The world depends on us overthinking,' says Cedric.

'Quite so,' says Ambrose.

They chat the length of the track leading to Randolph's garage, and no further sense is made of the possible Morse code two dots and one dash.

'It could be a non-code,' declares Cedric.

'Yes, a non-code,' agrees Ambrose.

Ninety-nine per cent of a code breaker's work is deciding what needs deciphering and what needs ignoring. Letters and numbers are sometimes just letters and numbers. And pinholes and scratches in a book are just that.

'As a clincher,' says Ambrose, 'Randolph was useless at Morse Code.'

Cedric opens the garage door, and rays of sunshine catch the tumbling dust particles like a projector's beam in a dark cinema. The untouched piles of folders and stacks of papers fill the rear shelf in the otherwise empty garage.

'I thought we knew everything about Randolph,' says Ambrose.

Cedric walks towards the rear garage wall and says, 'We did, apart from this mystery garage, and who killed him.'

'What does your intuition tell you?' asks Ambrose. 'I'm asking because we have two murdered spies, ten years apart, who worked every case together, and we pulled the strings of their operations from HQ.'

Cedric says, 'Do you think there's a possibility we could be next?'

Ambrose stops in his tracks. 'Maybe the Friday Street Spy Ring is being eliminated? What's your best guess?'

'I don't guess, dear boy,' says Cedric.

'We should warn Linus,' says Ambrose.

'Let's not jump to conclusions and make fools of ourselves.'

They decide to make a start on the shelves and begin by creating four piles of documents: one for personal papers belonging to Randolph, another for instruction manuals relating to the Jaguar and Elsie, one for operation files, and one for everything else. Each pile will be subdivided into varying levels of interest, eliminating documents with only little importance, although, at this stage, everything is potentially important.

During the Cold War, some spectacular code-breaking

came from seemingly unimportant sources. A Russian spy was caught because he used the wrong ink to forge a date stamp on an envelope. Another left a coffee stain from the wrong blend on a fake invoice, and once, an extra spoon in a cutlery drawer proved vital in identifying the photograph's authenticity.

Cedric and Ambrose begin subdividing the four piles into three stacks of low, medium, and high importance.

'It doesn't look much,' says Ambrose.

'It never does,' says Cedric. 'Clues are clever like that.'

They pack the pile of important documents into a carrier bag and lock the garage door. Winnie skips between Cedric and Ambrose as they circle the pond and walk along the track to Plum Pudding Lane.

'What do you think Charlie is doing?' asks Ambrose.

'Interrogating Yuri about the clues, I hope,' says Cedric.

Charlie steers her black Jaguar effortlessly toward the coast with one hand on the wheel and one arm out of the window.

'You're a good driver,' says Yuri.

'You sound surprised!' she says. Her response was a little snappy, so she eases up, saying, 'Thank you. I had a good teacher.'

She tilts her head while looking at the road ahead, which shimmers with a mirage of watery puddles. She half expects Cedric and Ambrose to pipe up from the backseat, informing her about the inversion layer leading the light rays from the sky that would otherwise hit the road curving upwards, thus creating the illusion they have bounced off a reflecting pool of water on the road.

Charlie quickly grew to love Cedric and Ambrose the way she loved her father—the way she still loves her father.

'Who taught you to drive?' asks Yuri, watching Charlie take the perfect racing line on a tight left-hand bend while avoiding the need to dab the brakes.

'My dad. How about you?'

'My dad was always away a lot on state business,' says Yuri. 'I didn't get to spend much time with him when I was younger.'

'My dad was a giant killer,' says Charlie, observing Yuri and checking for the slightest body language clue.

'What's that?' he asks.

Charlie explains about a smaller team beating a bigger one, but he shows no hint of recognition. Is he a trained agent, or does giant killer simply mean nothing to him? Charlie changes gear, and the exhaust bellows its enjoyment as they hurtle through the Sussex countryside.

Charlie knows that Verity would have Yuri tied to an oak tree in a quiet lane by now, begging for his young life.

Yuri glances over his shoulder, 'I can't wait to look inside the hamper. My picnics are normally a limp sandwich and a packet of crisps.'

'Mine, too,' she says. 'My two fussy experts at home are brilliant at things like this. They even made me wear a dress today.'

'You look wonderful, especially the boots,' he says.

Charlie brushes off Yuri's compliment, concentrating on his directions as she weaves through Eastbourne's lanes to a large house on a clifftop overlooking the sea.

'This place is spectacular,' she says.

'My father hates it,' says Yuri.

. . .

Linus follows the dot on his screen and directs Verity to park Elsie at the bottom of the lane that leads up to the clifftop house. They see Charlie's Jaguar parked in the driveway.

'How are you holding up, Linus?'

He couldn't speak or move; such was his tight grip around Verity's waist.

'You can let go now,' she says, levering his fingers off her jacket and stepping off Elsie.

Linus takes a few deep breaths. 'We're alive. I suppose that's something.'

'Oh, stop being a baby. Nobody's shooting at us, and it's a lovely sunny day. However, I need you to do something for me.'

Linus takes a step backwards.

Verity ignores his retreat, saying, 'I want you to edge your way up the driveway to the house and tell me what you see.'

Pope takes another step away. 'Why can't you go?'

Verity clears her throat, declaring, 'I think you misunderstand how this works: I tell you to do something, and then you go and do it!'

'You're not my boss,' says Linus, sitting on an exposed root of a huge oak tree.

'I've terminated dozens of spies, you know. Some British, and some of them weren't even spies,' says Verity. 'Mostly for simply being useless. Your only task is to peer around the corner and walk up to the house. How hard can it be?'

Pope groans as he gets to his feet and wipes his sweaty hands on his trousers. He takes a few tentative steps up the driveway, looking back at Verity every few paces—Verity waves at him to hurry up.

'Is it safe?' he says.

'The war is over,' she says, laughing and shoos him away while backing into the bushes to keep out of sight.

Linus edges around the second bend, where a teenager is smoking a cigarette with one foot against the wall while looking at her phone.

'Hello,' she says to Pope without looking up.

'Hello,' says Pope to the girl, and continues to walk on.

The house towers out of the ground and overlooks the sea. The refreshing salt air blows into Pope's face as he presses himself to the wall and peers around to the front of the house.

Three steps with a ramp on one side lead to a wide front door. Pope looks inside and instantly recoils before running back to Elsie.

'Verity!' he calls out. 'Verity, where are you?'

'Behind you,' she says from the bushes. 'What is it?

'You're never going to believe what's up there,' he says, gasping for air from his sprint down the hill.

'Vladimir's clifftop home?' she says.

'It's a nursing home,' says Linus. 'Vladimir is in a nursing home!'

Verity sits on Elsie in deep thought for ten seconds, and then she hands him an earpiece, saying, 'Go and find out what room he's in.'

He pushes the earpiece into his ear, saying, 'Why me?'

'We've been through all that. Go on, hurry up,' she says.

Reluctantly, Pope walks up the driveway, nods to the smoking teenager, and walks in through the main entrance. A curly-haired man sitting behind the reception desk taps away at the keyboard, and his thick, bulbous-lensed glasses capture the glare from his screen.

He sees Pope and says, 'Can I help you?'

Flustered, Pope says, 'I'm trying to find a place for my mother. I can see you're busy; may I scoot around and look at the gardens? I'll see you on my way out.'

The young man nods and returns to his keyboard, and his glasses fill once more with flickering colours.

'Testing. Testing,' Verity's voice pipes through Linus's hearing bud. 'Nicely done, you're in,' she says in a soft, quiet voice. 'Now mooch about and locate Charlie and Yuri.'

'Message received. I'm heading to the waiting room. Over,' he says.

'You don't need to say *over*,' she says, munching on a scotch egg.

'Did you steal something from Charlie's picnic hamper?' asks Linus.

'I stole it for us in case we were hungry from our spying endeavours. Go and find Charlie and Yuri. We don't have all day.'

Linus pushes the double doors open to the waiting room. It's empty. The next door leads to a day room, chosen, no doubt, for its light and panoramic views across the mirror-flat sea. Linus decided when his time comes, he'll stay in Friday Street—looking at the sea too long makes him queasy. There's nothing but a red yacht and white-crested waves. He's a village man.

'Found anything?' says Verity.

'Nothing,' he says.

Five people are in the sunny day room. Two elderly ladies playing backgammon, a man sleeping with the sun on his face, and a nurse helping a lady eat her soup. Linus heads next door to the library, where a couple in matching dressing gowns sleep holding their books.

'What's happening?' Verity whispers.

'There's no sign of Charlie or—wait,' he says.

Charlie and a young man, Yuri, Linus presumes, are chatting at the bottom of the staircase.

'What's going on?' says Verity.

'I can see Charlie and Yuri. What do I do?'

'Keep out of sight and follow Yuri to Vladimir's room.'

From a safe distance, Pope watches Yuri take the stairs and follows him along the hallway. Three minutes later, Linus runs down the driveway to the shrubbery where Verity is hiding.

He pants, 'Room eleven, top floor, but there's a problem.'

'There usually is,' says Verity.

'There's a square-jawed man built like a mountain on sentry duty outside Vladimir's bedroom door.'

Verity pulls a mustard-coloured cardigan from her bag and ruffles her hair—not that it needs too much ruffling. 'How do I look?'

'You'll fit right in.'

Verity creeps up the driveway and slips in through the backdoor unnoticed. Linus sketched a rough layout of the nursing home for her, and she follows the arrows to the bottom of the staircase.

To avoid the floorboards creaking, Verity takes her boots off and hugs the wall as she climbs the stairs. She peers around the landing on the top floor and sees the bodyguard, just as Linus described him, outside room eleven.

She waits for Yuri to leave before walking down the hallway. The tatty cardigan hangs shapelessly from her shoulders as she bends over, clutching her back as she creeps along the carpet.

Verity spent thirty years in hostile environments, side-stepping giant nose-breakers like the fellow outside

Vladimir's room, who makes his first mistake, assuming Verity is no threat.

'Has Yuri left yet?' asks Verity in a croaky voice. 'He's a lovely boy, always looking in on his old dad. I wish my son—'

'Yuri has been and gone already,' says the mountain.

'Did he bring his dad any grapes?'

'I don't—'

The karate chop to the man's windpipe was swift and unseen. He fell to his knees, grabbing his throat and gasping for air.

'Oh, don't be such a baby,' says Verity. 'It was a light tap to your Vagus nerve. You'll feel a bit sleepy, but you'll live.'

The mountain slides awkwardly down the wall into a pile of his own giant limbs. His unconscious head hangs to one side, and his tongue pokes out of his dribbling mouth. Verity steps over him and opens Vladimir's door.

And there he is—her Russian.

Vladimir faces out to sea in a high-winged, red leather chair, failing to hear the commotion outside his door. This imposing KGB mid-level mobster once ruled his small world with two fists and is now reduced to a south-facing view of nothing but an empty sea. Maybe this was his request, although Verity doubted he would choose such a slim existence. It looks like he's been put out of the way. The Russian way.

She steps up behind him and puts a few stray hairs back in place. Her beautiful man, now a thin bodily shell withered with age, makes no effort to see who is fussing over him.

'I'm Verity,' she says, stepping in front of his chair to block his view.

His mind computes the information slowly, and his lips

move as if practising to make an announcement. 'Who?' he manages.

'Verity!' Her voice is as crisp as an opera singer projecting to the back wall of the concert hall. 'Verity Fanthorpe, room six, down one floor slightly to the right. You have a lovely view up here.'

'Verity Fanthorpe,' he musters. 'Have we met before?'

'We were at school together,' she says with laughter.

Vladimir smiles. 'I like you,' he says. 'What's your room number?'

'Room four. Down three floors to the left,' she says. He looks confused by the conflicting information, and before he joins the dots, she adds, 'We should have tea on the lawn one morning.'

A flicker of recognition flutters across his face, and then it vanishes, slipping away like an uncatchable wisp of smoke.

'Giant killer,' says Verity.

'What was that?'

'I didn't say anything.'

'I'm losing my mind, not my hearing,' says Vladimir.

'Elision,' she says in a softer voice.

He looks straight into her eyes, and the flicker of recognition reappears.

'Are you married?' says Verity, pulling a footstall close to his chair.

Where once intense blue eyes busied themselves seeking out danger, watery, colourless eyes move slowly.

'Yes, I'm married,' he says, touching her hand. 'To you, my darling Katia.'

<><><>

Chapter Thirty-Five

Verity is not someone who loses her poker face when engaged with the enemy—even if the enemy is her ex-husband. Technically, Vladimir is her widowed husband, although she would technically need to be dead. Whatever he is, Verity lost her poker face when he called her Katia.

She clears her throat, regaining a minor percentage of composure, and says in her sweetest voice, 'Who is Katia?'

Vladimir's vagueness reappears, and the smoke of recognition floats away again as he says, 'Katia was the most beautiful woman in the world. She died in a car crash.'

'Do I detect a hint of a Russian accent?' asks Verity.

He tries looking over his shoulders as though checking if they are alone and whispers, 'I'm a former Russian KGB spy.'

'Nobody is a former KGB spy. Once a spy, always a spy,' she whispers back at him.

The old man in the chair looks like Vladimir and sounds like Vladimir, but Verity is face to face with the ghost of her former Soviet husband. He's not quite at the dribbling stage, but it's not far away.

'Who killed Randolph Vine?' she says.

'Never heard of him.' Vladimir winks. 'What was he: CIA or MI6?'

'He was murdered ten years ago in Friday Street.'

Vladimir yawns, pulling his blanket up to his waist, and looks at the ceiling. 'Friday Street,' he whistles. 'That'll be BW1189.'

'That's nice, dear,' says Verity. 'What's BW1189?'

Vladimir looks at her, 'My son never visits.'

Verity tucks his blanket into the side of the chair. She wants to kiss his head as it bobs around with the gentle force of the tucking. This man she tricked for their whole marriage and her death stares out the window into an ocean void. He doesn't know what day of the week it is or what he did in his adventurous life.

Vladimir stares at Verity, and the cloud of confusion lifts momentarily. He yells with joy, 'Katia!'

'Yes, darling,' says Verity.

'I love you,' he says, staring into her eyes and then the uncatchable smoke wafts away.

'I love you, too,' she says, touching the paper-thin skin on his spotty dry hands.

'Did Annika get to school on time?' he asks. 'It looks like it's going to snow. We should pick her up.'

'I'll take the car and collect her,' Verity says. Her eyes fill with tears. Their daughter, Annika, died at birth—a beautiful life of love lasting seven minutes and fourteen seconds, followed by a funeral in a quiet corner of Moscow. Only Verity and Vladimir attended, and both cried themselves raw in the following months.

'She's a good girl,' says Vladimir.

'She's the best,' says Verity sniffing on her sleeve as she stands to leave. 'I'll come and see you again.'

'Who are you?' he asks with the desolate face of an innocent boy.

'I'm Verity Fanthorpe from upstairs to the left.'

'I'll tell Katia I made a friend,' he says, closing his eyes to shut out the world.

Verity opens the door and takes out her syringe from her cigar tube. She jabs the mountain in his arm, and he starts to stir.

'What happened?' says the groggy sentry. 'Did you hit me?'

'An old lady like me? No, dear, you keeled over for a few seconds, but you'll be fine. I'm Verity Fanthorpe from downstairs. I'll check on you later.'

The mountain nods, and with her help, he gets to his feet and rubs his neck. Verity skips down the stairs and passes the preoccupied man behind the reception, and heads for the shrubbery at the end of the driveway.

Of all the patchwork of colourful towels on Eastbourne's sandy beach, there isn't one with a picnic as tasty and extravagant as the one assembled by Cedric and Ambrose.

Charlie offers Yuri a Wookey-Hole cheddar and cracker. He takes it and washes it down with a glass of Chablis.

Yuri says, 'I bet nobody else on the beach is serving a chilled Chablis in crystal-cut glasses.'

'Diamond-cut,' she corrects him, knowing that Cedric and Ambrose wouldn't be seen dead drinking from crystal-cut glasses even if they were dying of thirst in the desert. She gave them a set of crystal-cut whisky tumblers for their birthday. They immediately asked if she had kept the receipt.

'You should start a business selling picnic hampers,' says Yuri, finishing off his scotch egg.

She tells him the fuss Cedric and Ambrose went to since she told them about her picnic date.

'They sound like fun,' says Yuri. 'What do they do?'

'For the last ten years, they did everything for me after my father died,' she touches the hem of her summer dress. 'The boots were my choice, which caused them concern, but I can easily get my own way.'

Yuri selects a few grapes and offers them to Charlie. 'They know all about picnics and dresses,' he says.

'They would say they know all about everything.'

Yuri stares out to sea and sips his wine.

'How was your dad today?' she asks. Charlie learnt from Verity that when you ask a question, you remain still and silent, allowing your opponent to fill the uncomfortable void.

Yuri finishes his wine. 'Physically, he's in good shape, but dementia is cruel. Everything is normal one minute; the next, he doesn't remember that his wife and daughter are dead. Sometimes, Dad knows who I am, and on my next visit, I have to remind him. Today, he was on and off. I'm sorry for not mentioning his condition to you.'

'It must be hard,' she says, looking into the hamper and taking her time to select nothing. She nudges Yuri playfully, 'My dad used to drink in a pub in Fulham; maybe my dad knew your dad. Randolph Vine? Have you heard that name?'

Yuri looks vague, saying, 'No, I don't think so.'

Charlie pauses the conversation again. It's a good power play when you want to find something out. She leans back on her elbows, stretching her legs and lets her curly black hair brush the sand.

'How did he die?' he asks.

Charlie stares at the cloudless blue sky, contemplating whether to tell Yuri that his dad is one of the suspects who killed her dad. Instead, she says. 'He was a victim of a mugging.'

From the marine parade, Verity looks at the couple on the beach through her miniature telescope.

'You look like a pirate,' says Pope. 'I'm starving. Did you save a scotch egg for me?'

'Yes. I ate it,' says Verity, focusing the lens on Charlie, watching her take time to ask questions. 'Good girl,' she says under her breath. 'Good girl. She's playing the game really well. Charlie is a natural in the field.'

'So you keep saying,' says Linus.

Verity moves her telescope from Yuri and back to Charlie, watching them munch their way through their picnic.

Seeing Vladimir sinking into the abyss of dementia took her by surprise, and hearing Annika's name took the wind out of her sails like a punch to the gut. Annika's premature death drowned Verity in grief, leaving her with a hardened shell. She never allowed love to penetrate her heart again. Annika was unplanned—an accident, but seeing the baby's heartbeat on a monitor in a Moscow hospital during the height of the Cold War gave Verity sleepless nights deciding whether she should break cover and tell Vladimir her name was not Katia but Verity Fanthorpe: a sleeper spy from England.

"*Don't be stupid!*" - came the reply from Cedric and Ambrose in plain Russian in a non-coded message in the next edition of *Pravda*. And they were right. Her emotions were caught in a downward spiral of unimaginable agony.

Her darling daughter Annika was snatched from life before Verity could nurse her baby girl in her arms—no mother should endure such pain. And raising a child in a house of lies is perhaps not the best environment.

'Penny for your thoughts,' says Linus. 'I've never seen you drift off like that. Is everything alright?'

Verity swivels the lens and zooms in on Charlie. Annika would be the same age, a bit older, and should be the one sitting on the beach teasing information from Yuri—three slow, deep breaths calm Verity's racing pulse.

'I'm thinking about the case,' she says. 'Lots of moving parts and nothing to grab onto. What do you know about BW1189?'

'Nothing. Are you sure you're alright?' he says.

Verity swots his words away like an annoying fly buzzing around a food table. She messages Charlie from Linus's phone and watches the picnic wrap up a few minutes later.

Verity and Linus wander off to where they left Elsie and watch the dot on the screen move away from Eastbourne toward London.

Numbness, akin to an out-of-body experience, strikes through Verity's nervous system. Linus holds tightly around her waist, yet all she feels is the emotion from thirty years ago in that Moscow hospital. Elsie grips the road and peels away the miles to London as Verity rides on autopilot, responding to Linus's directional taps on her shoulder.

Cedric and Ambrose turn right into the bottom of their lane, taking in the majesty of Tanglefoot Farm. They agree their day was as satisfying as the afternoon they spent at Stonehenge, telling tourists the stones were erected by Mick Jagger and The Rolling Stones for a concert.

They walk around the farmhouse, where they come face to face with Colin, wearing his Hawaiian shirt.

'Good afternoon, gentlemen,' says Beard. 'I'm sorry to turn up unannounced.'

'Perfect timing for tea,' says Ambrose, slipping through the kitchen door.

Cedric leans left and right to stretch his back. A day of bending and sorting brings with it a host of aches and pains, and the dust triggers a bout of sneezing. He plumps up a cushion and eases himself onto the sofa, inviting Beard to join him.

'Where are Charlie and Verity?' asks Colin.

'Eastbourne.'

'Catching some sunshine?'

'Catching a murderer, I hope,' says Cedric.

Ambrose places a tray on the table and slumps on the sofa next to Beard. 'I feel like I've gone five rounds with a heavyweight boxer and lost!' He pours three cups of tea and grips a slice of lemon with his tongs, looking at Beard. 'Lemon?'

Colin Beard has the appearance of a man who drinks milky tea with three spoonfuls of sugar. He looks at the tray, noting the lack of milk and sugar and says, 'Lemon, lovely. Thank you.'

Ambrose serves three generous slices of homemade blackcurrant cheesecake.

'This is Ambrose's masterpiece,' says Cedric.

'Do you two cook a lot?' asks Beard.

'All the time,' says Ambrose.

Cedric points to a plot of land beyond the wildflower

garden to an allotment where they grow vegetables. 'To the right is our apple and pear orchard, and to the left, a row of blackcurrant bushes,' he says, pointing at the cheesecake.

'And a dozen beehives,' adds Ambrose. 'We make honey.'

The roar of Charlie's Jaguar booms around Tanglefoot Farm as she races across the courtyard and parks in the garage. Verity pulls Elsie to a standstill next to the humming Jag and steps off the motorbike—Linus remains glued to the spot, his hands still holding on to where Verity's waist was a few seconds earlier.

'Having fun, Pope?' says Cedric.

Linus removes his crash helmet, saying, 'Verity and Charlie overtook each other without paying attention to the highway code.'

'Come and have a slice of blackcurrant cheesecake,' says Ambrose.

Somehow, everyone squeezes onto the sofa, including an overly excited Winnie, while Ambrose refreshes the teapot. A hush falls as if commanded by an orchestra conductor while they eat their cheesecake.

Charlie finishes first, saying, 'The picnic was a success, almost too good as I nearly forgot to interrogate the poor chap.' She drinks her tea, adding, 'Yuri knows nothing.'

'And Vladimir's home in Eastbourne is not a summer getaway but a care home, and the old Russian remembers nothing,' says Verity.

Charlie asks Colin Beard, 'When will an autopsy be carried out on Joshua King?'

Linus Pope corrects her, saying proudly, 'Post Mortem. It's Latin.'

The word autopsy is a derivative of Greek and Latin,' says Cedric. 'You can use either term. Post mortem simply means after death. Autopsy, the term Americans use, means *seeing for oneself*. Slightly more poetic, wouldn't you say?'

Colin Beard follows the fast-moving conversation like a tennis umpire, with his head turning left, right, left, right, and says, 'It's too early for the results from the lab. And remember, I'm retired, so I'm getting dribs and drabs of information from old mates on the force.'

'So, was today a total waste of time?' Charlie asks Verity.

'Not if anyone knows what BW1189 means?' says Verity. She hands her plate to Ambrose, telling him it was quite simply the most incredible cheesecake ever made.

Cedric puts the bag they carried from Randolph's garage on his lap and flicks through the pile of papers and documents. He removes a faded cream envelope and says, 'You mean something like this?'

Verity holds the envelope up to the light and reads aloud the markings on the top right-hand corner, 'BW1189.'

'What does it mean?' asks Colin Beard.

'Berlin Wall, November nineteen eighty-nine,' says Cedric.

<><><>

Chapter Thirty-Six

Charlie

Yuri is lovely, but I already knew that.

He loved our picnic, liked my dress, and was polite about my steel-toe-cap boots. He's more than likely the stiletto-type of man. Giant killer meant nothing to him, and elision went over his head—it goes over everyone's head, and KPH brought nothing, either. I'm beginning to wonder if they're nothing more than a couple of holes and a scratch near some clues in a random crossword book my dad happened to have in his pocket when he was murdered. Or put there by the murderer to throw the police off track.

Nobody else is up, so I witness Tanglefoot Farm's morning rituals alone from the sofa in the ops room. The warm sun draws moisture from the ground through a misty haze to a soundtrack of chirping birds. As a student, I missed thousands of mornings and chirping birds. Not now. Well, not usually.

I've been staring at the five photographs for nearly an hour, and I fear I won't ever crack the case, and my father's murderer will never be brought to justice.

Joshua bloody King! He's dead: murdered, so if he is my father's killer, then justice I will not have, but he remains a suspect. As are Polly King, Kevin Hall, the lovely Yuri and Vladimir.

One of you did it, or two of them did it.

Is it possible that maybe all of them did it? Don't be silly. No, wait, it might not be so foolish. Vladimir is sidelined with dementia, and Joshua King is dead. So that's two down, with three to go. Who is next? No, wait, my thoughts don't make sense.

'Morning, love bird,' says Verity from thc door of her campervan.

'Coffee?' I ask, ignoring her jibe.

'Love one,' she says. 'I'm so happy you dodged Cedric and Ambrose's crazy rules of when they can and can't drink tea and coffee. If I want coffee, I'll drink coffee.'

Verity is about as no-nonsense as you can get in an adult. It is black or white with her about everything. She loves you or hates you. There's no middle ground, and there's no grey area for misunderstanding. I put the coffee machine on and wait for it to do its thing, and I see Verity going through her rigorous routine of star jumps, shadow boxing, and lunges in front of the ops room. I haven't seen this much energy in a seventy-plus woman before. Or man. Or anything. She is a. . . actually, I don't know what she is.

Why did my father have an envelope with BW1189 in his garage? And why, coincidentally, did Vladimir drop the code into conversation with Verity through his battle with lucidity?

The machine finishes spluttering and produces two frothy coffees. I grab a couple of soft croissants, some butter, and a pot of jam, then head for the ops room. We make ourselves comfortable and dip the croissants into our coffee, laughing at how Cedric and Ambrose would give us a twenty-minute lecture if they were here. But they are not, so we continue dipping.

'I can't see Yuri being our man,' I say.

Verity says, 'Too good-looking, is he?

I blush.

Verity slurps her coffee, adding, 'Vladimir could have killed your father, but his brain is tied in knots. So, as a lead, he's as good as dead.'

'Joshua?' I ask. 'Being dead won't get him off the hook.'

'He's a strong maybe,' she says.

'Polly?'

'She's a maybe, but why?' she says.

'Kevin Hall?' I ask, hoping for more than a maybe.

'He's a definite maybe, but again, what's the motive?'

And she's right. We don't have a leading contender for the Murderer of the Year award. Unless the police find a note on Joshua's person confessing that he killed my dad ten years ago, we can't do much more.

Verity snaps her fingers, which startles me from my thoughts.

She says, 'I'm going to break into Vladimir's house and rifle through his stuff and look for something.'

'When?'

'Tonight!'

'And what is Yuri going to think about your plan?'

'He'll have no idea because you'll be on a dinner date

with him,' she says. 'I'll send him a message from you from your phone if you like.'

'What about Cedric and Ambrose?'

'I don't think you should take them on your date, dear,' she says.

'I meant about your plan,' I say.

'Breaking into a Russian mobster's house is a man's job, so we better leave those two out. That goes for Linus, too. It's best if we go alone. It's a simple operation: you distract; I'll rummage.'

Verity has this way of making her thoughts sound like decisions. I suppose it's from years of living off her nerves while undercover as a sleeper spy in Moscow. What if Yuri doesn't want to go on a date with me this evening? What if I don't?

'I know what you're thinking, Charlie,' says Verity. 'The second date sexy time conundrum.' She stresses *sexy time* while looking at me and widening her eyes. This woman has no filter, and to prove the point, she adds, 'Shave your legs.'

Cedric and Ambrose appear in white v-neck sweaters, cream and purple polka dot cravats, brown corduroy trousers, and highly polished brogues.

'Where are you going?' Verity asks. 'The nineteen twenties?'

'You're an unpleasant woman at times,' says Cedric. 'But it so happens there's a Surrey Hills beekeepers' meeting in the room above the Stephan Langton pub this morning.'

I can't see the connection between beekeeping and their attire, but I don't need to because they'll have an explanation that will block my head. 'Do you need me to drive you down Plum Pudding Lane?' I ask.

'No, thank you. We'll use the walking time to plan our talk,' says Cedric. 'What are you two troublemakers doing?'

'We're planning to break—' I stop myself from saying anything about tonight's plan at Vladimir's house.

'Break-into-a-sweat over these clues,' adds Verity, performing a dramatic mop of her brow with the back of her hand and flopping back onto the sofa. It's all too much for Cedric and Ambrose, who, after checking their watches and muttering *morning tea*, scurry back into the kitchen.

Somehow, and I don't know why, I'm thinking about tonight's break-in at Vladimir's house. It makes sense only because nothing else does.

I pick up the envelope from the table and ask her, 'Where were you when the Berlin Wall fell?'

'Berlin, obviously. The Soviet Union was in meltdown because the Berlin Wall was much more than an Iron Curtain; it was their symbolic statement to the world.' Verity's words tail off as she looks at the envelope from my father's garage. It's still not much to go on; it all feels impossible to piece together. Verity flips the envelope over and removes a single sheet of blank paper—it's equally as faded as the envelope.

'Why would Dad keep this envelope with a blank sheet of paper inside?'

'This sheet of paper is certainly not blank,' says Verity, slipping it back into the envelope.

I need to message Yuri. What should I say without appearing too desperate or needy? *Hi Yuri, I loved our picnic yesterday. How about dinner tonight somewhere romantic?* I already sound like an idiot.

'What shall I say to Yuri?' I ask.

Verity looks up from the envelope, and without missing

a beat, she says, 'I'm coming to your house this evening because you're taking me to dinner.'

And there it is: the world through Verity's black-and-white lens. Everything is logical. You just say what you think and do what you want. I look at my phone and tap on Yuri's name, hovering my fingers over the message box.

'Oh, give it here,' says Verity, snatching my phone. She taps a message, and without showing me, she sends it. In desperation, I grab it back. Oh, Lord. She sent the forthright statement with five kisses.

I say, 'I think a bit of softness would have been better, Verity. You need some coyness, some elegance when attracting a—' I stop talking as Yuri's reply pops up. It says, *Perfect, what time?*

'Tell him seven-thirty,' says Verity. 'You kids are too touchy-feely these days.'

Winnie jumps up on my lap and looks like she's just climbed out of my bed. She's not an early riser.

'Fancy another coffee?' I ask.

'Yes, and more of those croissants,' says Verity. 'And then we'll prepare tonight's activities.'

How did I agree to be part of this? I thought I was an assertive, single-minded, strong woman, but when I'm with Verity, I go along with everything she says. I'm under her spell. I like it, and that's the problem; I like the danger, and I like her. Once we've cracked the case, she'll no doubt go her separate way, and life will return to normal. Not that it was ever normal—I live with Cedric and Ambrose.

I need to sort my life out!

<><><>

Chapter Thirty-Seven

Polly King sits in the front room of her cottage in Shere Village, her hands in her lap, listening to questions about her husband.

'When did you last see Joshua King?' asks the police officer.

'Ten years ago,' says Polly.

'Did you know King was visiting Shere?'

'Of course not. He died in a car crash ten years ago in Australia.'

The officer, dressed in a blue jacket and a white shirt, takes notes while starting his next question without looking up, 'Did you know Joshua King worked for the Intelligence Service?'

'It appears there's a lot I didn't know about my husband's activities.' Polly's eyes water, and she dabs a tissue at the tears.

The officer shows Polly a photograph found at the scene in the cottage opposite. 'Do you have any idea why Joshua King would be carrying a photo of you?' The man places the photo, sealed inside a plastic sleeve, on the table in front of her.

'I have no idea. I can't even believe he was alive, and now I can't believe he's dead!' she says, sniffing. 'How did he die?'

'It's too early to say, but it appears he died from a heart attack.' He waits a moment and adds in a softer, more sympathetic voice. 'Mrs King, why do you think your ex-husband was trying to kill you?'

Polly blows her nose into the tissue, 'What makes you think he was trying to kill me?'

'King died slumped in his chair in front of a sniper rifle, with its telescopic sights trained directly at your head in this very room.' The officer sits back in the chair as if to rest his case in a court of law. A round of applause would not have gone amiss.

Polly opens her mouth to say something, but nothing forms. After all, what can be said about a man who returns from the dead after ten years to train a rifle on your head from the cottage opposite?

The officer says, 'I think you're lucky he had a heart attack when he did, or you could have been his next victim.'

'Next? Why, who was his first?'

'Randolph Vine.'

'But that was ten years ago,' says Polly.

'Murder has no sell-by-date, Mrs King. It's safe to say we've got our man.'

Colin Beard walks up Plum Pudding Lane and circles Tanglefoot Farm.

Since leaving the force, he's gained weight around his waistline and Mrs Beard, who reads health magazines, insists he walks everywhere unless it's to take her shopping. However, with the magazine suggestions and endless walking, Colin's Hawaiian shirt is no looser.

'Morning, Charlie,' he says.

'Good morning, Colin,' says Charlie. 'Perfect timing.'

'For what?' he asks.

'For a walk to the pond and a woodland loop,' says Charlie. She taps on Verity's campervan door. 'Colin's here, and he's coming with us.'

The campervan door pings open, and Verity leaps onto the gravel courtyard. 'Morning, Beard,' she says, slapping his back. 'A quick five-miler will give us an appetite for lunch.'

'Perfect,' says Beard with all the enthusiasm of an overweight man entering a gym on New Year's Day. Winnie dashes in circles as Charlie laces her boots, and Verity rolls up her sleeves and then tries to remove a grease stain from her shorts.

'You have a spectacular home,' says Beard, admiring the ivy-clad architecture. Tanglefoot Farm's seasonal charms are best displayed late in the morning when the sun hits at the perfect angle. He looks longingly at the comfortable sofa in the ops room and the plate of croissants.

'Waggons roll,' yells Verity, grabbing Beard's arm and steering him across the courtyard. 'Now, tell me, how did Joshua King die?'

'The early indicators say it was a heart attack.'

'That's nonsense! What do you think?' asks Verity.

Charlie loops her arm on the other side, and with Beard in the middle, their stride pattern sends a rhythmic left, right, left, right into the Surrey Hills soft blue sky.

'It's far too convenient, King dying of a heart attack,' says Beard. 'One minute, he's staring through the sights on his sniper rifle into Polly King's cottage, and the next, the poor chap dies of natural causes.'

Charlie and Verity stop together as if under the watchful command of a fearsome Sergeant Major on a parade ground.

'Polly thought he was trying to kill her,' says Verity. 'But why would King kill King?'

Charlie stands in front of Beard. 'Are you saying our suspects are killing our suspects?'

Beard looks over his shoulder, saying, 'The police are working on the theory that he killed your dad ten years ago before fleeing to Australia a day after he was booked to fly and then faked his death in a car crash.'

'I sort of think that too,' says Charlie.

'I'm keeping an open mind,' says Verity. 'It's no good setting your heart on something this early in the game.'

'She's right,' says Beard. 'Ten years ago, the case was driven by the belief that Joshua King somehow killed your dad.'

'You said it was a mugging gone wrong,' says Charlie.

'That was the official report, not mine.'

They reach the bottom of the lane and take turns clambering over the wooden stile. Friday Street's pond has a stillness to influence and calm the busiest of minds.

An artist with his easel perched on the edge of the pond studies the weeping willows and then dabs his brush on the canvas to catch a thousand shades of green that seep into the crow-black water.

'I wish I had the patience of an artist like that old boy down there,' says Verity.

'Maybe you have a hidden talent for oils,' says Beard.

'There's nothing hidden about Verity,' says Charlie.

They slow their pace as they come alongside the

painter, who sits on a foldable stool. He's an elderly man wearing an old cardigan with paint splatters. He nods a polite good morning.

'Caught much?' asks Verity, pointing at the water. 'I hear it's good for pike.'

'I'm painting,' says the man.

'Excellent idea,' she replies, and they continue walking around the water.

There are too many cars for the small parking area at the Stephan Langton pub, where Charlie sees Cedric and Ambrose through the window, gesturing to an enthusiastic group in the upstairs function room.

Colin asks, 'Was Kevin Hall surprised to see you when you showed up unannounced at his cottage in Silent Pool?'

'Yes,' says Charlie. 'His gate was surprised, too, when Verity kicked it down.'

Beard says, 'I'd love to hear how he fits into all this. He seemed like a decent chap with a good job on the railway, but there was something about him I couldn't put my finger on. His alibi with his wife, Doreen, was solid, and two staff members confirmed they had dinner at the pub that night.'

Verity nods, 'I know. Linus Pope checked it, too. The pub keeps their booking diaries going back fifteen years. Kevin Hall's booking stated it was their anniversary, just as he said.' She stands with her hands on her hips, looking directly at Beard. 'Why did you tell Kevin Hall about Vladimir Nikitin?'

'How did you know that I did?'

'Hall mentioned a Vlad Niki from Fulham,' says Verity.

'I can't remember,' says Beard. 'Do you know this Vlad chap?'

'Yes, I was married to him!'

'Is he a suspect? asks Beard.

'He's on our wall,' says Verity. 'His son, Yuri, is up there, too.'

'Any plans to visit them?'

'Way ahead of you, Colin. Way ahead,' says Verity.

Charlie heads into the woods behind the pond and follows the trail up a steep hill. They walk up and over several hills at quite a pace until they find a place to rest on a fallen tree. Verity straddles the giant elm, and Colin lets out a long breath as he sits.

'I need to get fit,' he says, holding his stomach.

'I'm ten years older than you and could easily beat you to death,' says Verity.

'That's an unusual way to compare fitness levels,' says Beard.

'Stick with us, Colin, and we'll have you losing weight in no time,' says Charlie.

The Surrey Hills sprawl beneath them, and ancient church towers in each village poke through the trees—country lanes spider-web around the uplands and lowlands connecting each hamlet.

'I wonder why spies choose to live down there?' says Charlie, pointing at Friday Street.

'Spies are like antique shops,' says Verity. 'Where there's one, you'll find ten in a row. There's a house in Holmbury St Mary where four spies live together.'

'British, I hope,' says Colin, laughing at his quip.

'It would be more useful if they were enemy spies,' says Verity. 'It's easier to keep an eye on the blighters if you know where they live.' She tugs at the dry tree bark, and a cloud of dust escapes, sending bugs and ants scurrying for a new home. A woodpecker's beak rat-a-tat-tats against a sturdy trunk somewhere in the woods, and a distant dog barks with excitement but doesn't disturb Winnie, who sleeps during the break.

Over lunch at Tanglefoot Farm, Charlie tells the assembled team about Verity's plan to break into Vladimir's house while she's distracting Yuri over dinner. It doesn't go well.

'It's a ridiculous plan,' says Linus Pope. 'Vladimir is a paranoid Russian who's probably installed cameras all over the place.'

Verity holds up a black metal instrument the size of a shoe box and explains she stole it from a KGB agent forty years ago. 'This beauty interferes with the feed from any camera, putting it in pause mode.'

'How about bodyguards?' says Pope.

Verity takes out a large black aerosol canister, 'One spray of this, and you'll wake up two hours later.'

'What if Yuri doesn't want to go to dinner with Charlie?' says Pope. 'He might want to cook at home.'

Verity holds up a tiny black dress and a pair of high-heeled black stilettoes. 'Charlie will be wearing this number tonight.'

'Does everything have to be black?' asks Pope.

Cedric and Ambrose bring two trays of food to the garden table: Meatballs in a chilli sauce, stuffed mushrooms, egg salad, prawns in wild rice, curried potato and cauliflower, sliced peppers and humous, pickles and olives, and of course, a wide selection of cheese and biscuits. It's what Ambrose and Cedric refer to as their end-of-week-fridge-clear-out.

Hands bump into hands as the hungry gathering reaches across the table to spoon and scoop the dishes onto their plates. Cedric returns from the kitchen one last time with warm, crusty bread and butter.

Ambrose pops open a bottle of rosé champagne and fills everyone's glass. 'I think the team is all here,' he says. 'Tanglefoot Farm is always better at a noisy mealtime.'

'I'll drink to that,' says Charlie. She leans close to Verity, whispering in her ear, 'We'll take the Jag tonight because the dress you want me to wear is a little short for Elsie.'

'Good idea,' says Verity. 'Later, I'll set us up with earpieces so we can stay connected.'

'What are you two concocting?' asks Pope.

'Girl stuff,' says Charlie.

Linus Pope scoops a large spoonful of prawn rice onto his plate and dollops a few meatballs on top.

Colin tells nobody in particular that his diet will restart tomorrow, and Charlie hands him the basket of warm bread.

'You're not helping,' he says. 'I'm doing my best to lose weight.'

'You're a lovely big bear,' says Charlie, nudging him in the ribs.

Colin spoons a bit of everything onto his plate and turns to Verity, saying, 'Tell me about Berlin. The envelope and blank sheet of paper must mean something to you.'

Linus says, 'What a night. So much hap—'

Cedric and Ambrose kick Pope's leg under the table, and Verity glares like a laser beam boring through an iron plate.

'Secrets among spies are like bees in a hive,' says Cedric.

<><><>

Chapter Thirty-Eight

Verity places her bag with the camera jammer and the knockout spray into the Jaguar. Upstairs, Charlie changes from her jeans and leather jacket into Verity's short black cocktail dress.

'Can I wear my boots,' she yells from her bedroom window overlooking the courtyard and ops room.

Verity yells back, 'The plan is to seduce him, not kick him. Wear the stilettos, dear. Men can't resist how our hips thrust forward, and our leg muscles flex.' She demonstrates the action around the courtyard but looks more like a giraffe in difficulty.

'I'll take both pairs, you mad old thing,' whispers Charlie under her breath.

'I can hear you,' whispers Verity. 'These earpieces pick up everything.'

'I didn't say a word,' says Charlie.

'Quite so, dear.'

Cedric and Ambrose clear the garden table and carry the plates to the kitchen. They return with a pot of tea and sit in the ops room with Linus and Colin. Verity tightens the bolts to secure the sidecar back onto the motorbike, and Elsie is complete again.

Charlie appears at the back door wearing her cocktail dress, and the chatter in the ops room falls silent. She twirls as if in a fashion show, then stomps across the gravel to the Jaguar in her steel-toe-cap boots.

'And it was going so well,' says Cedric.

Charlie lifts her pair of stilettos above her head like a trophy and receives nods of approval and cheers from the tea drinkers.

'Men are so soppy about shoes,' she says to Verity.

'Men are soppy, dear. Are you ready to go?'

'We'll leave in five minutes, and you're driving,' says Charlie. She enters the ops room, where Ambrose pours tea, and Cedric serves Linus and Colin scones, jam and cream.

Linus says, 'While you and Verity are charging about on a wild-goose chase, we'll employ our brains to get closer to finding your father's killer.'

'We'll be using our brains, and Linus will be taking notes,' adds Cedric.

Verity revs the Jaguar and rumbles out of the garage, leaving a plume of exhaust smoke lingering around the ops room. The men wave the fumes away and then wave the Jaguar goodbye as Verity zooms off the courtyard. Neither Charlie nor Verity flinch as they accelerate through the pinch and head for the main road out of Friday Street towards Fulham, Yuri, and danger.

'What did Cedric mean over lunch when he said secrets among spies are like bees in a hive?' asks Charlie.

'Did he say that?' says Verity without removing her eyes from the road ahead.

'Yes, and you know he did.'

'Cedric is a funny old sausage. You never know what he means.'

'But you do know what he meant,' says Charlie. 'It's obviously something you all know because you all pounced on Linus to shut him up.'

A few minutes tick by before Verity coughs. 'You're not going to let this go, are you?'

'What do you think?'

Verity taps the steering wheel and looks at her watch, then taps the wheel again, looking across at Charlie. 'Listen, it was such a long time ago.'

Charlie remains silent, waiting for Verity to continue talking.

Verity exhales a long sigh of resignation, knowing that Charlie is not letting her off the hook and says, 'It would be much easier if your father had told you this.' She pauses another minute before adding, 'Our mission, the day before the Berlin Wall fell, was to intercept a letter destined to change the course of the world. The plan was simple. Distract the Russian courier and swap the letter, and after the mission, replace the letter with the original without the courier knowing.'

Charlie looked at Verity, 'What was the letter?'

Verity paused a beat, saying, 'It was a statement from the German Government together with a set of carefully worded answers to prearranged questions from the press.'

'Who did the letter belong to?' asks Charlie.

'A high-ranking official from The German Democratic Republic was tasked with reading a statement on live television about relaxing the rules for crossing the border from East to West Germany.'

'And what happened?' asks Charlie, indicating for

Verity to pull off the road so she can get her undivided attention.

Verity steers the Jaguar into a quiet lane and turns to face Charlie.

She says, 'It was the ninth of November 1989 when we intercepted the Russian courier from the Communist Party and replaced the answers with a blank sheet of paper. The courier didn't suspect a thing and innocently handed the envelope to the high-ranking official from East Germany. And that was the envelope and blank sheet of paper Cedric and Ambrose found at Randolph's garage in Friday Street.'

'So what happened?'

Verity taps her legs, looking down, 'The East German official read a short statement to the press about the proposed relaxation of travel permits. Afterwards, he was asked by a journalist when these rules would take effect to allow East Germans to cross the Berlin Wall. The official rifled through his papers, and only seeing a blank sheet of paper, he said, "Immediately, without delay." And that changed everything.'

Charlie takes in Verity's account and asks, 'What should it have said?'

Verity says, 'The answer he should have given was a detailed step-by-step process of how the East Germans could, over time, apply for passports and travel permits. It would have taken years, maybe ten years, for change, but that's not how it sounded when he said: Immediately, without delay. The German people took pickaxes and hammers and tore the Berlin Wall down that night.'

'What happened after that?'

'We distracted the Russian courier and replaced the letter with the original Communist Party questions and answers.'

'Who was there?'

'Randolph, Joshua, Cedric, Ambrose, and me. The five of us watched the night's events unfold from a park bench on a hill above Berlin.

Charlie says, 'And what happened to the Russian courier?'

'The courier was blamed for the blunder and was sentenced to death. His family were exiled, and the courier's wife took her own life and was found hanging from a tree by her children. And that's what *secrets among spies are like bees in a hive* is all about. It's our code, and now you must take that secret to your grave.'

In silence, Charlie stares through the windshield until Verity eases the Jaguar back into the late afternoon traffic and heads towards Fulham in south London.

Outside Yuri's house, Verity performs a thorough equipment check.

'Knockout spray, camera jammer, lockpicks,' she says. 'I'm all set.'

Charlie points to her cocktail dress and stilettoes, 'Me, too.'

'Did you shave your legs?' asks Verity.

'You are shameless,' snorts Charlie.

They wait out of sight of Yuri's house until a few minutes to eight. Verity slaps her thigh, saying, 'Let's get this done. And remember, I can hear what you say, and you'll be able to hear me, so just speak normally.'

Verity slips out of the car with her bag of tricks and skips around the road that runs along the back of Yuri's mansion and takes up a position behind his pool house.

She whispers that she's in position.

'I'm going in,' says Charlie.

'Good luck,' says Verity.

Charlie drives up to Yuri's front gates and toots her horn twice. The gate slides open, and she steers her Jaguar onto his driveway. The gate closes behind her. Yuri opens the front door and beams a smile directly at her before waving her inside the house.

Charlie whispers Yuri's instructions to Verity.

'Go on in, but let me know when you're leaving, and tell me if you see a guard inside the house.'

Charlie steps out of the Jaguar and enters Yuri's London mansion. She takes in the Russian splendour and opulence. Cedric and Ambrose would have a field day here with the clash of colours, fabrics and materials. The overuse of sparkly objects was on a different scale.

Charlie finishes looking around the front hallway and says, 'You must think I'm so pushy telling you to invite me out tonight.'

Yuri leans against the archway leading into the library. 'I quite like a pushy girl.'

'Stupid boy,' whispers Verity.

Charlie laughs, 'Well, that's good.'

'Kiss him,' whispers Verity. 'Kiss the stupid boy.'

Charlie slides over to Yuri and kisses him on the cheek. 'I'm ready when you are.'

'Good God, girl. Go easy on the boy!' says Verity.

'I thought we might stay in,' says Yuri, and he takes her hand.

Verity says, 'Twirl! Men love showing off their girlfriends. Charlie, twirl like a clockwork toy.'

Charlie twirls for him to witness the full effect of her black cocktail dress. She says, 'Staying in is a brilliant idea, but I thought we could go out first and come back later. I assume we'll be all alone in this huge house.' She walks towards the front door. 'We will be alone, won't we?'

'Of course, we will be alone,' he says.

'Good girl,' whispers Verity.

'I like your plan better than mine,' says Yuri, opening the front door. They walk towards his Italian car, and Charlie swings her legs elegantly inside. He fires up the engine and drives through the gate.

'Keep the boy occupied for as long as possible,' whispers Verity. 'I'm going in.'

Yuri zigzags through London towards Mayfair and parks outside a private diners club, where a doorman rushes out to park Yuri's car.

'Come here often?' says Charlie.

'My father has been a member for years, and I took over his membership when he found it too difficult to get around.'

Back in Fulham, Verity turns on the camera jammer box and creeps from behind the pool house. She kneels in front of the side door and picks the lock inside ten seconds, taking extra care not to scratch the brass around the keyhole. The door pings open, and she steps inside.

'I'm in,' she whispers.

The marble-floored hallway is cool to her bare feet as she steps through the archway into the library. Most rooms can be ignored during an initial search: kitchen, bathrooms, bedrooms, but you can never eliminate a library. The floor-to-ceiling shelves are packed with colour-coded books, more for show than usage. Verity looks for a worn book spine, the most common giveaway, and runs her eyes from shelf to shelf, but nothing is out of place. Across from the library is a small study with a leather chair behind a wide desk. The drawers are unlocked and empty. She sits and swivels in the chair and notices two light switches set side-by-side by the door, but the room has only one ceiling light.

She flicks the first switch, and the light comes on. She turns it off. The second switch does nothing. She flicks it again and hears a quiet click coming from the library—it's faint, like a door latch. Verity steps back into the library, and the bookshelf in the corner is an inch out of line. She pulls the middle shelf to reveal a door. A man like Vladimir could never resist the drama of a hidden door in a library. He should have kept his secrets under the mattress if he didn't want Verity to find them.

She swings the heavy steel door open and shines her torch down the pitch-black stone staircase. Her feet flinch on the cold steps as she holds onto the rail descending into the basement. Another door at the bottom of the stairs opens into a square room containing five white plastic boxes. She takes a photograph of the layout using the phone Charlie lent her so she can put everything back in the correct order.

The first box contains random unmatching shoes of different sizes. The second contains Russian electric and gas meter readings from 1971-1979. The third contains watercolour paintings of graffiti in Berlin—pre and post the collapse of the Berlin Wall. The fourth contains thirty unused diaries dating back to the mid-nineties, and the fifth has a stack of photo albums. Verity takes the top one and sits against the cold wall, flicking through the pages. Each album is dated, and she rummages in the box to find the dates she and Vladimir were married.

While she looks at photos of herself and her Russian husband, she hears Charlie chatting with Yuri. They talk about everything and nothing. Charlie steers the conversation from topic to topic without rushing or giving Yuri a reason to think this is anything other than a fun evening with an engaging young woman.

Verity delves deeper into the box and pulls out an album marked Annika. Verity's heart jitters and skips as she kneels next to the box, staring at images of her baby Annika. She slumps back against the wall. What might have been? Her short life left an indelible imprint on Verity's soul; sometimes, she daydreams through a list of maybes. On one occasion, she found herself in front of a green traffic light, frozen in thought as car horns sounded all around.

Annika had red cheeks and a twirl of curly hair, complete with Verity's eyes. She would have been a spy for sure, but for who? Verity smiled at the thought.

'How are you getting on?' whispers Charlie. 'Yuri has gone to the restroom. Have you found anything?'

Verity didn't answer. She was caught in a trance.

'Have you fallen asleep?' Charlie's words punch through Verity's dream state.

'Reminiscing, dear,' says Verity as she removes a photo of Annika and puts the photo album back in the box. There's an album tucked in the side of the box, and it's simply marked BW1189.

Verity flips through the blank pages until her eyes fixate on the only photograph in the whole album.

Verity shouts, 'Charlie, listen to me. Get up and get out of there. Run!'

<><><>

Chapter Thirty-Nine

Unable to tear her eyes away from the photograph, Verity slides further down the wall until her neck jars at an uncomfortable angle with her chin against her chest.

Charlie whispers through Verity's earpiece, 'I'm in the loo at the restaurant. What's going on?'

Verity's eyes flick from left to right as she gathers the words to describe the collapse of her beliefs. 'He knows!'

'Who knows? Knows what? Verity, what's going on?'

Verity explains how her life has just gone down the plughole inside a strongroom under Vladimir's house in Fulham while staring at a photograph taken the night the Berlin Wall fell.

Charlie says, 'I don't get it.'

'Vladimir has a photograph of me, sitting on the bench with Cedric, Ambrose, Joshua, and your father, the night the Berlin Wall fell.'

'Holy crap on a stick! How did Vladimir get hold of that?'

'He took it, so he knew I was a sleeper spy all along.'

'Then he must have genuinely loved you,' says Charlie. 'Yuri is waiting for me in the restaurant. What do you want me to do?'

Verity scrambles to her feet and tucks the photo in her pocket next to the photograph of Annika. She thinks for a minute and says, 'Come back with Yuri and make an excuse to leave right away. I'll wait for you.'

'Understood,' says Charlie.

Verity climbs the stone steps and tries opening the strong room door, but its self-locking mechanism is shut fast.

She says in a lost voice, 'There's more holy crap on that stick of yours. I'm locked in the room in Vladimir's basement.'

'What do you want me to do?' asks Charlie.

'Call Linus.'

Linus Pope takes the call from Charlie as he and Colin Beard are walking down Plum Pudding Lane. They do an about-turn and march back toward Tanglefoot Farm, where Cedric and Ambrose sit on the ops room sofa, sipping champagne cocktails.

'Verity is stuck in a basement strong room in Vladimir's house,' says Linus.

Cedric puts his glass on the table and asks Ambrose, 'What sort of lock would a basement strongroom have?'

Ambrose says, 'A high-grade strongroom in a basement will have a triple displacement double barrel outer lock and a flat surface door punch on the inside, but if it's locked from inside, then Verity is trapped like a rat.'

'Verity told Charlie where the study light switch is to click the library door open and that we should enter from the lane behind the pool house,' says Linus.

'We?' asks Ambrose. 'This sounds like a field operation, not for retired intelligence officers.'

'We must all go,' says Linus.

'We don't have a vehicle,' says Cedric.

Linus looks across at Elsie. 'Colin, you look like a man who rides a motorbike?'

'Back in the day, yes, but that was a long time—'

'That will have to do,' says Linus. 'How do we get into the strong room if it's triggered an inside lock and we can't open it?'

Cedric says, 'Gallium, of course. How can you not know that?'

Pope and Beard shrug their shoulders and wait for more detail.

Cedric glares at them and says, 'Gallium is a soft corrosive metal that you can pour into a lock. We have a tube in the shed.'

Beard says, 'Come on then, let's not beat about the bush.

Cedric says, 'It's beat *around* the bush, not beat *about* the bush.'

'That's nice, but I don't care,' says Colin kickstarting Elsie.

Ambrose returns from the shed, slightly out of breath and wearing an asbestos glove, holding a silver tube. They used gallium to corrode the locking mechanism twenty years ago when Randolph locked himself in a walk-in refrigerator while searching for some smoked salmon for a sandwich.

Colin gets a feel for Elsie by taking a few runs up and down Plum Pudding Lane. He nods his approval. 'It's a flying machine.'

Cedric and Ambrose settle in the sidecar, and Pope fastens the glass lid shut.

Beard shifts his large frame forward, giving Linus room on the rear of the saddle. At first, Elsie chugs down the lane at a sensible speed, and Cedric points to the intercom switch on the handlebars.

Beard flicks it on.

Cedric says, 'I'm not usually the one for speed, but Verity's body will decompose at this rate. So light this thing up and get going.'

Beard opens the throttle, and Elsie surges forward at a terrifying speed. Pope holds onto Beard's barrel-shaped waist, and Cedric and Ambrose close their eyes. The hedgerows blur, and Linus shouts directions through the intercom at Colin, who takes Elsie through the corners and roundabouts at speeds more in common with Charlie and Verity.

Beard turns left and right, following Pope's directions to the lane behind Yuri's house. They park Elsie out of sight next to the neighbour's garage.

'I can't believe we got here in one piece,' says Pope.

'I love Elsie,' says Beard, staring at the cooling motorbike.

Cedric and Ambrose, who decided on grey linen suits and pale blue shirts for the mission, crouch beside the pool house while looking for movement inside the house.

'Oh, come on, you sissies,' says Beard, striding across the lawn to the side door. He opens it and pops his head inside, taking a deep lungful of air through his nose.

'What are you doing?' asks Pope.

'People leave a smell of sweat, fragrance, feet, or something,' says Beard.

'Can you smell someone's feet?' asks Ambrose.

Beard walks inside and gives the all-clear signal. They walk along the hallway to the small study opposite the library. Pope flicks the switch, and the bookshelf in the library clicks open, just as Verity explained.

Ambrose steps down the stone staircase and studies the strongroom door. 'It's an Ancaster 700C series, model RBLM4E.'

Pope cups his hands against the metal door and shouts, 'Verity! Verity! Are you alive?'

'Of course, I'm alive, you fool,' came the reply from inside the strongroom.

Pope turns to the others and says, 'Delirium is setting in.' He cups his hands at the door again and shouts, 'Ambrose has a tube of gallium, so stand back and cover your mouth.'

Verity replies, 'Understood.'

Ambrose covers his mouth and nose with a white handkerchief and waves for the others to retreat up the steps. He squeezes the tube, and the gallium liquid bubbles and dribbles into the nooks and crevices of the lock.

'It would help if you lot had telephones,' says Linus, gesturing at Ambrose, Cedric, and Verity inside the strongroom.

'We don't want anyone to call us,' says Cedric.

'Then how am I supposed to contact you?'

'It's actually you who we don't want to speak to!' says Cedric.

Colin Beard laughs, 'You walked into that one, Linus. I'll keep a lookout for Yuri,' he says, climbing the steps into the library.

Pope cups his hands once more to the strongroom door, 'Where's Charlie?'

'She's trying to delay Yuri a bit, but he's intent on

getting back here, and who could blame him after seeing that dress? I've told her you're here releasing me from the room.'

'Sit tight,' Pope says.

'Excellent idea,' shouts Verity.

After thirty minutes of fizzing, the internal locking bolts give way, and the strongroom door swings open to find Verity sitting in the corner with her shirt over her head.

'Well done, boys,' she says.

Colin peeps through the front window and sees Yuri pulling into the driveway. He dashes back into the library and down the steps to the strongroom.

'We've got company,' he says.

Verity closes the door and whispers into her earpiece, 'Charlie, we are all in the strongroom. Whatever you do, don't let Yuri into the library. We will sneak out while you keep the Russian busy.'

Outside in the driveway, Charlie puts her arms around Yuri's neck and says, 'Thank you for dinner.'

'Good girl,' whispers Verity. 'That's the spirit. Keep him occupied until we're across the lawn, and then pick me up on the corner. If he spots us, I'll use the knockout spray.'

'You can stay here tonight if you like,' says Yuri.

'Oh, that will be nice,' says Charlie. 'But I'm dead tired, so I'm going to shoot off.' Charlie kisses him.

Verity whispers, 'You are a very noisy kisser. We're slipping out of the strongroom now, so keep kissing the boy. We're heading for the side door; keep up the kissing. We're crossing the lawn and heading to the pool house. Alright, Charlie, we are out of sight. You can put Yuri down now.'

'Do you have to go?' says Yuri. 'I thought we were spending the night together.'

'Another time,' says Charlie, stepping back from him,

then thanks him for a lovely evening. She opens the door to her Jaguar and changes into her boots. She fires up the engine and eases out of the parking spot and onto the road, waving at him until she's out of sight from the Russian house.

Verity is standing on the corner with her mission bag as the Jaguar pulls up alongside her.

'Get in!' yells Charlie.

The Jaguar slips into the stream of traffic, and Charlie steers towards Friday Street.

Verity says, 'Of all the rotten luck, I didn't get a chance to use the knockout spray.'

<><><>

Chapter Forty

Verity

Yesterday was pretty bad.

I don't usually do scales, but on a scale from one to dreadful, it was a dreadful day. How could I have not realised Vladimir knew that I was a sleeper spy? I don't know whether to feel stupid or useless. I take the two photographs from my pocket and study the faded images.

I look young, baby-faced and carefree. I remember feeling full of confidence that Vladimir knew nothing about my double life. What a fool: he knew all along.

In my mind, Vladimir and Yuri are our leading suspects in Randolph's murder. If Vladimir had known about me, he would have known about Randolph and Joshua. But why kill them? Vladimir couldn't have killed Joshua King because he was in his care home in Eastbourne when Joshua slumped to his death.

How about Yuri? But why would Yuri murder Joshua King? My head hurts with too many crushing thoughts, and I'm getting nowhere.

My campervan is cool from the shade under the giant oak on my side of the courtyard. I smile at the thought of Cedric and Ambrose coming to my rescue to free me from the strongroom yesterday with a tube of gallium. Only those two would have thought to bring such an element.

I'm angry with myself. Spies are like that. They reflect on their actions and are critical of their mistakes.

I stare at the photographs again, losing my train of thought as I smell Annika's hair and sweet skin—my baby. Tears will begin to fall if I think more about her, so I pop the photograph back into my pocket.

There's a tap on my campervan door. It's Charlie.

'Coffee?' she yells.

'Yes,' I say.

'Cedric is serving scrambled eggs and—'

I open the door, and Charlie pushes a small black coffee into my hand.

We wander to the ops room sofa and recount yesterday's movements and discoveries. Charlie sounds confident Yuri is clueless about her father's death.

Cedric hands me a plate of scrambled eggs on a slice of toasted sourdough bread. His signature dish of button mushrooms sautéed in butter and balsamic vinegar smells sensational, and I begin to eat. After my lock-in adventure in Vladimir's strongroom, I didn't eat last night, so I munch my way through a second spoonful of Cedric's scrambled eggs. How does he get them so creamy? If I ask, he'll take an hour to tell me, and I'd rather eat than listen.

'Winston Churchill drank champagne for breakfast on Tuesdays,' says Cedric.

'How do you know that?' asks Charlie.

'Grandma Lizzie told us,' adds Ambrose. 'She told us many stories about the Prime Minister, I especially liked the one when she drove him to visit her grandad to buy a bag of six-inch nails and brought Friston Village to a standstill.'

Cedric says, 'But we like champagne Tuesdays best of all.'

Charlie refills my coffee and asks, 'Why did Dad keep the blank letter and envelope?'

'He kept mementoes,' says Cedric. 'Everyone does.'

Ambrose adds, 'When we sorted Randolph's back shelf in his garage, we found lots of items from his missions mixed up with household bills and takeaway menus. His filing system was a hazard.'

I sip my coffee and feel my body self-regulating after yesterday's disaster.

Charlie asks, 'What's on the agenda for today?'

I know a thousand things need doing, but I fixate on seeing Vladimir again to ask him why he didn't confront me about being a sleeper spy.

'What are you thinking about?' Charlie asks me.

She knows too much for someone so young. She has a radar built into her head, and I tell her I'm not thinking about anything.

'You're frowning a lot for that, Verity Fanthorpe.'

I consider telling them my thoughts about seeing Vladimir. I'm certain they'll understand.

Cedric picks up the jug of freshly squeezed orange juice and half-fills our glasses, and in his other hand, he tops them up with chilled Pol Roger Champagne.

It must be Tuesday. It's my new favourite day.

Charlie says, 'Verity, you should visit Vladimir and find out how he took your photograph on the Berlin bench.

Maybe he'll have a brief moment of clarity, especially if you visit him as Katia, his dead wife with lots of blonde hair, a leopard print skirt, and gold jewellery?'

An excellent idea, I tell her.

Ambrose adds, 'We're having a Kevin Hall day, so it's best you're not here when he arrives. You frightened the poor chap half to death when you violated his garden gate.'

'How about Polly King?' asks Charlie.

Cedric taps Polly's photograph on the wall, saying, 'She keeps popping up in the wrong place. We don't know how or why, but she's involved.'

I tell Charlie I'll need her help if I am going to lose thirty years. We top up our Tuesday drinks and retreat to my campervan to bring Katia to life.

<><><>

Chapter Forty-One

Cedric and Ambrose lay the garden table with a late-morning spread of Danish pastries ready for Kevin Hall's arrival. They have their questions ready and will sit him facing the sun—dazzle the suspect, that sort of thing.

The wildflowers dance in the light breeze in the far garden, and the potted herbs by the back door scent the air around Tanglefoot Farm with rosemary and basil.

Charlie opens the campervan door and walks Verity down the metal steps. Cedric and Ambrose halt their conversation about the introduction of herbs into British cookery and stare, open-mouthed, at a ghost, Katia, from thirty years ago.

'Don't look too closely,' says Verity. 'The wrinkles are still there, hidden under the inch of makeup, but from a distance, what do you think?'

Cedric and Ambrose, yet to speak, are without a quip and remain silent.

'I think we can call that a success,' says Charlie. 'Take

the Jag,' she tells Verity. 'We can't have Katia turning up on Elsie.'

Cedric and Ambrose open the Jaguar driver's door and escort Verity to the car.

'Maybe I should go and question Yuri today,' says Charlie. 'I'll press him for more information.'

Verity says, 'You've squeezed enough juice from that boy for now. You can press him all you want when we've cracked this case—if he's innocent, of course.' She sprays Russian perfume in the car and all over her clothing, then lights an old Soviet Union cigarette, which induces spluttering and coughing like an ancient mariner sea dog.

'It smells of cow dung!' says Charlie.

'That is top-drawer Cold War nuclear tobacco,' says Verity. 'If these didn't kill you, you had a decent chance of surviving the war. God, I miss them.' She coughs until her eyes run.

Charlie grabs the cigarette and takes a puff; she coughs until her throat is raw. 'If these sensory smells don't kick-start Vladimir's memory, then he'll never remember you.'

Charlie closes the car door, and Verity fires up the throaty engine. She pulls out onto the gravel courtyard and swings around the house. Verity blasts the horn, and the sound disappears as she flies down Plum Pudding Lane.

Cedric and Ambrose are still in their open-mouth positions, holding a pile of plates and cutlery for Kevin Hall's visit.

'It was 1989 all over again,' says Ambrose.

'Let's hope Vladimir sees Katia and spills any beans he has to spill,' says Cedric.

Still recovering from her nuclear cigarette, Charlie pulls their suspect photographs off the wall and tucks them and the crossword book into a draw in the ops room. It's hard to tell if they're winning or losing or drifting further away from the answer. Being rudderless may be normal, but never knowing if you're getting closer to exposing the killer is exhausting. How will the truth reveal itself?

Charlie slumps onto the sofa and closes her eyes, trying to stop the constant flow of probabilities and endless unanswerable questions.

'What's happening with Joshua King?' she asks.

'Colin Beard is passing through later with an update,' says Ambrose.

'I like Colin,' says Charlie.

'Poor choice of shirts, but otherwise a very decent fellow,' adds Ambrose.

'You were lucky, Cedric, that the chap is so lovely, especially after all those terrible things you said about him,' she says.

Charlie slips into a momentary sleep, and Winnie skips onto the sofa and curls up beside her. Cedric pulls a blanket over them, and Ambrose tucks a soft cushion behind Charlie's head. There's no end to their fussing.

Ambrose whispers as he looks at Charlie, 'Who would have thought ten years ago that this skinny, unruly child would turn into this skinny, unruly woman.'

Cedric stifles a laugh. 'She's quite the force. Randolph would be proud of us.'

'Definitely,' says Ambrose. 'We should find out if they give awards for parenthood.'

Kevin Hall accepted the invitation from Cedric and Ambrose after Linus Pope told him they needed his advice on potted herbs. Hall couldn't resist.

Colin Beard appears, puffing and sweating from his walk up Plum Pudding Lane. Cedric puts his finger to his lips and points to Charlie on the sofa. They steer Colin toward the wildflower garden, where butterflies busy themselves on the swaying stems.

'Any news on Joshua's death?' asks Cedric.

Colin's forehead beads with sweat, and he dabs it dry with his white handkerchief. His contact in the police force supplies him with valuable titbits of evidence, offering a name here and a murder weapon there. Colin spent his last few years on the force training his protégé so he knows he can trust the information.

Colin leans against the gate post at the top of the garden for a breather, taking in the views across Friday Street, spreading out like a watercolour landscape.

'My officer says that the toxicology report claims Joshua King died from ricin poison,' says Beard.

'Oh, that's tasty news,' says Ambrose. 'Ricin was the favourite poison for the Soviet assassins because it's quick and deadly. There was this one time a Bulgarian dissident, the author Georgi Markov, was jabbed with a poisoned-tipped umbrella in 1978. He died at a bus stop in Balham.'

'That must have been bloody awful for him,' says Beard.

'What, dying from ricin?' asks Ambrose.

'No, dying in Balham,' says Beard.

The three of them laugh and take in the sweet summer air.

'How did the killer lay the poison?' asks Ambrose.

'Multiple spots,' says Colin. 'In his water jug, the rim of his glass, a small spike on the chair, and the eyepiece of his telescope. The stuff was everywhere. The killer didn't take any chances. Just one touch and it was goodnight, Venice.'

'Vienna. It's goodnight, Vienna,' says Ambrose.

'Are you sure?'

'Yes, quite sure,' says Ambrose.

'I've always said goodnight Venice.'

'Then you've always been wrong!' says Ambrose.

They amble through the wildflowers to the courtyard, where Charlie sits up, rubbing her eyes. Winnie doesn't stir.

'How long was I asleep?'

'An hour and three minutes,' says Cedric. 'It was blissful.'

Kevin Hall is due in forty-five minutes, so they prepare the scene. Ambrose removes their flourishing herb pots and hides them behind the shed, while Cedric turns some pots around and forces a couple of beautiful wild basil plants into pots that are far too small—allow your opponent to believe you are slapdash.

Earlier, over breakfast, Cedric and Ambrose compiled a list of detailed herb questions for Kevin Hall, deciding, after much debate, not to conduct the interview in Latin—sometimes, it's best not to overdo it.

Colin Beard joins them at the pots and says, 'Keep the questions subtle this morning. We need to tease the information out of this man, so don't ask direct questions about the case. Softly, softly catchy monkey.'

Cedric looks at an imaginary watch on his wrist, 'Oh, look at the time,' he says. 'It's not our first day on the job!'

Colin straightens his colourful shirt and rolls his eyes. 'As I said, go easy on the man.'

A brown Volvo pulls up in front of Tanglefoot Farm, and Kevin Hall rings the doorbell. Ambrose invites Hall to follow him around to the courtyard, where Cedric and Colin greet him.

Kevin Hall looks at the battered array of potted herbs and tuts and shakes his head. He says, 'Your herbs are in the wrong size pots, and some are facing the wrong way.'

Nothing annoys Cedric and Ambrose more than being

wrong, and nothing makes Charlie happier than seeing their faces droop. She beams from her hidden spot on the sofa at Kevin Hall's assessment of their poor herb attempt.

The decision to keep Charlie out of Kevin Hall's way makes sense. Beard suggested that Hall won't talk to Charlie after her raiding party at his home in Silent Pool. A suspect needs to feel comfortable chatting. So Charlie will remain on the sofa with Winnie in the ops room, safely out of sight.

Grandma Lizzie told nighttime stories to Cedric and Ambrose about captured German pilots during the war and how they housed them in lavish surroundings with good food and wine. Grandma Lizzie listened to their relaxed chats with other enemy flyers and gathered vital details.

'Tea or coffee?' Cedric asks Hall.

'Tea, white with three sugars, please,' says Kevin.

Cedric nods, 'How lovely.'

The plate of Danish pastries passes around, and Colin Beard declines twice before taking two.

'I'll be good tomorrow,' he whispers to nobody.

'What is the giant killer of herbs?' asks Cedric. 'You know, the small one who can beat the big one.'

Kevin Hall's face is blank, 'What's that?'

'Your Volvo, is it KPH or MPH?' asks Ambrose.

'Have you ever come across an elision?' says Cedric.

Colin Beard glares at Cedric and Ambrose while Kevin Hall tucks into another pasty.

Colin interrupts the persistent questioning from Cedric and Ambrose and says, 'The view across Friday Street is fabulous from up there,' pointing to the stile at the top of the garden. Kevin Hall joins Colin on the narrow pathway among the swaying flowers.

'What's upset Beard?' asks Cedric. 'Our questioning was on point.'

'We didn't put a foot out of place,' agrees Ambrose.

'What's Beard asking Hall up there by the fence?' asks Cedric. 'We already peppered the suspect with tiptop questions.'

Charlie checks to see if the coast is clear and calls out, 'How's it going?'

'We think it went extremely well,' says Cedric.

'I think Colin was impressed,' says Ambrose. 'They're coming back, hide!'

Verity checks her bright red lipstick in the Jaguar's mirror and fluffs her blonde curls.

Where did the years go?

From the Cold War, hiding in plain sight in Moscow to hiding in her campervan in Cedric and Ambrose's courtyard, was not what she predicted back in the day. Her back aches, and she would love nothing more than to perform a set of fifty vigorous star jumps. But not in this dress and not in these stilettoes.

She summons her inner Katia and growls her name with a Moscow drawl, 'Kat-ia.'

Standing in the driveway, staring at the care home on the cliff, she thinks about baby Annika. 'Come on, Katia,' she barks at herself. 'Stop drifting. You've got a job to do!'

Everything points to Vladimir's involvement in Randolph and Joshua's murders, and as the saying goes, there's no smoke without fire. Vladimir is guilty of something—what that is, is not clear.

Verity pushes the front door open and strides up to the

reception desk. The young man doesn't hear Verity approaching.

'I'm here to see my husband.'

'Your name?'

'Katia Nikitin. Vladimir's wife.' Verity walks toward the staircase.

'Hold on,' says the man.

Verity turns and snarls, 'What?'

'You must sign the visitors log.'

Verity dismisses him with a dramatic wave of her hand. 'You sign it, darling—K-A-T-I-A.'

She takes the carpeted stairs two at a time to Vladimir's floor, where the security has been increased. Three guards now lean against the wall outside the Russian's room.

Verity strides toward them like a model on a catwalk, wearing a scowl fit to adorn every angry wife's face.

'Smarten yourselves up!' she shouts. 'Stand up. You're a disgrace.' Her Russian cuts through their daze. 'Is my husband awake?'

'Husband?' says one, although his dry, husky voice barely registers.

The taller of the three asks, 'And you are?'

'In a bloody hurry,' barks Verity, reaching for the door handle.

'Who are you?' the husky one asks again, blocking her way.

Verity turns on him, using the old tactic that attack is the best form of defence.

'How dare you! I'm Katia Nikitin, Vladimir's wife. Are you going to keep asking silly questions, or shall I call Yuri?' It was a brave stance to take—*don't blink, don't melt, stand your ground*. The words of Grandma Lizzie flash in Verity's mind.

It works as the guards stand reluctantly to one side, and Verity barges into Vladimir's room.

Her Russian husband from yesteryear stares out to sea in his wing-back chair.

'It's me, darling,' she says in her softer, more loving voice. 'How are you this morning?' She lights a cigarette and blows the Soviet smoke into the air, then kisses his cheek, complimenting him on his blue shirt.'

Vladimir's cloud of confusion shows through his blank eyes.

Verity says, 'It's a beautiful sunny day, and there's a light breeze kicking off the sea. How do you fancy a walk in the garden?' She waits for an answer. Nothing is forthcoming. 'I'll ask the boys to lift you into the wheelchair and bring you down.'

She steps outside, and the guards follow her into the room and prepare Vladimir's wheelchair. All the while, Verity blows Soviet smoke through her nostrils, showing her impatience as the men fuss with blankets and pillows for the old Russian KGB mobster.

The tall guard wheels Vladimir to the end of the hallway to a small lift. Verity squeezes in with them and presses the button for the garden.

The guard says, 'We were told you were dead.'

'Nobody told me,' says Verity, offering the guard three packets of Russian cigarettes. He stares at them as though he'd been handed the keys to a sports car.

He says, 'My father smoked these, lots of them, right up until they killed him.'

Verity snorts, 'A sign of weakness.'

The guard smiles at Verity when the door pings open on the ground floor. The other two guards help the party into the garden and show appreciation for the packets of cigarettes.

Verity relieves the three guards from their duty and pushes Vladimir's wheelchair onto a smooth pathway away from the care home towards the cliff edge.

'Katia!'

'Yes, darling,' says Verity.

'I knew it was you the other day.' Vladimir's sharpness returns for a brief moment.

'You've known all along, haven't you?'

'Yes, dear,' he says. 'I've always known who you are.'

<><><>

Chapter Forty-Two

Verity

As a rule, I'm unflustered.

People who know me will tell you I'm cool under pressure—the sort of person who can handle the heat. Today, though, well, I'm not too above my station to say my Russian bear rattled me.

I put the key into the Jaguar's ignition and fire up the big cat. Vladimir's three guards wave me off the property, and I steer the car around the twisty lane and down the hill away from the man who knows all my secrets, past and present. I left the remainder of my nuclear cigarettes with the guards. If the smell reminds them of their Moscow mothers, then my deed was a good one.

I need sea air and head to the beach, and more than anything, I must de-Katia myself. The wig comes off, and I throw it along with the high heels into the back seat.

So, my time with Vladimir saw him float in and out of lucidness—if that's the term. One moment, he saw me as Katia, his mouthy blonde wife, and the next, he couldn't grasp who was pushing him around the garden. He asked about Yuri every third sentence, and I reaffirmed his son was coming later. Obviously, I don't know Yuri's schedule, and I would be long gone by the time Yuri showed up or not.

'He never visits,' Vladimir kept saying to me.

'He visits all the time,' I told him.

Apparently, he does, according to the guards. Yuri dotes on his father. Even murderers dote, I suppose. That's not to say Yuri killed Joshua King, but one thing is for sure: Vladimir didn't! Or rather, he couldn't.

I buy an ice cream and dangle my feet above the sand on Eastbourne Beach to run the afternoon's events through my head. I can't get around the fact that Vladimir knew all along I was a sleeper spy; I mean, he knew everything and did nothing about it. If the boot were on the other foot, I would have strung the lying weasel up from a lamppost.

But that's me.

I can't find the connection as to why Yuri would murder King, and he would have been too young to murder Randolph. There are no dots for me to join.

Vladimir talked about our baby Annika as if she were alive and me, her doting mother. In my head, I have a vision of a small coffin. So, on that basis, I would rather be in Vlad's head.

I went full-out and bought a double chocolate ice cream with twin flakes, which was a mistake as it's melting in the sun and making a mess.

Dementia creates havoc without the recipient knowing too much about what's happening. Vladimir knew I was a sleeper spy, and he knew I was Katia, and he knew Katia died in a car crash. And yet, he was chatting to her in his care home garden thirty years after my horrific fake death.

Having an all-hands meeting at the Stephan Langton pub in Friday Street will be a good idea this evening. We must ensure we've shared all we know about the case.

Being a lone wolf in Moscow was more manageable than being part of a team because I'm not naturally a sharer of information, and I'm guessing the others might be similar. We need a pow-wow to make sure we've left no stone unturned. On top of that, I'm starving.

Vladimir slipped in and out of being present during our walk in the garden. He struggled to pronounce a word, and his eyes bulged with effort. It sounded like *Ker* or *Curry*—I have no idea what he was trying to tell me, but he was getting himself in a fluster: *Ker, Ker, Ker.*

The Jaguar's reassuring engine growl drowns my thoughts apart from one. Was Vladimir warning me?

<><><>

Chapter Forty-Three

Kevin Hall takes a keen interest in Cedric and Ambrose's beehives from a safe distance.

'Do you see yourself trying a spot of apiology?' asks Cedric. Hall shows the faintest flicker of uncertainty, enough for Cedric to educate his new pupil. 'Beekeeping.'

'I'll stick to my herbs,' says Hall.

Far away from the beehives, Colin Beard lets out a long sigh as he sits on the sofa next to Charlie.

He says, 'For highly intelligent men, your uncles are useless with people. No tact, no grace, just whammo! They badgered the poor man with questions about giant killers, KPH, and elision. How the devil did they get into the Intelligence Service?'

'Firstly, they were kept away from people, and secondly, they aren't my uncles, but if I did have uncles, I rather imagine they would be just like those two.' Charlie cranes her neck around the ops room's opening, doing her best to see what's happening in the garden.

Colin dabs his forehead with his white handkerchief

and folds it neatly before putting it back in his pocket, saying, 'You have quite the odd family with two mad uncles and Verity Fanthorpe as your wild mother.'

'When you put it like that,' says Charlie, 'They're all as mad as teapots.'

Colin says, 'Kevin Hall was as plain today as he was ten years ago. There's nothing about the man that's remotely memorable. He's a beige man with a vanilla personality, and absolutely nothing about him sticks out.' Colin shakes his head and looks into his open hands, whispering, 'There's nothing to grab. I don't think I've ever met someone so understated and bland.'

Winnie pops her head out from the red blanket and yawns, and Colin runs his big shovel-hands over her little head.

Charlie asks, 'And what do you make of somebody with no memorable features?'

'Kevin Hall is the first person I've met who lacks any notable characteristics. An eye witness would struggle to remember anything.'

'Maybe the skill, to be forgotten, is one he's developed intentionally.'

'Or maybe he's just a dull man,' says Beard, smiling. 'My head tells me he's dull and forgettable, and yet my detective gut tells me there's something about the drab man I should remember.'

Colin Beard leaves Charlie on the sofa and strolls along the garden trail, where he re-joins the conversation, which somehow has morphed into the correct thickness of stitching on a sturdy English brogue. Kevin Hall agrees with Cedric and Ambrose about brogue stitching and mumbles about shoemaking for several minutes.

'Where are my manners?' says Cedric to Kevin Hall.

'Let me see you to your car. My brother and I have taken enough of your time wittering on about bees, flowers, and herbs.' Cedric steers Hall around the courtyard to his brown Volvo.

Hall starts the engine and snaps the fasteners on his open-back driving gloves. He gives a mock salute to Cedric, checks his mirrors, and drives steadily down Plum Pudding Lane, turning carefully onto the main road towards his cottage in Silent Pool.

Verity hides in the shadows in the Jaguar, waiting for Hall's brown Volvo to turn onto the main road before she rushes up the lane to Tanglefoot Farm.

Verity steps out of the car and runs on the spot for thirty seconds before performing a dozen alarmingly fast star jumps. She says, 'We've all got a snippet or two of information we must share with the group, so an all-hands chat over dinner at the Stephan Langton pub is needed to lay our cards on the table.'

'You don't mean Pope as well, do you?' says Cedric.

'Everyone,' says Verity. 'Send up the flare.'

'I'll put a note in the study,' says Ambrose. 'He'll see it soon enough.'

'I'll book a table,' says Charlie.

The round table in the alcove at the Stephan Langton pub houses the tight gathering.

'We should think of getting a new venue,' says Pope, trying to squeeze in next to Colin Beard.

'Don't be ridiculous,' says Cedric. 'The Friday Street Spy Ring can't leave Friday Street.

'I'm not a spy,' says Beard.

'Nobody's a spy except me,' says Verity.

'You're an ex-spy,' says Pope.

'Once a spy, always a—' begins Verity.

Charlie cuts her short with a couple of slaps on the table. 'Let's order food and make this evening constructive.'

Silence falls as they study the menu while Cedric orders two expensive bottles of wine.

'I'd rather have a beer,' says Beard.

'Oh, the claret is not for us, dear chap,' says Pope. 'Our palates are not developed enough by all accounts.'

A table for six takes three times longer to decide what to eat than a table for two. The *what are you having?* discussions go on and on until they all decide to have the beef and mushroom pie with garlic and rosemary roast potatoes. The wine arrives, and Cedric and Ambrose swirl the claret around their glasses before drawing it noisily through their teeth. They nod their approval in unison.

'We're not in The Savoy,' snipes Pope.

'I was handed a lifetime ban from The Savoy. Something to do with me tracking down an old Soviet spy who pretended to be a waiter,' says Verity. 'A fight broke out and—and, well, you know how five-star London hotels feel about their waiters getting punched in the face.'

Pope tuts.

Cedric and Ambrose study the label and discuss 1976's great vintage, and as they begin to list their top ten clarets in order, Charlie brings the meeting to order.

She whispers, 'Our suspects are dwindling, dead or incapacitated, and we are no closer to finding out who killed my dad.'

Verity says, 'Shame Joshua King was poisoned; he made an excellent lead suspect.'

'I must ask,' says Pope. 'Verity, did you poison King?'

'Darling, I'm a stabber, a puncher, a strangler, and a shooter. I'm most certainly not a poisoner.'

The food arrives, and the *oohs* and *ahhs* welcome the steaming beef and mushroom pies. A waft of garlic and rosemary precedes the tray of roast potatoes. You can't talk and eat unless you are talking about the food you're eating, so the conversations stay food-based until their plates are empty.

Charlie takes her notebook and pen from her leather jacket pocket and writes, "Murder on Friday Street", on top of the page and underlines it three times.

Pope points to her title and scoffs, 'It's Murder *in* Friday Street, not *on* Friday Street!'

'There'll be another murder on Friday Street if you can't keep quiet,' says Verity.

The all-hands meeting starts slowly, but after a few minutes, everyone offers their penny's worth of knowledge, and by the time the crème brûlée arrives at the table, Charlie's page is full of scribbles.

'Oh, and one more thing,' says Verity. 'Vladimir kept trying to say something to me.'

'Don't come back?' suggests Pope.

Verity says slowly, 'Ker or Curry, I've no idea what it means. He was not coherent, and his voice was frail. But he kept saying it over and over. He was getting worked up about not being able to speak.'

'Ker,' says Charlie as she writes it down. 'Ker—curtains? Ker—courageous? Ker—curve.'

'Curator? suggests Ambrose. 'Or curtail?'

'Curse?' offers Colin Beard.

The sweet aroma from the caramelised sugar on top of the crème brûlée distracts their thoughts, and they dig into the creamy puddings.

'Curfew?' says Cedric. 'It could be anything.'

Pope tuts, 'It's not much of a clue, is it.'

'Everything is a clue, no matter its size or importance,' says Verity. 'We must treat each clue equally.'

Coffee follows their pudding, to which Cedric and Ambrose recite their rules about when to drink coffee and tea.

Nobody listens.

Charlie closes her notebook, mouthing a silent *thank you* at Verity.

In return, Verity nods and whispers, 'We'll catch your dad's murderer.'

Cedric and Ambrose slip away to settle the bill. Colin Beard begins to stand with the suggestion he should chip in and pay his way.

'They love to pay. It's their way to contribute,' says Charlie. 'And they've got more money than Solomon.' Grandma Lizzie left her estate to them and a huge stock portfolio.'

Beard sits with a sigh and says, 'We must shift from a gut feeling to an evidence-based case. All crimes reach a point where the evidence points to someone. What does our evidence tell us?'

Charlie flicks the pages of her notebook back and forth, hoping a name will pop out and land in her lap. There's almost too much information now—lots of little details, but disconnected—no fingerprint on a smoking gun.

As Charlie bites the end of her pencil, she says, 'It has a Russian feel, with the ricin, but there's a hidden motive somewhere here we are not seeing.' She thinks about the crossword book clues, the blank sheet of paper in the envelope, Joshua's death at the hands of an assassin using a Russian drug, and Kevin Hall's lack of character. Polly King offers nothing, and Yuri is lovely, really lovely and is simply not a killer, while his father, Vladimir, is in a home on a cliff suffering from dementia. She stares back into her notes, mouthing *Ker Curry*.

'What are you thinking?' asks Verity.

'I'm thinking that I don't have a next step,' says Charlie. 'I've always had a next step, but now I don't. I'm stuck and lost.'

Beard puts his giant hands on the table. 'When you're stuck, it's time to eliminate your weakest suspect. Find reasons to prove they didn't do it, and remember, the murders might be linked, but the murderers might not be.'

Cedric and Ambrose return to the table with a tray of brandy balloons. 'This will keep the cold out,' says Ambrose.

'It's the middle of summer and a warm evening,' says Linus.

'So you don't want one?' says Cedric.

'You're absolutely right. We shouldn't take chances,' says Linus Pope, reaching for a brandy glass.

Charlie looks at her team around the table, sipping brandy. 'So, who is our weakest suspect?'

'Vladimir, without a doubt, is the weakest,' says Verity.

'Kevin Hall,' says Ambrose. 'The man is a herb expert.'

'Joshua King is the innocent one,' says Cedric. 'He was your father's best friend.

'I think Yuri is innocent,' says Charlie. Her face flushes, 'He's too handsome, and Winnie loves him.'

'Polly King is lovely. I can't see her killing anyone,' says Pope.

Colin Beard stands and downs his brandy in one gulp. 'I must get home to the good lady Beard before she worries about me.'

Charlie puts her hand up and stops him, saying, 'That didn't work, so what's next?'

'Stakeout!' says Beard.

'Stakeout?' says Charlie.

'Yes, stakeout,' says Beard.

<><><>

Chapter Forty-Four

Polly pours some wine and sits in her small garden at the rear of her cottage in Shere village, then raises her glass to her departed ex-husband. She believed he was dead for ten years, only for him to return to life and die again.

She thinks about changing her name and concludes that Polly King has a lovely ring to it, so she decides to keep it. Polly sips her wine and looks up at the stars in the nighttime sky.

Randolph Vine and Joshua King are both dead: that's quite a duo, she thinks. Did Joshua come back to life to kill me? She empties a packet of pistachios into a small dish and begins digging her nails into the shells, making a pile of nuts and then eating them in one go.

She'll make the funeral arrangements once the police have finished their investigation. Nothing fancy, a few drinks and snacks at the Stephan Langton and a few stories about Joshua will be perfect. Polly jots her ideas into a notebook and pours another glass of wine. A knock at the door snaps her from the funeral thoughts. She walks barefoot through her neat cottage and opens the front door.

'Good evening,' she says.

Kevin Hall nods politely, 'I thought I'd check in on you.'

'I have a bottle open in the back garden. Come on through,' she says, and a moment later, they're sipping wine and shelling pistachios.

'I was invited to Tanglefoot Farm to advise Cedric and Ambrose about their potted herbs,' he says.

'That's nice,' she says, topping up her glass.

'They didn't need much advice, of course. They are fastidious gardeners and beekeepers. They asked me strange questions about giant killers and my speedometer in my Volvo.'

'What does that mean?'

'I have no idea. Those twins are strange,' says Hall.

'They've always been odd, but Joshua liked them,' says Polly.

'And Charlie Vine was there, hiding out of sight. Colin Beard, the bear-like ex-police officer, was there too. We had a good conversation while walking in the garden.'

'Was he the one who hauled you in for questioning after Randolph was fished from the pond?'

'That's the one, yes.'

'That sounds quite the party.' Polly finishes her wine and pours another. She moves the bottle towards Kevin Hall, and his hand covers his glass.

'I'm driving, no thanks.'

Two hours earlier, Cedric and Ambrose walked down the stairs and into the kitchen at Tanglefoot Farm. They decided on the way home from the Stephan Langton the night before to dress in army camouflage, from top to bottom, with green and brown painted stripes covering their faces.

'It's the Rambo boys,' squeals Charlie.

'You should consider giving up wine,' says Cedric.

'I'm afraid if I did that, I'd have to replace it with murder,' she fires back.

Verity holds her stomach, bending double in a fit of laughter. She points at them, barely able to speak, 'What are you doing dressed like that? I can't breathe!'

'We can't perform stakeout duties without the right equipment.'

'We're in Surrey, not the Congo!' says Charlie.

Colin Beard, who was the most conspicuous of anyone, had been designated driving duties and Linus Pope, communications. Verity assigned herself lookout in Shere opposite Polly King's pretty cottage while Charlie opted for the Fulham task to lurk in Yuri's bushes. Cedric and Ambrose, clad in camouflage, were to be positioned in Silent Pool, staking out Kevin Hall's house.

Verity hands out walkie-talkie radio sets in the ops room while Colin revs the Jaguar. The team climbs in, and he eases the car down Plum Pudding Lane. The first drop is Verity in Shere behind the cottage opposite Polly King—the same place where Joshua King was murdered. She slips quietly out of the Jaguar and takes up her position.

'Testing, one, two, three,' she says into the mouthpiece.

'Receiving you, Giraffe One, over,' says Linus Pope, who sits on the sofa in the ops room at Tanglefoot Farm. 'Giraffe One, you must say over.'

'You didn't say over after you said *over*. Over,' says Verity.

'Are you in position, Giraffe One? Over,' Pope's annoyance pipes through the walkie-talkie.

Verity pulls her night vision goggles over her eyes, and a green hue, like an old computer screen, fills the lens. She sighs, 'Giraffe One, in position. Over. G-Zero, do you think the police cleaned up the ricin from this place properly? I'm feeling a bit—' she chokes and splutters.

'Giraffe One! Come in, over. Giraffe One!' Panic surges through Linus Pope's voice in his attempts to raise Giraffe One. Winnie does not stir from Linus's lap as he tries to reach Verity on her walkie-talkie.

'I'm messing with you,' says Verity after a long silence.

'You must say, over. Over,' says Linus.

'I'm messing with you, Linus,' she says.

'No names, Giraffe One,' he says. 'I'm Giraffe Zero. Over.'

The black Jaguar speeds away from Shere Village towards Silent Pool, with Colin at the wheel displaying a coolness under moderate pressure. All the while, Charlie laughs at the exchange between Verity and Linus.

Colin asks, 'Why the giraffe call signs?'

Ambrose says, 'Verity used them during her time in Moscow. A giraffe's markings are unique patterns, like fingerprints.'

'I'm Giraffe Two,' says Charlie.

'We are Three and Four,' says Cedric. 'And, Colin, you're Giraffe Five.'

They begin calling each other to test their walkie-talkies, and the cacophony is debilitating.

'You must say, over. Over,' shouts Linus.

Colin continues laughing as he pulls into Silent Pool's parking area.

Cedric and Ambrose slip quietly from the back seat and creep into the bushes. Charlie and Colin's walkie-talkies burst into life.

'Giraffes Three and Four are in position, and operation Silent Pool is now active. Over,' says Cedric.

'Message received, over,' says Linus.

'Linus takes it seriously, doesn't he,' says Colin, steering the sleek Jaguar towards Fulham. Colin's involvement with his new Friday Street gang has brought a fresh spring to his step and a revived freshness to his investigative thought process.

'You're loving this, aren't you?' says Charlie. 'All this rushing around with stakeouts and murders. You're back in the life you left behind.'

Colin shifts gear with his giant hand and fails to conceal his grin. 'The lovely Mrs Beard was beginning to wish I was back on the force, and she can see that I've bucked my ideas up since being on this case with you and the team.'

'We're a great team,' says Charlie. 'My dad would have been proud of us.' She leans back as Colin pushes the Jaguar at high speeds towards Fulham. Deep in her gut, she believes Yuri is innocent—it would make no sense for him to kill her father or Joshua King. However, the use of ricin keeps the Russians on the hook.

As if reading her mind, Colin asks, 'What do you make of the Russians? And by that, I mean Yuri because Vladimir is out of the picture now.'

Charlie inhales deeply through her nostrils as if creating a new idea and tells Colin her thoughts about Vladimir and the lack of evidence for Yuri to be involved, and they agree on the ricin conundrum.

'Some of the hardest crimes to solve are those where you can't possibly imagine the culprit to be guilty,' says Beard. 'Right now, your mind is batting away any suggestion that Yuri is guilty. Your job is to collect evidence and piece it together without prejudice.'

Their walkie-talkies burst into life.

Ambrose's voice pipes through the handsets with crackles and pips, saying, 'Giraffe Three and Four reporting in from codename: Silent Pool. All quiet, nothing to report, over.'

'Message received. Over,' says Giraffe Zero.

Colin laughs, 'Why have they gone all Special Forces?'

'I've spent my life with this nonsense,' says Charlie, opening the window, 'but I wouldn't change it for the world.' She watches the evening green hedgerows morph into outer London towns where drinkers stand outside pubs, and the hubbub of chatter and laughter fills the air.

'What's on your mind?' asks Colin, easing the Jaguar through the narrow streets on their approach to Fulham.

She contemplates putting her thoughts out into the ether. 'What happens if we can't solve the case?'

'Not every case is solved, and not every question gets answered—that's the real world—unlike in whodunnit novels where everything comes together in a neatly tied bow with the guilty party brought to justice. Audiences don't like unsolved murders, you see. So the good guys must catch the bad guys.'

Charlie says, 'In your experience, what chance do we have of wrapping this thing up?'

'The best I can offer you is fifty-fifty,' he says.

'So we might or might not catch my father's killer.'

Colin smiles and nods. 'It's the best I've got.'

Charlie can live with that; after all, she did nothing

about solving her father's murder for ten years, and now she can think of nothing else.

Their walkie-talkies crackle.

'Giraffe Three and Giraffe Four calling Giraffe Zero. Over.'

Charlie leans over to Colin and says, 'That's Cedric and Ambrose calling Linus Pope.'

Colin raises his eyebrows, indicating he's up to speed on the Giraffe codes.

'Go ahead, caller. Over,' says Pope.

'The herb potter is leaving Silent Pool. Repeat, the herb potter is leaving Silent Pool. Over.'

'I'm guessing that Kevin Hall is the herb potter,' says Colin Beard.

Charlie nods. 'You'll be spy material in no time.'

<><><>

Chapter Forty-Five

Verity puts the walkie-talkie to her mouth.

'This is Giraffe One. I know where the Herb Potter went when he left Silent Pool. He's just knocked on Polly King's front door. Over.'

The crackles precede Linus Pope's voice, 'Information received. Over.'

Verity watches Polly open her front door to greet Kevin Hall like an old friend—or are they lovers? Probably not. But from Polly's face, she's happy to see him. Verity's spy instincts kick in, and she wants a closer look. She sneaks away from her prime position in the cottage and exits through the rear garden gate, stepping into the alley that runs the length of the cottages. She runs to the far end and crosses the lane by the church, cutting through the graveyard under cover of night.

Nothing much else is moving in Shere Village except the lights shining through the pub windows at the far end of the lane and a few drinkers around an outdoor table.

Verity clambers up and over the churchyard's stone wall and drops down into the lane, edging her way towards

Polly's cottage. She turns off her walkie-talkie and eases open the gate next door to Polly's place, then sneaks into the dark garden. Polly and Kevin's voices float on the evening air, and Verity steps barefoot across the grass and presses her ear against the wooden fence. She closes her eyes and blocks her other senses, straining her ears to hear the conversation.

The sound of shells from the pistachio nuts dropping into a saucer and the glug-glug of wine pouring from a bottle waft through the wooden slats in the fence. Verity hears Kevin Hall tell Polly about his visit to Tanglefoot Farm.

They sit in silence for a few minutes.

'Do you think they know?' asks Polly.

Verity freezes. *What do they think we know?* She pushes her ear closer against the fence panel, waiting for an answer. Verity's pumping heartbeat pounds in her ears as her concentration focuses on Hall's next word, but nothing comes.

Come on, Kevin Hall. Say something.

There's nothing but silence until the unmistakable cold metal of a gun barrel tapping her temple. Verity's eyes ping open to see Kevin Hall pointing his pistol at her face.

Cedric and Ambrose stand in the parking area near Silent Pool with their walkie-talkies.

'Come in, Giraffe One. Over,' says Ambrose. 'Verity, are you there?'

Not even a crackle for a reply, just a silent airwave.

'She can be infuriating sometimes,' says Cedric. He presses the button on his walkie-talkie, 'Linus, where's Verity?' He's expecting a reprimand from Linus for his lack of communication protocol.

'Giraffe Three and Four, return to base,' says Linus. 'I repeat, return to base immediately.'

Ambrose stares at his brother, 'He didn't say over.'

'Then something's very wrong,' says Cedric. 'If nothing, Pope is annoyingly consistent and would definitely tell us off for not saying over. We have to return to Tanglefoot Farm as fast as possible.'

Ambrose says, 'It will take too long to walk, and Colin hasn't reached Fulham yet.

'Let's flag down a car and ask for a lift,' says Cedric.

'The driver might be a serial killer.'

'This is the Surrey Hills, dear boy. Although we have had two murders in ten years.'

'Quite so,' says Ambrose. He steps onto the verge next to the road and yells, 'There's a car coming down the hill.'

Together, they step onto the road and frantically flap their arms up and down. There's a screech of tyres and a strong smell of burning rubber as the car slithers and slides to a noisy standstill a few inches from Cedric and Ambrose's knees.

The man in the car screams, 'You idiots! What are you doing? I could have killed you.'

The driver is Wrong Kevin, the man they wrongly accused of killing Randolph Vine.

'Are you a serial killer?' asks Ambrose.

'What?'

'It's quite simple. Are you a serial—'

'Of course, I'm not,' says Wrong Kevin. 'What are you two fools doing? I could have killed you.'

Cedric stands next to Ambrose, 'We need a lift to Friday Street,' he says.

'Sod off!' says Wrong Kevin.

'It's a matter of life and death,' adds Cedric.

'Your death, I hope,' says Wrong Kevin.

'We don't have time to listen to you wittering on,' says Cedric, opening Wrong Kevin's rear door. 'Oh dear, God.' He points to the pizza boxes and piles of mess and closes the door.

Ambrose opens the front passenger door and throws the rubbish into the backseat. He climbs in and waves for Cedric to join him in the front seat.

'Get out!' yells, Wrong Kevin.

Ambrose, doing his best not to touch anything, says, 'Come on, we don't have all day.'

'I'm not a taxi service,' shouts Wrong Kevin.

'If I give you a thousand pounds, will you take us to Friday Street?' says Cedric.

'For a thousand pounds? Yes, I'm not an idiot.'

'Yes, quite. So, you're a man with a car who'll take passengers to their destination for a fee. You sound like a taxi driver to me,' says Cedric.

Wrong Kevin puts the car in gear and pulls out onto the road towards Friday Street.

Cedric says, 'Now, about your fees. I was thinking fifty pounds, not a thousand.'

'You said a thousand!' shouts Wrong Kevin.

'Yes, that was my opening offer to get the vehicle moving in the right direction. My new offer is fifty, but my next number is forty—you get the idea.' Cedric waves the notes in the air.

Wrong Kevin snatches the money and mutters under his breath to Friday Street and all the way up Plum Pudding Lane.

At Tanglefoot Farm, Linus Pope races out to meet them.

'Thank you, Wrong Kevin,' says Ambrose.

'What do you mean, Wrong Kevin?'

'It's a long story which ends with you being completely innocent and fifty pounds up,' says Ambrose. 'So, a good night all round for you.'

Wrong Kevin turns his head towards them, 'Get out of my car, you clowns.'

Cedric and Ambrose meet Linus, and together, they walk around to the ops room, where Linus explains the problem with Verity's walkie-talkie.

'Kevin Hall is not who he says he is,' says Ambrose.

'How do you know?' asks Linus.

'Because the man drove away from his cottage at high speed without his driving gloves and without looking in his mirror. We've not been able to raise Verity since,' says Ambrose.

'There are tracker beacons in each handset,' says Linus. 'As Giraffe Zero, I need to know where you all are at any point.'

'And?' says Cedric. 'Where's Verity?'

'In the garden next door to Polly King's cottage.'

'That's not unusual, is it? She is a spy.'

'She is an ex-spy, but that's not important right now,' says Linus. 'Verity hasn't moved a millimetre in twenty minutes. She's an annoying pro who understands fieldcraft better than anyone in the Service and would never be that amateurish to stand still like that.'

Cedric agrees with Linus, adding, 'Verity doesn't make mistakes. Let's call Colin and Charlie.'

'Maybe the walkie-talkie fell out of her pocket,' suggests Ambrose.

Linus speaks into his walkie-talkie, 'Giraffe Two and Giraffe Five, come in. This is Giraffe Zero. Over.'

No crackles.

Silence.

'G-Two and G-Five, come in. Over.' Linus's voice displays increasing agitation. He repeats his message twice more, then picks up his phone and rings Charlie. It goes to voicemail. 'Something's not right. We need to get to Polly's place and then onto Fulham. Is that cab driver still out the front?'

'That was Wrong Kevin, not a cab driver,' says Ambrose. 'And he hates us.'

'That's understandable,' says Pope.

The three of them weigh up the possibilities before turning as one towards Elsie, gleaming in the garage.

'Oh, no,' says Pope. 'I can't ride that thing.'

'Don't be such a baby. How hard can it be?' says Cedric. 'I've read engineering books.'

'And I've watched Charlie and Verity ride the thing,' says Ambrose. 'I can give you a brief lesson to set you on your way.'

'On *your* way?' says Pope. 'You two are coming with me. If we're to crash and burn, we will crash and burn and go down together.'

They wander across from the ops room towards Elsie. Ambrose bends down and points to a lever on the motorbike.

'I think you kick that downwards, and the engine starts,' he says.

Linus looks at Cedric for reassurance.

Cedric shrugs his shoulders, saying, 'I'm the engineer, not the oily rag.'

Linus sighs, then straddles the motorbike and partly

stands before kicking his foot down lightly on the kick-starter—the engine barely coughs and splutters before returning to silence. Linus tries again with the same result.

'You'll need to flip the fuel switch on,' says a coarse voice from the courtyard. Wrong Kevin stands looking at the three men around Elsie. 'You won't start it in a month of Sundays doing what you're doing.'

'Who are you?' says Pope.

'That's Wrong Kevin,' says Cedric.

'He looks dangerous,' says Pope.

'We thought so too,' says Cedric. 'But looks can be deceiving. He very kindly gave us a lift in his unpleasant car.'

'Do you know how to ride a motorbike, young man?' asks Pope.

Wrong Kevin scoffs, 'I'm a man! Of course I know how to ride a motorbike. What man doesn't?'

Linus, Cedric and Ambrose raise their hands.

Wrong Kevin steps over to the motorbike and sidecar, admiring its beauty. 'This is a classic,' he says, running his eyes over Elsie's lines. He sits astride the saddle, turns on the fuel tap, and then, with one swift kick on the starter, brings the engine roaring to life.

'Let's take your car,' says Pope.

'Unfortunately, Wrong Kevin's car has Lupus,' says Cedric.

'Very well,' says Pope, taking command of the situation. 'Ride us to Shere Village, then onto Fulham in London.'

'It's a bit late for you three lightweights to be roaming about, isn't it?' says Wrong Kevin. 'Alright, I'll take you to Shere, then to Fulham.'

A few minutes later, Wrong Kevin speeds down Plum Pudding Lane. Cedric and Ambrose tightly grip the sidecar's handles, and their cloth corduroy caps hide their fearful looks while Pope holds on for dear life.

Linus turns on the helmet intercom system and directs Wrong Kevin towards Shere Village.

'I've lived here all my life. I know the area like the back of my hand.' Wrong Kevin rode quickly but less enthusiastically than Charlie and Verity.

'Pull up in the churchyard,' Linus says, and when they come to a standstill, he unclips the glass canopy, and Cedric and Ambrose clamber out. 'That wasn't altogether a terrible experience,' says Cedric.

Pope whispers into his walkie-talkie, 'Giraffe One, this is Giraffe Zero. Come in. Over.' He repeats his message several times.

The walkie-talkie offers no response.

'Who the hell is Giraff—'

Wrong Kevin is silenced by Cedric's hand over his mouth. He says, 'It's best if you don't say another word. Stay here!'

Linus Pope leads Cedric and Ambrose to the far side of the graveyard and makes his first attempt to clamber over the wall—his arms don't have the muscle capacity to haul his body up onto the church wall. Cedric and Ambrose try lifting him, but they only manage to rub Linus's face against the brickwork.

'For crying out loud, stop!' shouts Linus, pointing to a long red graze on his nose.

Wrong Kevin stands with his hands on his hips. 'I've never seen such useless men. Move out of the way.' Wrong Kevin hops up on top of the church wall with one leap and reaches down to haul Pope up to join him.

Cedric reaches up, and with Ambrose's help from below and Wrong Kevin pulling from above, he sits on the wall. Wrong Kevin jumps down and pushes Ambrose upwards, and then vaults back up to join the three men who are perching on the church wall.

They jump down the other side and run along the lane behind the cottages until they reach the garden next door to Polly King's place.

'What's in there?' whispers Wrong Kevin.

'We don't know,' says Pope. 'But Britain's best ex-spy has gone missing, and the last place her walkie-talkie registered a beep was behind this gate.'

Wrong Kevin says, 'What are you waiting for then?'

Cedric says, 'A dangerous man could still be in the garden.'

'Who is this dangerous man?' says Wrong Kevin.

'Kevin Hall,' says Linus Pope.

'That's my name,' says Wrong Kevin.

'No, your name is Wrong Kevin,' says Ambrose.

Wrong Kevin pushes the gate open.

<><><>

Chapter Forty-Six

Yuri's garden is in darkness. On Charlie's previous visit, hundreds of fairy lights twinkled in the trees—but not tonight.

Charlie sits behind the pool house and tries contacting Colin on the walkie-talkie, 'Giraffe Five, this is Giraffe Two. I'm in position. Over.' Charlie releases her finger from the walkie-talkie and waits for his reply. She repeats her message, but nothing.

A twig cracks behind her like a rifle shot, and Charlie turns with her fists in a fighting pose, ready to take down her assailant.

'Calm down, it's me,' says Colin with his hands in the air.

'I could have killed you,' she says. 'You shouldn't creep up on people like that.'

'Our walkie-talkies are down. I can't get hold of anyone,' he says. 'We're on our own out here.'

Charlie signals for him to stay out of sight behind the pool house and then steps out onto the perfectly mowed lawn, edging towards the rear of the house. She can't see any lights inside the house—maybe Yuri is in Eastbourne again visiting his father. Charlie reaches for the side door's handle and gives it a pull. It's locked. Kneeling, she takes her lockpick tool from her back pocket and slips the curved blade into the centre of the lock, twisting it this way and that. She listens like a safe cracker for the tumbler to catch, then pulls the handle and opens the side door ajar.

A hand falls heavily on her shoulder, and she jumps like a cat.

'It's only me again,' says Colin.

'For a big man, you're light on your feet,' she says.

'I need to warn you that you're committing a crime,' says Colin.

'And you're the getaway driver!' she says. 'Keep quiet and follow me.'

Charlie eases the side door open and steps inside the darkened house. They stand in the hallway, waiting for the creaks and groans to fall silent. An empty building usually has an air about it, but not this one. There's someone here.

Charlie inches her way to the end of the hallway and peeps around the corner. It's clear, so she waves at Colin to join her. He reminds her that a stakeout involves watching a house from the road or a bush, not from inside the target property—it's too late now to make a stand against her decision to go in. Colin would not have worn his Hawaiian shirt if he thought for one moment he would be breaking into a Russian mid-level mobster's house.

The telephone on the desk in the study rings. And in a silent house, the sound resonates like a school fire bell; such is the echo in the cavernous place. Charlie and Colin jump for cover in the library opposite, and both have their hands over their hearts from the shock.

Heavy footsteps descend the staircase, then clomp

along the hallway and into the unlit study. The telephone stops ringing when the receiver is lifted.

A moment passes before, 'Yes, this is Vladimir.' There's another pause, then, 'I think they know.'

In the library, Charlie removes her hand from her mouth and, without a sound, mouths, 'Vladimir.'

Colin nods.

Charlie takes a half step towards the library door and stands in the opening. At the same time, a key turns in the front door at the end of the hallway. Charlie ducks back into the library, pushing Colin behind the leather sofa, but he's a big man, and at least two parts of him are exposed.

'Why is it so dark in here?' mutters Yuri. The sound of flicking switches follows, and lights in the hallway and kitchen ping on, casting light into the library.

'Dad! Are you here?' Yuri's voice echoes around the empty house.

'In the study, Yuri,' bellows Vladimir.

'Are you hungry?' asks Yuri.

'I'm starving. One more meal at that daft care home, and I'll take up killing again.'

Yuri says, 'I think we can safely say you've been discharged, Dad. It's served its purpose. Why are you sitting in the dark? Come on, let's get something to eat.' Their footsteps pad through to the kitchen.

Outside the library, Vladimir stops and says, 'I had a phone call from my handler.'

In the lane behind Polly King's next-door neighbour's garden, Wrong Kevin walks through the gate first. The lights from Polly's garden shine through the gaps in the fence.

Linus Pope puts his finger to his mouth, showing everyone to be quiet, and Cedric picks up Verity's walkie-talkie from the grass. The four men stare through tiny holes in the fence into Polly King's garden, where she's sitting alone, sipping wine and shelling pistachios.

After a few minutes of silent staring, Linus Pope waves them towards the garden gate and back into the lane. Then, without talking, they walk back to the church and clamber over the wall into the graveyard.

Cedric pulls them into a small circle, 'If Verity was taken, then it must have been Kevin Hall.'

'What?' says Wrong Kevin. 'How could I—'

'Not you, buttercup,' says Ambrose.

Cedric adds, 'Let's get over to Silent Pool and see if Verity is there with Hall.'

Wrong Kevin kickstarts Elsie and closes the glass lid on the sidecar. He eases the motorbike out of the churchyard and turns at the junction, where the outdoor drinkers chatter and laugh, completely oblivious to the evening's dangerous doings. The road is quiet, and Wrong Kevin opens up the power, whizzing Elsie through the small villages towards Silent Pool.

'Stop in the layby opposite the parking bay,' says Linus.

'How do you know your friend is here?' asks Wrong Kevin.

'Because, Wrong Kevin, this is not our first day on the job,' says Linus. 'Come on, follow me.'

Cedric looks at Ambrose, 'Has Pope been on a how-to-take-charge course?'

Linus leads the way along the path past the pool and into the woodland at the rear of Kevin Hall's cottage. There's no sign of the brown Volvo, and the cottage is in darkness.

'It's that one,' says Cedric. 'The one with a thousand potted herbs.'

Linus steps through a gap in the fence where a gate used to hang.

'Verity kicked it off its hinges last time we visited,' says Ambrose.

Linus marches towards the cottage door and knocks. There's no answer. He knocks again. Nothing,

Wrong Kevin pushes his face against the window, saying, 'I can't see anything.'

'Go and check around the other side,' says Cedric.

'Why me?' asks Wrong Kevin.

'Because you have extra special spy-like qualities,' adds Ambrose. 'Cedric can spot a spy in the making from a hundred miles away. You, my boy, have got what it takes, hasn't he, Linus?'

'Oh yes,' says Pope. 'The lad is top-notch, super-spy material.'

Wrong Kevin soaks up the buttery comments and strides around the cottage with his chin held high.

<><><>

Chapter Forty-Seven

Verity

I was taken by surprise at gunpoint once before, but that was a long time ago.

Of all the people. . . Kevin *bloody* Hall!

How did I let that lightweight fool creep up on me so easily in the garden? Of course, I know the answer. I was focusing all my attention on Polly and left myself unguarded. And for that, I now find myself chained to a damp wall in this damp basement in Hall's cottage. I hate to admit when I'm outsmarted, but I was outsmarted, and he caught me fair and square.

But Kevin *bloody* Hall!

So, here I am—ankles and wrists professionally chained to solid rings bolted to the dank wall, and I'm blindfolded and gagged. He did a number on me. Hall bundled me into his brown Volvo at gunpoint and brought me here, chained me to the wall, and then I heard him drive off.

Who uses a Volvo to snatch a top spy at gunpoint? I still consider myself a top spy, but to look at me now in the darkness, anyone would think it was my first day on the job.

There's no point getting het up in a situation like this. I've been caught, so now's the time I spend my full attention on getting away, not moaning about my predicament.

But, Kevin *bloody* Hall.

Alright, enough. Get a grip, Verity Fanthorpe.

The first question I always ask myself to get my mind to focus on the next step is, What do I know? Firstly, Kevin Hall is good—he snatched me, which makes him good, and I'm feeling slightly better already. It was a stealthy snatch at gunpoint, put into a Volvo, and chained professionally in the basement. So what is he? Rogue MI6, FBI, CIA, ex-KGB? He could be any of the alphabet agencies. I'll figure out which one later.

There's a loud knock on the door upstairs, and I hear Linus Pope's voice calling through the letterbox. I rattle my chains and yell out through my gag, but he won't hear me from my dungeon.

Am I being rescued by Linus Pope? That's a new low. Actually, I doubt he'll save me because he doesn't have what it takes to kick Hall's door down and search the cottage. I'm stuck here until I die.

I was a prisoner in Russia back in my spying days. The KGB suspected everyone of being a double agent in the Cold War, and on one occasion, I was the subject of their spotlight. And a pretty ugly spotlight, I can tell you. They didn't waterboard me. That was more a CIA torture method. The Soviets loved injecting you with hallucinogenic substances to get you talking, but the British produced some heavy-duty antidotes that worked like a vaccine. It might have been a placebo; either way, I didn't crack under pressure or under questioning and after a long weekend of imprisonment, I was free to return to Vladimir.

I pull against my chains and remind myself to focus on getting out of this pokey little basement. So, who is Kevin Hall? The murderer? Did he kill Randolph Vine and Joshua King? He's undoubtedly pushed himself up the charts of suspects to the number one spot. Why take me at gunpoint and chain me up if he's innocent? So, by definition, he's definitely guilty, but of what I still don't know, apart from kidnapping, of course.

Somebody is tapping on the back door and shouting my name, but it's not Linus. I don't know who it is, but his voice sounds young—a young man—I don't know any young men. That's sad as I used to know all the young men. Is it Yuri? No, it can't be him.

Kevin Hall chained me in a stress position. That's how I know he's good. I can't quite sit down, and my arms are slightly above my head. I used to chain people up the same way—it's the most painful and exhausting position because you can't rest or sleep. In a strange way, it's good news because it suggests Kevin Hall is coming back. He wants me worn down, not dead. Not yet.

A plan is forming—not a good one, but a plan all the same. The problem with plans is that they fall apart the moment you engage the enemy, and knowing this can save your life. It's not the plan that matters; it's the adjustment to your plan that matters.

I lean against the wall and try to relax my aching arms. There's no way to get comfortable, and at seventy-five, being comfortable is the focus of most days—every day. But I wouldn't want anyone to know I have a footbath.

'Kevin *bloody* Hall!' I scream through my gag.

How can I use my anger to turn this around? Usually, I'd shoot someone, but those days are over, plus I don't have a gun.

I didn't hear the front door open, but I hear it close, and then footsteps, not clompy footsteps, but they have a purpose. The lock in the door at the top of the basement stairs clicks, and the hinges give the faintest squeak.

The footsteps pound to the bottom of the staircase, and the fine hairs on my arms alert me to the looming danger. Whoever it is, I'll give them something to think about.

I can't see anything through the blindfold and do my best to muffle my words through the gag.

'Well done,' I say. 'Excellent timing. Would you mind scratching my chin? It's been itchy for ages. I should have asked earlier, but I didn't know you'd be gone so long.'

I say chin for a particular reason: I can't punch or kick with these chains. But I can bite and use my head.

The faintest slither of light is visible under my blindfold, and I see a man's hand reaching for my chin. The owner of the approaching hand makes a terrible mistake when they take a half step closer to me. Their hand leads to their arm, their arm leads to their shoulder, their shoulder is next to their neck, and their neck has a head on top. And I smash my head against theirs. I'm prepared, but they're not, and down they go, wailing.

The crying goes on a bit, not from me, followed by a lot of swearing, also not from me. The gag and blindfold are unceremoniously ripped from my face, and the rush of light fuzzes my vision.

In front of me, a man doubles over, holding his face. Finally, he stands up straight with blood pumping from a gash on the bridge of his nose.

He yells, 'What did you do that for?'

'Who are you?' I say.

'Kevin Hall!'

'My God, how long have I been down here? You had hair, and now you're bald with tattoos and, oddly, twenty years younger!'

Cedric appears at the bottom of the basement steps and says, 'Verity, this is Wrong Kevin.'

I say, 'Wrong Kevin should learn never to scratch a lady's chin when she's chained to a wall.'

Cedric says, 'Let's get you out of here before the real Kevin Hall returns.'

Am I surrounded by amateurs? They don't seem to understand that I am in complete control of the situation. It doesn't look that way, but I've got Kevin Hall exactly where I want him.

I ask Cedric, 'What happened?'

'We were on a stakeout,' he says. 'Kevin Hall left here, and we followed him.'

'First rule of a stakeout,' I say. 'Never leave your post. That's what the walkie-talkies are for.'

'That's true, but yours went dead,' he says.

Cedric made the right call to follow him. Most plodders would follow the rules and sit like a dummy waiting for an order. Cedric and Ambrose are thinkers. Annoying but clever.

Wrong Kevin, with blood down his shirt, says to me, 'You broke my nose.'

'Would you like me to hug you to my bosom and sing Kumbaya? I heard it helps.'

'No!' He manages to say between pitiful cries.

'Get out of here then,' I shout.

'Why?' says Wrong Kevin.

'Because I want to catch the real Kevin Hall. Now, put my blindfold and gag back in place and bugger off!'

Noses are messy when they break, and there's blood on the floor. I'll think of something witty to say to Hall when he returns. Wrong Kevin and Cedric run up the stairs, and I hear the front door close behind them.

My plan is based on bluster. Come to think of it, all my plans are based on bluster. I'll shout at Kevin Hall until he... until something happens.

I think thirty minutes, maybe forty, have passed since Cedric and Wrong Kevin left. I should have gone to the toilet.

I try crossing my legs. I can't quite cross them.

Yes, I should have definitely gone to the toilet. I'll have to explain more than blood on the floor any minute.

<><><>

Chapter Forty-Eight

Charlie

Colin Beard is a heavy breather. He could wake the dead.

He's a mountain of a man, and in a silent room, when he breaths in, he sounds like a wheezy old smoker, and his out-breaths sound like a rattling air conditioning unit. I'm not going to whisper to him to breathe quietly in case he's someone who can't whisper.

Yuri is with Vladimir in the kitchen, and we're held up in the library in the dark. My walkie-talkie is dead, and I can't get a signal on my phone. I should turn it off to be safe. No, I'll leave it on; you never know.

It turns out Vladimir doesn't have dementia. Instead, he sounds as sharp as a pin. Why would he trick Verity like that? I don't see the gain. Maybe he's giving her a dose of her own medicine—she faked her death—he faked his dementia. I strain my ears above Colin's rattling iron lung to hear what Yuri and Vladimir are saying, but I can't fathom a thing.

I edge myself along the library wall to the door frame and ease my head slowly into the hallway to look into the kitchen. Vladimir is leaning against the island while the lovely Yuri: no, wait, just Yuri, I must remain in stakeout mode, is pouring two glasses of wine. I take four steady steps into the hallway while staying out of their line of sight.

I signal to Colin for him to stay in the library with his loud shirt and even louder breathing. I don't know why I hadn't noticed it before. Honestly, he sounds like a giant pair of bellows you find at a glass-blowing foundry.

I watch Yuri pass his father a glass of wine. Vladimir takes a sip and nods. What are they talking about? I can get closer, but will I find they're talking in Russian? I'm caught in indecision. What would Verity do? She'd run into the kitchen, punch them both in the face and finish their wine, calling them a couple of losers.

But I'm not Verity Fanthorpe—I wish I had her confidence about making decisions. She's the most impressive person I've ever met. I summon my inner Verity and edge closer to the kitchen door so I can hear the mumble of their chatter, but I'm not close enough to determine what they're saying. Their body language suggests they're discussing a problem.

There's a firm tap on my shoulder, and I just about faint.

It's Colin again, and it takes every ounce of restraint not to shout at him. Instead, I freeze when I hear Yuri say my father's name. My ears blank out the world as I wait for any following words. None come.

I push Colin back into the library and tell him I heard Yuri say Randolph Vine's name.

Colin whispers into my ear, 'We need to get out of here.'

He's half right—he needs to go.

I'm staying.

The ever-perceptive ex-police officer reads my mind and indicates with his finger that both of us are leaving. Even when Colin presses himself against the library wall, Colin's waistline is visible from the hallway, and his shirt is probably visible from across the street.

I hear Yuri and Vladimir put their glasses on the countertop, and their voices grow louder as they approach the hallway. There isn't an excuse in the world I can use to explain why I'm standing in his library with a retired policeman.

Oh, hi Yuri, I was admiring your wallpaper.

Oh, hi Yuri, I left my purse the last time I was here.

Oh, hi Yuri, this is Colin, and he wants to buy a house in Fulham, so I thought I'd break in and show him yours.

I hold my breath, which is pointless because I'm standing beside Old Wheezy. Yuri and his father stand in the hallway, chatting in Russian. They are on the other side of the wall, no more than an arm's length away from me.

Verity, the super-spy, speaks Russian. She should have come here, and I should have staked out Polly King's cottage in Shere. I came here to be near Yuri, and how did that work out for me? My silly heart ruled my head.

I'm straining my ears to listen for another mention of my father, but it's impossible. And then, in English, as if for my benefit, Yuri says, 'Did the kill order come from your handler?'

'Kill order?' scoffs Vladimir. 'That's a little Cold War.'

They laugh, and I hear the stairs creak. I ease my head around the library door opening to see Yuri helping his father up the stairs. I signal for Colin to follow me, and we dash for the side door and run out into the garden. Behind the pool house, breathing like an old diesel generator, Colin gives me the thumbs up.

'Are you having fun?' I ask.

'Loving it,' he says. 'It takes me back to being on the serious crime squad, chasing bad guys and putting them in jail.'

'Did you hear Yuri say, Kill order?'

Colin nods as he finally catches his breath and says, 'Do you think Yuri was referring to Joshua King?'

'Or my dad?'

'I don't speak Russian, so I'm useless to you,' says Colin.

'We are the only two non-Russian speakers on the team,' I tell him.

Colin shrugs, 'Cedric and Ambrose would not have broken into the house so they wouldn't have even heard the Russian chatter.'

I agree.

Verity Fanthorpe would have grabbed Vladimir and Yuri and punched them until they confessed. It's funny because here I am in Vladimir's garden while Verity is doing absolutely nothing, staking out Polly King in the sleepy Shere village in the Surrey Hills.

She got the easy one.

Next time, Verity Fanthorpe, you get the tough assignment.

<><><>

Chapter Forty-Nine

Verity is close to peeing her purple dungarees. However, wetting herself is momentarily postponed as someone opens the basement door and stomps down the stone steps. 'Thank goodness you're back. I need to pee!' she yells through the gag and blindfold.

Kevin Hall unshackles her hands from the chains and places a yellow bucket in front of her. 'I've got a pistol trained on you, so don't do anything stupid.'

Verity unclips her dungarees, removes her blindfold and gag, and grabs the bucket. Kevin Hall watches her every move.

'I can feel you watching me. Turn around, you creep!' she orders.

He turns away while keeping his hostage in his peripheral vision.

A string of oohs and ahhs follow from Verity as she pulls her dungarees back up, saying, 'Thank you, Kevin, that's much better. You can chain me back up again if you like.' She offers her wrists to him for re-chaining.

He dismisses her hands, saying, 'No funny business.

I've still got my pistol and won't miss from this range.' He slides a wooden stool towards her with his foot and indicates for her to sit.

Verity pushes the yellow bucket aside and makes herself comfortable on the small stool. She stares at Hall for a minute, then says, 'What are you, ex-KGB?'

'What makes you say that?'

'I can see it in your eyes,' she says. 'I met your type many times. You can leave Russia, but Russia can never leave you. You sound English, you look English, you grow herbs, and you'll fool everyone except those who know better.'

Kevin Hall smirks, 'And you know better? It's laughable how little you know.'

'I know you killed Randolph Vine and Joshua King,' she says.

Hall's laughter borders hysteria.

Verity whispers, 'I planned to be here in your basement, and now I've got you just where I want you.'

Hall doesn't catch her words and waves his pistol in a circular motion for her to repeat. She whispers even more softly about her plan to be in his basement, and he moves closer to hear what she's saying.

That was his second mistake. His first was not re-chaining her hands to the wall.

Verity punches Hall on his chin with a beautifully timed uppercut, and he crumples in a heap on the damp floor. He lets out a squeal as his eyes roll and close.

Verity reaches into Hall's pocket for the keys and unlocks the chains around her ankles. She drags him into a comfortable position and loosens his clothing. The chains lock tightly around his ankles, and she puts the key in her pocket. Verity moves the yellow bucket within easy reach—there's never a need to be unkind, she thinks.

She takes Kevin Hall's phone and slips quietly up the stone steps and out of his cottage into the night air, then runs across the fields to Friday Street.

Wrong Kevin handles Elsie with ease as they speed towards Fulham.

Linus Pope speaks into his mouthpiece, 'Wrong Kevin, you should see Charlie's black Jaguar on the corner of the street up ahead. Park as close as you can to it.'

Wrong Kevin salutes to show receipt of the message. On arrival, Linus Pope points to Vladimir's house and says, 'You enter the house from the rear, and while you're in there, I'll guard Elsie because, as the communication officer, I can raise the alarm if anything happens.'

'You big sissy,' says Wrong Kevin.

'I like him,' says Cedric, pointing at Wrong Kevin. 'He has an eye for a big sissy.'

Ambrose pats Wrong Kevin on the back. 'Lead on.'

Linus sinks into the sidecar and whispers into the walkie-talkie.

'Giraffe Two, come in. Giraffe Two, come in. Over.'

The line is dead. He calls Charlie on his phone, and instantly, the call diverts to voicemail.

Wrong Kevin runs across the road and clambers through a hedge. Cedric and Ambrose follow. The three of them gather at the rear gate of Vladimir's garden. It's open ajar, and Cedric encourages Wrong Kevin to peer through.

'What can you see?' whispers Ambrose.

Wrong Kevin brings his head back through the gate and

says, 'There's a giant man wearing a Hawaiian shirt and that girl who looks very mean.'

'Good. That's Colin and Charlie,' says Cedric. 'Wave them over.'

Wrong Kevin steps inside the gate and catches Charlie's attention. He waves her over, and a few minutes later, they all walk towards the black Jaguar and Elsie.

'What's Wrong Kevin doing here?' asks Charlie.

'Saving the day,' says Wrong Kevin.

'Is that why you have a red nose and your shirt is covered in blood?'

Wrong Kevin sniffs and says, 'I met Verity and—'

'Say no more,' laughs Charlie. 'Where's Linus?'

'On the front line,' says Cedric. 'Hiding in the sidecar.'

'I know who killed my dad,' says Charlie.

'So do we,' says Ambrose.

Verity arrives at Tanglefoot Farm and breathes deeply while stretching her legs against the sofa in the ops room.

Did Kevin Hall murder Randolph Vine and Joshua King? When she caught him with her uppercut, she thought there would be more to him if he had the wherewithal to kill two highly trained agents—he's too soft to be a killer. If anything, he's too much like Linus Pope.

Verity pours herself a large brandy from the drinks cabinet in her campervan and sits on the metal step, sipping and thinking. There's always something staring you right in the face: a clue that doesn't look like a clue. She takes Kevin Hall's phone from her pocket.

It's locked: facial recognition is required.

She finishes her brandy and considers the fastest way to get to Silent Pool to use Kevin Hall's stupid face to open his phone. Her campervan has a dead battery and won't start, so she enters the garage and removes a dusty old blanket covering boxes and oddments.

And there it is an old bicycle. The rusty chain hasn't seen action in thirty years, but after a dozen generous glugs of Cedric and Ambrose's expensive extra virgin olive oil, the bicycle was ready for the ride of its life.

Verity climbs aboard the heavy machine, tucks her dungarees into her socks, and begins peddling down Plum Pudding Lane as if she's leading the peloton in the Tour de France.

Each jarring bump in the road is met with an equally loud yelp from Verity as the hard leather saddle catches her in all the wrong places. By the time she reaches the bottom of the lane, it occurs to her that this is not the best time to test the brakes.

'Oh, buggeration!' screams Verity as she repeatedly pulls on the non-responsive brake levers. She crosses the junction and weaves onto the dark road leading to Silent Pool. She misses three cars by inches and decides that speed is her friend, so she continues peddling like fury. It's too late now to consider the inherent dangers of cycling at night on unlit roads without bicycle lights or brakes.

Verity rides as far up Kevin Hall's rutted track as possible before leaning the bike against a tree and running into the cottage. She barges through the front door and races down the basement steps to find a groggy Kevin Hall leaning against the damp wall.

'I need your daft face to access your phone,' says Verity, panting.

Hall closes his eyes and turns away, burying his chin into his neck.

Verity kicks his foot, saying, 'I can always take your ugly

head with me in a shopping bag if you prefer.' As she speaks, she makes a sawing action across her throat, 'What do you say, Kev?'

Aware of his limited options, he sighs, showing his face, and with a few taps on his phone, Verity disables any need for future face recognition or passwords. She walks towards the steps.

Hall shouts out, 'Are you leaving me here like this?'

'Would you like to hear the other option?'

He says, 'Can it be any worse than being chained up?'

'Of course, it can, you chump. The other option involves butter and a carrot!' Verity climbs the steps and runs back to her bicycle. She pedals to Tanglefoot Farm and pushes the bike into the corner of the garage.

Taking her refilled brandy glass, she slumps onto the ops room sofa and scrolls through Kevin Hall's phone. And what a treasure trove it's proving to be.

Charlie's black Jaguar with Colin Beard at the wheel squeals around the courtyard, followed by Elsie and a full team on board. Within a few minutes, they all have a glass of something strong and squeeze onto the sofa, except Cedric and Ambrose, who don't care for proximity sitting.

'I know who killed my dad,' says Charlie.

'That's great, me too,' says Verity.

'I'll go first,' says Charlie. 'It's Vladimir.'

'No, you're wrong, it's Kevin Hall,' says Verity.

They look at each other with an edge of disbelief.

'You can't both be right,' says Cedric. 'But you can both be wrong.'

<><><>

Chapter Fifty

The silence in the ops room lasts a few seconds before a full-on debate takes place about who killed Randolph Vine and Joshua King.

'I know it's late, but would anyone like some cheese on toast?' asks Ambrose.

Food is so often the best way to change the direction of a heated debate, and a chorus of oohs and ahhs soon replaces the bold claims of who murdered who.

'Is it always like this?' asks Wrong Kevin, who somehow is still there.

Linus Pope shakes his head, 'Goodness, no, Wrong Kevin. Sometimes it's a lot worse. For example, fights have started in this courtyard over a spelling disagreement, and fierce arguments have lasted the whole weekend over a disputed answer in a general knowledge quiz.'

Cedric leans over, adding, 'And Linus Pope should know. He is the A-to-B of general knowledge.'

Linus says, 'Don't you mean A-to-Z.'

Cedric says, 'No, A-to-B is your limit.'

Wrong Kevin asks Pope if he's a spy like Verity.

Cedric, failing to contain himself, says, 'Linus Pope dresses up as a shepherd when he's a spy.'

'Why does he do that?' asks Wrong Kevin.

'Because he's a shepherd's pie,' says Cedric.

The laughter took a while to settle, and with perfect timing, Ambrose puts a colossal tray of buttered toast with melted cheese on the small table in the ops room, and calmness returns once more to Tanglefoot Farm.

Verity puts a finger in the air, claiming the airwaves to make her point. 'Kevin Hall took me at gunpoint and chained me to his basement wall. He must be the leading suspect.'

'A lot of people want to take you at gunpoint,' says Pope. 'We can't all be guilty of murdering Randolph Vine.'

Charlie reaches for another slice of cheesy toast and delivers her case as if in a courtroom. 'In Fulham, I heard Vladimir say on a phone call, *I think they know.* A few minutes later, Yuri asked Vladimir *if the kill order had come from his handler?*'

Verity puts her hand up to stop any further conversation. 'Wait! Vladimir was in the house in Fulham?'

Charlie gulps down her toast. 'Yes. And he was fully coherent. I mean, no sign of dementia. He was talking on the phone as clear as day.'

'Dementia comes and goes. It means nothing,' says Verity, defending her ex-husband.

Holding three pieces of cheese on toast, Colin Beard says, 'The man skipped down the stairs like Fred Astaire in a Broadway musical and made a phone call. I can tell you, Vladimir looked like a man with no hint of a disorder.'

Verity sinks into the sofa as if the weight of the new revelation is too great to shoulder.

Colin Beard gestures as if he's about to make a further

point, but before he speaks, Charlie says, 'And the winner for the noisiest breather and nearly giving away our hiding spot goes to,' she points to Colin with a wide smile.

Colin takes a half-theatrical bow.

Charlie asks, 'And where's Kevin Hall now?'

'Chained to his basement wall,' says Verity. 'Even though I'm convinced he's ex-KGB, we can't leave him there all night. He might die.' She takes out Hall's phone and shows it to the group before handing it to Charlie.

Using a short double-width cable, Charlie plugs Hall's phone into her phone and, with the dexterity of a teenager, begins tapping a long code into a private Government app. She scrolls through his contacts and looks up, saying, 'Well, this is interesting. Kevin Hall knows Vladimir and Yuri. They are hidden contacts in his address book with coded names.'

'When was their last contact?' asks Cedric.

Charlie flicks into the call log. 'Hall made a call to Vladimir's home phone number that lasted three minutes and forty-one seconds at the exact time Colin and I were hiding in Vladimir's library.'

'A call that long is not a misdial,' adds Ambrose.

'Any messages between them?' asks Beard.

'No,' says Charlie. 'Hall could have deleted them, and I'll need my work equipment to find those.'

Verity takes the last piece of cheese on toast and says, 'We should mix things up a bit. Let's send Vladimir a message from Hall's phone asking for a face-to-face meeting.'

Cedric adds, 'We should round everyone up in one place, so let's send the message to Yuri and Polly as well.' He looks at Verity and Charlie for confirmation.

They both nod in agreement.

'How about inviting them to The Stephan Langton pub,' says Ambrose. 'Shall we say tomorrow evening at seven-thirty? It's poetic for the murderer to return to the scene of their crime.'

Charlie taps out a message on Hall's phone and sends it to their suspects: *Meet me for dinner in Friday Street at the Stephan Langton Pub tomorrow at 7:30.*

Yuri responds first with a simple – *Yes.*

Vladimir replies – *Yes, why are you messaging in English?*

Polly replies – *I would love that. See you tomorrow, goodnight.*

The late evening drifts on until all is quiet in the ops room, and Charlie and Winnie cuddle on the sofa.

Charlie sees Cedric and Ambrose's heads bobbing around in the kitchen, cleaning up from the epic mountain of cheese on toast. Verity, who finally ran out of steam, began nodding off on the sofa and finally headed off to her campervan. She'd had quite the day.

Wrong Kevin drove Colin to Kevin Hall's basement with a supply of food and water.

Charlie opens the crossword book and looks at the three baffling answers as if the solution will appear because of her concentration. *Elision, KPH, giant killer.* Her tired mind draws a blank, and she concedes the day is over.

<><><>

Chapter Fifty-One

Good ideas rarely interrupt you at a convenient time.

A few minutes after three in the morning, Charlie sits bolt upright, throws the duvet cover to one side, and leaps out of bed. Winnie didn't move a muscle; she never does in the middle of the night. Charlie reaches for her leather jacket, slides it over her pyjamas, and wriggles into her jeans. She bounds downstairs and out into the ghostly, quiet courtyard. The gravel crunches underfoot as she marches over to Verity's campervan.

She taps on the door.

Nothing.

'Verity,' she whispers—still nothing.

Charlie bangs three times on the thin door with the side of her clenched fist: what her father called the Gestapo knock.

The door swooshes open, and Verity appears naked, her bird's nest hair more out of control than usual. It's hard to think of something to say to someone who is nude.

'Grab your dungarees,' says Charlie.

Verity grabs her clothes and steps outside onto the gravel.

'Why are you naked?'

'It's an old spy trick,' says Verity.

'What sort of trick?'

'For the life of me, I can't remember,' she says, buckling up her dungarees. 'Where are we going?'

'To look something up. Get in,' says Charlie. They climb into the Jaguar, and the meaty exhaust bellows over the silent hills. Halfway down Plum Pudding Lane, Charlie jumps out, clambers up the slippery bank, and runs across the field. The damp grass claws at her ankles as she stomps her way to Linus Pope's house.

Instead of a quiet tap, she employs the Gestapo knock while praying Pope doesn't use the same naked spy trick as Verity. The door opens ajar.

'Oh, it's you,' says Pope.

'Good, you're not naked!'

'Why would anyone answer the door naked?' he says.

Charlie shakes her head to dismiss the conversation and starts a new topic. 'I need to get into the office.'

He looks at his watch and makes no attempt to stifle a yawn, 'Why are you telling me this at three-fifteen in the morning?'

'Because we're going now. Get your shoes on.'

Pope opens his mouth, but before he can protest, Charlie repeats her demands, and he puts his hands in the air in defeat. A moment later, they are striding across the field to the burbling Jaguar in the lane. She points for Pope to sit in the backseat, and the Surrey Hills once more is alive with the Jaguar's roar.

At that time of night, Friday Street is asleep. The road leading to London is asleep, but London life is far from comatose. Stragglers coming out of clubs meander on and off the road as Charlie navigates past the American Embassy with its numerous tower block buildings to the goliath cream and green building of MI6 at Vauxhall Cross.

On the journey, Pope made a security call to gain access for an out-of-hours visit, and the guards at the barrier took less than a minute to wave them through to the inner spiral road leading down to the basement.

Two armed guards stand in front of the vehicle, and three members of security open the car doors.

Verity steps out of the car and says, 'Oh, I remember now. You're seventeen per cent less likely to get shot if you're naked.'

'Did you make that up?' asks Charlie.

'There's an eight-two per cent chance that I did.'

MI6 is a twenty-four-hour operation with activity on every floor serving intelligence operations around the world.

Charlie sits at her desk and switches her attention from giant screen to giant screen on two desktop computers with the aptitude and speed of a hacker on the run.

Verity lurks over her shoulder while Linus potters about in his office.

'What are you looking for?' asks Verity.

'A Russian news story from the late eighties.'

'Berlin Wall era?' asks Verity.

Charlie nods without taking her eyes from her search, which has the potential to take several hours. She explains to Verity what to look for and sets her up with a screen next to her workstation. The side-by-side screens scroll with countless Russian newspaper articles.

After three hours of scrolling, searching and reading,

Charlie and Verity head into Pope's office with a box full of printed material.

Pope is on the phone and points at two leather chairs, indicating for them to take a seat. He continues to take notes while listening with a furrowed forehead.

'Are you sure?' he says. Pope pulls a face and adds, 'Thank you for your help. I really owe you one. Goodnight, or rather, good morning.' He leans back in his chair.

'Did your troublesome paperclip order go through alright,' says Verity.

He looks at her and says, 'Verity Fanthorpe, I know you think I do nothing other than order stationery, but you told me to ask my paymaster how Randolph Vine was murdered. On that phone call, I heard the transcript from the toxicology report, the official one.' He turns to Charlie, 'Your father was poisoned with ricin. Just like Joshua King.'

Charlie opens her mouth, but nothing comes out. Verity takes over and thanks Pope for unearthing the truth.

'Did you get what you came for?' he asks.

At first, Charlie struggles to get her words in the proper order, then says, 'To be honest, it's not conclusive, but it gives us an edge.'

They make their way to the basement, and Charlie fires up the Jaguar. She drives back up the spiral track and exits through the security gates.

The wispy layers of pink and blue clouds high in the mackerel sky suggest a lovely day ahead. Charlie turns right and follows the Thames to the outskirts of London and back into the Surrey Hills.

Halfway up Plum Pudding Lane, Linus steps from the car and scrambles up the grass bank. Charlie shouts a hearty thank you, and he waves and disappears across the field in the early morning sunshine.

'He puts up with a lot from us,' says Charlie.

'Now you come to mention it, you're right,' says Verity. 'And another, but a far more important thing, I'm starving. What shall we have for breakfast?'

Charlie swings the Jaguar around Tanglefoot Farm and parks in the courtyard where Cedric and Ambrose are watering their potted herbs with a long spout watering can.

'You're up early,' says Charlie.

'We're always up early,' says Ambrose. 'It's you who hasn't seen this part of the day too often.'

'Breakfast?' asks Cedric.

Charlie and Verity slump on the ops room sofa and study the pile of printouts, and within a minute, Ambrose reappears with a pot of coffee and two glasses of freshly squeezed nectarine juice.

The Russian newspaper stories follow the events before and after the fall of the Berlin Wall. Charlie lays the pages in date order from left to right on the floor. The fifty pages show the developing story of the Russian courier blamed for the inevitable downfall of communism—a scapegoat in the extreme. Who would have thought swapping a page of questions and answers with a blank piece of paper would have brought down the Berlin Wall and communism? However, the courier faced a gruesome execution as a result.

Charlie says, 'Do you think my father would have carried out the envelope swap knowing that the Russians would execute the courier and the subsequent suicide of his wife?'

Verity alternates between sipping coffee and nectarine juice.

She says, 'A spy must follow orders from central command because only the person running the operation can see all the pieces on the board. Your father would have been too close to his part of the op to know the consequences of his actions. Saying that, I think Randolph and Joshua would still have swapped the list of answers for the blank sheet of paper because the lives they saved far outweighed the courier's life and the life of his wife. However awful, it's what we are trained to do.'

'But that's a bit like playing God,' says Charlie.

'Yes, it is,' says Verity.

Charlie sits in contemplation.

Neither move until Cedric brings two plates of scrambled eggs on sourdough toast, sauteed mushrooms and homemade hash browns. The deepest thoughts can only be interrupted by breakfast. It's a fact.

<><><>

Chapter Fifty-Two

Colin Beard and Wrong Kevin take shifts through the night, watching Kevin Hall, who remains chained to the wall.

'Cup of tea?' asks Wrong Kevin as the sun starts peeping through the cracks under the basement door.

Kevin Hall opens his eyes and nods wearily.

Wrong Kevin climbs the stone stairs and wanders into the kitchen, where Colin Beard is making a ham sandwich.

'So what's the deal with the old boy down there?' says Wrong Kevin. 'He spent the last hour muttering in Russian or something.'

'He's the chief suspect in a ten-year-old murder,' says Beard.

Wrong Kevin asks, 'Who was he supposed to have killed?'

Beard bites into his sandwich. 'Randolph Vine, Charlie's dad. I was the investigating officer and pulled Kevin Hall in for questioning, but there was not enough to hold him.'

'So you've got some unfinished business then,' says

Wrong Kevin. He makes two cups of tea and ponders his next question. 'That Verity, she's not normal, is she? My nose still hurts.'

'I think you can add Cedric, Ambrose and Linus to that list,' says Beard. 'They're all a bit unusual.'

Wrong Kevin leans against the sink, drinking his tea and says, 'I've never met anyone like them before. I thought my life was full of the unusuals, but this lot is off the chart.' Wrong Kevin slaps a piece of ham between two slices of bread and places it on a tray next to the cup of tea. 'I better feed the accused. And to think, I'm only here because we share the same name.'

Colin smiles at the stupidity of it all. At the time of the murder, Kevin Hall had a solid alibi, but knowing he's probably ex-KGB and the fact that he kidnapped Verity at gunpoint makes him the number one suspect. Colin takes another bite of his sandwich and realises he's nearer to closing this case now than ten years ago.

Following their hearty breakfast, Charlie and Verity set off across the fields for a morning powerwalk to get their brains going. Charlie stomps through the dew-laden grass, knowing tonight is her moment. The Stephan Langton pub will be her court and her moment of justice to point the finger at her father's murderer.

Verity strides ahead, panting like a horse on the morning gallops, and without breaking step, she asks, 'Are you sure Vladimir was—you know, back to normal?'

'Verity, nothing about any of this is normal, but he was coherent. He and Yuri chatted for a long time in the kitchen in the dark. I couldn't hear anything above Colin's breathing, but it looked like a genuine father-son conversation.'

Verity picks up the pace, and at the top of the hill, she vaults the tree they sat on with Colin during their previous walk. She says, 'Colin's a good sort. He's dependable, and it's always useful to have a clever ex-police officer around.'

'Around for what?' says Charlie, doing her best to keep up.

'For our team,' says Verity.

'Our team? What team?'

'Oh, do keep up, dear. Our team, of course,' says Verity. She pushes through a thick hedge and follows the overgrown pathway around the field, and adds, 'There will be other crimes to investigate, and we're the perfect team to solve murder cases.'

Charlie looks around from the summit of the hill at the multiple shades of green fields surrounding the valleys and woodlands.

She says, 'What crimes? Wait! What murders?'

Verity stands to admire the view for ten seconds, then marches on. 'Murders! Unsolved ones,' she says over her shoulder.

'We should crack this one first.'

'I'm looking ahead,' says Verity.

Charlie chases after her, saying, 'This team of ours, who is on it?'

'Us, obviously.'

'Obviously,' says Charlie.

'We need intelligence, so Cedric and Ambrose.'

'They've got nothing else to do,' says Charlie.

'And Colin Beard. Every team has to have a Colin,' announces Verity as if reciting the law. 'He can handle all the police business.'

'How about Linus?' asks Charlie.

Verity kicks a grassy tuft with the force of an angry

mule. 'I suppose so, yes. The thing is, whenever I'm with him, after about five minutes, I find myself plotting to put him in a headlock, but he's a good organiser, and he has access to the Service.'

'And Winnie,' says Charlie.

'Goes without saying.'

They plough alongside a small meandering stream running through the bottom of a valley and take deep breaths as they climb to the top of another hill. The sun shines across the Surrey Hills just as the mackerel sky promised earlier in the morning.

'Any tips for tonight?' asks Charlie.

'Don't accuse someone on an empty stomach,' says Verity. 'Let's get back to the ops room and see what Cedric and Ambrose have up their sleeve for lunch.'

'You can't possibly be hungry,' says Charlie.

'I possibly can,' says Verity.

They climb over the fence in a gap in the hedge that leads into the far field behind Tanglefoot Farm. They march through the wildflower garden and into the courtyard, where they find Cedric and Ambrose drinking tea.

'You two are regular as clockwork,' says Charlie.

Cedric looks up from the newspaper articles gathered from MI6 earlier in the morning. He says, 'We've been reviewing your printouts, and while it's fairly conclusive, we still think you need a knockout piece of evidence: something that points directly at the killer.'

'Like a name carved in marble, next to the smoking gun,' says Ambrose.

<><><>

Chapter Fifty-Three

Cedric sautés shallots, mushrooms and garlic in oil and butter until they shine. He adds a healthy glug of white wine, fresh herbs and spaghetti; it's his favourite fast food.

He fills four bowls with the aromatic spaghetti, grates some parmesan cheese over the top, and then walks across the courtyard to the ops room for a working lunch.

Verity and Charlie eat while studying the newspaper stories and photographs. There's a lot to churn through before they can confidently announce the killer in five hours in Friday Street's pub. Charlie leans back on the sofa, running scenarios through her head.

Verity eats as if it's a contest and tears off half the baguette, using it to mop up the oil, herbs and garlic, then puts her empty bowl on the ops room table. She says to Charlie, 'You take the lead tonight. Let them hear one confident voice, your voice.'

'Where will you be?'

'Out of sight, but close by,' says Verity. 'I'll bug the table and put something in your ear so we can communicate.'

Charlie stands and walks about, kicking at the gravel in the courtyard. A bombardment of questions force their way to the front of her thoughts. 'So, what do I do? Do I circle the table of suspects and place my hands on the killer's shoulders and say, I know what you did ten years ago?'

'That's one way of doing it,' says Verity.

Charlie shrugs. 'Maybe I can shine a torch in the murderer's face and shout, killer!'

'That's an option,' says Verity.

'Maybe I should run up to the murderer and tell them the game is up?'

'You could,' says Verity.

Charlie kicks more gravel and says, 'When you were in this position, back in your spy days, what did you do?'

'They were usually dead by this point,' says Verity.

Charlie slaps her hands against her head, yelling that she's not ready and then grabs the crossword book before setting off at pace to the top of the garden. She finds an area of warm grass and kicks off her boots.

'Dad, give me the strength to finish this,' she says and lets out a long sigh, and asks for him to send her a sign.

She thinks over the past few weeks and how different things would be without Verity by her side, guiding her in and out of trouble. Mostly into trouble. Was she serious about forging a team and solving crimes? Maybe she'll forget about it by the time Dad's murderer has been rumbled. She let her imagination meander while watching the swaying wildflowers and butterflies zigzagging from stem to stem. . .so many doubts.

Of course, Verity was right to appoint her as the single spokesperson tonight; it was her father's cold case, after all. She wanted to make him proud. There would be no judge, no jury, just the accused, their accuser, and her day of justice. Her calculations, at best, were part evidence and part guesswork to fill in the blanks.

Charlie begins to wish she never started the process of finding her father's killer. What if she's wrong? What if? Her thoughts are cluttered with endless what-ifs.

Charlie sits upright and pulls her knees under her chin in time to see Verity running up the garden like a sprinter towards her.

'They've cracked it!' says Verity. 'They've only gone and done it!'

'Who has cracked what?'

Verity reaches Charlie and bends over with her hands on her knees, trying to regain her breath. 'Cedric and Ambrose have solved the crossword clue. I always said your father was a genius.' Verity reaches out her hand and pulls Charlie to her feet, adding, 'The last piece of the puzzle is in place. We've got our name on the smoking gun.'

Verity and Charlie sit among the wildflowers for an hour, putting the evening's session together.

'I should feel ready, but I don't,' says Charlie.

'Come with me,' says Verity, striding back to the courtyard. She points to Elsie and says, 'Hop on, girl, you need inspiration.'

'Where are we going?' asks Charlie

'Somewhere to make you feel inspired,' she says, kick-starting Elsie's engine. Verity blasts around the corner and down the lane in a cloud of dry dust and spiralling petals.

Charlie taps Verity on the shoulder to switch on the crash helmet intercom.

'Give me a clue,' says Charlie.

'At unique times like this, you've got to go back to the beginning,' says Verity and pulls to a stop in Friday Street.

'Your lovely dad was murdered right there,' waving her arm in the general direction of the far side of the pond.

Charlie sits and stares at the water, doing her best to avoid drumming up an image of her father floating face down in the pond. Over the years, she forced herself not to imagine her father in the water. But now, just hours before she reveals her father's murderer, a bit of anger might give her a helpful edge.

They step off Elsie and wander up to Randolph's secret garage and open the door. Charlie stands at the entrance, admiring the neatness of it all following Cedric and Ambrose's day of sorting.

She says with a dry voice, 'This is one of the last places my dad came.'

'Your dad left us all the clues to point the finger at his killer. You've got this, Charlie-Girl. Randolph was proud of you. He boasted about you all the time at work. It was Charlie this and Charlie that.'

'Sorry, it must have been boring hearing about me all the time,' says Charlie.

'You're just like him, and he was the best of us.' Verity wraps her arm around Charlie as they saunter back to Elsie, climb on and roar back up Plum Pudding Lane.

In the courtyard, Charlie looks around the ops room and takes in all the ground they've covered as a team. 'I think I'm ready,' she says.

'I know you are, Kid,' says Verity. 'Let's go and catch ourselves a killer.'

Every table in the Stephan Langton pub displays a *reserved* sign. Cedric and Ambrose telephoned ahead to book every table and paid handsomely for the pub's loss of takings.

They asked the manager to remain on hand to show an element of normality when welcoming the pub's only booking and then not to return until she received the *all-clear* text.

'It's all such a mystery,' says the pub manager, arranging colourful flowers in the vase on the small front desk.

'Look upon it as a surprise rather than a mystery,' says Ambrose. 'Your flowers are beautiful. Are they from your garden?'

Ambrose's artful yet effective distraction makes the manager forget about the unusualness of the evening ahead and carry on with her flowers.

Charlie checks her watch for the third time in a minute. In half an hour, her four suspects will walk through the door. Verity is fiddling with a bugging device under the alcove table while Cedric and Ambrose wait outside, looking for approaching vehicles.

Wrong Kevin pulls his brightly-coloured car into the parking bay opposite the pub, and Colin Beard steps out of the back seat with Kevin Hall close to hand.

Hall is cleanly shaved, wearing a brown suit, and looks surprisingly fresh for a man chained to a damp basement wall all night. Charlie's brief to Colin and Wrong Kevin was simple: bring him to the Stephan Langton in smart clothes without any visible marks.

Cedric and Ambrose greet them and walk Kevin Hall to the alcove.

'What's going on?' says Hall.

'You don't know?' says Cedric.

'How could you not know?' says Ambrose.

'Is that mad woman here?' asks Hall.

'Which mad woman do you mean? We have two on our books?' says Cedric.

'Verity! The one who chained me to the wall,' says Hall.

'Oh, you won't see her for a while,' says Cedric.

'The woman is unhinged.'

Cedric and Ambrose agree with Hall as they settle him into the alcove. They pour him a glass of water and offer him bread from a wicker basket as if they are head waiters in a five-star hotel.

Charlie walks into a dark corner on the opposite side of the pub and stands next to Verity, who looks at home in the shadows.

She says, 'Hall looks totally confused.'

Verity nods and whispers, 'Confusion is good. Now, get in position, and good luck. This is your moment, so don't bugger it up.'

'Was that your first pep talk? It wasn't very good,' says Charlie.

'Listen, kid, your father was murdered, and you're about to put his killer away for the rest of their life. Not many people get to do that.'

Charlie looks down at her feet. 'When you put it like that!'

Verity gives her a playful thump on the arm, and with a warm smile, she says, 'Afterwards, I'll take you for ice cream and buy you a pony.'

'Really?'

'No, you clod,' says Verity, pushing her away.

Charlie stands out of sight from the front door at the side of the alcove and waits for the others to arrive. Her mind ticks through the evidence they've gathered to nail her father's killer to the mast. Ten long, painful years since his murder, and now she stands on the brink of bringing the murderer to justice. Two cars pull up in the spaces opposite the pub and snap her to attention. Yuri and Vladimir get out of the first car and share a word before they walk across the lane to the pub.

What is Yuri going to think?

She's snubbed him for two dates in the last five days and is about to stand in front of him as if in a court of law. Polly King, dressed perfectly, steps out of the second car and walks into the pub behind the two Russians.

The pub manager welcomes them warmly, and they follow her to the alcove to join Kevin Hall. On her return to the front door, Cedric and Ambrose give her a friendly thumbs up and see her safely out.

Colin Beard and Wrong Kevin lock and bolt the door.

The show is about to begin.

<><><>

Chapter Fifty-Four

Charlie

My heart is beating like a nervous drummer boy on his first day of band practice. I can hear Yuri and Vladimir making polite conversation with Kevin Hall and Polly King. The next hour is about my ability to pull the evidence together and get it right—so no pressure.

It was insightful of Verity to suggest we visit the pond and my father's garage earlier. It gave me perspective on the case and time to calculate my thoughts. I promised Dad I'd catch his killer.

So here I am.

Everyone is at the Stephan Langton pub, shoehorned around the table in our alcove. It feels odd to see people at our table—our alcove. There's a crackle in the air, an intensity identical to the atmosphere of those few moments *curtain up* at the theatre.

God knows I'm nervous.

A pip, a crackle, and a pop from my earbud precede Verity's impatience, 'You're on! Chin up, chest out, and let your nerves feed you. You've got this.'

With Verity's power in my head, I grip the crossword book and step into the alcove. My nerves do feed me; she's right. I start positively by thanking them for coming. My voice is strong, my chin is up, and my chest...well, my chest is doing its best.

Yuri half stands and says, 'Charlie, do you work here?'

I smile and tell him to sit.

'Nice start,' says Verity softly in my earpiece.

'I've waited ten years for this,' I say, and on cue, Ambrose arrives with a bottle of champagne, and Cedric carries a tray of glasses—the invited four will need a drink. As Ambrose pours, I begin my deliberation.

'Randolph Vine, my father, was murdered in the pond behind the pub. I was young, eighteen, and devastated, as you can imagine.'

'What's this all about?' says Vladimir.

I'm prepared to deal with interruptions calmly, and I've thought about most questions they'll ask, so without looking at him, I say, 'I think you'll find this evening interesting.'

Verity whispers, 'Give Kevin Hall one hell of a bloody nightmare for kidnapping me at gunpoint.'

I edge my way around the chairs and stand behind Hall. I place my hands on his shoulders, ready to present my first statement. 'Kevin Hall, you are a handler for Russian agents. Ex KGB.'

'Don't talk such nonsense,' he barks. 'I work on the railways.'

I press my hands down on his shoulders, preventing him from standing, and put my mouth near his ear, saying with a whisper, 'I know everything you've done. You're a deep sleeper spy who became a vital handler for Russia's top asset.'

I like how my voice controls the small area. I exhibit no nerves, my hands are steady, and I pace the floor with ease, but my insides are churning like a cement mixer. There's no doubt I've got their attention as four pairs of eyes follow my every move around the alcove.

Ambrose walks in and tops up everyone's champagne glass like a professional wine butler, then leaves without a word. If this were not so serious, I would laugh at his performance.

'Time to ease into the information,' whispers Verity.

I open my laptop and place it against the ice bucket, ensuring everyone can see the screen and press play. The janky pictures from yesteryear begin unfolding the story of the night the Berlin Wall fell. The slideshow captures their attention. You can find anything online—if you know where to look—and we finally knew where to look.

The news stories, some movie clips, and some newspaper articles reveal the Russian authorities rough-handling a man. The man was identified as Ivan Petrov, the courier responsible for handing the prepared statement and sheet of answers to the high-ranking official to read out on a state live broadcast. Ivan Petrov, the courier, played a small part in a powerful chain of command. His task was to guard the envelope, nothing more.

I press pause, saying, 'Moments before the handover, my father and Joshua King switched the envelope with the prepared answers for a blank sheet of paper, so when a news reporter asked the question, "*When will these restrictions be lifted?*" the response should have been, "*Over the coming months and years*", but the sheet of paper was blank.

Then, after a moment of thought, the trusted East German official, Günter Schabowski, said, "*Immediately, without delay*". And those immortal yet accidental words started in motion the scenes witnessed by the world when thousands of Berliners began tearing down the dreaded wall with hammers and their bare hands.'

I press play, and the screen comes to life with the mob of Berliners ripping the wall down. Men, women and children wielding pickaxes and hammers sent sparks into the night sky, and history changed on live television—all because the sheet of paper was blank.

The film clips show Ivan Petrov, the courier, being marched away by authorities. It was clear from the black-and-white photographs the courier was assassinated. However, it was the following story showing a few grainy images of a woman hanging from a tree in a tiny snow-covered garden that changed the mood in the alcove.

Ivan Petrov, blamed for the defeat of Russia's Communist party, became the patsy for the decline. Ivan Petrov was Moscow's Lee Harvey Oswald.

Yuri made another half attempt to stand, but Vladimir held his arm, indicating for him to remain seated.

I think the penny is beginning to drop.

I clear my throat to continue and pace around the table. I stand behind Kevin Hall and place my hands on his shoulders.

I say, 'Ivan Petrov had a son, and I imagine that son would be angry at how his father was blamed and assassinated. I'd also imagine the son could not control his rage when his mother, unable to contain her sadness, took her own life.'

Kevin Hall is motionless. I feel his breathing quicken, and his body temperature rises a degree.

I ask the gathering, 'The courier, Ivan Petrov's son, is called Kieran Petrov, and I'm guessing everyone wants to know what happened to him.'

A few nods and a few murmurs from the group suggest they do want to know.

'Kevin, do you have any idea what happened to him?'

'No,' barks Hall. 'How the hell should I know?'

I ignore him and say, 'Kevin Hall, formally known as Kieran Petrov, the son of the unfortunate courier responsible for reducing Russia's power, was undoubtedly angry about what happened to his parents. And I can understand that.'

I press play on the screen, and a second raft of headlines with images appears. Verity and I cobbled them together in a rush, and somehow, we did a good job.

My earpiece crackles with her soft, encouraging voice, 'You're doing really well—time to drop the axe.'

She's right, it is.

I look at Yuri, smile and tell him it's nice to see him.

A smile spreads across his handsome face. I urge myself to concentrate. Maybe he's still thinking I'm the pub manager and I'm about to hand out menus. It's time I put him in the picture.

'My father, Randolph Vine, knew he had to cleverly conceal the clues that would reveal his killer so the murderer would not find them. You see, I think he knew it was just a question of time before he was murdered. He also knew Cedric and Ambrose would put their sizeable brains to the task and solve the complicated clues.'

I wave the crossword book as I speak, using it to punctuate my points in a way a pipe smoker prods the air with their pipe. It's an old trick my dad used when he told funny stories.

'This is a lot of nonsense. It's factless and ridiculous,' Hall says, trying to stand. My hands on his shoulders keep him in his seat.

I say, 'Kevin, please tell the group where you were last evening and all day today. Actually, on second thoughts, I'll tell them as you'll miss out on all the good bits.' I take a deep breath; here it goes, 'Now, where to begin? Oh, I know. Kevin Hall took Verity Fanthorpe from a garden in Shere at gunpoint and kidnapped her in his brown Volvo, and then chained her to his basement wall.'

'I—' Hall manages to utter only one word before Verity races across the pub floor, dives into the alcove and slaps his face.

She introduces herself to the wide-eyed audience before taking a long look at Vladimir. Finally, she says, 'It's good to see you, Vladimir, looking so free of a consuming illness?'

'Katia,' says Vladimir. His long, exhaling breath carries the last syllable of her name. He tries to say another word, but she puts her hand up to stop him.

She says, 'It's Verity, not Katia. Try not to speak. We can catch up another time. We have much to discuss.'

And they do.

I watch Verity handle the Russian with ease. This is the part of the evening I've been looking forward to the most. A few weeks ago, I never knew Verity Fanthorpe, and now I can't imagine a day without her. Verity paces around the tight alcove with graceful agility.

She says, 'Randolph Vine and Joshua King were the best two agents the British Secret Service had in operation, and together they unwound the Russians with a sheet of blank paper without firing a shot. It had the hallmark of a Winston Churchill trick played against Hitler.'

I step back a little and let Verity take the whole stage.

She adds, 'Randolph's empty lock-up in London led us to a garage back here in Friday Street. To the untrained eye, the garage was nothing more than a messy, clueless location with an old motorbike and sidecar. But Randolph knew Cedric and Ambrose would be unable to sleep at night with the untidiness. And he was right; they spent the day sorting through the documents until they came across this,' Verity holds up the envelope with the blank sheet of paper.

Verity compliments Kevin Hall's considerable ability as a Russian deep-sleeper spy. She says, 'I was Hall's opposite number in Moscow, so I know what it takes to live a double life. Kevin's loving wife, Doreen, provided the perfect cover as the suburban couple with an abundance of potted herbs. It helped Kevin Hall, I mean, Kieran Petrov, move about his business undetected.' She adds, 'So, credit where credit's due, you stayed undetected for decades.'

As Verity mentioned earlier, it's time for me to drop the axe.

I take her place on the prowl around the table and say, 'One of you murdered my father, and ten years later, you murdered Joshua King.' I let my words filter around my audience.

Cedric and Ambrose join Colin Beard at the entrance to the alcove, and Linus Pope is peeping through a small gap.

I look at my team and drop the axe, and with a release of ten years' worth of pent-up energy, I shout, 'You are the murderer!'

<><><>

Chapter Fifty-Five

The jarringly silent members in the alcove slowly turn to look in the direction of Charlie's accusing finger.

Kevin Hall jumps to his feet.

'This is a joke!' His harsh Russian accent booms through his once quiet English disguise. He flounces, losing his cool, and slams his fists on the table, sending cutlery and condiments in all directions. Champagne glasses crash to the floor, sending glass shards spinning under the table.

'Temper temper, Kevin,' barks Colin Beard. 'Charlie's finger of blame has been pointed, and there's no going back. The evidence is overwhelming—you know it.'

Vladimir waves for Kevin Hall to sit, adding, 'You're making a fool of yourself,' he repeats himself in firm Russian. Kevin Hall slumps into his chair—a lost soul—a defeated man.

During a bout of commotion, as any good agent will attest, is the best place to make your play. And Polly King didn't waste a second. She picks up a steak knife from the floor and, with the speed of a panther, she thrusts the blade against Charlie's throat.

Yuri stands as a natural reflex to assist her, but Polly is swift and has taken the dominant position, pushing the steak knife against Charlie's throat and holding her chin up with her other hand. It's classic combat training. Polly is no amateur.

'Easy, everyone,' says Verity, whispering the phrase several more times. 'Nice and easy.'

Polly guides Charlie to the alcove opening and motions with her eyes for Cedric and Ambrose to step aside. They are powerless to do anything else. Colin Beard begrudgingly steps back along with Linus to let Polly approach the front door. In a well-rehearsed move, Polly pushes Charlie back into the pub and dashes towards the open front door. Charlie clatters into a table, turning it on its side, and scrambles to her feet, shouting a curdling cry for Wrong Kevin to stop Polly King from getting out. He's standing at the far end of the narrow hallway leading to the front door.

'What do you want me to do?' he yells.

'Stop her! Hit her! Kick her! Anything, just don't let that woman pass.'

Wrong Kevin lands a perfectly timed left hook on Polly's chin, and she stops dead in her tracks, slumping against the brick wall. Polly groans and moans in an attempt to stand, but her legs prove lifeless as she looks entirely resigned to her capture. Her eyes flicker and then close in a state of unconsciousness.

'Lovely punch,' says Verity, shadowboxing a couple of left hooks like the one deployed by Wrong Kevin. 'I love an unfair fight.'

Colin and Wrong Kevin drag Polly back into the pub and sit her on the leather sofa in the bar area. Charlie throws the freezing water from the ice bucket into her face, and Polly stirs. When her eyes open, she attempts to run, but Colin's substantial body mass keeps her pinned to the soft couch.

Yuri asks in a staccato rhythm, 'So, Polly King murdered your father, Randolph Vine?'

'She did,' says Charlie.

'And Joshua King?'

'Yep, she killed him, too. Polly King is a double killer,' says Charlie.

The alcove empties and everyone gathers around Polly King to witness the final deliberation. Charlie stands in front of the sofa and takes a deep breath, exhaling fully before putting her hands on her hips.

She says, 'Polly King is Kevin Hall's sister, and therefore, she's the daughter of the courier Ivan Petrov.'

'That's a lie. You have no proof,' shrieks Polly.

Charlie steps into the alcove to retrieve the crossword book and looks back at Polly over her shoulder, saying, 'I must admit we were struggling. We had clues but no way to tie them together because you covered your tracks so well that we needed something to point the finger, so to speak.'

All eyes were first on Polly and then on Charlie. The case had distilled down to two people: the murderer and the accuser.

Polly King doesn't flinch or offer any sign of emotion. But the body can't lie. Everyone gives off signals, but most people miss them—but not Charlie. She's waited ten years to meet her father's murderer face to face.

'This is my trust fund,' says Charlie, waving the crossword book in Polly's face. She turns to Cedric and Ambrose, adding, 'They cracked the most difficult anagram I've seen. My father told me who his killer was in the three clues:

Elision, Giant Killer and KPH. You have no idea how long I stared at those words. But if you have bionic brains like Cedric and Ambrose, you'll spend hours rearranging the letters until it reads: Polina King is the Killer.'

There's a tiny ripple of applause from Verity.

Wrong Kevin says, 'But who's Polina?'

'It's Russian for Polly,' says Charlie. 'Polina means grace in Russian. My dad had to bury his killer's name, trusting we would somehow crack it, and we did. Polly poisoned him and tossed him in the pond to make it look like a mugging.'

Colin Beard takes his phone from his pocket, calls his contact in the police, and explains Randolph Vine's murderer is ready for collection. He looks at Charlie, 'And how about Joshua King, Polly's husband?'

'Polly murdered him, too, with the help of her brother, Kevin Hall.'

'Joshua died in a car crash in Australia,' snarls Polly.

'We thought so, too,' Verity says. 'Joshua King hid in Australia for ten years to keep Charlie safe, but he received an urgent postcard from Kevin Hall, pretending to be me, explaining Charlie Vine was in danger. Kevin Hall and Polly King knew some evidence might surface and needed him out of the way. They knew all along he was alive and tricked him into coming back. The poisoning was easy. Polly King slipped into the cottage opposite hers and laced everything with ricin. It was heavy-handed and clumsy, yet very deadly.'

Beard redials his police contact, 'We have Joshua King's murderer here, too.'

Linus Pope steeples his fingers, saying, 'I must admit I truly believed this case was unsolvable. So Polly murdered your father to avenge the deaths of her mother and father?'

'Yes,' says Charlie.

'And what about Vladimir?' asks Pope, directing his question at Verity.

'Vladimir and I have a lot of catching up to do involving apologies and explanations, but as far as I can tell, he's not involved with the murders.'

Charlie looks at Yuri and flashes a wink so slight only he can see it—he winks back.

Cedric taps a teaspoon against a champagne glass. 'When the police have collected our murderer, let's retire to Tanglefoot for a late supper. I don't know about you, but I'm famished, and this charming pub seems very low on staff.

<><><>

Chapter Fifty-Six

The embers of the sun melt slowly across the wildflower garden at Tanglefoot Farm.

Cedric and Ambrose scurried up Plum Pudding Lane half an hour before the others to prepare the supper spread.

'Let's go rogue,' says Ambrose. 'I'm thinking blankets and cushions rather than tables and chairs. It won't hurt us to try a little informality dining for once and sit up at the far end of the garden.' He loads food onto three large trays.

Cedric says, 'Excellent idea. Sitting on a blanket is like living on the edge. I'll warm the bread and chill a few bottles of cider.'

The two men operate like seasoned veterans, producing sandwiches, dips, an assorted cheeseboard, cold meats, bowls of pickles, salads, chilled curried eggs, tangy fish-cakes, and baskets of warm bread. They carry the food trays to the edge of the wildflower garden, where Ambrose spaces the cushions around the matching blankets, and Cedric lights the garden torches and candles.

'What should we wear?' asks Ambrose.

'I'm considering we go with white shirts, gold polka dot cravats, sky blue shorts and deck shoes,' says Cedric.

'No socks, dear boy? Is Verity's campervan living rubbing off on you?'

'You can't live on the edge while wearing socks,' says Cedric.

A distant splash of twirling blue lights are from the attending police cars extracting Polly King and Kevin Hall from Friday Street.

In the warm evening, Charlie walks beside Verity and leads the party up the lane to Tanglefoot Farm.

'Well, you did it, Kid,' says Verity.

'We did it,' says Charlie. 'It was a team effort.'

'Yes, but you had total control as you pushed and pulled and made things happen. Your dad would have loved to see you in action.'

'You think so?' asks Charlie, her voice barely audible.

'I know so,' says Verity. 'He loved a feisty agent.'

Charlie loops her arm through Verity's, and they skip into the courtyard—the flames from the torches and candles in the far field light up the darkening sky.

Yuri catches up with Charlie, 'So this is where you live?'

'I've been here ten years since my father—,' Charlie's words trail away, and they walk together up the garden path towards the lights.

Vladimir wanders sheepishly towards Verity, 'And do you live here, too?' he asks, giving her the slightest hip nudge.

'Lord, no,' she says. 'My exotic high life of luxury living is behind me.' She points to her campervan. 'That's me in there.'

Vladimir squints to focus on the rusty campervan. 'I like what you've done with it,' he says. 'You can live off the grid in one of those. You'll have to show me around one day.'

Cedric and Ambrose appear at the kitchen door to greet the party assembling in the courtyard.

'Do you have a different outfit for every meal?' asks Wrong Kevin.

'Obviously, dear boy. We aren't animals. Go and wash your hands,' says Cedric.

Ambrose leads the way to the torch-lit supper spread in the wildflower garden, and Cedric points to the seating chart he tied to the ice bucket, which is promptly ignored.

Colin Beard grabs a few bottles of chilled cider and pops the lids, handing one to Wrong Kevin. They chink bottles and begin chatting about the evening's incredible events.

Wrong Kevin says, 'I've got no idea what happened in the pub, and I don't know who everyone is, apart from Kevin Hall, and if I forgot his name, then I would be the village idiot.'

'Firstly, Vladimir, the older Russian man, is innocent. His son, Yuri, he's innocent,' says Colin.

'How about the other two?'

'Kevin Hall and Polly King are guilty of pretty much everything. They are brother and sister who took revenge for what happened to their parents. Between them, they murdered Charlie's dad and Joshua King.'

'And Polly, the lady I stopped from leaving the pub, was she some sort of spy?' asks Wrong Kevin.

'Polly King was Russia's top spy, and you punched her in the face, you might get a medal,' says Colin.

'I'm going to get some food,' says a happy Wrong Kevin.

Verity opens her bottle with the heel of her boot and

takes a long swig, then wipes her mouth on her sleeve before handing the bottle to Vladimir while she grabs another.

Vladimir hands Verity a glass.

She says, 'I'm seventy-five, I don't need glasses, I drink straight from the bottle.'

'You're still as delicate and as lovely as always,' he says.

She smiles and takes his arm, steering him away from the gathering onto a pathway that weaves around the garden. They amble like an old married couple taking a last lap around the garden before bedtime, neither saying anything and yet both with much to say.

Eventually, and without preamble, Verity blurts out, 'Your dementia must have been one of those famous forty-eight-hour bouts.'

Vladimir looks straight ahead, saying, 'A bit like your twenty-four-hour death in a car crash miracle.'

'Yes, that must be it,' she says.

They walk to the top corner of the garden and turn down past the beehives.

'I have a confession to make,' says Vladimir.

'Only one?' she says.

'I listened to the Friday Street Spy Ring meetings when I was in Russia,' says Vladimir. 'I put a bug inside the bug under the table.'

'That was my bug,' she says.

'That's nice.'

'And what did you learn?' she says.

'Absolutely nothing,' says Vladimir. 'The spy ring talked utter nonsense.'

'I told them to speak gibberish in case someone was listening,' says Verity.

Vladimir says, 'Well, it worked, especially Cedric and

Ambrose because they talked nothing but complete rubbish every Friday evening for years.'

Verity bursts out laughing. 'I didn't tell them,' she says. 'I only told Randolph and Joshua.'

They reach the courtyard and slump on the sofa in the ops room. Vladimir looks at the photographs pinned on the corkboard and smiles.

He looks at Verity and says, 'When you came to see me in the nursing home. I tried to help you by giving you a clue. A big clue.'

'Clue! What clue? You didn't give me a clue.'

'I virtually told you to look at the courier.'

'No, you didn't,' she says.

'I kept saying, ker, ker, ker,' he says.

'And I thought you had dementia and were just not quite with it,' she says.

Vladimir half laughs, 'Can I ask you the question I've wanted to ask you for so many years?'

She nods.

'Why did you choose to die on me?'

Verity's eyes water with tears she's held back for a lifetime. 'My mission was complete,' she says. 'It was my time to go home. But you knew I was a spy and didn't say anything—why not?'

'Because I loved you forever,' he says. 'But I thought that if you chose to be dead rather than be married to me, you must have never loved me the same way, so I sadly let you go.'

'But I did love you,' she pauses a minute. 'It was a lifetime ago, Vlad,' she puts her hand on his.

He looks into her watery eyes. 'We have a lot to talk about.'

'Yes, we do.'

'Shall we meet for coffee one day?' he asks.

'I'd like that,' she says. They walk up through the garden together to the torch-lit supper. 'One more question.'

He looks at her. 'I think we will have a lot more than one.'

She says, 'Before we rejoin the others, tell me about the nursing home?'

'I own it. Yuri told me about his visit with Charlie, and I pretended to be a resident.'

'You know about Charlie?'

'I know about everything, Katia.' Vladimir takes her arm and says, 'Look at things from my position. After years of silence, Randolph Vine's daughter turns up at my house, asking questions. I didn't know what mission you might be on, so my best play was to sit and say nothing. I had nothing to do with Vine or King's murders. Those days are far behind me and you, by the looks of things. Kevin Hall and Polly King have been uncontrollable for too long, and I should have asked Moscow to extract them, but you know how difficult that can be.'

'I can buy that,' says Verity.

Vladimir says, 'Britain isn't the only country who does theatricals. Russia also loves a bit of smoke and mirrors.'

Linus Pope collects a plateful of food and walks over to Charlie.

'You were amazing this evening,' he says. 'Polly King and Kevin Hall will serve long sentences for their crimes, and it gives Britain some much-needed leverage over the Russian Government in upcoming negotiations.'

'Thank you, Linus. You are like family, you know that,' says Charlie.

Yuri joins them and says, 'You pulled the impossible out of the bag this evening, Charlie.'

'It was a team effort,' she says.

Linus butts in, 'She's definitely our team leader.'

Yuri shuffles his feet and looks down.

'Nervous?' she asks.

'A little.'

'Why is that?' she asks.

'Because I have something to tell you.'

Charlie taps Linus Pope's arm and says, 'Could you get me some cheese and another cider, please.'

Pope nods and slips away to leave them a moment to talk.

Yuri lowers his voice and says to Charlie, 'I've toyed with not telling you some information, but after this evening's performance of yours and how you conducted this whole murder case, I think you should know what I learned earlier from my dad.'

Charlie looks puzzled. 'What else is there to know?'

Yuri smirks, saying, 'There's always something else to know.' He takes a swig of cider and finishes his cracker, then lets out a long sigh. 'My father told me that twenty years ago, there was an unsanctioned assassination in England by two of our operators. Dad was in Moscow when the news reached him about the killing, and it meant nothing to him at the time. He told me he never connected the dots until this evening.'

'Who was killed?' asks Charlie as if asking what the weather will be like tomorrow, such was her calmness about the crime. Verity's influence has fully rubbed off.

Yuri leans closer, and in a quiet voice, he says, 'It was the wife of a British agent. Apparently, two cars purposely ran the woman off the road into a tree, where she died instantly. The Russian agents made it look like a tragic accident, and the police were none the wiser and didn't investigate. However, the agents reported their deed to Moscow.'

'And these two agents would be Polly King and Kevin Hall?' asks Charlie.

'That's true,' he says.

'And the British agent would have been my father?'

'Correct again,' says Vladimir.

'And the woman...' Charlie's voice trails off. 'The woman would have been my mother.'

Yuri puts his arms around Charlie and whispers in her ear, 'Dad says that Polly King wanted your dad's entire family to suffer just as hers had suffered.'

'Well, she got that right; we did suffer,' sniffs Charlie.

Still holding her tightly, Yuri says, 'I have no comforting words for you, but maybe somewhere in this tragedy, you'll get some sort of closure and, ultimately, some peace.'

She takes Yuri's hand, guiding him to the far wooden gate, leading him through to Tanglefoot Farm's top field, and as chatter from the wildflower garden fades, they walk to where a giant oak tree protects two gravestones.

'My mother and father,' she says, touching the granite tops. 'I promised them I'd find—'

'You did,' he says.

The sweet-smelling summer grass and light breeze peeling off the Surrey Hills make this a perfect resting place.

'I could stay here for hours,' she says. 'But we should rejoin the others. I just wanted to introduce you to my parents.' Charlie wipes her eyes, and they head back.

Cedric and Ambrose stand by the far gate and help Charlie back through into the wildflower garden. She loops her arms through theirs, saying, 'Polina King is the killer.

Wow, that is a great anagram, and you said my dad was useless at crossword puzzles.'

'He was,' says Cedric. 'But seemingly, he was excellent at setting anagrams.'

Charlie looks at the noisy mixed group on the blankets and says, 'This is my family.'

'You don't mean Linus Pope as well, do you?' asks Cedric. 'I'm not sure I could take being related to that man.'

Ambrose laughs. 'He's got a point.'

Verity brings the tray of assorted cheeses to where they're standing and says, 'I've been thinking.'

'Oh Lord, no,' says Cedric. 'That never ends well.'

She says, 'We can't bring the Friday Street Spy Ring back to life, but we are a team who solve Friday Street Murder Mysteries.'

Cedric and Ambrose nod their approval.

Charlie raises her glass, 'I'll drink to that.'

Verity says, 'That's good because I received a postcard from—'

Charlie puts her arm around Verity's shoulders and says, 'That sounds like a lovely story. Why not tell me all about it in the morning.'

'You're an ungrateful child, Charlotte Vine.

<><><>

If you enjoyed reading *Murder On Friday Street*, please leave a review on Amazon. Each review makes a huge difference and with your support I can write more books.

Thank you.

"A SECRET TO DIE FOR" (READ FREE BONUS)

Download your free bonus mini murder mystery story, *A Secret To Die For,* straight to your email inbox:

RussellCooperBooks.com

This mini mystery starts when Verity receives a postcard from her sister in the Cotswolds. Follow the clues and help the team solve the blackmail case.

READ "EASIER DEAD THAN DONE"

Order your next Friday Street Murder Mystery: *Easier Dead Than Done*

Acknowledgments

A special thank you to this group for their help and encouragement:

Anita (Mini) Davis, Greta Cooper, Wendy Wilson, Martin Cooper, Emily Mace, Emma Sheppardson, Patrick Collins, Sally Gamble and Neil Gamble.

An extra special thank you to Rachel for her cheerleading and expert advice to make *Murder on Friday Street* a reality.

And thanks to you, my lovely readers, for your enthusiasm and support. Without you, none of this is possible.

About the Author

Russell grew up on a rich diet of Sunday afternoon television mysteries. Following a hectic career in the restaurant business he did a couple of undisclosed stints with NATO & GCHQ.

Russell lives with his partner in the beautiful Surrey town of Weybridge, where the Rivers Wey and Thames meet. He spends his days writing, dreaming up delicious meals, and meeting the incessant demands of their bossy toy poodle, Winnie.

Books by Russell Cooper

Florence Fairweather Spy Mystery Series:

Milton Park

Aubrey Hall

Red Cottage

Friday Street Murder Mystery Series:

Murder On Friday Street

Easier Dead Than Done

A Murder Worth Dying For

Murder ME Tomorrow

Printed in Dunstable, United Kingdom

82828326R00224